Pr

NORTH

"A damn good book . . . the sort that gets you quickly in its grip and keeps you there, hanging on for the ride until the final secret is revealed. And then wishing there were just a few pages more."
— *The Washington Post*

"Riveting and incisive, the tension vibrantly builds at a relentless, thrumming pace as Jack confronts dangers both real and imagined in veteran novelist Busch's electrifying psychological thriller."
— *Booklist*

"While I was reading this novel, the phone rang, there were knocks at the door, coffee got cold; the story's emotional velocity held me fast to my chair. I love the memory-haunted protagonist, Jack, whose world seems nocturnal, even during the day. I love Busch's noir sensibility here. He is—and always has been—one of the best novelists we have." —HOWARD NORMAN, author of
In Fond Remembrance of Me and *The Bird Artist*

"*North* bears the standard of this excellent [crime novel] tradition. It is a crime novel whose soul is a meditation on life lost and found, complete with all the touchstones of the form."
—ROBIN VIDIMOS, *The Denver Post*

"Few authors link so tellingly the outer and the inner dark, and Frederick Busch here extends his chart of the terrain. The Jack we met in *Girls* is on the loose, the prowl again, and where he leads we readers follow line by fateful line." —NICHOLAS DELBANCO

"*North* is a riveting psychological novel of small-town secrets, intrigues, tragedies, and ultimately surprises. Busch is a master storyteller whose novel will appeal both to readers of noir detective fiction and those who simply love good writing."

—*The Independent*

"Filled with potent atmospheric effects, wrenching dialogue, and a sure sense of its middle-aged protagonist's weary apprehension of the facts of his limits and his mortality." —*Kirkus Reviews*

"The much-anticipated sequel to *Girls*, *North* is a hard-boiled trip into the hard-luck backwoods townships of upstate New York. With his spare, lyrical style straight out of Hemingway and Chandler, Frederick Busch has crafted another smart, big-hearted country noir." —STEWART O'NAN, author of *The Good Wife* and *The Night Country*

"Noirish and nihilistic . . . Busch has written the rare psychological thriller that cares more about the psychology than the thrills."

—*The New York Times*

"A signature grace of a Frederick Busch novel is its pace, a narrative drive that gathers powerful momentum without ever seeming to hurry. It's such a momentum that masterfully animates *North*. Beneath the lean, alert prose lurks a disturbing, ominous tension that seems at once disproportionate to the controlled violence of the book, and wholly in balance with the haunting, psychological portrait of its hero." —STUART DYBEK

"No one can balance toughness and tenderness like Frederick Busch. *North* continues his remarkable journey through the chilly environs, both geographic and emotional, of lonely towns and lonely people in search of a place to warm themselves. He knows more than most of us about violence and betrayal, but even more about love and its costs. Add this to your Busch shelf; it's another keeper." —ROSELLEN BROWN

"Busch puts some interesting twists on the hard-boiled detective genre. . . . The accomplished Busch is known for exploring domestic themes and for creating characters struggling with life's hardships, and here he does not disappoint. This novel should satisfy both Busch's long-time readers and fans of the genre."
—*Library Journal*

"I want to call *North* a thinking man's thriller, but it's tougher than that. I want to call it 'novel noir', but it's darker than that. This book will keep you up until you finish it, and then it won't let you get to sleep." —DAVID BRADLEY, author of
The Chaneysville Incident

"A tale that almost aches on the page with accumulated grief . . . It's not a new subject, but Busch handles it with economy, empathy, and grace." —MISHA BERSON, *Sunday Seattle Times*

"Frederick Busch is one of those authors everyone respects, but it seems that not enough people actually read his works. That's a sin, given his seemingly inexhaustible ability to churn out compelling stories free of the unnecessary razzle-dazzle that so often passes for literary style. . . . Busch manages to ladle out the drama and the melodrama in equal servings and smartly uses both to keep the pages turning. . . . *North* is a fundamentally sound, well-paced potboiler committed to carrying the reader on a bumpy, backcountry roadtrip with an old-fashioned, black-coffee-swilling action hero at the wheel." —ANDREW ERVIN, *The Miami Herald*

"If you can imagine a past-paced detective story with a broken heart, you have a pretty fair idea of Fred Busch's *North*. What Jack, the hero of the earlier novel *Girls*, uncovers in the course of his laconic sleuthing may be criminal cruelty, but what he carries in himself is the abyss. A wrenchingly wonderful book."

—JANET BURROWAY, author of *Writing Fiction*

"With the restraint of a master storyteller, Busch unfolds before us a tightly spun tale of past secrets and sadnesses, allowing us to enter Jack's loneliness in a way that makes us less lonely, sheltering us in moments of luminous transcendence. This is a tender and tough and wonderful book."

—ELIZABETH STROUT, author of *Amy and Isabelle*

"Ghost story, love story, literary thriller, Frederick Busch's *North* is an exhilarating exploration of the dangerous terrain between memory and experience, a journey to the borderlands where the delicate interplay between a haunted landscape and a man's psyche exposes the cost of compassion." —MELANIE RAE THON

NORTH

NORTH

A NOVEL

FREDERICK BUSCH

BALLANTINE BOOKS • NEW YORK

JUDY BUSCH: TRUE NORTH

2006 Ballantine Books Trade Paperback Edition

Copyright © 2005 by Frederick Busch
Reading group guide copyright © 2006 by Random House, Inc.

Published in the United States by Ballantine Books, an imprint of The Random House
Publishing Group, a division of Random House, Inc., New York.

BALLANTINE and colophon are registered trademarks of Random House, Inc.
READER'S CIRCLE and colophon are trademarks of Random House, Inc.

Originally published in hardcover in the United States by
W. W. Norton & Company, Inc., in 2005.

Library of Congress Cataloging-in-Publication Data

Busch, Frederick.
North : a novel / Frederick Busch. — 1st ed.
p. cm.
ISBN 0-345-48683-8
1. New York (State) — Fiction. 2. Loss (Psychology) — Fiction.
3. Missing persons — Fiction. 4. Widowers — Fiction. I. Title.
PS3552.U814N67 2005
813'.54 — dc22   2005001531

Printed in the United States of America

www.thereaderscircle.com

2   4   6   8   9   7   5   3   1

BLOWBACK

I N A MARRIAGE, you have to tell your secret. I came to believe that. But I also came to believe that my wife would die of ours. So I kept it to myself. The marriage ended. Fanny moved on in upstate New York. I went west and south. I didn't know what to look for so I looked for work. I was all kinds of hired security in the usual dark, cheap uniform that was always tight across the chest and shoulders or too short from the tails to the neck. One way or another, I worked with a patch of skin showing.

When we were together the dog tried to look after us. Whenever Fanny cried he thumped his tail against the floor. He'd done it since we got married. Sometimes it was the sound of his tail that lifted us out of that minute's misery.

He always knew what he was supposed to do, even after Fanny left with nothing but a couple of suitcases and some cardboard boxes and a cheap urn filled with ashes. He and I were together in New York and then New Mexico and across the Southwest. We went directly west for a while and then we went south and then we headed east. We stopped on the Carolina coast. I had been a military policeman, a deputy sheriff in three counties and two states, a campus cop in northern New York, a head of strip mall security in Arizona, department store security in Portland, Oregon, and a guard in a private psychiatric clinic not far from Eugene. I was climbing slowly down the ladder of police work. I figured soon I would be a half-drunk bouncer in a porn palace in a medium-sized city I hadn't heard of yet in a state I hadn't meant to visit.

Sometimes I still couldn't get warm. I woke up out of my life in air-conditioned rooms and the hot, wet countryside of the Carolina coast. Then I was back in the world made of snow again and the winds that came down from Canada. I would brew a pot of coffee in the tiny kitchenette of my efficiency apartment. Maybe I would sweeten the coffee with sour mash. I would stand there cupping the white china mug like it was a bowl of live coals in a blizzard.

It was me and the dog before the marriage and during it and afterward for fifteen years. I was the one who questioned everything I did. He was the one who always knew what he should do. His work included guiding me on missions whether or not he understood what they were or where we had to go. He protected me under any circumstances. He assisted me by carrying objects encountered on the ground. In the truck he rode to my right. He was at my left ankle when we walked. He was in charge of observing any creature that wasn't us.

He usually came with me when I did my rounds of the resort that employed me to keep the guests safe from each other and the usual infiltrators of places like that. I watched for whores of both sexes, petty thieves, the occasional rapist, a variety of grifters. Security was made up of me and moonlighters from area police departments and Maurice Pettey. He was known as Mo. He was a guard at East Carolina and a B+ student in economics the color of weathered cherrywood boards. He was the size of a small bulldozer. The football season of his senior year was coming up and he thought he might get himself drafted the following spring by the NFL. "This here is my ticket," he said while he pounded his own hard ass with his giant fist. "My muscle is my *mo-dus-op-or-end-I*," he said. "You want the ticket, you got to hump the bale." He grew short-tempered because he was working out harder in his off time and he was cutting down on snacks. "I am growing agile, mobile, hostile, and erectile," he told me. He felt peckish, he said. That was his grandmother's word. On the job he'd grown mean. He was watchful and bright. He talked a mixture of television and what I thought of as poetry and the teachings of his grandmother.

He was peckish, he said, when he dismissed from the beach-view dining room an ensign, the ensign's new wife, and her parents. He got offended when the drunk ensign kept calling the chilled Pouilly-Fuisse "pussy foosy." Several days later he dislocated the finger of a woman who tried to cut his face up with her long fingernails after he mistook her for a hooker working the bar. "Wouldn't you of mistook her for a whore?" he asked the night manager as the woman sat on her barstool behind him. She went for his face. He turned and caught her hand and then tossed it away from him. The move dislocated her index finger and brought in the first law enforcement convention of the summer season. There were state police, sheriff's deputies, a carload of Shore Patrol and enough emergency medical technicians clustered around the weeping guest to give you the impression they were treating her for a shotgun wound to the upper thorax. I begged the management to keep him on for two more weeks so he could leave for early practice with another salary packet in his jeans.

The second law enforcement convention occurred in the first week of August. I wasn't on duty but I decided to hang around the resort that night because Mo was now two days away from reporting to campus for practice and he was hungry all the time. I came alone because the dog was in pretty bad shape. He had to work hard to breathe these days. His muzzle was much milkier. His eyes had the dull glaze they get when the lenses harden. But it was his breathing that told you he was in trouble. The larynx muscles were paralyzed so his airway didn't open wide enough for him to draw a decent breath. The surgery with heavy anesthesia was a long procedure and neither of the vets I'd talked to would promise he would survive or even feel a good deal better. Generally I tried not to ask for promises. This time I did. The vets couldn't give me a guarantee. So the dog and I walked very slowly together while he heaved for breath and growled down whatever air he could. He sounded like the drain of a kitchen sink when it emptied. It didn't help him that his hips were crippled from dysplasia and the forelegs stiff with arthritis. We walked side by side. We took our time.

I was in the big bar on a Thursday night when it was crowded with a package tour on a long weekend as well as the usual officers from the base. As far as I could see there weren't any female whores. There was one man you might call a gigolo. He was a service reject in his thirties named Jason Arnold who worked the available older women with some success because he was tall and tan and what I guess you might call sleek. I had banned him but I was only a costume cop and he knew it.

I asked Robbie, the college kid bartender who shaved his head daily but his chubby cheeks rarely, for a glass of mineral water with ice. I held the cold glass against my cheek and stared at Jason Arnold. Nothing intimidated him but I thought I ought to try. He was talking to a woman nearly six feet tall with big shoulders who was wearing a dress cut off in back under the shoulder blades. She looked uncomfortable and I couldn't tell whether it was because of the dress or Arnold. He was moving his hands in the air imitating how pilots do it. They usually did it gracefully. Arnold looked like his hands were going to fall onto her shoulders or her chest. Her back blushed and I enjoyed watching the color come up over her skin. She had shiny dark hair and a crooked nose. She was trying to keep acting dignified, I thought. And he was probably talking about sex. I waited to see if she needed me. I reminded myself that my job consisted of maintaining a pleasant social atmosphere and not of deciding which women needed guidance and protection.

Arnold put his hand on her back. She sat on her barstool a second or two without moving. Then she leaned forward away from the hand. The hand went with her. She looked up sharply. He put his hand on her ass and held it there. She said something I didn't hear and I went there.

I stood behind Arnold. A chunky, bucktoothed woman to his right who I recognized as local turned around on her stool to ask me, "You going to break anybody's hand tonight?"

"No, ma'am," I said. "That would be my young colleague, Maurice. He's patrolling the grounds right now, I believe. But he'll be here soon. Excuse me."

Arnold's back was rigid. I told it, "I wish you'd consider working someplace else tonight."

The woman to his left with the blushing back was facing me now. She said, "Working?"

"I'm sorry," I said.

She said, "Oh, Jesus. I didn't—well, I did. Can you believe it? I did. And I'm a *lawyer*."

"Well, ma'am, they say he's a charmer."

Arnold got down from his stool and tried to tower above me. Since we were pretty much the same height, that wasn't easy for him. He was broad enough, with thick forearms to prove how hard he worked with weights. His jeans were tight and they had a crease pressed into the legs. They were cut to show just enough of his cowboy boots for you to appreciate they were made of the skin of something unusual that was dyed black and red. He looked at me like I amused him.

The bucktoothed woman struck me as a lot of fun. Her eyes were merry and fond of trouble. She said to the older man to her right, "I think he's going to break somebody's hand."

"It was a dislocated finger, ma'am," I said, "and you'll have to consult with Mr. Pettey about that."

"Well, we'll see," she said.

The lawyer with the uncomfortable dress and the blue-green eyes had a broad mouth that must have been a liability in the court-room. It told me just how silly she thought she had been and it was asking if I might be able to give her a hand. Her voice was low and a little harsh. I couldn't imagine it whining. She said, "What kind of mess are we in?"

"He and I will get the whole thing done in a minute or two. I'll try and make sure you aren't embarrassed."

"Oh," she said, "I've *been* to embarrassed. Now I'm halfway to humiliated on the number Nine express. That's on the New York City subway system."

"Yes, ma'am," I said. Then I said to Jason Arnold, "We need to exit the premises."

He stepped back. He spread his long, thick arms. He crooned, "I stand before you, ladies, free, white, and twenty-one."

The bucktoothed woman said to the man beside her, "He's ten years older than that if he's a day. And *I* wouldn't wave no hands around in the air inside of this place, with its reputation for break-ing them and all."

"No, ladies," Arnold said, "I have the strength of twelve tonight, and I am ready to serve and service one and all." His face was very sweaty, dark red, and I didn't think it was only from the Manhattans on the rocks he'd been drinking.

"Okay," I said. "I want you to do your service in a tavern some-place down the road. You're a free man and this is a free country. But it's a private hotel. I get to pick who stays and who goes. You go." I went for the basic come-along. You grab a finger and you turn their hand palm-up and then you lift, bending back, at the same time. It's fast, simple, and no one resists. The body doesn't allow it.

"You told me you wouldn't break no fingers," the bucktoothed woman said.

"I really don't want to break anything," I told her. I lifted his hand to move him along and he couldn't help rising onto his toes. But he was gritty and maybe he was flushed from chemicals. Something drove him right through the pain and it must have been considerable. He went for my Adam's apple and he squeezed it. He snarled. I reacted without thought. I'd been trained to. I snapped his pinky or his ring finger and freed my right arm. He was still throttling me when I used the right. If there is trouble and a man leaves his midsection exposed then you go for it, and especially if he seems drunk or amped on coke or amphetamine. Someone that highly cranked is all energy and no mind. The solar plexus will stop them. I swiveled my hips and drove my fist maybe six inches into the meat below where his ribs met above the stomach. I got into those nerves with enough power to make him stand absolutely still. All his motion stopped and then his mouth opened while his face went white. Then he caved in over his gut and went down into a ball on the floor. He made awful noises and I felt sorry for the guests who had to hear them. I noticed that the lawyer was looking at me and not at Jason Arnold. I noticed that I was looking at her instead of him.

Robbie put a glass of mineral water over ice on the bar where I could see it and I nodded to thank him. Whenever you fight you run the risk of breaking someone up a good deal worse than you want to. I didn't think I'd tried to do anything permanent to Arnold. I would say so to whichever cops and even prosecutors I might have to deal with. But I didn't say a lot when the Shore Patrol arrived. They didn't have jurisdiction since Navy or Marines weren't involved. But the room was filled with noise and loud music and women not wearing too many clothes so they stayed on. Maurice Pettey was there and he seemed to know instantly that an approach to the bucktoothed woman might be rewarding. She held one of his giant hands in both of hers and examined it. Lester Golden was the sheriff's deputy who was a former Air Force mechanic. He came next. He squatted beside the heaving victim and went through his pockets. Then he stood above him. He cocked his head at me. I shrugged. The EMTs came next and they left with Jason Arnold.

Lester took some notes and I told the story again for Mo. He said, "You are the man with the moves, baby," and pounded me on top of the head to show his approval.

Then I went over to the lawyer. She looked confused.

"You all right?"

She nodded. "I'm feeling a little humiliated, but that passes. Right?"

"I'll walk you out to the lobby," I said, but she shook her head. "You'd prefer to get out of here altogether?" I asked. She nodded. She was blushing now and I wondered if that was a liability for a lawyer. I took her upper arm, which was nicely muscled and very smooth. "Come with me, why don't you, ma'am." I aimed us toward the fire door that went out the side of the hotel.

She said, "It makes me feel a little old if you call me ma'am. Say Merle, if you would. Merle Davidoff."

"Jack," I said, "and I'm plenty enough older than you."

"And violent," she said.

"I suppose."

"And—what? Gallant? You were coming to rescue me. All the way across the floor of that terrible lounge. I watched you in the mirror behind the bar. You were looking at me and that what's-his-name, and then you came over when he set his sweaty hand along my ass."

"Your back blushed. It was like a flag going up."

We were walking on the gravel outside the bar. The vegetation smelled sweet and maybe a little rotten. Usually the salt of the sea came in on the wind and cut the rankness of whatever it was that bloomed with fleshy white petals and a high, sweet perfume.

"The thing was, Jack," she said, "all I was after was feeling something. Is this an imposition to have to hear?"

"No."

"I'm not talking about sex," she said. I steered her toward my truck. I enjoyed holding the upper part of her arm.

"No," I said. "Feelings. In the—where? I guess you'd say heart. Would you?"

"That's what I would say," she said. "That kind of feeling. I'm three years into being divorced, and I don't do it well, apparently. First I felt battered, and then I felt so lonely I thought I was going to have to hire teams of people to keep me company from after dinner until bedtime. And then I thought I wasn't ever going to have emotions again. Where are you in all of that?"

"You mean which do I feel?"

"Or not feel."

I didn't know what to tell her. I didn't know what to tell myself.

"Well, isn't it absurd for me to barge in and stroll through your life like that," she said.

"No," I said. "I'm pretty dull and everyday. I try not paying too much attention to how I feel."

"Sure," she said. "But does it work?"

I opened the passenger-side door of the truck. "Would you like a cup of coffee?" I asked her. "At my place? It's safe. There's a chaperon there. Or I can drive you for a hamburger or a beer someplace and then get you back to the hotel when it's a little less crowded in the lobby or the bar."

"Do you make good coffee?"

"I sometimes add sour mash to sweeten it."

"I drink Scotch," she said.

"That's okay," I said. "We can drive you someplace for coffee and Scotch. Or we can just walk back around to the lobby. Whatever you want."

"Your coffee," she said. "And I can try some sour mash with it, please."

We didn't talk in the truck. I hadn't ridden alone in a vehicle with a woman who wasn't a prisoner or a cop for a very long time. I looked at the road and the beach houses. I was aware of the heat off her body and the smell of perfume and soap and skin.

Inside my place she headed for the kitchenette and stooped down in front of the little refrigerator. "There we go," she said, taking out a bunch of radishes I didn't remember buying. They were held together with a heavy blue rubber band that she stripped from the wilted radish stems. She gathered her shiny dark hair and slipped the rubber band over it to make a loose ponytail that showed me her ears.

Then she went back to the living room. He didn't make a fool of himself with her. He was never one of those goofy Labradors who try to pick you up like a stick and carry you around. But he seemed to approve of her. He stood beside her with his tail slowly brushing back and forth while she took off her high-heeled shoes. She sat down on the floor with her back against the front of the dark tan sofa that came with the place. She crossed her legs at the ankles. He walked over them to lie down beside her. After a while she was leaning her weight against him. He took it easily and they seemed all right together. I went around the corner into the kitchenette to brew coffee.

"What's his name?" Merle asked.

"He doesn't have one," I said.

She didn't ask me why. She apparently said something to him. I heard his tail along the carpeting. Then she called, "I'm supposed to be attending a legal seminar at that terrible place. That hotel of last resort. But I am not going to a single meeting."

"You're going home," I said.

"First flight out to New York that I can book."

"Good idea," I said.

"Why? Are you tired of rescuing me?"

"I think *you're* tired of feeling what you've been feeling."

I brought two mugs of coffee with sour mash around to where she and the dog sat together.

"And what have I been feeling, would you say?"

"Something that would make a woman like you sit at a bar with Jason Arnold."

"Is he really a male hooker?"

"Well, let's say his white teeth and his healthy physique do him more good in the bars around the island than his service record. He was washed out of basic on account of theft. He claims to sell insurance for a living. I think he does sell some. But he seems to make most of his money off of drugs brought into the States by service personnel. He isn't pressing charges against me because the sher-iff's deputy found a ladies' powder compact on him. Maybelline, I believe was the brand. Only he emptied out the face powder and replaced it with cocaine. Which he was snorting, I believe, shortly before he laid his hand on you. That would explain his energy and speed when he was able to get onto my throat."

"And didn't you punish him," she said.

"That wasn't very smart. It was automatic."

"Fighting is automatic to you?"

"I was a military policeman. I was a rough kid who got made sergeant in the Military Police of the United States Army. I was one of the stalwart MPs who rescued hookers from stoned dogfaces, ser-vice personnel from the hookers' pimps, and the diplomatic corps of the United States from the unhappy citizens of South Vietnam. Then in '75, the Marines rescued us all from the NVA coming down from the north. Once in a while after that I was an honest and efficient deputy sheriff. The rest of it's a downhill story."

"You're leaving out all the other rescues, aren't you?"

"What rescues?"

"The ones you can't help doing," she said. "You don't need to comment about that. But I know a rescuer when I see one. Do you ever do what private detectives do?"

"Follow husbands for their wives and get people's debts paid?"

"I had in mind something more like trying to find people who drop out of sight."

"I imagine you would know that kind of detective in New York. You know, given your business."

"It's a kid," she said. "Not such a kid, but young enough. Twenties, late twenties, my dead sister's boy. He's the love child, if love ever came into it, of my older sister's next-to-last, failing effort to be happy for more than an hour. She died." She swallowed coffee. "I'd forgotten how sweet the sour mash could taste. And her final husband. They were married for maybe twelve hours. He didn't want the kid back then, and he sure doesn't want to know him now. Tyler's more or less on his own, though he's demonstrated a willingness to accept whatever money I send him, so I send him some. And he's her kid. So I've tried to look out for him. And if I sent anybody after him, this person would have to be someone I trust. And who is, as you describe it, trained. There are unfriendly parties involved. His name is Tyler Pearl."

"He sounds like four teenaged singers and a used set of drums in someone's garage."

"Well," she said, "it's almost that innocent. Except for his full-time jones for gambling, he's kind of a sweet kid. He's my nephew, and I suppose you could say I love him. I suppose you could say he breaks my heart a little. He's got problems, and I'm who's left to try and take care of him. And now I can't find him."

"As in he's missing?"

"Missing, at least. At least."

"I'm sorry," I said. "I don't do that kind of work."

"You rescue women like me?"

"Like you?"

"That's what you said a few minutes ago. 'A woman like you.' What *is* that?"

"Smart," I said. "Sad, a little. With a nose that goes crooked a little, from left to right. Eyes that aren't only blue or only green. And who blushes."

"I hate that," she said. But she seemed to enjoy my saying it. The dog was sleeping but his tail rose and fell on the carpeting a couple of times. I wondered if he knew that Merle Davidoff might cry. I hoped not. I enjoyed watching her smile. But by then the brushing of his tail had set me thinking of Fanny. I saw how Merle Davidoff noticed something in my expression. She said, "And a woman like me is going to ask a man like you to drive me back to the hotel, please. I want to call people at airlines and get myself headed for home."

"You could call from here," I said.

"I'll call from the hotel. But you can give me your number," she said. "We might want to be in touch."

"Sure," I said.

She took a card from her long, thin purse. She left it on the floor beside the dog. She made to get up and I went from my chair to stand in front of her and stick my hand out to help her. Her palm was broad and her fingers were long. When I pulled her up her forehead came almost to my chin.

"You just went away for a minute," she said.

I didn't know how to answer that.

"Do you do that to be interesting?"

"I think I just thought of something."

She said, "I should have taken the plane down here just for a cup of coffee with you. Too bad we don't live closer."

"You don't strike me as a person who would hang around with cops."

"But I am. I practice criminal law. I spend hours and hours with cops and their victims." She waited for me to react and then she said, "It's a lawyer joke. Forgive me. I started out, before I went into this practice, as an assistant district attorney in Manhattan. I worked with the police. I even dated the police."

"I'll bet only detectives."

"One lieutenant. Once. I ended up marrying a professor, though."

"I used to know some of those."

She put the fingers of her left hand against my chest very lightly. Then she took them away. "Did you date any of them?"

I nodded. "One," I said. "Once."

"I take it you did not marry a professor?"

"No," I said. "I was married to a nurse."

"And now you're not."

"And now I'm not."

She closed her eyes and nodded and then opened them. "All right," she said. She looked at me like I was supposed to say something back. I didn't. She turned and squatted in her wrinkled, short black dress with its thin shoulder straps. She touched the dog on his muzzle, just below his eyes. He pushed his big brown head up at her hand.

"I miss you already," she said to him.

We rode in silence on the sandy road past dunes whipped by wind. Autumn storms would move the dunes to cover the road. Maurice Pettey would be knocking over linebackers at East Carolina. Drunk officers would wobble in and out of the hotel with their girlfriends and wives and even boyfriends. It would get to be Christmas and this woman would want to go shopping in New York City to find a gift for someone who cared about her needing to give them a gift.

"What is it?" she said.

"No," I said, "I was thinking."

"You went off to that place where you go."

"Sorry," I said.

"We could possibly try to be friends, Jack. We interest each other, I think."

"I like your nose."

"I got punched in Girl Scout camp. They were teaching us interpretive dance and one of the girls flapped her big, sweaty arms around a little too violently."

"That's the story of my life," I said. I saw she was looking out the window at the darkness or the sand. I said, "Well, you let me know if you need any help before you go. All right?"

"If I need any rescuing, Jack, I promise you I'll call. You gave me your number, right?"

"Yes," I lied.

She kissed me on the cheek when we stopped outside the hotel. She was out the door and on her way before I could react. I realized that I had just spent more time alone with her than with any other woman since I learned that Fanny was dead.

That night I thought about three women. I also thought about some of the kids I had looked after at the college in upstate New York. I remembered the sweet, skinny patient named Sue Ellen McGreavey in the psychiatric center who kissed me on the cheek when her parents took her home for good. When they brought her back two weeks later she didn't know who I was. I thought about Elway Bird, who was the best policeman I had known. He told me about what happened to Fanny late in the night when I decided for no reason I understood to call him up after something like a year of not calling.

Of course, it *was* for a reason. I remembered hoping that maybe Elway's wife Sarah would answer the phone. The news he gave me was my punishment for that. It was a night full of thoughts like itchy skin you can't quite manage to reach. Whenever I woke up I heard the dog panting hoarsely. He was chasing after air. I remembered the feeling on my face of her kiss.

So we were out while it was dark that morning. We went walking

very slowly along the eastern beach I liked to be on while the sun
came up. We investigated kelp and periwinkles in tide pools and we
had ourselves a pee. He moved off on his own and I looked at the
small white hairs under his tail and along the backs of his legs. That
doesn't happen with Labradors until they're plenty old. I decided to
look at the sun sit on top of the horizon. It was fat and orange and
uneven. A big man with long, thin muscles and a high, tight haircut
came jogging through. I could tell from his bearing that he was an
officer. He ran close enough to me so he could say, "Morning," and
for me to smell his alcohol and sweat. He'd be one of the lieutenants
who rented a beach house. It sometimes was a dozen of them at a
time. They'd sleep a few hours a night on beds and cots and sofas
and the floor. They'd burn off the last night's drinks and get to the
base to pound on the lowly. The sun was climbing and the dog had
walked through the fringe of the surf. Salt and the smell of seaweed
blew in at us and a small white Coast Guard cutter made its way
north parallel to the shoreline at high speed.

Merle Davidoff would be arranging a ride in the hotel jitney to
the airport. She'd go home to her apartment house and she would
think about her nephew who nobody loved and her practice of the
law. I'd have bet that she would wear her hair down over her ears
and she'd have slacks on. She would stride through the airport like
someone on a serious errand. It would have been interesting if we
had drunk a second cup of sour mash in coffee together.

The gulls were lining up on the jutting rocks a hundred feet or
so to the south. They assembled in groups and though they mostly
looked alike to me they had to be different varieties. They jumped
up off into the air and held in place. Then they rode the air currents over the ebbing tide. There were four different levels and
each bird as far as I could see returned to the one he'd started from.

All four levels were in the air at once. It was complicated traffic. All of them were looking for the same food at the same time. The one that saw and dove and rose the luckiest swooped back over the beach in a kind of arc and dropped the shell or the little crab onto the rock to break it open. They made more noise than people.

I thought of Merle and how the night before in my apartment when I had described her to herself she had cocked her head like she was laying it on her own right shoulder. I realized that some of my waking time during the night had been spent searching for what was so familiar in that. This morning I remembered. I was a very young sergeant of Military Police and I was finishing my tour at our embassy in Saigon. It was springtime in 1975 and we were pulling out. One of my nastier kids was a champion high school wrestler from Ambler, Pennsylvania, named Richie Postillo. He smacked his truncheon onto the side of a tiny woman's neck. She was shouting at him. She wanted to go out with us. She had got up onto the roof and was fighting her way toward one of the helicopters. She must have frightened him into taking her down. I didn't know if she did laundry or translated intercepts or just knew which way to aim for safety. But he laid his truncheon onto the side of the tiny woman's neck and she went down with her head cocked the way Merle's had been. The small, frowning face bounced on the ground.

If she translated, she might have worked with a civilian in Saigon who was a tall, thick man we all knew as Mr. Loomis. Mostly we called him Five. He wore metal-rimmed glasses that were tinted light green. His straw-colored hair was combed the way rock 'n' roll stars in the fifties combed theirs so the pompadour rode a couple of inches above his forehead and then swept back over the top of the ears into a duck's-ass point at the collar line. He wore civilian khaki trousers and white button-down shirts without a tie. He always wore a brown leather holster that was clipped over his left hip with the pistol butt turned forward for a right-hand cross draw. He wore heavy brown leather engineer's boots and he never rolled up his shirtsleeves. The MP detachment that guarded the vehicle shed and gate perimeters got our information from the Marines who guarded the entrances and diplomatic personnel. Sometimes they fed us dirt on the bosses, though mostly they scorned us. I couldn't blame them. Most of us Army were young, stupid, tough, but not well trained and not as groomed or just plain ready as the Marines. But one of them told one of us that Mr. Loomis went back to Phoenix Project days and had personally minused five local leaders found to be working for the north. He drove himself because he didn't trust the local drivers and he didn't want military personnel knowing his routine. Whenever he was on his way to one of the cars, we'd signal each other by holding up a hand with its fingers widely separated.

She leaned her head to the right and went down and bounced. I didn't see her stand again. It was a panic, a riot, and the Americans were as terrified as the South Vietnamese regulars and civilians. My corporal and the privates didn't trust me enough and I didn't trust my lieutenant enough to entirely believe we'd be extracted to the carrier *Hancock* that was lying offshore. The Marines knew their officers would take care of them. They always did. None of us believed anything until we were up in a Huey that buzzed and bucked over a country we swallowed some of and couldn't stomach and vomited out.

I thought Merle Davidoff set her head to the right that way because she couldn't help showing you she was interested in seeing who you were. I imagined her doing that in a courtroom to a judge and really annoying him. I had to smile. We were standing on the shore in the hot wind and the cries of wheeling gulls and an increased traffic in jogging military. As if they were flying cover, a squadron of nine pelicans worked single-file from behind us. They pumped on in that absolute silence of theirs low over the surf and then headed toward where the shoreline curved and the east-west roadway began. It was very good to see something so orderly.

We went back to the truck. He usually put his forepaws onto the cab floor and I gave him a shove from behind so he could scramble in and then up onto the passenger seat. This time he stood on the sand and looked ahead. Then he looked at me. He didn't move and I knew it was because he couldn't. I picked him up and placed him inside. After I shut his door I went around and sat in the truck with the engine running. I looked at him. Then I couldn't. Then I put it in gear and we drove the two lanes edged by that fine sand that blew onto the road and that also was carried away to the sea. There were areas fenced off to preserve the shore and then there were the one-story box-shaped vacation houses rented out to the junior officers. That was the summer we took three hurricanes in seventy days, and dozens of batten-board homes were leveled. Most of them didn't have cellars so what you found along the roads after the winds died were rectangular rain-soaked cement pads and fragments of living arrangements. There would be a grape-colored toothbrush driven like a nail into a piece of wood that had been the molding in the corner of a room. There would be undershorts wrapped around a skeleton of hedge. There would be a refrigerator on its back like a pale coffin.

Mo had his last weekend of work and he didn't break anyone up. Neither did I. When we said goodbye I told him, "You'll need to be nimble, Mo. I'll look in the papers for your name. I would love to hear you made it to the big time."

"Oh, you'll hear, Jack," he said, "because *I* am the Jack be nimble. *You* be the jack of spades. You like the smack I can run? I am full to the neckbone with electric jive. Ipso facto, Mo' ready for the En Eff of El."

"Well, you go to class all year. Don't forget to be smarter than you look."

He grinned a very broad, very white smile, like Louis Armstrong when he performed. Then he smiled like he meant it and he hugged me goodbye. It was like being embraced by a rhino.

The dog heaved for breath whether we walked or simply stayed in the air-conditioned room. I kept him there when I went to work. Then I spent more than I should have for a new used truck I didn't need. I reasoned that the 4WD would get us onto the beach so he'd have less of a walk to the sea. The air-conditioning would make it easier for him to sit up on the seat next to mine when I delivered him there so he could act like a puppy in charge of an errand. He'd been bred for missions and I thought he ought to have them. His breathing grew worse. On the hottest afternoons he lay himself flat on the bathroom floor between the tub and the toilet where it was cool. His muzzle was hard against the tiles and his tongue was stiff. When he lifted his head to suck for air he panted harder.

On the third from my last day there I bought a new shower curtain. I put it in the bed of the truck along with an old bedsheet. I lifted him up onto the passenger seat and then I went around to belt myself in and start up. He stared out front and seemed to watch with his usual intensity. He was serious because we were in the truck and that meant we were on a mission. His excitement caused him to work very hard for breath. I talked to him. I talked about what a fine fellow he was and how necessary our trip was. He was patient but he ignored me because he knew that what I said was unimportant. This was an errand and errands meant you kept an eye on the world and went straight ahead. You were supposed to be silent. As usual he shamed me into shutting up. He seemed to recognize the beach and the small road that left the blacktop which was traveled by Shore Patrol vehicles and boys and girls intent on getting into trouble and each other. When I stopped he gathered himself and he came behind me as if he was younger. He almost jumped and didn't quite fall from the seat down onto the sand.

He didn't go ahead of me as he often tried to on these trips. He knew to stop. We were surrounded by very high mounds of earth moved aside for the construction of vacation houses. I didn't take any tools from the bed of the truck. I stood next to him close to the truck. I looked at the sky that was going gray with ranks of cloud that were curly and welded together.

I waited to say something. He waited because I waited. He looked at me and he must have sensed how coiled for it I was or how coiled away from it. But I think he knew I was in trouble. He readjusted his stance on the sandy earth. His tail was up. His breathing was hoarse. It sounded damp and obstructed. But his nose worked the incoming winds. He leaned his bulk against me and we stayed like that. We inspected the world together.

I was going to say something.

I stayed where I was. I heard the gulls groan and scold. I heard the tide smack the sand. I said nothing. I reached past him to the open door of the truck and took the .32-caliber Taurus 741 from the side compartment and looked only at the back of his head. I had taken the pistol away from a kid I arrested in a whorehouse in Saigon and I'd kept it oiled and clean. Every now and again you need certain tools. The gusting winds took the sound of the shot away. It was like a puff of ocean air coming straight down. I could see the coarse, glossy hair on the back of his head shift. I remembered looking down out of the air from a helicopter flying in low. The vegetation stirred and then you were past it watching something else. I was not looking at the blood or fragments or the spatter of the blowback on my jeans. I was studying the mound of earth off to our right past the truck. I finally looked. I had made a mess of him. He was like objects in a reddish brown sack. He was disorganized. His teeth were exposed and you could have decided he was snarling. Or you could have said he wore one of those loopy dog grins. His tongue stuck out. He looked ridiculous, like everyone else who died.

"You silly boy," was what I finally said.

I wrapped him in my bedsheet and then in the shower curtain. I took my old long-handled pointed shovel from the truck bed and I dug. The earth there was soil mixed with sand and there was enough of a clay base for burial. I didn't want the winds moving cover off his grave so I went deep. It took me all of the morning to work him in right. A Shore Patrol four-wheel drive vehicle slowed and a midshipman looked at me through squinted eyes. I squinted back once and kept digging. He moved on. I tamped the dirt into hard layers four times. It was the best privacy I could give him. I'd thought about one of those veterinarians' cremations but I couldn't see myself not doing all of the work on his death. I didn't want to let a stranger burn him. I was supposed to take care of him and I did. There had been others in my life I was supposed to take care of in the same way but I hadn't. I wasn't letting that happen again.

I threw the shovel into the truck very hard. I'd carried it for years. I think I'd hated it for years. I went forward to the cab but then went back to his grave again. I wished then that I had a map with me so I could mark the place. I waited to see if there was anything to say. But there wasn't and I left him there.

I bought a cap for the truck so I could lock my clothes and my household gear inside. I didn't like the look of it but the metal rectangle with its useless little side windows and the silly small door at the back was going to be all the home that I had. I gave notice at the hotel and I told my landlord. I tried to iron the wrinkles out of my blue-and-white-striped seersucker sport coat. I hung it off a gun rack hook behind the passenger seat. The weapon I could have set on the rack was a Korean War vintage .30-caliber M-1 carbine. I locked it back in the cap. I had a big jug for keeping coffee hot and some compact disks to play. I was going through my Linda Ronstadt phase. I did that every few years. She and I started to sing "It's So Easy" when I rolled out on the long drive to New York City to see if Merle Davidoff really had work for me.

I was working with Linda on "Ooh Baby Baby" when I went past the dunes at the end of the beach where I had dug him in. I stopped singing. I shifted down and then into neutral and let the truck idle while I looked at where I'd left him. I let myself try to remember him from when Fanny and I lived together in New York State and had plans. Then I stopped. You need to be able to stop that. I put the truck in gear and let Linda Ronstadt sing on her own while I drove north.

BUSHWHACK

I WENT WEST and north on 40 to I-95. When I got crazy with highway traffic I ducked off to 301. It was a slower road with more to look at if you can stand looking at little used car lots and unpainted motel cabins and hamburger stands. The middle of August was a bad time for highway traveling and not only because of the heat whenever you stopped or the strain on the engine. There were too many vehicles on the road and too many people at the rest stops. Every large rest area had a special place for people to walk their dogs. I saw Rottweilers fed fresh water from a plastic jug and collies with heads too narrow for brains and the occasional Newfoundland laboring in the heat under what looked like a hundred pounds of black hair. I saw mutts who leaned toward the rodent side of life. And of course there were Labrador retrievers everywhere. There were plenty of yellow or black imperfect ones who were too stalky on their legs or too skinny in the snout or too thin at the flank. But there was a liver-colored, well-muscled, big-headed, slightly gutslung, short-legged Labrador who had been placed in charge of the entire rest stop and knew it. I had to look away. I'd read once about a famous man who was a drunk. Apparently he mistreated one of his Labradors. I never heard what he did but he knew and that was enough. When the drink got to him very badly he hallucinated his own death. He had to face a council chamber of Labradors. They all stared at him with that serious face that can look inside you. Their alertness to your feelings is terrible sometimes. They get dopey and cocked sometimes like they're about to hurl themselves off somewhere if you'll just make clear what you need them to do. But if you're annoyed or hung over or too lazy they will know it. You'll have to look away ashamed. When I saw the biggest and most intelligent of them during that trip, I thought of the famous drunk man and his dreams about dying. And of course I thought about putting my dog down.

I found a motel room off the throughway near Dale City and I slept awhile. I left before dawn. I was furious to get there even though I hadn't much of an idea why. I needed work. But I didn't have to drive to New York City to find it. It wouldn't be a burden to see Merle Davidoff. But once I saw her I'd leave town. I knew that. Maybe I wanted to work for her because I would have to drive upstate again to where her nephew disappeared. I would have to see the countryside my daughter and my marriage died in. It was the land that the missing girl was buried under. Maybe it was that.

Later on, I slept a few hours in the parking lot of a truck stop in Pennsylvania someplace, maybe a hundred miles from New York. Because it was hot I kept the windows of my truck open. I heard the idling of the tractors while I shut my eyes and tried to fool myself into thinking I slept so I could fall asleep. A wind came up toward dawn. It blew hot grease fumes from the restaurant and it carried the noises that the truckers made tightening lashed loads on pallets and filling ice chests and calling home on cell phones and radios. I had slept a little so I knew I could do the rest of the drive. I went into the bathroom and then the restaurant and ate one of those official truck-driver breakfasts of fried potatoes and maybe half a dozen eggs and six or seven pieces of bacon and rye toast soggy with butter. I filled my jug with coffee and took off again. I complained along with Linda. We were just some broken-hearted toy who someone played with. We tried and we tried, but we couldn't let go. Poor us.

When I did reach New York I was impressed coming in through the tunnel from New Jersey by all the separateness I saw dancing around every other separateness. The heat was heavy and full of diesel hanging like an invisible grease on the lighter stink of burnt-up leaded gasoline. I found myself happy for so much action. We all pretended to ignore each other but we were wary. I had fun with our mistrust. We hung alongside each other in the tunnel at fifty when it should have been twenty and we were six inches apart when it ought to have been plenty more. We made believe we didn't worry. We were suspicious as hell. It was a dangerous and foreign-feeling place. It was more concentrated and a little faster than any city I'd been except for Tokyo. I found myself grinning at it. You never know what kind of a change you might need.

It was close to two in the afternoon when I exited the tunnel. I worked through traffic to Third Avenue and made a left because the lane I was in went that way. According to the map left meant north. That was where I was headed. I pretended to be making decisions. I found a twenty-four-hour parking garage that would take the truck. The attendant told me pickup trucks were illegal on many of the roadways around New York and I'd been risking a hefty traffic citation. I told him I'd been illegal before and I tried not to give him any of the Carolina twang I might have acquired down there. I'd been southerly for a long time. Before I left the garage I put on the seersucker sport jacket I had pressed some of the wrinkles from. I wore it over a clean white T-shirt and the same jeans I'd been driving in. I had my fairly new half boots on. To look like a professional I carried a notebook I had bought at a rest stop. It was about the size of my hand and spiral bound and bright red. The cover said in white letters that I had a friend in Pennsylvania.

I walked from the parking garage on Third Avenue in the 40s up to 57th. I cut one block east by mistake and then made my way back west to Madison. It was good walking and I was like every hayseed you hear about. I studied the carved stone over the entrances to buildings. I watched the buses kneel to take on hobbled passengers. I looked at the men and women passing me like they were part of the scenery provided by the chamber of commerce for my entertainment. I kept wondering at how many people there were and how few of them knew anything about me or each other or possibly even themselves. I thought I might better leave that part of it to someone specializing in the field. The only real experts I knew were a psychologist and a chocolate Lab and both of them were dead. I was beginning to yawn a lot and I wanted a nap. I gave coins to street people who seemed very competent about being stripped by their lives to the bone. I was surprised how few beggars there were for the simmer of people that the streets were in. I speculated that they might round them up to keep them away from the well-fed people who owned a place to live in. Inside a very swell restaurant they told me very quickly that there wouldn't be a table for half an hour. I sat at the bar and drank an Amstel that cost me seven dollars and change. I scooped up some salty little fish-shaped crackers from the bowl in front of me and I decided to skip the meal and go up and get started. I left change from a ten on the bar when I left but no one applauded.

The streets smelled damp and sour. People looked like the air they took in tasted that way. It was a time when your energy might dwindle. The city seemed to make it evaporate like sweat. When I walked into the ice-cold narrow lobby made of orange-brown marble I was reading her business card. That apparently marked me as a tradesman. The security man was dressed in a dark blazer and crisp light slacks and shiny shoes. He said, "Who you want, brother?"

It meant *what* do you want and it sounded like what *could* you want?

I told him and he consulted his list. Then he stepped back to a desk and pushed some computer keys. He shook his head. "I ain't got you."

"I don't have an appointment."

"Then you don't go up."

"No," I said, "I want to go up and *make* an appointment."

"You ever hear of the telephone?" He shook his head and smiled at the man he was issuing a visitor's pass. This was a person on the list. He said to me, "You call upstairs, they make you an appointment, do they want to see you. Then you can show up here and get you a pass. But you *got* to be on my list."

"It's for a job."

He looked past me, then around. "You out of work?"

I nodded.

"Bad times," he said.

"Bad."

"And you got you a plan? I mean, they going to *want* you?"

"I'd bet money on it."

"What kind of money?"

"Twenty bucks."

"Win, place, or show?"

I lifted my foot, wiggled it, then set it back down. "Just for this toe inside their door. Give me a half an hour. You get worried, you can come looking for me."

"No, sir," he said. "I am the man lets people through. They want you out, they pay me to hold the door for the po-lice. I do strictly *low* skin contact work. You place your bet now if you like. Place it right."

I palmed a folded twenty, and I shook his hand. He pocketed the bill and he wrote out the pass that he slipped into a clear plastic carrier attached to a metal clip. "Wear this on that wrinkly jacket of yours, hear? Give me the pass when you leave. I hope you get some work, you buy you a *war*drobe."

So I had dropped thirty dollars on a beer and admission to a public building. I figured that parking would cost me another thirty. I was sure I'd be able to find a way to make it an even hundred before I left town.

It was a shallow alcove that was paneled in what I thought was black walnut and lined with a dark blue carpet so thick you could misplace a foot. The pale, sad, heavy woman at the wide wooden desk buzzed me through the glass entry doors and told me that I didn't have an appointment. I agreed. I asked if I could have one for today. She stared at me like I'd said something personal. She made a call. Then she pointed to a broad black leather sofa facing black leather chairs. I sat.

Ten minutes later a woman came through a corridor to my left. She was tall and very slender and was the same cherrywood color as Mo but with a lean face and thin lips. She stood before me. She was wearing a clear plastic telephone headset that was connected to a power pack at her waist. Her voice was very low. The smell of her perfume was delicious like a kind of creamy soap with something dark in it. I didn't know what else to do so I stood and I smiled. I realized that I was so used up I could sleep standing in front of her.

She said, "Wait a minute. Do that again, will you?"

"What?"

"Give me that tired smile."

I shook my head and bared my fangs.

"No," she said. "You've got another one. Give me the other one."

I shrugged and smiled. I was going to have to work my way out of the city into New Jersey, where I thought I stood a better chance of finding a clean cheap hotel.

She said, "That's right. You're the one from down South, aren't you?"

"I've been there."

"No, she talked about you. Some kind of fracas at her hotel, and you were a good guy about it. If I can make some time, she'll see you."

"Ms. Davidoff," I said.

"She's who you asked for. You're who she talked about. Unless I'm wrong and you aren't who you look like and you're maybe an attorney licensed to practice in the state of New York. Or perhaps you're serving papers?"

"I am not an attorney," I said. "Or the other thing—papers."

"Well, that's fortunate," she said. "Sit over here and read a business magazine and make believe you enjoy it."

I sat with *Barron's* on my lap and I closed my eyes and slept. What wakened me was the shifting of her heel on the carpet. She was wearing the same perfume as her assistant. Her hair was over her ears. She was in a loosely woven suit of coarse texture. It looked like a kind of canvas that was the color of sand. She wore an amber necklace and a matching bracelet with silver settings. Her nose went left to right, just a little, and I still couldn't decide whether her eyes were green or blue. She stood with her hands clasped before her and she was blushing as she smiled. I thought I might be blushing too.

While I was driving up north and even when I was making my way into the city I'd gone over with myself what I might say if I got to meet her again. I had wondered if I'd come up to New York because my dog was dead and because at my age there was nobody left alive I could think of except maybe Sergeant Elway Bird of the New York State Police and Sarah his wife who would possibly be pleased to see me.

I stood. I watched her face. I saw her assistant down the corridor studying us. I was going to tell her my dog died. I wondered if I had to say I'd killed him. But what I heard from my mouth was, "What do they think, all those people walking behind their dog with a plastic bag over their hand? You must have some heavy-duty leash laws here."

She opened her mouth to reply. She didn't seem to know what to say. Of course not, I told myself. She isn't used to exchanging views on dog shit.

She finally said, "Hello, Jack. I'm very happy to see you." She gave me a fine handshake with her arm extended low and the palm and fingers long and strong. "What was that about the pooper-scooper people?"

I shook my head.

"How's your dog?"

I found that my throat had closed. It was always risky coming off something tough when people were nice to you. She looked at me and said, "We'll go to my office." She turned and led me and I was glad to follow. The office was small and not filled with antiques and good wood like I'd expected. Her desk was stacked with briefs and some thick books with place markers sticking out. There were piles of magazines on the floor under the broad window that looked out onto a side street and maybe, I figured, Madison Avenue or the one that was east of it, Park. There were two water-colors framed under glass that hung on the wall behind her. One was of ocean and sand and the other was of rocks and kelp and the surf striking. The sky was dark in each painting and the light was kind of yellow. I knew the colors of coastal storms and I liked see-ing the pictures. On my right between bookcases opposite her desk I saw a large poster for an exhibition in London of the etch-ings of George Cruikshank. I stood and looked at the paintings behind her and then back at the poster. Then I sat in one of two clients' chairs. Instead of sitting behind her desk she came around to sit in the chair beside mine.

I smelled that perfume again and wondered whether she'd given it to her assistant or if the assistant had given it to her. There was something good about their being on those terms.

She said, "Cruikshank was famous in the 1800s. He illustrated books. Dickens used him. He was very famous for his stories in pic-tures, and for claiming that he'd thought up *Oliver Twist*."

"I never heard of him," I said. "Cruikshank."

"Well, who did? Why would you? My husband was a teacher," she said. "I told you that, right? He was an art history teacher. He did his work on Cruikshank. We thought the dispute over *Oliver Twist* bridged the gap between our fields. Dickens wrote a lot about lawyers."

"I knew some teachers when I worked upstate. We got one free course every term, and I took some. I was a late bloomer, one of them told me. I'm still waiting to bloom. Was it a tough divorce?"

"He was the one who did the divorcing. I became divorced. He was enchanted. His word. By an art student. According to my former husband, she had perfect breasts, springy and taut. Those are his words. And everything else was just right, and he once more sensed the possibilities, end of quote. He loved giving her volumes of what he liked to call lyric verse."

"Lyric verse," I said. "Instead of giving them to you?"

She closed her eyes and nodded tightly. "Thank you," she said.

I said, "Poetry."

"The very same. Tell me why you're here. No," she said. "Don't. How's that? Don't tell me why you're here. Let me take you to dinner. Let me make you dinner. I can't cook. Let me take you to dinner. Where did you leave your dog?"

She looked away for a bit, then she looked at me hard. I could see the lawyer in her calculating. She finally said, "Damn it, Jack."

I nodded. I couldn't think of anything I might say to make it easier for either of us.

"Jack," she said.

"I like the rocks in that painting. I feel like I've seen that place."

"It's in Maine, up past Portland. Down east, they say, but it's really up along the coast. I painted that."

"I know that country a little. Anyone can paint like that ought to be receiving the volumes of lyric verse," I said.

"You know, you're a swell fellow," she said.

I had said that, said something like it, to the dog when we were driving to the beach to finish things or afterward. I couldn't remember which but I could hear myself saying it. I didn't mind if she said the same to me. I had meant it and I'd wanted him to know. I wouldn't have minded if Ms. Merle Davidoff meant it too. At the right time that feeling could be worth the drive to New York. But I wanted to be very careful about not banking on it for more than the second I'd felt it most powerfully. It's like looking at good countryside when you drive though it. Appreciate the land but keep moving.

"And let's not talk about Les," she said.

"The one with the friend with the springy—"

"Him," she said. "I'm divorced over two years, nearly three, and I still talk about it too much."

"Children?"

Her face went tight. "No," she said. "You?"

I shook my head.

"Divorced?"

I nodded. I hadn't been to court about it but I couldn't imagine any distance larger than the one between Fanny and me.

She asked, "Are you used to it?"

"No. I don't know. I don't feel like I *improved* because of it. I think we corrected something we couldn't find any help for. Does that make sense?"

"As much as anything else," she said.

"No," I said, "you're still wounded, you're saying."

"I am?"

"Sorry," I said.

"And you know that you can really get past that feeling?"

"It's what I've heard."

"And the wound thing would account for my acting like a high school virgin at your bar. Former bar?"

I nodded.

"Do you suppose," she said, "there *are* high school virgins any-more?"

Her assistant leaned into the office and said, "Some calls you need to take, Merle."

"I can walk around for a while," I said.

"And I can call somebody who might be able to get us a table at a very nice place I think you'll like. Why don't you go back to the hotel and take a nap, and I'll call you."

"How about I call you," I suggested.

Her assistant came back to scold. She waved me goodbye and I waved back.

In the lobby, I returned my pass to the security man. "Are we employed?"

"We're in business," I told him.

"Horse comes in *win*," he said.

"I'll start shopping clothes."

"You better," he said.

I walked, I yawned, I found a place on Madison a few blocks down from her office that would sell me a cup of coffee and a buttered English muffin for under ten bucks. Then I walked south a long distance. I ended up at Madison Square which was a little park in the 20s. I sat down opposite a huge bronze statue of a military man on a horse. I was on the other end of a bench from a man who sorted through small pieces of cloth. He wrapped and unwrapped them. He set them in four piles on his legs. He moved pieces from one pile to another. He gathered them. He studied them. Sometimes he waved one in the air before him and muttered words I couldn't make out. It occurred to me that I might wake up with my shoes gone or my seersucker sport coat shredded or my eyeballs swiped. But I listened to the traffic and to the whispering of my neighbor on the bench and I gave in and catnapped. When I woke I saw that the textile man was sleeping. His hands gripped the cloths. He started out somebody's son and he seemed all alone in New York now except for the cloth he clutched and whatever it meant to him. I walked down a few blocks and cut over on a side street and found what I'd have called a diner where I ordered coffee. While I drank it I thought that I was also somebody's former son who was all alone in New York but without the cloths to hang on to. I called Merle's firm and her assistant told me the name of a restaurant and where to find it. We figured I was maybe three blocks away from it.

Her assistant said, "You behave yourself."

I said, "I can't remember how not to."

"Not true," she said. "The way I understand it, you're condemned to be a gentleman."

I needed to kill several hours, so I walked awhile. My knees were getting sore. I decided to blame that on city pavement. It was as good an excuse as any. The streets were filled because work was letting out. I began to get annoyed by having to sidestep small men with large parcels and fast-darting boys on Rollerblades cutting along the curb. I went into the nearest movie house and bought a ticket to see an English film about middle-aged men who carried their friend's ashes to throw into the sea. My eyes began leaking when I sat down and I was blinking them hard when it was time to leave. I figured I would probably have wept if they'd shown two hours' worth of Donald Duck cartoons.

She smiled at me when I entered the restaurant. I thought for a minute that I knew the short, dark-haired woman in the navy linen dress who stood at the end of the bar near the entrance to check reservations. Then Merle smiled at me when the woman took me to her table and then the waiter smiled at us when we ordered drinks.

"This is a happy place," I said. "I mean, they seem to *mean* to be friendly."

"Yes, they do," she said. "They're the best-trained staff in New

York. And of course that's how commerce works. Profits make you smile. Except for me, " she said. "I'm smiling because I'm happy to be here with you."

"Same to you," I said.

She drank a martini and I drank sour mash on ice. She ate what seemed to be uncooked tuna, and I ate duck that had lemon and pepper worked under the skin. I suspected myself of eating duck to show her I was skilled with a knife and a fork. She'd ordered a bottle of wine that filled my mouth with flavors and she talked a good deal about a case she'd appealed involving a Mexican-American man arrested for possession of a plastic bag of dope who had been sentenced to four years in prison. He was one of the pro bono cases her firm did. She intended to save the prisoner, whose heart was shutting down.

"I'm gonna get them to pay for bypass surgery, the bastards, on account of his being afflicted by conditions *they* created in his life." Her eyes got wide and shiny, and she waved her fork at me. "How old do you think I am, Jack?"

I shook my head.

She poured more wine for us.

I told her, "Thirties. That's all I intend saying."

"I'm thirty-eight," she said. "Was it the eyes?"

"Was what?"

She looked at me and pulled on her sleeves. "Or I heard it could be the skin at the base of the hand where it goes into the wrist. It gets slack."

"You're worried about looking old?"

"No. Not worried. Not— Sure. Yes. Exactly. Worried. Why not?"

"I'd worry about not being able to paint a painting like you. Or practice law. Or order wine in a place like this. You're a fine unit, Merle."

She pushed her fork against a slice of what she had told me was pickled ginger and then she set it down. She clasped her hands and looked at them. Then she pulled her sleeves over the base of each hand. When she looked up her face was merry and red. "A fine unit."

"Yes, ma'am."

"Thanks, Jack."

"Thank you."

"For . . ."

"Company. Pleasure. You know. Fun."

"Are you here about my messed-up nephew?"

"Might be," I said. "I really don't know. I got paid off, I packed my stuff, I got in the truck, and then I drove here. Here I am."

"What else could it be besides my nephew? Work, I guess you'd call it."

"I don't know," I said. "I had to put my dog down. And I don't know a lot of people."

She said, "Did you come up here for *me*?"

I almost did. I could have told her that. But I was also there for other reasons. She was giving me the job but I also had other business north of New York. I couldn't say it clean and clear. Her face was so open to me. She was ripe for being hurt. I held my palms open. I shook my head.

"Disgraceful question," she said. "A sure sign of a drunk attorney, asking a dumb question like that."

"Listen," I said. "I came here. I surprised hell out of myself and I imposed on your entire afternoon and evening. I hope you forgive me."

"You need to do something, first, for me to forgive," she said. "Have you ever heard of Sniffen Court? Nobody's heard of Sniffen Court. Come there and have coffee."

She told me the dinner was on the firm and she paid the bill. When we left, the same people smiled at me and I felt good because I ate there. I said to the woman in blue linen, "If I came back, would you smile at me like that?"

She gave me the smile. "Even if you don't," she said.

We walked up to what Merle said was called Murray Hill. The streets were crowded and a lot of the stores were open. I liked the wakefulness of the evening there. We cut east and by the time we were at 36th and halfway down the block from Lexington Avenue she was holding my left arm with her right. She pulled it against her a little. Her softness and firmness together felt good. In her left hand she swung a cordovan briefcase in pretty wide strokes. She looked like a schoolgirl coming home happy. Sniffen Court turned out to be a broad alleyway inside a tall iron gate she unlocked. Cobblestones paved the courtyard. There were small buildings jammed together, six or seven on either side. The one we went into was at the back on the east end. It had a narrow entryway and narrow stairs off to the right. There was a little living room and then a dining room of the same size and a small kitchen in the back. It was very old and I felt like I was in another country. The cooled air smelled of her perfume. Her living room was littered like her office. I thought a dark painting of the ocean was by her.

She stood on the other side of a coffee table made of oak with red tiles set into the top. I was sitting in a thick, deep chair covered with a nubby brown cloth. It felt like a date. I was too old to remember exactly what a date felt like. But this felt nervous and dates were always nervous. It felt like one of us or both of us expected something. I was pretty sure I expected nothing. That was what I wanted to expect.

"I'm making coffee," she said, "and I'm not drinking any more alcohol. I get a little stupid when I drink. If you would like some single-malt, or a beer, a glass of wine, would you let me know? Look. Help yourself. In the cabinet over there, under the bookcase. I'll be back."

I was glad to sit in the chair and let my knees go slack. I felt my arms loosen and then my neck. I was almost asleep when I heard a latch click and I opened my eyes. She was wearing jeans and a light gray V-necked cotton sweater with long sleeves. She carried a square wicker tray with dark brown pottery mugs and a dark pot.

It was very strong coffee and I found myself smiling. Then she said, "Your dog died."

Her harsh voice seemed harsher. She was tucked into her dark brown easy chair with her legs underneath her and her hair drawn back the way it was at my efficiency. I understood from the tones of those few syllables that she knew how to be cruel. The words landed like gravel someone threw at a wall.

"Yes, he did."

"When?"

"Last week. This week, maybe. I lost count. It was not too many days ago. Why?"

"So you chucked it all and drove up here."

"Yes."

"Because . . ."

I waited for her to finish.

She said, "I was waiting for you to say the rest of it."

"I'm not interested in doing that," I said. It was a kind of deposi-tion. They did it to you before a trial. They swore you in and the lawyer for the defense could all but draw blood. I had been deposed a few times as arresting officer or first officer on the scene. I had always come out breathing hard and looking for something to pound my head or hands against. She was after something. But I figured she was also taking care of herself.

"You're all alone," she said.

"Meaning what?"

"It's the impression you gave. That you had no place to go."

"I never have *no* place to go," I lied.

"Not your ex-wife, I'm guessing."

"Not her," I said.

"And not your place of work."

"No, I left that."

"And you came here."

"Yes."

"I mean *here*, Jack. My city. My office. My apartment."

"Your very own Sniffen Court."

She leaned forward to gesture with the carafe. I nodded and she poured. "You take it black," she reminded herself.

"Milk would be an insult to coffee like this."

"What college courses did you take?"

It was one of the tactics in a deposition. You shift the angle of approach. You change the topic. But you always come back to your primary topic. I tried not to show the deposing lawyer when I was losing my patience. That was the only pleasure in those sessions. You kept them from seeing how their prodding bruised your ribs.

"Starting-out stuff. You know. How primitive societies are organized. How complex societies get disorganized. Why Margaret Mead can't be trusted anymore. Or read this poem or short story and write a composition telling the professor what he told you

about it in class. Wordsworth, I remember something by him we
had to write on. I said he was an arrogant writer. I'd only read about
a half a dozen poems since high school and two of them were on
birthday cards in the IGA. That's a chain of country markets," I
said.

"Did you write that, about the IGA?"

"No. Just the arrogant part."

"What did the professor say?"

"I believe he called it a not-unperceptive reading."

"Were you married at the time?"

"Why?"

She looked at me, then looked away. She shook her head. "I was
wondering," she said. "That's all."

"Yes. I was."

"And you said there weren't any children?"

"Not for very long," I said, looking first at her painting of the sea
and then at her.

She pulled her sleeves up along her arms, then changed her
mind and pulled them down so they came to the middle of each
palm. Her face was very sad. She said, "I'm sorry."

"It was a long time ago," I said.

"I'm sorry," she said. "I also wanted to ask you what did happen
to your dog." When she looked at me like she was evaluating me,
her face got set and her eyes were hard. She was as interesting to see
as she was when her eyes got softer and she looked like she could
be hurt.

"What happened to my dog?"

"Yes, please."

"I had to put him down, Merle."

"God. Because he was sick?"

"Yes."

"And you—"

"I killed him."

"Jack!" She sat forward in the chair. She looked like she needed to get somewhere. Then she looked like she forced herself to sit back. "You were able to do that," she said.

"I'm afraid that I'm good at things like that."

She said, "Maybe you just think you should be."

I said, "You're checking me out for a job. So I can understand that you might feel you need to ask that kind of a question."

"For a job," she said. "Did you really come all this way for work? Just—you needed work?"

"It's something to go after, Merle. When you're not sure what to do. Grown-ups have to do something. It's all that I know to call it. Work. But it's *your* job I came after."

She looked at me awhile. "Yes, it is. Yes, it is."

"Your nephew. Tyler Pearl."

"I'm astonished you remember the name."

"I used to do a lot of work with people and names. I checked a lot of people out."

"You were a policeman for real. Not that you didn't do real work down there, down South, and come in real damned handy for me. But—you know. Cop stuff. You did that."

"I did."

"Maybe I shouldn't ask any more questions."

I thought and then I said, "That's right."

"I should either trust you or not."

"I don't know if that's a good rule to live your life by. But if you and I might end up being friends of some kind, now would be the time to slack off of the questioning."

She said, "All right."

I watched her, and she watched me, and then we both kind of let go a little. Something in the air of the cold, messy room felt like it relaxed.

"Tyler Pearl's pretty young, you said."

She shook her head. "Well," she said, "I mean, he's old enough to vote. He's old enough to be running a life that might go someplace. He's twenty-three. Tyler is the son of Verna, my dead older sister. His father hasn't had very much to do with him since Verna died. Charlie's a nice enough guy, considering he makes a generous living by selling rugs. Can you imagine someone who spends his time selling *rugs*? 'Carpets,' he would say. Some of them are very nice, the Iranian, the antique Afghan. But he spends his life fingering cloth."

"And Tyler?"

He spends his life—he *ran* for his life—upstate. I was able to find him some money, and there are ways of hiding yourself. I hear this, in my practice of the law, that there are ways, though I wouldn't know what they are."

"Of course not."

"So you can get someplace and, if you stay there, and you work hard, and you stay out of trouble, the heavy boys might not find you. I hear one of the prime choices in the federal witness protection program happens to be upstate New York. It apparently has a lot of corners. He *could* be safe. But he gets in trouble, he possibly engages in practices the canons of your profession and mine might not approve of. And he's backed into bad debt, which is what set him running in the first place. He borrowed from someone who borrows from someone who is connected to what I call the heavy people. Is that a meaningful term?"

"I imagine I've done business with them in the past. Or with their friends. With friends of their friends. It starts in pretty respectable-looking places. It ends up with men who swing baseball bats but not at baseballs. They have their own accounting practices."

"Yes," she said. "That's who I mean. I gave him some money and he ran. There was no witness protection program I could get him into, since he didn't know anything he could sell in exchange for the protection. He made it upstate and he stayed put in a place called Vienna."

I nodded. It should have surprised me. It didn't. I said, "I know where it is."

"That's more than I know."

"I used to live a couple of dozen miles away from it."

"When you—"

"When I had a wife and a child."

She nodded. But she was a lawyer. Nothing unpleasant slows them down for long. She said, "It makes it easier, you knowing the area. It sounds very peaceful, from what he says. Except 'peace' and Tyler don't belong in the same sentence, much less the same area code. But when he gets in touch, which is infrequently, he insists he's safe. I don't believe it. Now it's been a very, very long time since he called. It's been like holding my breath." She lifted the carafe, then put it down. She looked at me and there was some power in it.

"I know about that. Holding your breath in that part of the country."

"It wasn't very good for you, then."

"Bad times are supposed to help your character. So maybe it was very good for me. Though I sure took off from there and stayed away."

"Then why go back?"

I shook my head. "I don't know. Maybe to see if I can?"

"And you're not afraid it might be unpleasant for you."

"Maybe we'll find out if I go back."

"Jack, he's a good boy. He's a child. The trouble is, he isn't anybody in particular's child anymore. He's alone, he's rash, he isn't brilliant. He gambles, and he gambles badly. I think he wants to lose. And nobody loves him."

"Except you," I said.

"Maybe so."

"There are worse fates."

"No. He doesn't know what to do with it."

"So he peels his skin off over—what? Casino gambling at the Indian places?"

"Horses. Cards. I know he loves blackjack. He plays poker. He'd play bingo in the basement of a church. But for stakes he can't afford."

"Let's say I do it. Let's say I go up there."

"Where you obviously don't want to go."

"Where I thought I couldn't stay. But let's say I go. Let's say I even want to go. Let's say I manage to find him. Then what?"

We looked at each other awhile. Then she looked down and poured more coffee for us. She reached for her briefcase and took out a large envelope. She removed a photograph. There were traveler's checks she'd been able to buy unsigned that she wanted me to sign that night. She said, "You use that money for expenses. Let me know if it isn't enough. And there's a check drawn on my own account. It's a retainer. I hope it's enough."

"You don't need that for me," I said.

"No, let's do it as business, Jack. How much of a fee should I pay you?"

"I don't know. I never did this sort of work privately before, getting paid for it."

"What did you work for privately that didn't pay?"

"There was a missing girl, one time. She was a minister's daughter, one of those really decent kids that the world gets hold of and it tears them apart for no reason anybody can understand. She disappeared from the side of the road. Her parents wanted me to help. I was working campus security. I'd been a sheriff's deputy. I knew the local cops. I tried to help out."

"And you found her?"

"I found who took her. I did get hold of him."

"And the girl?"

"No," I said, "we all looked but we never could find what was left of her."

"That's so terrible, though."

I nodded. She watched me and I fiddled with my coffee mug. "But what would you like me to do if I can find your nephew?"

"Bring him here?" Her face was crimson and she looked angry. Maybe she was angry with herself, I thought. You could get in trouble, loving someone.

"Sometime," I said, "I could take you out to dinner. All right? Or—I don't know. We can go someplace you like."

"You're saying you think we might go out on a date sometime."

"That's right. Especially if I bring him back down here for you."

"You've been worrying all evening, haven't you?"

"Most of the afternoon too."

"Because it might have turned into a date?"

"I couldn't really tell you," I said. "But I have been concerned."

Her harsh voice got lower because she was amused. "Listen, Jack. You're a good citizen. Or you seem to keep trying to be."

I wanted to say something snappy back to her. I couldn't think of it. I said, "Thanks."

We nodded at each other a couple of times.

She said, "Well, we'll be working together."

I nodded.

"And we'll stay in touch."

I nodded again.

"My father was an attorney," she said. "He did patent law, mostly, and his clients were always desperate. It seemed like they always thought, all of them, that they were getting cheated by large firms that had stolen their brilliant ideas. You couldn't believe some of the inventions. A cherry pitter that ran off household tap water, I remember. I swear it. A traveling, battery-operated coffee grinder. Some of them were junk—most of them. But some of them had very large commercial applications. These people were frantic about companies capitalizing on what they'd dreamed up. And my father tried to always reassure them. He said the same thing to every client at the end of a phone call. 'Take good care,' he said, 'and we'll be in constant touch.' So," she said. "You have my numbers, and you'll make sure I have yours."

I took the envelope and I sipped the last of my coffee. She stood up and walked to the door and I followed her. We kissed goodnight the way people in business kiss each other. Except I kissed her goodbye. I couldn't help thinking that way. I carried the envelope out of the little courtyard and I walked toward the parking garage. After a couple of blocks, I thought about the job. I had a name. I had a place to travel to. I had a very generous check with no bank account to put it in. I had no dog and no family and no real plan for finding Tyler Pearl. I had a new friend in New York. According to my little red notebook I had a friend in Pennsylvania. I had a couple of friends near Vienna, New York. I thought about them while I walked.

The parking tariff brought my expenses to just about a hundred for the day. I used the garage attendant's directions to get uptown on the west side of the city and then I took the Henry Hudson Parkway to the George Washington Bridge. Then I was in New Jersey on the Palisades Parkway. After a few miles I pulled in at a rest stop that looked over the Hudson River. I opened the windows and turned off the engine and closed my eyes.

Winds came off the river. The wheels of cars rolled over gravel in the lot. I heard the two-note call of a bird from the slope below. A few hundred yards behind the lot I heard the gusting of high-speed engines. I dreamed about a field that was thigh-deep in snow. Volunteers from the state police, the sheriff's department, and local small towns were out in the field with poles and tools with long handles. They were feeling beneath the snow for the resistance of the body of a girl. Whenever I dreamed it, I was frightened that I was about to feel her flesh at the end of the shovel haft I stuck down and lifted out, stuck down and lifted out. My dog was there and my wife was standing at the edge of the field next to the little girl's mother. I looked at where the shovel went in and then I felt flesh. I lifted my head to tell them I'd found her and I saw that Fanny was gone. I heard the dog snarl. Every time I reached this point in the dream I woke up. I knew that the snarl was mine. I opened my eyes in the truck and I felt the wheel. The bird called twice again and then again. I looked across the river at night to the lights in New York. It wasn't cold out but I thought of soiled bright chunks of slowly rolling ice that the current carried up the river and then back down.

IT TOOK ME not quite five hours to get upstate because I stopped at the end of the Palisades Parkway where it ran into New York 17. There was a giant mall with stores representing every brand of merchandise I'd heard of. I bought some clothes. I was able to find some gear in the mess of designer camping toys. On my way out I got myself a pizza and I ate it at seventy miles an hour. I left a good deal of the traffic behind after another hundred miles.

I was on the two-lane roads now and often behind local drivers. Unless they were kids or drunk on beer they tended to go slowly. This was a part of the state known for not very much. It was north of trout fishing towns like Deposit. It was south and east of the Adirondacks. It was above the Catskills. It was west of what was called Leatherstocking Country where you could go to the Cooperstown Baseball Hall of Fame. It was countryside that was in the books of James Fenimore Cooper. Nobody I knew ever read him except of course the English teachers I wrote compositions for during my time on the campus. They claimed to read his books. They didn't admit to skipping a book by anyone. It was rough country. It was as battered-looking as the worst I had seen of New England. It was more scoured out by poverty. It was some of what made them crazy up there. The brutal winters were part of it too. I knew that. People there kept a distance from each other. That used to comfort me. But I also knew it had to be bad for them. I knew it had to be bad for me. In the end, I ran away from it all.

Then I came back. When you travel off the trail in difficult country and you improvise your route it's called bushwhacking. So is the attack you make from a hiding place when you conduct guerrilla warfare. If I was attacking anyone I think it was myself. But I knew that I'd been bushwhacking as a kind of navigation over the

years. I traveled in my life the way outdoorsmen travel according to
the sun and stars and sometimes with a compass and always
according to dumb luck and not much of what a business or a government person would think of as long-range planning. I had been
a husband and a father and a pretty responsible employee in the
north. That died and I went south with my dog. After a while, I was
coming back north where home used to be. There were reasons.
There was my dog. There was the work Ms. Merle Davidoff, attor-
ney-at-law, was offering me. She might be offering more. I would
mostly have to call this trip bushwhacking.

I didn't look for someplace to sleep. Up there as long as you kept
away from college towns or Cooperstown you could find a room. I
gassed up the truck and bought myself a cup of coffee and went
looking for Sergeant Elway Bird. He had seen action as a Marine.
He was a tight and tucked-in man. He was as drawn together and
ready for anything as anyone I had known. He kept just enough
hair on top of his head so you could tell he trimmed it high and
tight every few days. He worked out of the Vienna barracks in
another county but not far from the college. We had connected on
cases. He was the third person on the scene and I was the first when
a drunk student crashed his crowded sport-utility vehicle into a
campus tree at high speed. There were a lot of dead children and
he got me and the village cop over our sniveling by the time the
sheriffs and the EMTs arrived. When I looked for the missing girl
named Janice Tanner I'd relied on him. He acted impatient with
me sometimes but I thought he trusted me. I remembered counting on his approval. I suspected you might think about your father
or a close uncle that way. I didn't think about mine if I could help
myself. And of course I tried not to think about Sarah his wife. She
was almost five years older than I was. She was seven or eight years

younger than Elway. She had her degree in music from the state university college at Potsdam, New York. She taught piano to grade-school kids and part-time to students in the local colleges. She was small and lean and muscular. Her hands were stronger than mine. She smelled peppery and sweet at once like wild thyme if you crush it in your fingers.

I went past their place by mistake on the first pass. It was a long time since I'd visited. After turning around at a four-corners I found it above a steep, short driveway off Burton Walsh Road at the top of Chicken Farm Road. It was a white, two-story farmhouse with a gallery along the front. The roof looked soggy around the ridge-pole. The house needed painting, I thought. When I looked closer I saw it needed new clapboard first.

A minute or two after I knocked I heard a hushing sound. It was soft shoes or slippers on a wooden floor. A big man came to the screen door and looked out at me.

"Can't be," he said.

"I'm afraid so, Elway."

He opened the door and said, "Have I done something to be punished for, Jack?"

As usual, I couldn't think of anything to say. His hair was long and thin. It was all gray. He looked shorter because he had put on weight. His long-sleeved shirt was buttoned to the neck. His neck used to be powerful-looking and thick, but now it was scrawny at the collar. His skin seemed loose and it looked grayer than brown. His eyes were moist and yellow and furious. I thought they grew milder while he looked at me but that could have been wishing.

"At least *you* look fit," he said. "Jesus, say something, Jack. You're standing there all yawped up and staring like you see some kind of middle-aged state trooper with a case of cancer."

I said, "Oh, shit." I thought of Janice Tanner's mother dying of cancer while I tried to find her child.

"That's what Sarah said. Actually, it's also what I said. But that's what it is."

"What kind, Elway?"

"Come in. You get the news, you can at least get some iced tea or coffee or something. And you'd be after something else, if I know you. And I do. Tell me why you're back here, and tell me what you had in mind to get off of me."

He pushed the door open, and I came into the short parlor hall with the wall crowded with slickers and jackets hung on pegs. The opposite wall had a metal-framed mirror, and I watched him look away from it when we passed. He moved slowly. He was wearing the sort of fleece-lined deerskin slippers you'd use in winter. His khakis sagged off his hips. His body struck me now not as fatter but softer. He was once the trimmest man and now he was losing himself.

We sat in a living room that was almost filled by the piano. There were some framed photographs on it and stacks of sheet music. I thought of the stacks of briefs in Merle's office. Elway sat in an upholstered rocking chair and I sat on the footstool nearby.

"You can have a whole chair," he said.

"I'm fine."

"All right. You were counting on me for something, right? That's why you came? Not to pay a sick call?"

"Hell, Elway, I didn't *know* you were sick. Otherwise—"

He shook his head. "You're pitiful. You're this big, quiet, scary fellow to a lot of people, and then something—I don't know. Some kind of emotion leaks into the room, and you get all pink and then you get all pale, and then you start staggering around *feeling* things. Don't you?"

I shrugged. I nodded.

"Good," he said, "don't commit yourself." Then he said, "What?"

"About what?"

"What do you need?"

"I need you to get better."

"Name me something I can do."

"You can't get better?"

He blew air out and put his lips together. "I don't know," he said. "*They* don't know. It's blood cancer."

"Is that leukemia?"

"I believe it is," he said.

"They can fix it."

"You know a lot about the leukemia?"

"I read once that they can. It was in the papers down there."

"I appreciated all the mail, Jack."

"I sent you postcards, didn't I?"

"And I appreciated both of those."

"Well."

"Well," he said.

"It's—maybe you could call it an investigation," I said. "It isn't one, though. That's ridiculous. A favor, maybe. It's a favor to someone. There's a nephew maybe on the run from some maybe mobbed-up downstate people. I'm supposed to look into it."

"You couldn't find any more maybes on a maybe farm."

"And I was thinking maybe—well, there I go. I was thinking backup with the system. Information. General, all-around help. I mean, *I* don't know what I'm doing."

He said. "You were once a decent investigator for a pretty competent sheriff, I remember."

"That was so many years ago. I've been a rent-a-cop and nothing more for so long, Elway."

"You sound a little ashamed of yourself, Jack."

"I don't know."

"How *do* you feel?"

"Okay."

"No," he said. "How do you *feel*?"

"Nobody dead got better, Elway. Nobody who left came back."

"Well, you did. That counts, doesn't it? You?"

I said, "I still can't figure out what you're thinking, how you think."

"Of course not," he said. "You'll miss me."

I looked at him.

"You will be sorry when I go, I'm saying. And you know it."

I said, "So do me a favor and don't go."

He looked at me with his red-rimmed, yellowish eyes. He nodded. "All right," he said. "I'll see what I can do about not going."

"Sarah already put in the same request, didn't she?"

"Yes, she did."

I tried to read his eyes when he spoke of her. I wondered what he read in mine when I said her name.

"And your son?"

He blinked his eyes and looked away from me.

I waited a minute. Then I said, "My dog's dead, Elway."

His eyes came back to me the way I thought they would. "Oh, you poor man," he said. "How can I let you lose your dog *and* the meanest cop you know?" He rocked a little, then he sat still. "Bad times, Jack," he said. "I'm sorry. You lost all you could lose, and you came back. Would that sum it up?"

"Why bother to sum it up?"

He rocked a little more, and then he said, "Why did you really come back?" He put his hand up. "Please don't tell me about a nephew on the run. I'm sure there is one. I'm sure we can have a little fun with it later on. And I can rag on you about no calls and letters and all of that. And you can dodge and weave some. But you were *right* to stay away. So I mean why *really*? This is where it all blew up in the air in pieces on you and the pieces never all came down. Why in hell would you ever come back?"

I heard wheels on their driveway going around to the back of the house. It was probably Sarah. I tried to breathe like someone who wasn't in trouble. She could have told him that nothing sums it up. You need to get at all of it but you can only do it one piece at a time. But I had no right to tell him a word about his life or even mine. And I hadn't the words.

"I sure hope you feel sorry enough to invite me for dinner," I said.

He smiled a tired smile. "You and Sarah can eat. I'll watch. I'm drinking milkshakes, these days. Of course, I'm allergic to milk, so I'm drinking make-believe shakes made from make-believe milk made from soy. The taste is a lot like synthetic motor oil."

"That sounds like all of my cooking."

"Hey," he called out, standing to greet his wife when the back door opened in, "guess who's crazy enough to come back here."

I heard the rattle of stiff paper bags, and then Sarah came, all five feet of her with her strong, slender brown arms and those wide, long piano player's hands. She looked straight into my eyes when she walked toward me. I wondered what she saw there. She laid one on my cheek and patted it and I felt ashamed of myself. I also remembered what we had done and what we had said and how she had tasted to me. Before she kissed me hello on the cheek at the edge of my mouth I saw the tears in her eyes and I wondered if they were for herself or Elway or me.

She smelled of spices and something ripe and sweet. She saw me working at the odors. The tears could have been for all of us, I thought.

"You just sniffed me over like a dog," she said "How is the old fellow?"

Elway said, "Well—"

"He's done," I said.

"Oh, Lord," she said. "You poor fellow. Oh, Jack, that is terrible news. Oh, I miss him." We stood that way, and then she said, "So how must *you* feel?" I think she waited for me to tell her. I couldn't. She said, "I'll cook us a dinner. His Highness over here won't eat, and he'll get grouchy because you and I will sit around and *watch* him not eating, but that's what we all should do. Grumble and eat and not eat. And I will try to think of anything that anyone can say about that dog and you. I can't imagine, Jack."

"Me neither."

She ran her hand through her hair. She looked like a five-foot version of Elway, even to the cloud of dark brown freckles on either side of her light brown nose. She was watching my face and I shifted my eyes away. Then she said, "What brought you back, honey?"

"You."

"I figured that from all the mail."

"Elway pointed out I wasn't very mail-y."

"Mail-y? I guess I couldn't call you that," she said, pointing to one of my postcards propped against a photograph on the piano. It showed a little man in chaps and boots who wore a big cowboy hat. He had lassoed a cactus.

Elway said, "Jack's working." He sat back in the rocker and let his shoulders droop. Then he moved back and forth a little and then he stopped. "He's looking for somebody. Or looking out for them. We're not sure which."

Sarah turned to head for the kitchen. She said, "As long as he doesn't have to call them up or send them mail."

Sarah walked in and out of the kitchen while she cooked. Each time she came into the room, Elway stopped talking. If I was talking, he stopped listening and I shut up. She smiled at someplace in between us and then she looked at me. She asked questions. One was about where I lived in New Mexico. Another time she asked about women on the pueblos. And another time, she said, "Can you bring yourself to get another dog?"

Elway said, "Oh, hell." She looked at him. He shrugged.

"Jack," she said.

I didn't know what to say. She stood there and then came over to stand next to my chair. She pulled my head over and held it with her hands like it was an animal separate from me. It felt very heavy and I wanted to lay it down on her. Elway watched us.

It was a short meal. It was quiet. She had roasted a small chicken stuffed with lemon and garlic and herbs. There was rice—a pilaf, she said. Elway ate a little of the rice and none of the chicken. We drank iced tea while he sipped at the thick drink he called his motor oil. I told him about Tyler Pearl. I told him stories about cop work on some of my jobs. When I talked to Sarah her eyes pulsed and her forehead furrowed. We had fallen into each other when she and Elway were having the kind of rough time a cop's family goes through. They got trapped in the silences. Fanny and I were caught in our own. I knew I wasn't any better for Sarah than I was for Fanny. I didn't think I could help her feel better than Elway could. I thought I wasn't much good for her at all. None of that stopped me.

"I'm your brown older woman affair," she said, with one hand on my chest and the other pushing against the ceiling of the passenger compartment in my old station wagon.

I called her my brown older woman after that when we made love. We were together three times. The first two were wild hours. I couldn't think of a motel he wouldn't know about so we got into the back seat of my brown Ford station wagon held together with duct tape. We liked being mostly naked in a car parked high up in the state-owned logging lands. We were closed away but we were open to a couple of thousand acres. We were crazy twice. The third time, we were sane so we were frightened every minute. The sex was more desperate. The last few minutes were sadder because we knew they were the last. I think we were also relieved.

But here I was in their house again. She and I cleared up while Elway went into the living room. We didn't speak. We didn't look at each other. We circled in the kitchen. When we ended up face to face, it was in front of the dishwasher we were trying to load without touching each other. She looked up at me and shook her head. I didn't know what to do so I leaned down and kissed her fast on the forehead. It's the way you'd kiss your sister, I thought. It also wasn't. She reached up and I bent down and she kissed me softly on the mouth.

She said very softly, "Hello, Jack. And don't you have the gift of getting yourself in trouble?"

"Can Elway make it?" I was whispering.

"You ask yourself that, all right? You keep him in mind. And I will too," she said. "But you damned well make certain you come back."

"Yes, ma'am," I said.

"Two cards. One phone call. After—"

"After what?" Elway called from the living room.

"After he promised us he would stay in touch."

"You know those going-away promises," Elway said.

She said, "Yes, I do." Then she said, "Jack, go in and keep Elway company."

He said, "Come in here and give me your excuses, Jack."

THRASHER

I PARKED IN THE LOT of a defunct supermarket half a mile from Vienna. The plate-glass windows were replaced with plywood sheets. The front end of the trailer of an eighteen-wheel rig was propped on cinderblocks near the locked entrance doors. I slept in my truck instead of the Birds' place. I didn't want Elway angry with me because I saw him sick in intimate ways. And it was close quarters in their farmhouse. I was more comfortable not hearing Sarah's bare feet on the floorboards. Vienna was too small to have much of a police force. I figured it was mostly patrolled by sheriff's deputies. One of them idled alongside me toward dawn. He gave me the once-over with his light and seemed to think it was all right. I waved. He didn't. His cruiser took off and I sat up and watched the sky get bright.

I ate breakfast in a convenience store attached to six gas pumps and then I parked in the lot of a strip mall at the edge of the town. It featured a realtor, an automotive parts place, a liquor store, and a supermarket. I shopped some supplies for the place I didn't live in yet. At ten minutes of nine I saw a woman opening the realtor's office. It was like banks and insurance offices. A middle-aged woman did the work and the man came in later to authorize the decisions she wasn't paid enough for making and setting in motion. Her name was Ms. Penny Putney, and she gave me three addresses. She said that was a surprisingly large number of furnished rentals outside of town. She gave me descriptions of how to get to them.

"We don't usually send the renters off on their own," she said.

"But I have an honest face?"

"No. Rentals that far out of town are hard to move. We're a little desperate. And I can't go with you because I need to be in the office this morning."

"And I have an honest face," I said.

She said, "Well, you've got a face. I'll give you that."

When I walked out a tall man with a long nose was coming through the door. He was portly and on the edge of just plain fat. He wore a double-breasted blue blazer with gold buttons over light gray slacks. His maroon-and-blue-striped tie was fastened with a knot that wasn't quite as large as a baseball. He looked shocked that a rowdy-looking fellow in jeans and work boots occupied the space he intended stepping into. He pursed his wide lips and backed away in two jerky motions to his right. Then he waved me through. He had an oval bald head and a jowly face. His eyebrows were either faint or falling out. His complexion was red. I thought he had been born so you could tell a foreigner what our word "impatient" meant by pointing at him.

"Penny," he said, walking through the door I held for him from outside the office.

"Hi, Dan," she said. "Here are the ads. Everett's in the back."

I heard him say, "Who—" as the door closed. I was the who.

Two of the places were candidates for being torn down and rebuilt by some optimist who loved old dry point foundations and not much privacy from traffic or neighbors. One seemed pretty good. I needed a base to work from that was convenient to Vienna and the countryside. I wanted privacy. I always did. I needed a roof and running water. I turned the kitchen tap, but nothing ran. I figured the power that worked the pump was shut off. Anyway, I seemed to have found a roof. I drove back to Vienna and chose between two rural banks and opened a savings account. I thought I wouldn't be there long enough to write many checks. I drove to the realtor's office and gave Ms. Penny Putney a damage deposit and a month's rent. That used up quite a few of Merle Davidoff's traveler's checks. Ms. Putney answered my question about the big man called Dan by saying that he was Mr. Bromell who owned the newspaper and the radio station. In a place like this one, I thought, he ate lunch with the president of either bank or both. He knew the personal Washington, D.C., phone number of the district's congressman. I drove a dozen miles to an office of the power-and-light, and I gave them more traveler's checks.

Moving in consisted of driving there on 12 south to 80, east on 80 to Albert Kelley Road. I went a couple of miles over ruts and rocks and occasional oil-and-stone paving to a short, very steep drive I'd have worried about if I planned to be there when snow collected and ice set up. The house was at the top of the hill, set back on the left and facing east. There wasn't a barn, but there were several tilted, unpainted sheds. Out back, there was a garden between the shed and the house. I could see the remains of compost heaps and rows that were once planted with beans under collapsing trellises made of pieces of weather-darkened lath fastened with twine. Straw hung on the mud in some of the rows where the gardener wintered over. It seemed a shame to leave a place you tended with so much care.

There were a lot of bottles, some from screw-top wine and some from what I thought of as bar whiskey, Schenley's and Black Velvet. Most were from cheap beer stored in pulpy cartons in the nearest shed. The other sheds were empty except for a shallow red metal wheelbarrow with an airless tire and the snapped handle of a rake or hoe. I thought of the snow-choked field and the men and women stabbing down to feel for the child.

It was a dark house. Without lights the day seemed over, edging into the dinner hour instead of bright forenoon. It made me nervous to feel I had lost all that time without getting work done. I told myself not to panic. That was what it was. You look up and you're alone in the middle of a house in the middle of the countryside and you're not getting anything done. It was like being lost.

"You slow down," I told myself. Living with the dog for so long, I'd grown used to speaking my thoughts out loud and getting a feeling of response. Hearing nothing but me, I felt more worried. I believe someone else might have said I was anxious, but I hated that word. It seemed to me to work better when it was applied to people with gentler impulses.

I carried in some sacks with extra lightbulbs and a box of stubby storm candles, two lanterns, matches, and a plastic jug I'd filled with kerosene. I got the lanterns going in the kitchen and I put the canned goods in a kitchen cabinet. I stowed the refrigerated goods in the dark, warm refrigerator. Then I brought some gear in and found places to store it. I put the pistol and a box of .32 shells in the drawer where I'd keep silverware when I bought some. I would have to use either my sheath knife or my pocketknife until then.

"Problem solved," I announced. I was making myself feel silly. I decided that I was going to get over talking like I lived with another mammal.

I brought in my tool kit and pounded twelve-penny nails above the kitchen doorway that opened in from the front yard. I hung the carbine there and stored cartridges with the ammunition for the pistol. The yellow light of the lanterns set on the scarred pine kitchen table made me feel like I was in a tent. I realized how happy that light made me. I was like a kid in his fort. I was glad to be. There were three old chairs at the table, and two of them took my weight without trouble. I didn't need to sit in more than that, I thought. I went out to the truck for my broad manila envelope from Merle Davidoff's office. I read over the page and a half of scrawl from my red Friend in Pennsylvania notebook. I had written that in the parking lot of the big mall. I set the pages on top of the big envelope along with her business card. I pinned them in place with a rock from the dooryard.

The picture of Tyler Pearl had the artificial light blue background you see in high school graduation photos. I knew him to be twenty-three. His skin was bad, especially on his lower jaw and around his mouth. The lips were full and dark red. The nose looked greasy. He was smiling. But I didn't believe the smile. His eyes were angry. His sandy hair was dull. I couldn't find Merle in him. He looked unhappy and sad. Upstate, they called these kids woodchucks when they're younger. The best they hoped for them was early enlistment in the armed forces. That way they'd get their bodies cleaned up. They would have a half a chance. That's what I had when I was seventeen. I was scared to let it go by. It could have been a picture of me grown to Tyler Pearl's age and state of confusion if I hadn't been frightened enough to work harder than the others in my basic training intake.

I put the picture back in the envelope because his face made me sad. I thought about the hunt for Janice Tanner. Her parents stuck a poster with her photo on it under every windshield wiper of every car that was parked on the campus or in town. She had a sweet smile but sad eyes. I used to think you could tell from the picture how much trouble she was in. It was an older man who took her. She was buying sexy underpants to wear for him. I went through her underwear drawer and found them. Her parents never looked. I think they found her underwear embarrassing. I almost killed him when I cornered him in his kitchen in the farmhouse at the edge of the cornfield he buried her in. He told us where to look and we searched the field. We never found her. I thought that it would be good to find this one.

I lined up objects and used a piece of dry paper towel on a stain on the stove. It stayed there. I looked at the chalky paint on the kitchen walls and walked outside for the sleeping bag and toilet kit. When I brought them in, I noticed the can opener screwed to the wall on the other side of the refrigerator. I didn't need too much more.

I opened some windows. I could smell the damp of the packed-earth cellar, the rot in the beams and posts. Almost motionless cluster flies snarled against the clouded glass. When I shoved the windows up, some of them flew out, sleepy and slow. Most of them stayed. They would soon be gathered in corners of the ceiling, dropping onto the table, circling my head, buzzing while they died on counters and floors. I made a list in my pocket notebook to buy sliding half-screens, some silverware, some flypaper strips to hang off the light fixtures. The dooryard tree was an old sugar maple that was easily a hundred years old. A humped lilac bloomed in the maple's shade. I saw the red of the breast of a bird I didn't know and the gutsy little black and white chickadees I did. I added seed for birds to the list, and a feeder. Then I put a question mark next to it because a bird feeder sounded to me like setting up housekeeping on a longer-range basis than I thought might be called for. I might be able to pick up Tyler Pearl's track. I might even find him. If not I might find some information for Merle. And then I would leave. I wanted to look the old countryside over and then I wanted to find someplace else to work.

It was a warm day for upstate New York but mild compared to where I'd been living. I had gone there to get away from the cold. I thought maybe the cold made me feel the other feelings stronger. It was like a signal just then. The house breathed, paused, then kept breathing. The electric power was on. The refrigerator hummed. The cellar pump for what they told me was a ninety-foot well began to chatter. It was filling tanks in the upstairs bathroom and the one off the kitchen. So take it as a signal, I thought.

Of what? I wondered.

There was a live bulb in a wall fixture in the living room behind the kitchen and I left it on. Then I flushed the downstairs toilet. It was like answering someone after they greeted you. It was like what hadn't passed between me and Mr. Daniel Bromell. I blew out the lanterns but I kept them on the kitchen counter where I could get to them if a storm took wires down and cut the power. Thinking of storms sent me back out to the truck for my rubber boots and heavy rain jacket. I set the boots on the floor near the door. I hung the jacket on a nail above them. I left a canvas coat and watch cap on the passenger seat and brought my seersucker sport coat in. That got hung in the closet in the downstairs hall where I'd put the rest of my clothes. I'd sleep in the living room and I'd live downstairs. In a short time I had begun to turn a house into an efficiency apartment. You can't get more efficient than that, I thought. I wrote "bed" with a question mark on my list.

Upstairs I found two volumes of a *Collier's Encyclopedia* that someone had probably purchased with a coupon book, so many dollars a month for information about geography, politics, and science that was useless by the time the set was halfway paid for. I found a flat, dirty hand puppet with a bear's torn-up head. Some kid might spend the rest of his life being worried about that bear.

He might never know how worried he was. They should have checked more carefully before they left, I thought. I put a bulb in the ceiling light of the bathroom and of the upstairs hall in case I had to get around up there. I found a blanket that didn't look too filthy though it had several small tears. I could wash it up in the kitchen sink, hang it on the line out back that ran from the house to the shed. Maybe I could use it sometime. I liked arranging for emergencies. I was good at them. And that was lucky, I thought, because I seemed to make a lot of them happen. I was pleased to notice that I didn't say any of this out loud.

I put some lightbulbs in downstairs fixtures. I had two left over to keep in the cupboard. I ran the hot water to see if the heating element worked and decided that a little warmth now meant heat later on. I looked at my notes and thought about reading them over. I decided that looking from a distance was good enough, so I left. I didn't drive north and west as I did years ago when I left my house to go to the campus to look after kids. I went south about fifteen miles into Vienna. I could buy what I needed there and then drive up into the hills to look for Tyler Pearl.

Thinking of him brought Merle to mind. I didn't know how much I wanted to let her stay inside me. So I thought of Sarah in the time just before everything went as bad as it could get and the Tanner girl was lost for keeps and Fanny went her way and I went mine. Sarah and I were sitting with our legs mixed up together on the seat of the Ford. We were surrounded by dark fir forest. Instead of feeling like a thief I was feeling that I wanted to get under her coat again because she was naked beneath it.

"Are my hands too cold?" I'd asked her.

"No," she said, "they're hot. " She said, "Why do you *want* me, Jack?"

I shook my head in the darkness.

"Would Fanny kill us both if she found out?"

"Yes. So would Elway."

"He would," she said. "He'd stick his service pistol down my lying throat and cancel me," she said. She leaned over and burrowed her head into me. "Keep me warm," she said. "Get me warm, Jack."

We had searched in forests like that one for the Tanner girl. We had broken into abandoned barns. State police and sheriff's deputies roughed up kids in country bars and set up roadblocks on randomly selected roads. At the end of it, I'd unloaded a pistol at the man who stole her and killed her and hid her way. I was a terrible shot and his fear of me shooting so wildly did the job. He told us to look in the frozen cornfield that went from behind the houses in his town out to the river that broadened miles downstream and flowed into the Susquehanna. That was where I saw Fanny watching me. She stood next to the mother of the missing girl. We were in snow to our knees. I looked up and Fanny was gone. I never saw her again. The dog remained. The girl's mother remained. We plunged the handles of tools down into the snow but didn't ever reach the child. The cold of the snow in the field remained. I wanted to find this boy Tyler Pearl and return him to Merle. Then I wanted to stop looking for anyone lost.

Get me warm, Jack.

I shopped furniture. I settled for a mattress but no bed frame. They'd deliver it to the house and leave it outside for me. In a giant all-purpose store, I bought flatware and the screens, flypaper, a forty-dollar bird feeder, and fifty pounds of bird seed. I wondered what it meant that I would settle for a mattress on a dusty floor instead of a bed but needed to provide expensive black oil sunflower seeds to summertime birds. In the furniture store, I showed

Tyler Pearl's photograph to the lean, hairy salesman in his dirty white short-sleeved shirt. He smelled of talcum powder over old sweat. He told me that he'd seen him, sure. He couldn't remember where. He wondered why I asked.

"His aunt's looking for him" I said. "Friend of the family."

I went to a small pizzeria. They weren't busy and the waitress as well as the nervous, short man who stood at the cash register said they recognized him. They wondered why I asked.

"Where do you know him from?" I said.

"He bought a pizza," the man said. "What else?"

"What'd he say? Where was he living?"

"He said, 'Thanks,' when I gave him change. What's with the where?"

They recognized him at the Kwik-Stop gas station at the edge of Vienna. Then one of the tellers at one of the banks said she saw him. She refused to look for an account in his name until I showed her my Southwestern Law Enforcement Association membership card. I called it a license. She clacked on her computer and told me that he had no account. He hadn't made himself a secret. It was only that nobody knew him. I thought that might cover half the people I saw on the street.

I went back to the realtor's. Everett was the male whose agency this was. He sat in his large, glass-walled office at the rear of the shop. He was smoking a cigarette while he read a newspaper that he spread flat on his desk and leaned above. That would be Daniel Bromell's paper, I thought. Everett looked studious. I'd have bet he was reading the comics. A short, smiling woman with a head of blue-lavender curls was on the phone. Behind her desk, she waved her hand back and forth. She seemed to enjoy the conversation. Ms. Penny Putney was wearing a suit the color of the inside of a lime. She was typing at a word processor. I sat down at her desk and told her that I liked the house. Then I explained how this was my return visit to the area. I said how much I'd missed the old agricultural life. I inquired about available dairy farms.

Her bracelets rang on each other and the gray metal of her desk as she worked the computer and then turned transparent plastic pages in a big three-holed notebook.

"Dairy," she said, looking at listings. She looked up through horn-rimmed glasses. "You must know how bad things are. The milk prices haven't kept up, the cost of equipment will kill you, and the subsidy's a joke. You know what these winters are like, forget your global warming or whatever. It gets cold enough, and your cows get sick, and the price of feed's not coming down. You'll work all year to break plenty less than even."

"It's good to be back," I said.

"It isn't a joke. I guess you know that."

"It isn't a joke," I said.

"I've got four I'd love to sell you, one I'd feel a little unhappy about you buying but not so much that I'd tell you which one, and a very sweet operation that could have made it if the farmer hadn't rolled his tractor over on himself and sheared off his leg. Wife had a heart attack trying to pull him out from under. He bled to death watching her die. That's how they put it all together after they found them."

"It's a beautiful day," I said.

"Farming's grim business," Penny Putney said.

Everett was studying her, and I could tell from the tightening around his small eyes that he worried about what she said to me. I gave her a big, phony smile so the boss would feel he could return to the funnies.

"You going to drive me around the countryside and keep me laughing?" I asked her. "Or would you like to copy off those listings and send me out with directions?"

"I'll type up the particulars," she said, "but I can't let you see the listings. We've got some comments on the page that Sonny wrote down when he took the listings. Sonny does the farms."

"He's the one back there?"

"That's Sonny Buck," she said. "He's Everett, but everyone calls him Sonny."

"Lucky man."

I asked her to show me detailed maps of every listing. She or Sonny believed in using the geodetic survey maps with detailed topography and I was able to figure out the kind of place I needed to see. Tyler Pearl was not attracted to legitimate sources of income. Merle had made that clear. So he would look for dirty work. Vernon Downs racetrack was flypaper to the people Merle called heavy. But that was pretty far from Vienna. If anybody commuted to Vernon Downs they would come over from Oneida, Rome, or Utica. I had to assume he was in this area. He might be running hard drugs or collecting bad debts for shady people except he wasn't tough, Merle said. He was gentle and maybe a little stupid. He had a gambling habit and he was plenty scared. I thought he might be involved in something to do with drugs. The Onondaga reservation near Syracuse was once supposed to be a distribution point for drugs from Canada. And the countryside was perfect for farming marijuana. There were all these isolated farms and unpatrolled back roads. A lot of corners is how Merle described it. Kids were after dope from the fifth grade on. Lawyers in their sixties trawled dangerous neighborhoods looking to buy it. Marijuana was a solid cash crop. He might have worked the growing end or the delivery end. Elway could ask around the cops and I could look directly for the robbers. So I went up into the hills with Ms. Penny Putney to find isolated farms run by suspicious characters. There couldn't have been more than several thousand in the county. That was the plan Merle Davidoff was paying for.

Only two of the places were occupied. The other places were emptied out by death or bankruptcy. "The usual miserable auction," Ms. Penny Putney said. "You know, the farmer and his wife are crying when their diskers and spreaders get sold off cheap once the cattle are auctioned. Then they sell the pots and pans. Then there's one more empty barn and a house with a kitchen in it that echoes." When she finished softening me up for the sale, she was pleased to hold the door of her Mercury for me and she started our travels on the small roads.

It was a long day. She and I exhausted everything in common very quickly because most of it was our being in the same car. We were too polite to admit it so we discussed local politics until she remembered that I didn't know anything about that topic. She asked three questions about my work and my history in the area. I think I wasn't very satisfying to investigate. Then we talked farming for a couple of minutes.

"Where did you used to farm, did you say?"

"Did I?"

"Did you what?"

"Did I say?"

"Oh, my," she said. "I'm prying."

"That's all right," I said. "You're smart and you're alert. But listen. I'm not a flim-flam man. Honest."

She laughed and said, "Honest, huh?"

"Pretty much," I said. "More or less."

"How *much* less?"

"I'm a serious man, Ms. Putney."

"I can see that for myself," she said. "But you don't know shit, excusing my Latin, from Shinola about anything to *do* with agriculture."

"That's cold and cruel," I said. "Anyway this is America. We start new lives. Why couldn't I buy one of these places and learn how to do it? And you'd get the commission. Are you confident enough about skipping the chance?"

"*You're* confident," she said, "I'll give you that."

"I'll take it. With thanks." I pointed at the giant round rolls of hay wrapped in shining white plastic. They were all over the fields alongside the roads we drove. I said, "Don't you miss the old-time bales of hay? Kids could always make some summertime money by throwing them around for farmers."

"Familiar with balers and haying, are you?"

"My uncle sold farming equipment. He pushed balers and the twine for baling, tractors, hay wagon wheels, all of that. He used to find me jobs when I was in high school. I'd go up there for the summer and work all day for very little money. I liked feeling strong by the time I had to go back home and start school. He had a place outside of Portland, Maine. Hay bales and lobsters and those tall, rich blond girls from Brunswick who knew how to sail."

She said, "I never thought of hay in Maine."

"Just lobsters and blondes driving Boston Whalers, right?" I said. "They farm there too."

She said, "I suppose the kids in Maine drink milk the same as here."

One young farmer with bright white hair talked to us over the idle of his tractor and then Ms. Putney walked me through the barn. She started to talk about the milking system, but after she looked at my expression she stopped. We walked in silence and went to the car without returning to the farmer. At the second place, miles from the first, we sat in her car in the farmyard and I looked at the barn and then we drove off again. The smell of her deodorant rose up in the car.

I said, "Are you worried whether you're safe with me, Ms. Putney?"

"I had some fear that crossed my mind," she said, looking only at the road as she drove, "but you could have done what it was in your mind to do a dozen times already."

"Don't be worried," I said. "I promise you it's all right."

"And I believe you," she said. "But it's late, I'm hungry, and I'm losing the best of the day."

"I'll pay for it," I said. "A consultancy."

"What's that?"

"Research assistance. Show me one more farm. It's on your list. After you turn onto—what was it? Potter Road? Potter Road. And then a half a mile and you turn again and we're there."

"No. Look again. It's marked 'sold.'"

"But that's the one I need to see. It's perfect—never mind for what," I said. "Just get me up there."

"And I'm—what?"

"Helping with research."

"For what?"

"I'm a consultant for a lawyer. That's the truth. You're the consultant for me. Nobody's getting sued," I said. "No one's in trouble. It's all what the lawyers call background. In case there's what they call an action. This one is something about somebody's nephew is all I really know. Here." I took out the photograph and held it so she could look while she drove. I saw how clenched his mouth looked. This was a kid nobody was going to please.

"I may have seen him in town," she said. "You know, walking around. Or in the market maybe. I never talked to him. He doesn't seem much more than a boy. Why's the law involved with a boy? What'd he do?"

"He apparently got born into the wrong family."

"Are you telling me the truth?"

"Yes, ma'am."

"And you're just an honest workingman doing an honest day's work."

"Yes, ma'am."

"Then I'm a belly dancer."

"Why not? You've got the figure for it. And you're making a hundred bucks consultancy."

"Then I can afford to give up belly dancing," she said, "figure or not."

Dirt plumed behind us. Her Mercury waddled over the ruts when we drove up the hill to the farmyard. We turned off to the right directly into the sun. I was able to look down at miles of forest and fields bordered by hedgerows and some wandering stone walls. The corn out behind the house would be high soon. The white farmhouse was low. It looked chewed rough by the winds that must have been fierce and steady up there in the winter. The barn looked to be in excellent repair. It was a story higher than the house.

"Why not stay in the car?" she suggested. A St. Bernard was up on his hind paws resting his forepaws on the roof her car. He made some noises that could have been grumbling or excitement. "And you're just looking for some farm property and all of that."

"It's research," I said. "Nothing else."

A big man in a short-sleeved dungaree boiler suit he wore over boots walked up behind the St. Bernard. He talked to him and the dog dropped down. Ms. Putney lowered her window. She chattered so fast, I wouldn't have believed anything she said.

He leaned in and looked at us. Then he stood straight. I said to Ms. Putney, "I'll do this."

I got out and came around the car, watching the dog. The dog watched me back. He drooled a quart or two. His tail moved in the barnyard dirt. I couldn't really make out his little eyes.

Standing next to the car, I nodded. The farmer nodded back. He appeared very eager to please. His face was as wet as the dog's. He seemed to vibrate. He was running with sweat. My first thought was crank but maybe he was sick, I thought.

"Hello," I said. I introduced myself and Ms. Penny Putney. "She's a real estate person from over in Vienna?"

"That's like the principal municipality around here," he said. His eyes were a very bleached-out pale blue and moist and on the move. His nose was hooked a little, and his nostrils seemed flared. You might have expected to see the scars from harelip surgery but there weren't any. There was the red of the skin that wasn't from sunburn and there was all that sweat. He looked like he clenched his jaw to keep his mouth from trembling. In a way he was handsome. "Boy," he said. He smiled with plenty of white teeth. "You try saying *that* one fast. Practical Mutationality. You see what I mean?"

He stuck his hand out. "I'm Clarence Smith. You could call me a brand-new New York State farmer from Vermont. Happy as hell to see you." The smile got wider and then it disappeared. His muscles couldn't hold it. They were racing inside of his skin.

We shook and he rolled the bones in my hand back over when he pumped my arm. Maybe I was supposed to be intimidated by his strength. I gave him the easy grin we're taught to use when we answer domestic disturbances. It's submissive so they don't think you're a threat. That way they don't kill you or the wife they've just been pounding on. Of course, he might have just grabbed hold of me like that to keep from flying away. I could feel the tremors in him before he let me go. His hand left my hand damp.

I said, "I'm looking over dairy properties, and I wondered about this one. I'm in the market."

"You what—you saw this from the road?" He shook his head.

I smiled. "I don't believe you can see your place from the road."

He shook his head again. "That's because we're invisible, man. Now you see us, whoops you don't. You know? So what can I do for you?"

I said it again. "I'm looking for dairy properties?"

He stared at me. He was trying to find my words. He said, "Oh! Right. Right. No, we don't have any up here. You know, we're like not for sale?"

The St. Bernard was lying down and working on his breathing in and drooling out.

Smith said, "You like dogs?"

"I used to have one."

He nodded. He paused. Then he nodded again. He gave you the feeling he was really thinking about giving you help with something. "Jack," he said, "right? Just what kind of a place are you looking for?"

"Someplace I could work alone with maybe one hired man. You know. I can afford maybe twenty head, a few more. I'd put the money into the milking equipment and tanks. I'd save on the other gear. I'm pretty good at getting machines to work. I'd like to sidestep the government loans if I could."

"Tell me how," he said. He smiled the big smile again. Then he forgot what he was happy about. He shook a little and took his left hand in his right and held himself together.

I said, "I guess there's no shortage of hired help."

"This is the saddest county in the state, man. No work! Everybody down here's on one form of assistance or another. Food stamps, senior agricultural certificates, SSI. You could hire a dozen if you liked. Of course, you'd have to pay them." He burst into a laugh that he clamped his lips around. He rubbed his wet face the way kids in school do to try and make the giggling stop.

"How's the dairy co-op? You know, with strangers. They treat you all right?"

"You know, man. Rural people are suspicious. I mean, not me, on account of I live, let live, you know, the gamut of hospitality. That's just me. I was raised that way. This is a tight place, though. You say Vermont, they think you're a hippie. You say New England, they think you're a Methodist. You say po-tatoe, they say pa-tawtoe. Everybody up here's tight around strangers. Not me, man! You know. I'd help you if I could. What's the thing again? You needed—" He moved one of his big hands across the air in front of his face. You'd have thought he was swatting at a fly instead of something in his head.

I said, "You mentioned Vermont."

"You heard of it?"

"I've been in it plenty, but I never lived there."

"I used to run a CD music store, man. You know, thongs, bongs, beads, tie-die shirts, Dead posters. I did all right for a while. Do you know St. Johnsbury?"

"I've driven through it, I believe."

"You probably saw my store."

"Glad to place the face to the name, Clarence. How's the new life treating you?"

"You called it. New life. I got reborn down here. I put on ten pounds, I made new friends, I'm a happy man. I heart New York."

"Sorry?"

He shook and sweated and moved his hands. "The chamber of commerce slogan? With the heart in the ad? It says I and then it shows a heart and then it says New York! You know. It's a landmark in the human communications field."

"Right," I said. "And what kind of an operation do you run?"

"Excuse me?"

"I was wondering what you farm."

He got the sly look you'd expect from a little boy. "You know. A little of this, a little of that. I tell you what. It's been a sopping wet summer. I'd say we'll have some gorgeous corn."

"Corn," I said.

"Sweet corn, man. Slide it over a bar of butter and you get that salt going, it's better than popcorn. It's better than sex. It's better than candy corn. You remember that? The little pointy, they're like kernels but sugar? Orange and black and white and your mom—"

His pupils were tiny and his eyes were wide. He was dripping sweat from his nose. He covered his mouth with his hand and whispered into it. He nodded. "Yes, siree," he said. "Yupper. I mean, I'm into a kind of eclectic mélange of like all of the rural life. I came down here, man, out of the northern kingdom of Vermont on account of stresses and strains from my mercantile days. Money was killing me. Money was killing me. Money—"

"Must have really had you worried," I said.

"Well, that varied day to day, you know." It was like a string tied to his ankle got tugged. He looked up and said, "Hey, man, I need to get to work, talking about, you know, work? Neat talking to you. Gotta go. Gotta go. Gotta go." He turned away, walked back, nodded, and said, "All right?" The dog groaned himself onto all fours and swung in loosely connected chunks to follow him. He had to slide the door open to let them into the barn.

I was thinking about the dog when I worked myself onto the passenger seat. Dope farmers usually patrolled their grounds with dogs but I had never heard of their using St. Bernards instead of Rottweilers or Dobermans. Ms. Penny Putney had us rolling away before I could buckle my seatbelt. As she turned off the farm road I counted out five twenties and stuck them, folded, into the ashtray.

"I'm grateful," I said.

She said, "And I'm a retired belly dancer."

Back in town and back in my truck, I got myself to a public phone at the edge of a little municipal park attached to a Greek Revival courthouse. Two young adolescent white boys with Technicolor hair were slouched on a bench nearby. Another sat cross-legged on the trim lawn. All of them smoked cigarettes self-consciously. They tapped ash off before it could collect. It might make sense, I thought, to draft them at that age and use them for latrine duty until they reached eighteen. After that we could try to train them to be soldiers. I didn't want to be the one who trained them.

I called her office collect and I heard the receptionist tell the operator, "Collect? We don't do collect here."

"Operator," I said, "ask them to check with Ms. Davidoff's assistant, please." We did a little dance about who would talk and when and why.

Merle finally came on to say, "You could buy yourself a cell phone. I'll pay for it."

"No," I said, "because then anybody with the number could call me up."

"Hi, Jack." She said it a little like the sound you would feel if you were very sleepy and just about to fall back onto a freshly made bed.

I was embarrassed to hear that. I didn't know why.

"I need some information," I said.

I heard her adjusting to my tone of voice. "Right."

"I don't mean to be short with you."

"No, that's fine."

"I seem to be bad about anything to do with being relaxed. I apologize."

"Are you saying you *were* happy when you called?"

"I was glad to hear you," I said.

"Were you glad to think about me?"

"Yes."

"So that means you did think about me."

"Yes."

"Would you say something besides 'Yes,' please?"

"Could you give me a little information about your nephew?"

"You're such a cop, Jack."

She gave me the answers and then I told her what I thought. "He was here plenty. The town isn't small enough for everyone to know him, but plenty of people noticed him and did everyday business with him. He didn't make any friends that I could learn about but I didn't hear about enemies or trouble."

"No. The poor bastard. Nobody ever taught him about friends."

"He could have learned a little from you about that if he paid attention."

"I don't know. I mostly lived my life and was happy not to know too much about his. My sister surely didn't have time to teach him much, and her husband wouldn't know how. Tyler learned to try and act tough because he thought nobody much cared about him. He learned to run a bluff because he was always afraid. He learned minor league ways of conning and thieving. He got picked up once by the police. He wasn't identified by the victim because he looked like any other punked-out middle-class boy who needed a bath. So he doesn't have a felony record. He might have the will to earn one someday," she said in her harsh voice. She sounded like a different woman now, tough and competent and used to the mess and slop made by people who lived hard lives.

"I'm not looking for gay bars or rural brothels," I said. "On the surface of things I'd say there's one bar like that with maybe some homosexual action and I don't know about a whorehouse. They'd need a bouncer."

"He wouldn't bring anything to the table at someplace like that," she agreed. "He isn't physically tough and he's definitely heterosexual."

I said, "I'm not looking for true blue gangsters because that would be Utica up north or Binghamton to the south. Cousins of what's left of the Mafia run those operations. It's the same with Verona amd Sherrill and more so in Syracuse. He isn't tied in to Rome because it's part of the Utica people. I doubt Oneida because the Onondagas have the franchise now and they wouldn't throw the work to a non–Native American."

"Aren't you enlightened," she said. "Native American."

"I got halfway beaten to death by a carful of Native Americans a few years ago. They got my attention. I call them whatever they want to be called."

"So what's left," she said, "is—"

"Marijuana. It's all I can think of, unless he got involved with

those psychos in the hills around here who eat their dogs and sac-
rifice their first cousins to moon gods. Dope is a crop that earns big.
There's hundreds of thousands a year in a sizable operation. The
people wearing the suits need to invest in land, a barn, crops or
cows that camouflage the real plantings, lights and nutrients. Then
you work out distribution. I'm getting in touch with local law
enforcement through a friend of mine and his wife. I'll learn more
about how it works around here. I can't think of anything else. It's
probably a one-try operation for me. If I don't find something fast
that's tied to what this countryside is about, which is privacy,
then—"

"Who's the wife?"

"Why?"

"You mentioned her. He's the cop who's your friend. Right?"

"That's right."

"But you also mentioned *her*. So . . ."

"You're very good," I said.

"That's right. So tell me."

"She and I are friends. We used to be friends."

"What kind of friends? Never mind. I don't want to know. Yes,
I do."

"Friends."

"Can I ask you something?"

"Sure."

"Are *we* friends? You and I?"

"Yes."

"The same as you and her?"

"No. And what does that tell you?"

"Nothing."

"I've also been thinking about your office."

"The office I'm sitting in?"

"That one," I said. "You shouldn't ought to be hanging that poster under glass on your wall. The what's-his-name."

"Cruikshank."

"You might think about taking it down."

"I see."

"You've had the same idea. I'm sure of it. Only it reminds you that the marriage failed. So you keep it there."

"I've got all kinds of calls coming in, Jack. I need to run."

"You do that," I said. "I'll let you know how it goes."

"Thank you," she said. "It's good to hear from you."

Wasn't it, I thought. Man lives out of a pickup truck and makes a shopping list that includes flypaper. He calls up from a public phone in half a park in Noplace, New York, to tell a well-constructed criminal lawyer how to decorate her life. His feelings get hurt when she needs to run her life without him.

I drove back to the house and hung the feeder from a wire coat hanger that I twisted and looped. I filled the feeder with sunflower seeds and dumped a pile on the ground. I remembered from our house up here that some of them fed only off the ground. They jumped back and forth in the husks of the seed and bits of leaf and twig to dig up food. Brown something, they were called. I couldn't remember. They were dark cinnamon-colored and they spent the day kicking at the ground until they found what they were looking for. I needed to store the seeds someplace safe from squirrels because a gray squirrel will chew through a plastic garbage pail or a wooden box. Finally, I tied the top of the sack and tossed it into the cap of the truck.

I walked the yard and went into the garden between the dead rows. Fanny hadn't ever gardened because her hours at the hospital were hard and her legs were too tired when she came home. I didn't garden because I never believed that I could make much live. The sun was heavy back there. It felt good on my neck and head. It couldn't compare to the weight of it in the southwestern places I had lived or places due south. I enjoyed it when I'd stood near the sea, how it seemed to be blown all to tatters by breezes coming in. Once in a while the dog would decide that this tidal nonsense had gone on long enough. He would wade on his stiff legs until the ocean was belly high on him and he would bark at it for a minute. Then he'd shake himself and turn his tail around and stalk back.

I found what was a ghost of a trail. There was a sense of wear that might be a track. It went through the brush behind the garden. I followed it through hawthorn and snaky young growths of plum up a rise. It led to a little pond the realtor hadn't mentioned. The water was low. It always was low in upstate ponds in August. But it was clear. A platform of weathered silver one-by-eights was tilted at the far edge. I walked around past clumps of brush to press with a foot on the boards. It was locked well enough in place to stand on. I saw small shadows under the surface ahead of me. It would be trout or bass. Behind me in the grass I saw a bare patch and watched it with my back to the water. Ground wasps forced themselves out and then suddenly rose up. I heard something jump. It might have been a frog in the coarse grass and floating weeds along the bank to the left of the little dock. Brown female blackbirds dived around me. The red and black males stayed away. One harangued me from the safety of an ash tree and another from the top of a cattail.

Sitting on the tilted dock and facing into the low sun to watch the brave female blackbirds, I remembered the birds I thought of as jumping back and forth and kicking up a mess while they

searched. They were called brown thrashers. I remembered the
dog wheeling to face the incoming tide and telling it off. I remembered Fanny bringing flowers home that belonged to a Mrs.
Ardmore. Fanny thought she ought to make something grow but
she couldn't. She thought we could use some color in the house. I
knew Mrs. Ardmore didn't need the flowers because she died.

And I was reversing the charges to tell Merle Davidoff how to
decorate her life.

I STORED THE mattress box in the shed closest to the house. I set
the mattress in the living room with my sleeping bag laid out. I'd
use some rolled-up clothes inside a shirt until I remembered to buy
a pillow. If I couldn't remember then I would have to make do with
putting my head down for the night on top of dirty laundry. I fried
up a chuck steak smeared with mustard and I washed it down with
coffee. I knew I was too old to be eating like a kid. I promised
myself I'd broil some fish soon. I wasn't certain I believed me. I
really enjoyed the spiced, greasy beef. I didn't pull out the sour
mash for dessert. I went to bed like a virtuous man.

I woke up before there was sun in the sky. I lay in the sleeping
bag curled tight. I tried to remember what I had dreamed that
frightened me. The earliest birds began to call. It was probably the
field, I thought, and the long poles going down into the snow to
find her. She'd have been curled tight the way I was now. I made
myself straighten because I wasn't dead under the crust of ice and
foot after foot of snow. Or was I trying to straighten for her? You
can't uncurl all the dead ones, I thought. I raised my knees toward
my face again and closed my eyes.

I stayed bent around myself like that until first light. Then some kind of woodpecker began to hammer against the house. It sounded like a nail gun on a roofing job. I'd have sworn the bird was banging on one of the old aluminum runoff spouts. That was plain damned misguided. You can hammer all you want against a rainspout but the chances of uncovering insects or a vein of sap were pretty slim. Most birds knew their business, though. Otherwise they learned a lesson. Or they starved. That was how it worked. I had to smile. I'd think of the stubborn woodpecker all day long. I intended to go and hammer on the farm patrolled by Smith. Sometime I might hammer on Smith himself. And it might not have had anything at all to do with the little girl lying under the snow. It might have been my cooking that gave me bad dreams.

I wore black sneakers and camouflage cargo pants and a cammie T-shirt. I had a small pair of binoculars, a compass, a map page I'd torn from a New York State gazetteer, a plastic bottle of water buttoned into the thigh pocket of the pants, and a jug of coffee to keep in the car. I wrapped a nutritionally questionable sandwich of chuck steak and white bread joined by mustard and held together by the plastic wrapping from last night's package of steak. I put kitchen wrap on my list and took off. Each time I left the house, I was tempted to tell someone to come along or say I'd be back soon.

The farm was less than half an hour north of my place. I went to the vicinity and drove the nearby roads for a while. I found an entry point and settled the truck in the brush off to the side of Kramers Barn Road. I headed in from there. I cut through an evergreen forest where the growth was regular. I thought it was likely a state plantation. I walked under giant spruce without having to bend over too often because the shade from its neighbors kept each tree from putting out branches much lower than seven or eight feet in the air. It was cool there and it smelled of sweet resin. The slightest wind made a sighing sound that I could hear as it began a half a mile away and came on toward me and then went past. When the wind was down, I heard insects buzz and I thought I heard the soft rasp of deer that drifted and fed at the border of the forest.

The walking turned steep. The plantings seemed to be pine instead of spruce. The trees were farther apart and the branches were lower to the ground. There was a good deal of shale. In the spring, it would be black with water that seeped from the hillside. I came out into bright sun and in the crevices of the rock I saw wild thyme that grew in springy clumps. Sarah's peppery smell came up over the smell of the pine needles I was crushing as I walked. Then there was very little cover on the hillside, only clusters of brush and tufts of low weed. I went very slowly as the angle got steeper. I found myself working uphill on all fours. I wanted to make it to a forest of aspen ahead of me. I was exposed here and I had no idea how energetically Smith and his friends worked at security. Of course Clarence Smith might simply be some harmless, stoned, smiling farmer. Cops were always being blamed for watching certain people closely or putting a little pressure on them. Sometimes they were wrong about it. Sometimes they did it because they were racists or drunk or both. But sometimes they did it because a law enforcement officer has an instinct. Even if you don't like it, there it is. Ask a cop why he followed a certain car for some long distance and he'll tell you he had a feeling. That's all it is. But it can be plenty. And I knew Smith might be all right. But I also didn't. He might be the man who hired Tyler Pearl. If the boy was alive Smith might be the man who hid him away. If he was dead Smith might be the one who killed him. It didn't seem likely they'd use a long gun on me here. They didn't know who I was or whether I was dangerous. But I was remembering what Elway Bird told me after dinner at their place.

"We never knew it was them. We never knew who it was," he said. He leaned forward on his elbows. I knew he missed his cigarettes. He kept kneading his fingers. The right hand cradled the left and then the left cradled the right. Maybe they ached. He looked awfully uncomfortable.

Sarah said, "Who it was *what*, El?"

"Oh," he said, "I was thinking of it so hard, I thought I'd said it all out loud."

"I do that a lot," I said.

"Senile dementia," Sarah said. She didn't smile for the joke. Her large brown eyes were studying him. She shifted her eyes to me. She shook her head to tell me she knew precisely what was right and what was wrong. Nothing of it had to do with his memory. "You're tired," she said to him, her eyes still on me.

"I'm tired," he said. "But I wanted Jack to know this. There was a DEA plane around here. They spent half a summer here one year, circling different areas all day long. It must have driven people nuts. Over and over, in big, loopy circles, over and over."

"The infrared," I said, looking back into Sarah's eyes. "They were searching."

"The infrared," he said. He told Sarah, "The lamps they use to boost an indoor marijuana crop, they have an infrared signature. It's from the heat of the lights. That's what the plane was searching for. And these characters brought the airplane down. Shot it out of the air. Took its little engine apart when it came in low, using I guess a regular deer gun, probably a thirty-ought-eight. It was low, and it was slow, and it came down gentle enough so the pilot wasn't killed. Man, they sealed that area off! We had state Environmental Conservation police up there armed with Glocks and ever so anxious to cap a cop or, you know, if they had to settle for it then they'd shoot some kind of an outlaw. We stayed at the perimeters, sealing off roads, and the state Bureau of Investigation and federal people—they brought the FBI in from Syracuse—they went through the wreck like it came down directly in from Mars. The sheriff's people I talked to, because it was really their beat, figured it was marijuana growers. Could have been these people you want to check out. It's a very profitable business, so we need to be careful, Jack—"

"Because," Sarah said in a gruff voice imitating his, "this is the United States of Money we live in, and the money owns the laws."

"Did you mean 'law' or 'laws'?" I asked them.

But she shooed him off to sleep before we could talk about that. I ran like hell so she and I wouldn't be alone together in the downstairs of their house.

I made it into the aspen growth and I sat with my back to a thick one, my legs pointing downhill. I drank some warm water. It turned out I'd bought carbonated water by mistake. When it's warm and bubbly, it's like drinking a kerosene soda. I oriented the compass and map, found the sun and studied shadows so I could navigate by sight alone. I stowed things in the big pockets of the pants and went up. At the other side of the aspens, I saw that I would have to be exposed when I covered the final distance I needed to cross. So I went low. Once I was out of the shelter of the trees, I crawled on elbows and knees. Sometimes I went on my belly and my chin. I pushed with my toes against the stony ground. I smelled the rabbit droppings I went over. I got bitten by deerflies. They didn't hurt much. I hoped I would avoid the bees that were drawn to the thyme. Judging from the angle of the sun, it was close to eleven in the morning. I was at the spot I'd aimed for—a couple of stunted white pines that grew together crookedly. They looked like a broad bush at the rocky edge of a hill face that looked down on the farm. I worked water from my right pocket, binoculars from my left, and I wet my mouth. Then I took a look. I had planned to be here earlier so when I used the glasses on this eastern hill, they wouldn't catch the sun and give me away with reflected light. I was late. I figured I would have an hour at the most before the sun was westerly and lighting me up.

There was no movement at the farmhouse. Nothing went in or out of the barn that was across maybe 150 feet of barnyard at right angles to the house. Then the St. Bernard came trotting around the barn. Saliva whipped behind him. His tail was up and his ears were cocked. I saw Smith in the same stained work clothes standing in the door. He motioned. The dog followed him into the barn. I didn't think I could call the law down on him for making hand signs to a large, wet dog.

There was a big John Deere tractor in the farmyard but there wasn't any haying gear. It might have been inside the barn. I saw no sign of cattle but of course they might be in a pasture I couldn't see. Or Smith might farm soybeans, I thought, or wheat. This wasn't good wheat country and you needed a lot of soybeans to make a crop. I'd heard of farmers up here trying to raise llamas and sun-flower seeds and even buffalo. But I never heard of anyone making much of a profit. But this farm looked prosperous. If Merle was right about her nephew, he was drawn to what was crooked. Smith seemed wrong in a number of ways. Of course they could all have to do with me being surly and prickly and suspicious and nothing more.

I wanted to work in closer. I wanted to trespass and linger and loiter and skulk. For now I had to settle for another half an hour's peeping through my 7 by 13 binoculars and the long trip back down to the truck. The sun and shadows at the house moved. I thought I saw a slim woman or a tall young boy in the doorway. When I tried to lay the glasses on whoever it was, they'd gone in.

I was studying a barnyard. It was empty except for the St. Bernard. He'd wandered out to lie in the dust and breathe in and out and scratch at himself. I turned my head so the breezes didn't break against my ears and deafen me to someone coming on foot. I heard nothing. Then there was the faint call of a hawk lying on the thermals high up, but I couldn't find him with the binoculars. I turned back to the farm and I still saw nothing. I thought of the woodpecker banging his brains against a rainspout. So much for the expert reconnoiter. I had worked very hard to get here and see nothing. It was time to go.

I went back low. I slid on my butt and guided myself with my heels. When I had cover I walked in a crouch. You tend to be careless when you retreat. We'd been told that in the service and I had seen it for myself on duty with sheriffs. You're more apt to get clipped going out than coming in. I was far enough from the lip of the overhang to stop for a pee and a drink of my kerosene soda. I tried to tell myself that the panting noise I made was what you'd hear from anyone on a hot August day like this one. I wasn't quite convinced.

Maybe I was eating too much meat, I thought. That made me think of my sandwich. I thought I might start to drool like the St. Bernard. I did compromise. I squatted in the shade and ate only half of it. Then I wrapped it. Then I unwrapped it and ate the other half. I was drinking a lot of coffee and of course that could make you pant. Couldn't it? I thought of Elway and his synthetic milk-shakes. I wondered if there was truth to speculations I had heard about marijuana being a comfort to people with cancer. If that was the case and if Smith was farming it I wouldn't mind lifting some for Elway.

I remembered a lieutenant I worked under. He was Walter Lee, a Korean-American just out of college where he took one course in depth psychology. He told me the Army believed this qualified him to be an officer in the Military Police. His broad smile and hooded eyes seemed merry enough although I always thought he was hiding behind them. He had been doing stockade duty. That suggested the source of his supply. He never shouted. He never complained. He did his job by letting me know that I was to run the detachment for him. He smoked immense amounts of marijuana rolled into spit-glued cigar-shaped blunts.

"I'm going to rely on your judgment in this case," he said maybe a couple of dozen times a day. He told us that his permanent appetite for the blunts came from the stresses of attending Dartmouth College, which he described as isolated in the countryside of New Hampshire. He praised the generosity of his fraternity brothers who apparently were plugged into suppliers working out of Canada. He had grown used to the tranquillity he found in spending every day in a deeply stoned state. I wasn't tempted by it except when I was trying to deal with a private who after six months' service had discovered that his wife and kid were living on borrowed money because he hadn't arranged for his salary to be sent to her. He didn't understand that he shouldn't be spending his money on whores and whiskey. It was a man's right. He'd earned his pay. I thought maybe I ought to just shoot him. I thought maybe the kid and I could use one of Lieutenant Lee's big smokes. I never did try one.

"Thanks, sir, but I won't," I told Lieutenant Lee after he offered to roll me one.

"How come, Jack?"

"Chickenshit, sir."

"Enough with the *sir*, okay?" He drew in after a big hit, and the words came out mangled. He sounded like he was suffering. He wasn't. He held the smoke in his lungs and I waited. Then he slowly, happily sighed out. He shook his head and smiled at me. "You're not scared of anything but a satchel charge," he said, "and the tall dork assistant chaplain who keeps wanting to get his hands on your nuts. You just don't like the idea of losing control, do you? Am I right? What you are *is* control. Am I right? Oh, I'm right. If I'm anything, I'm right. Right?"

I stuffed the sandwich wrapper in my pocket along with the water bottle. I buttoned the binoculars in the other pocket because I wouldn't be needing them now. Flies circled me and I waved my arms to keep them off. Then I stopped. I didn't know who might see me. I was prepared to take these people seriously. I'd found that it's always good to start out respecting them. You could make fun of them later on when they hadn't hurt you.

THE LATE AFTERNOON was sultry. I changed out of the camouflage outfit and walked naked except for sneakers to the pond. My place was situated out of sight like the Smith farm. I wondered what I would do with that invisibility if I lived here full-time. The first idea was I'd get my scrotum and ass cheeks bitten by bugs. I sat on the little dock and let myself down slowly, scraping my lower back against the silvered wood and coming to rest about chest high in the water. I walked out toward the center of the pond. The dropoff was quick and I did a bit of flailing around. Of course, you could say that was what I'd been doing for the last several years. Some people would say for more years than that. I'd kept the sneakers on because the bottom of a pond is slimy and it will prove whether you have an imagination. I'd been surprised to learn that I had one.

I floated on my back and watched the storm gather. I finally relaxed. I let the water hold me up. I let my mind empty the way your breath sighs out before you fall asleep. Crows barked in the high branches of the pines around the pond. I kept my eyes closed and I tried to keep my mind closed too. I knew I didn't want to think about anything to do with finding lost children. Knowing that meant I was thinking about finding lost children. I opened my eyes and looked at the massing clouds and rolled and kicked and went down. I held myself down there. It wasn't much use. The thoughts were in my head and not on the surface of the pond so I let myself float up.

The winds were high by the time I was home and using a couple of the resort towels to dry off. Then the storm stalled and the humidity climbed while the winds slacked off. I sat in the house and sweated. I drank coffee and moved my pad on the table in the dim kitchen. I told myself that I was preparing to make notes. But there wasn't anything to say.

It reminded me of a time in New Mexico. We had to wear navy blue short pants as part of the uniform. We'd brought in a man outside of a drive-in liquor store on a charge of loitering. We were waiting for information to be faxed because if anyone had a sheet this character would. I thought at first he was part of a movie troupe who got lost. He would have been playing the evil loan shark's knee breaker. His gut was fat, but there was hard muscle underneath. His arms were ropy-muscled and thick. He had enough tattoo ink on his body to make him look more green and blue than Caucasian. His teeth were badly cared for and they looked very yellow against his tattooed skin and bloody scrapes. He had resisted arrest and we'd tussled. I used my club as a prod into his armpit when he raised his hand to pound on the other deputy. He spun away from the pain and I kicked him into the brick wall of the store with my foot flat on the base of his spine. His face hit right after his chest did. His shirt tore when the skin of his nose and right cheek gave way on the bounce.

He sat in the hot little interrogation room breathing noisily because his nostrils were stuffed with dried blood. He refused to say anything. We got our information from his wallet. It contained a Social Security card under Richard Davenport, an Arizona driver's license under Dave Richards, and a Visa card under Llewellyn Elizabeths. Even Davenport-Richards shook his head when I read out the credit card.

I said, "Which one do you think might be stolen? Compared to which ones might only be false?"

He clasped his big fingers together. The backs were covered with thick hair the way his arms were. The curly blue-black hair of his head sat low over his eyebrows. With all the tattoos and all that hair he looked like another species. But he was nothing more or less than one of us.

Sharon Bishop was a deputy who once told me sadly that I looked better in my uniform shorts than she did in hers. She brought in two sheets of paper. Her left eye was black and she had painted the left cheek with mercurochrome. Those were her souvenirs of Davenport-Richards. She was short and broad and she was a decent single mother who was a veteran of the marriage wars. She was the best marksman among the deputies and a cinch for promotion because she closed cases and handled the domestic calls with confidence and tact.

"Cantwell Richardson Thorp," Sharon sang out. "From Oak
Park, Illinois. He went to college. You son of a bitch. I got one year
of junior college and you went to school in Minnesota. High tech-
nical aptitude, your parole officer says. You probably had a date for
the friggin prom. Didn't you?"

Thorp knew where he lived. He was meant to be in prison.
That's where the amateur tattoos came from. He'd go back into the
system to drink homemade white lightning and cluster with the
white supremacists to keep himself safe from the other-colored
gangs. He'd be back there because like ninety percent of the others
he'd driven himself to make a stupid mistake. He had earned no
profit. He'd had no fun. He'd run out of places to hide from himself. He went back because it was what he knew.

I looked at the empty notebook page and decided to wash the
blanket I'd found and scrub up the cammies. I would defrost a
frozen lasagna and wait to see if it rained. I hadn't bought a pillow
yet so I was going to sleep with my nose in my soiled clothes. There
was my agenda for the late afternoon and the night.

Bird had arranged for me to meet him the next morning at the
Kwik-Stop on Route 12. In the years since I'd been south and southwest the diners I'd known had mostly gone out of business. They
were where the townspeople had clustered over fried ham and
hashed browns and sugared pastries and coffee. Now it looked like
you had to be an extension of your car to get some company in the
morning or at least some friendly noise. You had to drive to a gas
station and it would be attached to a rectangular building made
mostly of plastic and filled with what used to be in candy stores and
markets like the IGA or your local Big M Superette. You filled the
tank with gas and then you sat inside while customers for lottery
tickets or cigarettes or coffee-to-go went back and forth behind you.

Part-time clerks who couldn't cook were the cooks. You ate microwaved cheese-and-egg sandwiches with unlovable coffee.

Elway Bird was drinking what looked like water at the counter. He sat next to a man who was very broad and very tall. His extra-extra-extra-large gray deputy's uniform was stretched tight across his back and chest. I thought he'd have a patch of belly showing between the puckered buttons when he stood up. His face was round and mean under his very flat crewcut until he smiled. Then his eyes came out of hiding. His hand seemed twice as big as mine when we shook and Elway told us that I was me and the deputy was Jerry Gentry. He remembered the Janice Tanner kidnapping and the series of kidnappings that had taken girls of fourteen, fifteen, and sixteen during that time.

"I remember *you*, matter of fact." His voice was lighter than you might expect and his huge fingers were surprisingly able to lift the cup and maneuver what he told me was a sausage surprise.

"The surprise," Elway said, "is when you can keep it down."

Gentry shook his head. He seemed to have a good deal of affection for Elway and that was good credentials for me.

"You were the guy with the handgun," Gentry recalled. "I heard about you and the bastard that took the girl. I didn't get to the scene until you'd captured his ass. But I heard it. How you'd walked into the man's back door squeezing off rounds, just blowing all hell out of his pots and pans and wall phone and cupboard. I heard he wet his pants. I heard he ended up begging to be saved from you. That pus bastard."

"I'm not much of a marksman," I said.

"You don't need to be. You can *scare* them into submission."

"I have to tell you," I said, "I think I wanted to kill him. I think I was hedging my bet. I was hoping I could shoot him dead on purpose by accident."

"Well, we all wanted to kill him," Elway said. "Every one of us."

That surprised me and I guess I showed it. The woman behind the counter slapped down a plastic plate. There was something on it that was cylinder-shaped and mud-colored. It was the breakfast burrito I ordered. I was happy to look away from it. I stared at Elway's slack-skinned face and muddy color. He looked awful today.

"No need to look at me like that," he said. "Even wound-up troopers have feelings. They just trained us how to not give in to them."

"Amen," Gentry said. "I've seen you people watch a man die in shock in front of his family in a one-vehicle DUI wipeout. We're all standing there wet-eyed and these state people are marching back and forth, measuring the skid and sweeping the broken glass off of the road." He smiled when he said it because he knew that Elway fancied being thought of as wired as tight as a human could get. I was surprised by his letting that mask drop down a little. Gentry said, "So how'd you miss that big guy in the house with a full clip?"

I shook my head, chewing the burrito. I hated to admit I enjoyed it so I made a face. "It was a revolver," I said, "a .32. Six in the cylinder. I'd have needed a tripod mount, tail winds, and a spotter to put him down."

Gentry said, "Nah. I've seen a man die, he was shot with a little .22. Caught him in the upper leg, the femoral artery came up like a fountain."

"Bled him out," I said. He nodded. "Anyway, I caught a lot of shit for being armed and for firing the piece and for scaring the neighborhood to death. Then in private some guys like Elway here beat me up over missing him six times from maybe six yards."

Gentry snickered. He sounded like a boy.

Elway said, "Jack gave him to us, though. He was the one kept after him and he was the one nailed his ass."

"Yeah. But we never found Janice Tanner."

"Her mother was the one sat wrapped in blankets out there, near the big wood fire, just watching, when we were all out in the field?"

"You were there in the field?" I asked.

"I was. I saw you there, saw her. I saw your dog, didn't I? Big brown Labrador? Wonderful dog."

"He was there," I said.

I put the burrito down on the plate and worked on my coffee.

Elway said, very low, "Hell."

Gentry got a refill and he turned to me. His knees hit the platform of the counter and brushed against me. He shrugged for his bulk, then said quietly, "You're doing exactly what?"

I looked at him and finally said, "I don't know what to call it. Looking out for a friend's nephew."

"Name of . . . ?"

"Tyler Pearl."

"Never heard of him." He wrote the name in his notebook.

"He's supposed to maybe be working on a farm up here. According to his aunt's recollection. According to how I've guessed."

"And you're what? Her detective?"

"I'm nobody's detective. I'm out of work. I'm just in the area for a while and then I won't be."

"And Elway said something about marijuana."

I said, "If there was something crooked going on up here on a fair-sized farm that was far up in the hills. You know, so the crops might not be all that visible—"

He nodded. "Could be. How's the water there?"

"The table's high. It looks like it seeps out of the hillsides."

"Yeah, I know the area a little. Sounds sorta right. There was an airplane came down not far from there five or six years ago. Am I right, Elway?"

He knew he was right, and he didn't bother to check Elway's expression. He was simply being polite. I tried to remember him from the big cornfield that stretched on until it reached the river. The day was frigid when we all were out there and the river looked like it steamed up into the cold air. The little girl's mother had sat with an awful yellow blanket around her in a chair that someone had carried over from their house. Nearby was a giant drum stuffed with kindling and stove wood set alight so that the flames came up into the air. The dog followed me whenever I got very far from him. He looked to me like someone who was an expert at digging things up who'd been sent out to supervise. I'd been jumped a few days before by the Native Americans I told Merle about. I was recovering from a broken rib and some smaller injuries. I made it my business not to make noises when I lifted the haft of my pointed shovel and stuck it down into the high snow of the field and then lifted it out and tried someplace else. I estimated the size of a small fourteen-year-old who might have curled up in pain or fear and I kept the insertions of the pole a couple of feet apart. I looked over at the dog every now and again and he was panting slowly. His eyes were winking and his nose slowly flared while he sorted through whatever there was to smell.

Elway said, "In a couple of days, maybe."

Gentry's voice sounded far away. It seemed like someone calling over the surface of a pond I was under when he said, "You bet."

Elway said, "Jack?"

"Sorry," I said.

"Well, you were out of town, weren't you?" Gentry said.

"Jack lives out of town on a full-time basis," Elway said.

Gentry told me he would run Tyler Pearl to see if he'd been arrested, jailed, hospitalized as a result of an auto wreck or otherwise entered into the system. We shook hands and gulped coffee and took off. I stood next to Elway's car and I reached in and patted his cheek. "Take care of yourself," I said.

"You're a sentimental man," he said. Before I could answer, he said, "It isn't a crime."

Elway drove a light blue Ford Crown Victoria, which was a civilian version of the car used by the state police for their navy blue cruisers. He sat straight and taut and from a distance he looked all right. Gentry's patrol car was a red and white four-door sedan that looked like a little economy coupe when he hunched inside it and then followed Elway onto Route 12. I stayed where I was because I wanted to use the phone booth outside near the air hose where you could pay a dollar to fill your tire.

I rang Merle Davidoff's direct line and then I hung up because I had nothing to report. It felt like I needed an excuse to call her. She wouldn't have agreed. I knew that. I also knew that wanting to talk to her worried me. I wasn't sure why. I went back inside to ask directions and then went to the three suppliers of feed and large-scale agricultural supplies within a thirty-mile radius. I shopped leather work gloves in one place, a bottle of gun oil in another, and a plastic container of chain saw lubricant in the third. I asked about local farming operations and where someone might work as a hired man. It was cruel and underpaid labor and you had to be desperate to accept it. When I left I had a little of the retailers' scorn and I had a little useless information in place of leads. Among a lot of local farmers one woman required the delivery of a great deal of potting soil in sacks. One farmer purchased large quantities of bagged lime and bales of peat moss. You could use them for planting in earth as heavy with clay as the ground off Kramers Barn Road seemed to be. Connecting those people to marijuana farming would be desperate work. None of the supply store clerks knew anything about interesting crop experiments or a farmer named Clarence Smith. I knew roughly what I had known earlier. It wasn't much.

I drove the back roads for a while with the truck windows open to the warm air and the bright green light of the countryside. My hands felt cold. I was thinking of the time at the cornfield when we searched for her. I remembered a lot of the faces of the off-duty cops who'd volunteered. I knew some of their names. I couldn't remember Jerry Gentry. There were so many looking for her, though. Mostly I had focused on the girl's mother sitting by the fire and waiting for us to find her. I saw the dog following me as I worked farther and farther out. I liked it that Gentry with his blond-haired buzz cut and his giant head with small eyes had been there.

I had thought about it for years. I came to believe that I hadn't just been looking for the daughter of Mr. and Mrs. Tanner who was stolen off a country road to end up huddled underneath a field full of snow. It was more than helping out. It was more than rescuing. It had to be that I was searching for my kin. It had to be that I was digging to find my own child. Once I had a baby daughter. I knew that Elway Bird knew about her. So did Sarah. I was sure that Jerry Gentry didn't. But I did. And Fanny did when she was my wife and afterward.

COYOTE

W HAT I DID next was mostly nothing. I drove back toward my rental place and I took my time because there weren't important chores at the house. I had always tried to study roads and countryside. It was a habit by then so I suppose I got to know Hamilton County a little better. I had started the day all full of intention. I was going to make an important contact through Elway and probably I had. Jerry Gentry seemed like a decent man. So now I knew two decent men in the area and I had also met someone who might get in my way if he could stand still long enough. Or I would try to get into his. I had a glow inside my belly from the breakfast burrito. I hadn't any more resolve.

It had been the thinking about my child and how she had died and what had happened afterward. It took my energy away. It always did. Thinking about her, I always got like this. I drove back going not much more than maybe twenty miles an hour. I just barely kept my foot on the gas pedal. I tried not to cry. I couldn't have said whether I'd have wept for the child or her mother or both of them.

So I didn't go for the frontal approach I'd been considering. I'd speculated on a drive up into the barnyard and finding a way to get Smith mad at me. It's often useful when they're mad at you because they make mistakes. On the other hand, they can also hurt you. Then you have to deal with pain, breakage, and varieties of mess. I didn't return to Kramers Barn Road and work my way back up to my observation place and stare down at the people on the farm in their lives. That had been the other plan. But I didn't have the feeling of being organized enough to work safely or usefully. Often enough at times like this I would turn to the passenger seat and say something I wouldn't have said to anyone else. I'd been working at not doing that anymore. I had some distance to go.

I could do a wash, though I'd forgotten soap powder. I didn't have a clothes washer either. I could haul my laundry to town and sit and watch the clothing tumble and wait for someone to approach me with secret information about the farm. Or I could sleep when I got home. Sleep appealed to me. I felt like I'd worked a long day. But the idea of information about the farm came back and it stayed. I stopped the truck next to a section of government land that had been timbered and maybe by someone with the state's permission. This section of the countryside seemed awfully unsupervised. Someone had clear-cut several acres of very old, tall spruce that would become lumber and big profit for the sawmill. I was looking at stumps and scrap that were what was left of fifty years' growing. But while I drove I was thinking about thinking about information. So I headed in the direction of Vienna.

It took about fifteen minutes and the patience of two clerks in the tax office upstairs in the county office building near the Greek Revival courthouse. I learned that Tyler Pearl was the owner of several hundred acres of land that made up the farm Smith claimed was his. It had belonged in three allotments to farmers named Mackenzie, Taft, and Schulmeister. Now it all belonged to Merle Davidoff's errant nephew who needed money from her to keep going but who had somehow found a way to buy a lot of land at prices ranging, I estimated, from $500 to a couple of thousand an acre. His taxes amounted to several thousand a year. The prices compared to what I'd seen anywhere else were very low. They should have been. The land didn't seem useful for dairy cows because so much of it was steep hillsides that looked to be mostly rock. I supposed you could have used a lot of it for feed for the livestock. So you'd have halfway well-fed cattle producing milk you couldn't get much money for.

Merle Davidoff had never given Tyler Pearl enough money to buy the land. The compound of house and barn plus maybe some old equipment thrown in but not that handsome new John Deere tractor would be worth more than several hundred thousand. If the capable Ms. Penny Putney did the deal it would be two to four hundred thousand. A young man who looked like a bad boy from out of town who didn't have long-term job references or dairy experience or a bundle of money to put down could never get a local bank or farmers' credit union to give him the mortgage. So Tyler Pearl, I figured, had been given front money to buy the farm where Smith didn't grow cattle or crops, as far as I could see, except for some corn.

Walking back to my truck I passed the public phone I'd used while I watched the mouth-breathing naughty boys of Vienna. A woman who had been my friend when we were looking for Janice Tanner had phoned me several months after I left the Northeast to work as a deputy and live with the dog in a southwestern efficiency apartment no different from a half a dozen others we would live in over the years. She was the professor I mentioned to Merle. She was the daughter of a cop. She had good research skills and she hunted me down. Once she confirmed where I was she telephoned every now and again. I'm afraid I discouraged her by not phoning back. And I wasn't good company when she called. I was thinking all the time in those days about Fanny and our child and how I'd failed with my daughter and failed with my wife and failed to find the Tanners' little girl.

She'd said, "I'm not going to call again, Jack. I phoned to tell you that." She laughed, and it was a bad, snorting giggle. It was the kind of noise you make when you don't mean your laughter. "Isn't that ridiculous?"

I said, "Please don't feel bad, Rosalie. I've never been good company for anyone. I'm sorry. You were terrific. You were good to me."

"That's right," she said, "I was a nurse, just like your wife. Except I wasn't your wife. God, Jack. I hope you get to someplace in your life where you have a good night's sleep. Where you can smile. I can remember every time that you smiled."

I got stuck in the long emptiness you get in telephone calls. I felt sorry for myself and sad for Rosalie. She was young and full of energy and she hadn't lost anyone yet. I figured she thought she'd lost me. I wanted to tell her about some of that. But she wasn't looking for anyone to instruct her. By the time I'd thought of what I should and shouldn't say she was off the line.

There were telephone calls with Fanny before we split up for good. The last time I saw her, she was standing near Mr. and Mrs. Tanner between the barn and the fire in the metal drum at the edge of the cornfield. I'd looked up to see the off-duty cops and local volunteers exploring the thick rind of snow that covered the cornfield. I saw the dog watching me. Far beyond him I saw the gray, leaning barn. There was Mrs. Tanner with a blanket around her shoulders. She was watching us all. And there was Fanny in her parka and her slacks and boots. She wore a woolen cap and her hands were in her pockets. I thought she was looking at me. I was pretty well beat up by then. I focused on getting the haft down into the snow and back up. The next time I looked she was gone. I learned later on that she had packed up the car beforehand. She came to look and then she drove away and then she stayed away.

I made calls to her apartment near Utica and later to the satellite health clinic where she worked outside of Watertown. This was long after our baby died. There was another call and then there weren't any.

By then, I was in the truck and heading north. It wasn't half an hour to the campus, which was built like a kind of vertical country club. The old stone buildings and the newer ones were on the upper slopes. Down below, it was all fields and tree plantings. Tractors dragged grass-cutting rigs and trimmed the fields into lawns. I drove onto the central campus road and went up past the library. I remembered some events there, and I felt good for a minute when I thought of Rosalie in her cheap, lightweight car on an icy morning when I'd given her a push uphill to get her to her class on time. This was where a man named Archie had run the counseling office for the kids. He tried to help me. He was homely and funny and smart. He was a man like Bird. He was tough enough for the work and very decent. I missed him a lot when I drove down a different road and off the campus and back toward Vienna. It wasn't the college. It wasn't upstate New York, I thought. *I* was the haunted house. Then I drove past the low, brick hospital where Fanny used to work. All right, I thought. There are other places with ghosts in them. I was holding my breath and when I let it out, I made a sound deep in my throat.

I thought of Tyler Pearl, who I really ought to find. Then I thought of Janice Tanner, who'd been stolen from her parents forever. I really ought to find her too.

You could always try driving up to the farm and knocking on the door if the St. Bernard lets you and telling them Aunt Merle wanted to know if Tyler was all right. Why not try *not* sneaking? Because you'd started off stealthy and lying. They wouldn't believe you now if you were honest. And because they are financed in secret and that is the surest sign of crookedness.

I picked up Ivory Flakes in the giant store outside Vienna that sold everything for less than it could have cost anyplace else. I carried a pillow to the checkout counter, then carried it back to the housewares and bedding section because I felt too domesticated. Then I gave in to the fact that I was happy about setting up my little fort in the country. I took the pillow back with me and paid for it and left. I went to the house and tried to fill the kitchen sink to do a laundry. There wasn't any stopper to keep the sink filled, so I made one with a section of the cardboard box my mattress had come in. It leaked very gradually while I did the wash, and it was a kind of slow-motion race to get my laundry done and then the blanket I had found. I also washed the bear doll I'd found and hung it over the line that went from the house to the shed. The blanket's weight would hold it on the line, and a paper clip in the papers Merle Davidoff had given me was enough to keep the soaked brown bear puppet doll in place. I knotted my socks on the line and hoped my undershorts and shirts would stay in place.

I was putting the Ivory Flakes away when I realized I had bought them and not just any detergent. It was what we had used for our daughter's clothes. When it began to rain on the wash I'd hung out to dry I made a pot of coffee and sat in the kitchen with a cup, debating whether to sweeten it with sour mash. I worried that if I did I wouldn't get any more work done.

I wondered what I meant by done. I called somebody and made her impatient or unhappy. I felt sorry for myself. I went back to some of my old life. I remembered what I didn't want to. I bought what I shouldn't use. I made coffee.

"Well, no wonder you're so tired," I said.

But I didn't drink the sour mash. If I started in treating myself too generously, I thought, I might come to expect that sort of kindness from me all the time.

It took a good deal longer to get to morning than I'd thought it would. I was glad there was no one else in the house with me when the woodpecker started in on the aluminum drainpipe. I had planned to put on a clean pair of jeans but they were draped on the line after a night of intermittent rain. They hung there along with my shirts looking like casualties. I washed clean in the narrow shower with the transparent plastic door and then I used a clean towel and put on dirty clothes. I was more sour now than when I'd first decided not to consider sleep anymore and to wait for the sun to come up. I made coffee and toast and I didn't burn either of them. When I started the truck it didn't burn either. I was grateful. And there was no question now about the approach. I was out of patience with any kind of gradual work. I'd do it directly. If there was anyone around to talk with I'd have bet them even money on my coming out of the doing it directly with scars and scabs. But after a night of thinking about Fanny and children and dogs, that didn't seem too terrifying.

When the morning settled in I was on the road. The road steamed. It looked like that because hot air came down on the wet unpaved surfaces and the soaked oil-and-stone roads that were pitted and potholed from the frost heaves of the winter. Around here, winter was always just over or on its way. I'd seen houses with their piles of logged twenty-foot oaks and maples, a number of them already covered with sawdust and ringed by fourteen-inch rounds that had been sawed from some of them. Men were already cutting firewood because if it's August upstate it's nearly December. They would use power takeoffs from tractors to run the splitters and there would be men using sledgehammers and steel mauls to split enough wood to feed a stove all winter. I remembered the ache in my lower back from doing that chore.

If there had been someone to ask that kind of question I thought I might have wondered out loud how come you can just about feel the muscle pain from splitting wood but you can't remember well enough to actually feel the good soreness you used to feel in the morning after a night of a little too much sour mash and a lot of making love.

I braked in time to miss the doe that slipped and slid and then made it across the road. I knew to wait. Three young ones followed her. A human person might stand in the road and pilot her kids across but these animals ran like hell and hoped for the best. I couldn't imagine a deer hoping so maybe they just ran like hell with no hope at all. I wasn't one of those people who got to thinking Bambi was the target during deer season. But I had come to wonder if they thought and how much of the thinking or not thinking had to do with fear. I'd figured fear was a safe assumption for anything with a brain much larger than my thumb. So I'd stopped hunting. Bambi had nothing to do with it.

I drove up without raising a dust plume because the night's rains had soaked everything halfway to mud. The truck did spit some muck out behind me and I knew some of it would coat the panels over the rear wheels so it would look a little more like I belonged here in spite of the foreign license plates.

The St. Bernard was up and on the alert when I pulled into the barnyard. I thought I'd best come to terms with him as quickly as I could. Before he'd arrived at the truck I was standing next to the door with my arms at my sides. If you don't want a strange dog who might be fierce to feel challenged you ought never to look it in the eye. Look away and move slowly. I did move slowly but I looked directly at him because I wanted to get through the part about challenges and pissing on each other's leg. I moved my hand slowly toward him and I said as evenly as I could, "We might be able to keep from chewing on each other's throat, don't you think? Sure you do. I sure do hope you do."

I had seen an infant mauled by a St. Bernard that was not much more than a puppy. He was a household pet everyone liked. He picked a newborn up with his jaws and swung him once before the owner got his hands into his mouth. The puppy dropped the child, and the child survived. This fellow could pick *me* up and swing me by the head. I'd just as soon he didn't. He cocked his head, he stood, and he waited.

I moved my arm slowly. He stepped in and smelled it and sat down.

I heard him panting and snorting. I heard no machinery, no livestock of any sort. I heard wind in the trees that ringed the farmyard and I saw the hard, dark clouds which were all about rainfall and in wintertime that would be all about snow. They were lining up now over the hills. The bright green of the leaves and brush were turning dark as the sun got sealed away. The joe-pye and all the reds and yellows and blues of the other weeds went darker too. The light brown mourning doves and the slate-colored pigeons kept rising up off the barn roof to fly in long half circles and then come back. Ground doves rose to sit on the electrical wires and then to float down into the dirt of the far end of the yard. I was waiting because I had heard the latch at the house slide very slowly. Someone wanted to see me before I saw them. I took the folded slice of bread out of my shirt pocket and let him see me bring it down. He sniffed. He came close. He opened his mouth, took in my hand and the bread and let the soaked hand slip out. Then he swallowed the bread and licked his slimy chops. He cocked his head for more. He lay down with a huge sigh to wait.

The dog heard the engine first. I watched his ears move. Then I heard it too. Smith came across the barnyard from around behind the barn where I could see the end of the trunk and taillights of a shiny black car. He was on a four-wheel all-terrain vehicle with swollen, small tires with heavy-duty treads. He crouched above the handlebars with his knees flexed. I watched him set the smile on his face and wave. He slowed and then turned off the loud engine.

"Hey," he called. He waved again like he wasn't a few steps from me.

He walked over in his farmer's clothing and bright tan boots. He was full of friendship. He kept the smile on.

"Mr. Smith," I said.

He said, "Well, hell. Call me Clarence, Jack. Am I right? It's Jack? How the hell are you, buddy?" He sounded like he was talking to his dog. He was red and sweaty again. I tried to see into his eyes but all I got was shininess. "Damned hot day today. Full of, you know, sunlight all over. That's what you get when you work out-of-doors."

"Sunshine," I said.

"*You* know," he shouted. "You been there. You're a farmer too. It's a philosophical position as much as it has to do with nutrients and solutions."

He shook a little and his eyes jittered.

"Clarence, I hate to waste your time. I'm wondering. Did you ever run into a kid named Tyler Pearl? In his twenties, looks maybe a little younger? He might have come up here from New York?"

"The city? New York City?"

"That's right."

"God, I don't know anyone from New York, man. Well, I had some cuckoo friends down there maybe fifteen years ago. But that was in connection with my old business interests. Olden days, you know?" He laughed the way you cough. "No. No, I haven't run into any New Yorkers. Unless I count you—"

"No," I said. "I'm not from there. How about have you ever met Tyler Pearl? Just to cut the bullshit a little?"

"No," he said, "I don't want to be wasting your time. It must be urgent. No. I never met him. What'd he do?"

"He disappeared," I said.

"Ouch. It's the worst kind of thing you can do. Disappearing like that, everybody gets worried, the people who counted on you feel let down and the civil authorities get in a tizzy. A *tizzy*." He looked sly and scared. "I sure hope the civil authorities aren't involved in this, you know, this missing thingy problem. You never want the authorities pissed off, you know?" He tapped his damp temple with a shivering finger. "They never forget."

"What'd you ask me, Clarence?" I wanted to see how far gone he really was.

"What—I—what?"

"About the cops?"

"What cops, man?"

Some of it could have been an act. But I really thought he was pretty far into panic and drugs.

"Hey," I said, "I'm costing you time and you need to get back to your farming."

"The farmer in the dell, man. But I sure do want to be helping you if I can be. I can look for this kid. What's he look like?"

I reached into the truck for Tyler's photograph and held it for him. The dog watched carefully but I thought it was because he wanted the picture to be a piece of food. I looked at Smith's face while he looked at Tyler Pearl.

He said, "Wow."

"Wow?"

"Well, you know. Missing and all. I don't think I ever saw a missing person before. You can get solemn over it."

"If you're not careful, I suppose."

"Who wants him back? I mean, you know, who sent you and everything?" Before I could answer, he said, "Are you like a private detective? Like television?"

"I'm doing a favor for his aunt. Like not television."

"Not-TV, baby. It sounds like a new cable system." He giggled and put his hand over his mouth. "Never mind. Never mind. Did you ask— Oh! No. No, man. I never saw the guy. Sorry. Sorry to his aunt, you know, if you happen to speak in the next few days. Sorry."

I said, "I appreciate your time."

"I'm a citizen, right? We got to look out for each other."

"I'll tell his aunt. Thanks again."

Driving off Clarence Smith's land that was owned by the Tyler Pearl he'd never seen or heard of, I asked the empty passenger seat, "I handled that awfully well, didn't I?"

Sarah was over the hills in Oneonta where she taught piano twice a week at the state university college. Elway was sitting in the late afternoon sun in his yard. They had set up a little yellow plastic pool. Their grandson would use it when their boy Michael and his wife came from Buffalo. Elway said it was his hope that by then we would be done with our case.

"Would you really call it a case?"

He said, "If what seems to be hincky really *is*, then yes I would. Yes."

"This guy Smith is a strange hombre."

"You became a regular John Wayne down there, didn't you?"

"No such luck. But he *is* malo. He's a bad guy, Elway, in the only other language I don't talk."

"No," he said, "you used to talk—this is when I first knew you— you used to carry on sometimes in that singsong Vietnam half-in-English half-in-whatever-you-might-call-it."

"Pidgin. That must have been when I drank a little more."

"Drank a little more than most of us, you mean. Yes."

"But Smith," I said, moving the cedar chair around to face him more directly, "he really is a problem. He's doing something crooked. I just don't know if it's any of my business or not."

"The problem," he said, "being that if it isn't your business, the way I see it from what you said, then you'd be *out* of business. On account of there not being any other reference in the county to your girlfriend's, client's, lady friend's—whichever she is—cousin, son, or nephew. Is that right? Smith is all that's left to you after a good deal of not doing very much except renting a house."

"I took a swim in the pond behind the house," I said. "And I did put a bird feeder up."

"And did you, for Christ's sake, get a telephone put in?"

I showed him the telephone card I'd bought at a convenience store. "I can call from anyplace with this," I said, "and I bought an hour's worth of talk."

In the shadows of the day's late sun he looked a little browner than gray. The freckles across his nose didn't stand out so much. He had one of his soy milk substitute shakes on the little white metal table next to his cedar chair. We sat in the Birds' backyard that ran to a field with old apple trees in it and then a hedgerow of ash and plum. He tensed up over his gut every now and again, but he looked all right. He did look softer than I had ever seen him. He wore khakis and a terra-cotta-colored polo shirt and sandals instead of shoes. The sandals troubled me. I was able to see his toes. That was pretty personal for Elway and me. He had old man's toes even though he wasn't much more than sixty-two or sixty-three. I could make out chips and split-lines in the clouded yellow nails. His biceps were hidden by the puffy sleeves of his polo shirt but his forearms looked spindly. If he and I got into a physical situation side by side sometime I knew I'd devote a lot more attention to looking after him than I had thought I'd need to. It used to be Elway bailing me out. He looked up to see me staring at him.

"What?"

"Nothing," I said. "Just taking it all in."

"Listen," he said, "I'm lucky to be back here in the daylight *breathing*. Understand? I know Sarah's getting home in a half an hour, forty-five minutes, and I will stand up and say hello when she arrives. A while back, I knew she wasn't certain she could count on that. And I had my own doubts. So I'm all right. I maybe couldn't take you in a bar fight anymore, but that would only be if we had to play fair. So don't look sorry when I catch you looking."

"You know a fight's never about fair," I said.

"I am assuming you're too intelligent to be looking to fight in a bar or anyplace else." He stared with his red-rimmed eyes, and he still had the hard expression for checking someone out. "And I will back your sorry ass down onto the floor if I need to," he said, looking out toward the hedgerow.

"I know that."

"You know I will."

"I know," I said.

"I can take care of myself," he said, "and I can take care of you." He picked up his shake and put the rim of the glass to his mouth. Then he returned the glass to the table. I sipped at my iced coffee. It was a little warm and bitter by now. We sat that way while a pair of delta-winged fighters came over low and noisy. They said all you needed to know about the world catching up with the countryside. There was too much time passing and a lot less country for it to pass in.

"They're from Syracuse," he said. "We must be going to war someplace."

"You can always find one," I said.

"I'm not looking."

"Me neither."

"No?" he said. "For sure?"

"Sure."

And then he said, "But you will get yourself a phone, right? I set you up with Jerry Gentry for a little information-gathering, and then when he called me I had to tell him you were hard to get hold of. We're asking people for favors, we can't be hard to get hold of, Jack."

"I can get hold of you," I said. I patted my shirt pocket.

"I know," he said, "you got yourself an hour's worth of calls. You are a modern warrior. And I'm your antique telephone exchange."

I leaned forward so I could touch his knee. I didn't. But I was that close. I said, "Elway, I came to you for help. I've done it before. I know you know who I am."

Now he leaned forward. I could feel his breath on the skin of my face. He said, "So we know what we know." He smiled his small smile and then his face went tense. The muscles weren't as tight as they once were. But they still locked down in the same way. And he was nothing but stern and attentive. "So *you* know," he said, "that I knew Fanny and I knew you in the day. Back in the day."

"Yes, you did."

"And we all went through that time together, the four of us. Five, eventually, if you count the child."

"Yes, we did." I had to put the iced coffee down because I didn't want the remaining slivers of ice to go banging against the glass in case my hand shook. I didn't expect it to but there's only so much you can control. I tried to snatch an insect out of the air to give me something to focus on besides what Elway was talking about. But what he was talking about took up most of the space before me. What was left was full of the one-note warnings of a slate-gray nuthatch on the sugar maple that shaded their kitchen. I watched him moving upside down to peck into the bark.

"It was some kind of rainstorm," he said, pretending to be look-ing past me. I knew he was waiting to check me out. We all did something like that at a highway incident or a domestic call. We made it seem we were looking away. That was just before we let them see how *now* we were thinking hard about them while we stared into their eyes. "This was before your baby girl, early on when I first ran into you. It was the Hosbach Trail, wasn't it? She'd got pissed off at you and stomped away like a kid. You tracked her, though."

"No," I said, "it was what you said before. About people knowing each other. I just knew where she'd walk. The trail goes as far into the woods as you can get out of town on foot very fast. It was either there or the ski trails above the campus. She was angry, and when she's—that was where she often went. She always took off when she got mad." The Hosbach Trail was named after a local doctor everyone loved. He'd delivered and cared for half the people of the town where I worked campus security and she worked at the country hospital. Dr. Hosbach dug for Indian artifacts and liked it that the townsfolk could walk where he calculated the Indians had walked. There was a small river and a lot of dark forest and a narrow track of earth and stone that went from the town to the forest. Fanny had gone there in her yellow slicker. Sitting in Elway's backyard in the sun I could see her as a yellow glow disappearing from the old station wagon's lights into the blackness of the woods while it thundered and poured down rain. Every now and again lightning would strike close enough to brighten everything. But Fanny had got herself out of sight. "And the answer, Elway, is no. I don't remember what we were fighting about. We were pretty good at fighting about not too much."

"I was on patrol," he said, "and some deputy must have got scared of the nasty dark woods and the mean old storm. He called in for support in a major way, and I responded. Two deputy's cars, then mine, and your old station wagon fastened together with silver tape. Everybody was inside their car, scratching their nuts and waiting for a grown-up. We had all got onto the same frequency," he said, slouching now, enjoying his own story and how I had to be polite enough to hear him tell it on me. "One of them whispers, you know, like we're in hiding. Only three vehicles with their engines running, all lit up, and this clown thinks he's mounting a major stakeout. His voice is real sharp, real excited, when he whispers, 'Movement!' I expected to hear them rack their shotgun slides. And down the trail, out of the woods, there comes Fanny.

She was marching. That was the way she moved when she was frosted at you, right?"

"Right," I said. "Right."

"That honey-brown hair of hers was soaked dark and her head was up. She looked at the cars the way she'd look you in the eye. That old fuck-you stare of hers."

"Right," I said.

"And there's you, then, halfway running, no raincoat, your hair too long to be respectable and plastered down over your eyes. You looked like a big dog. Except there comes your big dog after you. Fanny stops. You stop. The dog doesn't. He walks past you and he gets to her and he kind of nudges her. Then the two of them, her still staring the fuck-you stare, walk over to your terrible station wagon and they get in, and she takes off. Leaving you to stand there in the lightning and the rain and the lights and tell us there was nothing the matter. It was the first time I saw you off the campus. It was the first and last time I ever saw that dog leave your side. And that was when I thought—I don't know exactly. But it was something like, This guy could use a little looking after."

"And that's what you did," I said.

He shook his head. "It's what I *tried* to do," he said. He folded his square hands over his belly and he smiled, then let the smile relax away. He shook his head again. She let me walk home that night and it wasn't too bad. I couldn't have gotten any more soaked. I made it in time to take a hot shower, change my clothes, walk on my very stiff legs to pee in the yard with the dog, feed him, let him wander outside a while, and then go to work. Fanny had left in her car for the seven A.M. shift, and we'd both be too tired to fight that night. We'd be friends again. I knew we were friends even then when it was early morning and I was sleepless and drained by fighting over what finally wasn't much. It was because I knew what she didn't and I couldn't say. She hated my distance from her so she found reasons to fight. I couldn't tell her that I stayed away so I wouldn't tell her. Because it would be impossible for her if she ever found out. Though she did find out some time afterward. I ended up smiling with a kind of pride in how she fought. She was all tomboy-tough and hurt by the fighting at the same time. She made me want to hug her while we fought.

"Well, shit, Elway," I said. I hid behind drinking my coffee.

"I did try," he said.

"What?"

"To look after you some."

"Oh. Well, that's right. Yes."

"What did you think we were talking about?"

"Fanny."

"We were. No. *I* was talking about Fanny. You were wishing I wouldn't. I was enjoying the privilege of being the unwell elder."

"You are tougher than I'll ever be, Elway."

"Oh, I didn't say I wasn't tougher than you," he said.

As banter it was boring to us both. Each of us knew the other one well past locker room jokes. But at least it wasn't about Fanny when she was my wife and then later.

"I'll meet up with Gentry," I said. "I'd love to find something out about Smith. I can't believe his name *isn't* Smith. Nobody would be dim enough to pick it for an alias. Right? Now, your guys really have the best computer network," I said, meaning the terminals at the state police barracks south of Vienna that Elway had worked from. They were tied into the main frame at Albany.

"But we don't want to be begging my guys as a special favor, *and* completely illegally, to do just minor-league homework, now, do we? We want them for the big stuff, if it gets to that. So you see what Jerry can do. That would be a first step. And see what he thinks about that farmer you've got your eye on."

"I will."

We sat without talking. Then Elway said, "Why did Sarah marry me, do you think?"

I made sure not to freeze in the headlights when he said that. I kept myself ready when I was with him. I thought it was suitable punishment to never be able to enjoy our conversations because he might mention her to me. I said, "Because you're a nice man, Elway."

"I am a lot of things. And some of them are interesting, maybe. But I am *not* nice."

"She might think you are."

He laid his eyes on me hard. "You buy groceries from nice. You don't marry nice."

"I guess not, then."

"Don't be scared of the question, Jack."

"Why would I?"

"Because it's personal."

"It is?"

"Shit," he said. "She married me because I begged her to. I'm eight and a half years older than she is. She was a kid. She still is, it feels like. We started out because she could talk to me, she said. Came out of a terrible home life. Her old man was a drunk who whaled on his wife and kids. She had to keep me from whaling him back before we got married. She—you can imagine this on account of her work—she was always playing music on the piano, on the hi-fi. Listen to this, Jack. I am a tone-deaf African-American retired state trooper. Understand?"

"No."

"Music to me sounds like hens getting fucked by bulldogs. It sounds like one-armed carpenters banging away with ball peen hammers on a galvanized roof. I can't hear any of it without hurting."

"Elway, I don't know what to say. My goodness."

Elway laughed from his belly. "'My goodness' is right. That was pretty to hear, coming from you. 'My goodness.'"

"Did you tell her?"

"No. Never will."

I thought of the secret I didn't tell.

"Do you think she knows?"

He nodded. "I do. I think she knows. She never plays music as much as she used to. I think it's to spare me. I ask her to play, but she doesn't, all that much."

I said, "So where's the secret in it, then?"

"In making believe it doesn't hurt. We both do that."

I shook my head. I looked at my coffee but didn't drink it.

He said, "What?"

"I don't know what to learn from this, Elway."

"Well, Jack, who ever said I'm here to teach you? I'm as much of a father as I can be to Michael. Your old man had his shot."

"Yes, he did," I said.

"Was it that bad?"

"He had his shot," I said. "He took it. His aim was even worse than mine."

We sat with each other for a half a minute more. Then Elway said, "What?"

"You're a big-time man, Elway. She was right to marry you."

"Yes, she was," he said. "*I* shouldn't have married *her*, of course. I should have let her be. But I am a selfish man."

"As you should be."

"Yes?"

"To have Sarah."

"Don't you tell her. Don't give me away."

"I'll cover your back. You covered mine enough times. I worry about secrets, though. Keeping them from people."

"That's what they're for," he said.

"You think so? I don't know."

"I do," he said. "You keep what's left of your secret."

I tried to read his face. I couldn't.

"And you stay in touch with Jerry Gentry," he said, "maybe get something on that farm, maybe get some kind of a line on that woman's son."

"Nephew. Tyler Pearl."

"How did you get to be working for Aunt Pearl?"

"Aunt Merle," I said.

He closed his eyes and said, "Is this complicated, Jack?"

"Would I be in it if it wasn't? I don't have the gift of simple."

"No, you don't. But listen to this. Her people—her brother or sister—decided on calling their child Tyler? Our Michael married a girl who had to name their baby Sergei."

"A traditional African name," I said.

"Sure. She does what they call film theory. Sergei's the name of someone in that."

I shook my head.

"You don't quite hear my voice, do you? Because you're maybe only one-half here?"

"I'm a little bit pushed," I said.

He nodded.

"You too," I said.

He nodded again. He looked into his drink. "These outlaw farm-ers might just whip our asses, then," he said.

I thought he was right. I said, "I doubt it."

"Not a chance," he said. "But you do sound tired as hell. You got hunted through your dreams last night, didn't you?"

"Are they dreams if you have them awake?" I drank the rest of my coffee and set the glass down, and then I stood. "Elway," I said, "I'm tuckered out."

He said, "I'll sit here and nap, and you go home and do the same. If you had a phone, and if you needed it, you could call me up and I could tell you a story and it would put you to sleep."

He smiled up at me in a way that I liked. I surprised us both by stepping in and bending over and kissing him on top of his thin, gray hair.

On my way home, I stopped to buy a drain stopper for the kitchen sink, a bright yellow-orange pillowcase, and a large, oval-shaped wicker basket. I was spending Merle's money all right. But I wasn't buying her very much. I filled the bird feeder and brought my laundry from the line into the kitchen and folded it. As usual that reminded me of Fanny folding an infant's tiny white T-shirts and pajamas with feet. Coming back up here was not doing me a world of good, I thought. On the other hand, I hadn't exactly pros-pered as the rented law-and-order of the coastal Carolinas. Some people, I thought, can find a way to be miserable north or south. It doesn't matter which.

"It's a gift," I said to my stiffened laundry. "And probably," I said, like a man replying to himself, "you ought to get yourself a dog."

That didn't deserve an answer. I made a couple of grilled ched-dar cheese sandwiches with a ham slice in each. I drank well water with the meal because it was sweet. I was washing dishes and looking ahead to the evening's entertainment. It would consist of stuffing my day-old pillow into my brand-new pillowcase. And I was trying out explanations I might make to Merle Davidoff. They'd really be excuses. But they'd also be true.

I can't find your nephew, I'd tell her.

I probably couldn't help him anyway, I'd tell her. Because he is or was mixed up with bad people called Smith and whoever was running them.

The "was" refers to his possibly being dead, I'd tell her.

Putting my dishes away I heard what I'd heard in southwestern places. I heard coyotes. They were shrill and frightening because they sounded so purely wild. Their crying made me turn to look at the carbine hung over the door. So that can follow you around, I thought. You don't leave that behind.

And anyway, I'd tell her, I have lost at least a step. There's this kind of *caution* I'm noticing. It might be all right if you're looking to see has a person gotten more mature or composed or sociable. Something along those lines. In certain situations this could be seen as a serious and thoughtful response. But the problem is, I would tell her, thoughtful might not get the job done. It might be useful to get down to it with Smith and start barging in with some force. That's what someone like me was once best used for, I thought I should tell her.

The sound that came in was of a big engine on the short, steep driveway. I also heard the coyotes. I went outside and saw Gentry standing next to his patrol car. His big-rimmed deputy's hat looked small in his fingers. He was shaking his head and smiling the smile that made him less terrifying.

"Elway didn't have your phone number," he said. "I'd have called instead of dropping in. I caught this sector for patrol anyway, though. I needed to tell you, we have to change our meeting time."

By then we were near enough to shake hands. Mine isn't small but it seemed that way inside of his. He smelled of aftershave as sweet as a stale candy bar. Then the passenger's door clicked open and I saw the reason. She had gray-black hair cut like a man's crew cut gone shaggy a little. Her face was young and oval and her nose was long. She was slender though her long arms and wide wrists looked muscular. She wore a dark sleeveless top that showed how her muscles moved. It was dusk but she put on sunglasses with wire rims when she got out of the car.

Gentry held an arm out to point across the hood of his car at her. "Jack, this is Georgia Bromell. She's a writer. Well, she's a newspaperwoman. Newspaperperson."

"I write things," she said. "For hire, kind of. When I can find somebody to pay me." She made a wincing face to suggest she knew she might not be impressing me. I couldn't tell how much she meant to be modest. I sensed some salesperson in her. But she was interesting and her low voice was pleasant. She walked around the front of the car with her hand stuck out to shake. It was cool and strong enough. I figured all that typing would make for powerful hands and arms. Her slacks were the same gray-black as her sleeveless top. She wore black leather clogs and she didn't hold a pen or notebook or recorder. I appreciated her waiting before she hauled out the tools of her trade.

"Probably also when you can find somebody to talk to you. You know, give you the story. Whatever that might be." I looked at Gentry to make sure he was getting the message. "Has anybody agreed to give you a story on something up here?"

"As opposed to down where?" she asked.

I shook my head. "*I'm* not a story, is what I'm saying. And I don't have one to offer you."

She said, "Okay. I thought otherwise, though. But whatever you say."

I had met up with all sorts of reporters. I'd known kids who thought the metro beat in a chewed-up southern city was the best a soul could wish for. I knew grim, tired alcoholics who understood their next step down would be writing product information for gadgets advertised on television at two in the morning. They all always looked for the story. For me the story was just whatever happened. That was tough enough to understand. But the reporters I knew were always convinced the story was hiding someplace under or behind what went on. This Georgia Bromell seemed to be one of those. It took me a while to understand how much. I asked her, "What's your story about, Ms. Bromell?"

Gentry said, "I need to get out on the road, Jack. I'm not on a break. Let's meet up at the same place as before, all right? Nine o'clock for breakfast?"

"Two of us or three, Jerry?"

"Three, please," Georgia Bromell said.

I thought about it the best I could while I was standing out in front of my place like a security guard outside a bar. I asked her, "Is it about law enforcement in rural New York or something more specific?"

I smelled cigarettes on her breath when she talked to me. She said, "What would you suggest?"

I said, "Jerry, I'm not sure we'll be doing this."

"I kind of promised," he said. "Georgia went to high school here. In Vienna. We go back."

"That's what it's about," she said. "My piece. Going back and what you find there. Or what finds you."

"You're writing about Vienna, New York? Okay. But you don't need me and why I'm partnering up with Jerry because I haven't happened to you," I said.

Jerry said, "I'd say it's her call, Jack."

"Let me take a goofy guess," I said. "You two went to the high school prom together. You were voted something, I don't know, and it was a pretty important romance in the senior class of nine-teen-whichever in Vienna, New York? And it's part of whatever the story's about?"

"We never went out," Jerry said, looking at a stainless steel watch that seemed small on his wrist. "I never asked."

Georgia said, "I would call that a pretty smug analysis of me and Jerry and the work I do. I would say you ought to be embarrassed to be so wrong. Who appointed *you* in charge of understanding me? And by the way," she said, "I didn't date anyone in high school. I was too busy being bulimic and scratching lines across my wrist veins with my father's executive desk-set scissors. I don't need to defend myself or my work. Jerry needs to get back on the road now, so goodbye. It wasn't that terribly nice to meet you. But maybe you can make up for it."

"Tomorrow, Jack," Gentry said. When she was back in the car, he said, "She's a hand grenade, isn't she? Sorry about the lecture you got. We can try it just you and me in the morning. Then we can see how it goes with her."

"She's one pissed-off person, Jerry."

"I really would like to help her," he said. I didn't enjoy hearing him sound like he was begging me. I thought of how bitter the cold was that day at the cornfield where he was one of the off-duty peo-ple who looked for her under the snow.

"Did your wife know her in high school?"

He winced. "They all hated her. She was the rich man's daugh-ter, and she was the—I guess you'd say the sophisticated girl in the school. She got into plenty of trouble. My wife is, like, not thrilled."

"And the sheriff said she could ride with you?"

"He said she could have whatever she wanted. She's still the rich man's daughter. You read his newspaper."

"No, I don't," I said.

"And you listen to his radio station, AM *and* FM. He's Daniel Bromell." He looked at me. "All right," he said, "no, you don't listen to his stations either. But you know what I mean."

"Yeah, Jerry, I do. I shouldn't give you a hard time and I should have kept my mouth shut with her. But I don't think it's the best idea—for *me*, anyway. For Tyler Pearl's aunt. Well, for him, for that matter."

"She's had stuff published," he said, "in magazines."

"Let's you and me talk," I said. "Then we'll see."

He said, "I need to get on the road, Jack. We'll try it."

Behind the wheel he nodded at me. I waved. The light from the house fell on his windshield so its reflection covered the passenger's side. I couldn't see her face. To be polite I moved my hand in her direction before I stepped away. He backed out hard and raised some stones and dust. We were one step closer to out of control. And I had seen Ms. Georgia Bromell before. I was sure that I had seen her. I didn't know where. I could feel myself making a face while I tried to think of when and how I'd seen her. The face never helped and neither did the thinking. My memory coughed stuff up whenever it wanted and not when I needed it to.

It got so I had to focus on the calls of the coyotes to really hear them because they were distant enough to get lost in the rattling of branches or the sound of my footsteps on the kitchen floor. But they were there. They repeated their shrill calls. I suspected that I might have heard them since I'd moved in but had drowned them out with my remembering and speculations. They did seem

to be coming closer. But of course they wouldn't be, I thought.
Otherwise they'd be a dozen yards from the house by now. If you
didn't think of them as animals telling other animals something
about whose patch it was to feed on you might have thought they
sounded desperate. But they were just wild dogs that called over a
long distance.

Although anyone could step through half a dozen screened-in
windows I'd left open I did lock the front door. Someone could kick
in the back door or for that matter the locked one in front. I turned
out the lights in the downstairs rooms and corridor. I realized that
I was living in a larger space than I had since Fanny and I lived
together. It occurred to me when I set my head on a pillow that
there were new places like the far Northwest that I could consider.
I told myself that there were always jobs because there was always
plenty of disorder. I wasn't too old to work yet.

Then I thought that might not be true. I was forty-nine. I'd turn
fifty this year. It would happen in the autumn. I had every intention
of being away from upstate New York before the snow flew. Snow
and the deep cold of this place would make it all worse. I thought
to hear the coyotes now. It was like tuning a radio in and I wanted to
hear them more than I wanted to hear my thoughts. So I listened.
They yapped. It was a stupid sound. Finally, it was more stupid than
frightening. It was the same sobbing sound in a high register over
and over and over. It helped to think of their calls as stupid. When
dogs barked again and again you just told them to shut up or you
stopped listening. But the coyotes sounded different. I invited their
noise in and I listened to it hard so that I wouldn't think about Fanny
and our child. She'd be thirteen, I thought, if she had lived.

It took a long time for me to keep from blinking my eyes. It took
longer to keep them shut. Then I slept. Then lights hit the house.

I felt them before I opened my eyes. They flooded the kitchen and the brightness spilled over into the living room I slept in. I reached for the Mag-Lite I kept on the floor beside the mattress. I thought it was a little dumb to consider fighting light with light. But the three-battery flash was heavy and it had a good grip. It was a useful weapon for close-in work. I kept it with me after I put on boots and took a few seconds to lace them. You may think you're in a hurry so you haven't time to fasten your shoes. That can get you tripping ass over teakettle at a time when you need to stay on your feet. I thought this might be that kind of time.

A horn went off over and over. I wondered whether the coyotes would think the horn was answering their calls. Maybe they'd start calling louder in reply. Apparently I was supposed to be frightened by the light and the sound. And I was supposed to think that I lived so far from anyone that the noise wouldn't bring help. I wondered what I was supposed to need help from. The car or truck had a big engine that ran raggedly. It nagged through the firing cycles more than it idled. They began to rev it. That wasn't going to help their valves any. They surely wanted to make plenty of noise. I wondered what they'd decide to do when they understood my heart wasn't going to stop because they were blowing up the nighttime with their truck.

I walked through the kitchen even though staying low made more sense than moving upright on my way to the door. I took the carbine down and went to the drawer where I kept the pistol and cartridges. I took a loaded clip from the drawer and armed the carbine. I left the flashlight behind me because I had decided what I ought to have in my hands. I walked through the front door and into the light in my combat gear consisting of boxer shorts and T-shirt and work boots and a Korean-war weapon. Veterans told me the mechanism very often froze up during the Korean winter. The carbine didn't punch you down like the Garand. The .30-caliber military ball didn't tear through your soft organs like the 5.56mm of the M-16. But the carbine was an elegant little weapon for fairly close combat. I intended to be close.

I figured that whoever it was outside the house had the idea of more or less scaring me to death. Or they wanted to scare me the two-hundred-odd miles south to New York City. That was where the questions about Tyler Pearl had come from. I thought that standing in their headlights on my little raw-lumber front porch might indicate I wasn't scared. Later on I worried about that. It was true. I wasn't. It's stupid not to be scared of standing like a firing-range silhouette in front of hostile elements. But I was that stupid. I stood in front of them and I didn't care. I aimed at the right-hand headlight. I had to be careful not to shoot anyone because protecting your home and hearth has to take place inside the sill, as far as I knew. If they didn't invade the house I couldn't kill them. I really didn't want to. There's always a civil suit even if the authorities clear you of manslaughter. And you *can* do time for heroics with a weapon. So I decided on no heroics.

There was a lot of shrieking from the vehicle and somebody pumped the horn and raced the engine of what I thought by then was a clapped-out truck with a sulky muffler and laboring valve lifters. It was one impressive concert if you could make it all out. There were the coyotes, the horn, the engine, the shouts, and now there was me. I squeezed two rounds off at the right-hand light.

I shot twice more in groups of two. Trigger, trigger, then hold. Trigger, trigger, then hold. I fired six rounds and missed with each one. It's true that I was in the high-beam headlights of the truck. But it's also true that I qualified in marksmanship only because the staff sergeant at the firing range cheated for me. He allowed me extra targets. I was a very good military cop who shot badly. I was in my usual form on the porch in front of the truck. I thought I might have put a hole in the radiator grille. I hoped I hadn't ruined the core. I didn't want them stuck for the night in my rented front yard.

The engine did stop racing. The horn cut out. The shouting stopped. Over the uneven idle of the engine I thought I heard the coyotes' crying. I sighted on the left-hand light and fired for effect with two more rounds. I hit the usual nothing. I heard a door slam. What I'd decided was a big GMC truck backed down the drive. I squinted at it while it moved away slowly either because the cylinders were too worn to give much compression or because I was supposed to believe that whoever I'd frightened off wasn't frightened off. I chose the compression theory because their retreat didn't strike me as tactical.

In the morning I would be tidy. I'd come out and hunt for the casings ejected by the carbine. You don't want to litter a rental property with brass. This is especially true if you aren't the kind of tenant who mows his lawn. I wasn't. For now there was mess enough to deal with. There was the sharp stink of the fired shells and the very heavy smell of my own sweat and the banging of my heart.

Of course, I couldn't call Merle Davidoff tonight and tell her that I ought to quit. You could call what just happened a sign of success if you knew what to do about it. Or else you could think of it all as a joke. They blow their horn. I shoot off rounds. I could call it planning and progress, but I thought we were all pathetic. I leaned at the sink and drank two full glasses of tap water. I listened to myself suck for air between drinks. I dripped gun oil down the barrel. I'd clean it some other time. I hung it back over the door. I went into the room where I slept and I didn't sleep. I set my head on the pillow and pretended that I was able to sleep.

It would be best not to shoot someone. And it would probably be wise to not get killed although I did think that I didn't care. Walking out onto the porch and standing in the light should have worried me. It didn't. I was cold inside my chest until after it was over. I had thought only about the placement of the shots. If they wanted me dead they could have me dead. That seemed to me how I had felt. All of that sneaking around on the hill above Smith's land was only tactical and more or less professionally done. But I knew tonight that I didn't care if they sighted me in and finished me off.

"I don't watch movies where the good guy gets killed," I said. No. I was remembering something I said to Fanny a long time before. It wasn't about the good guy. It was about the wife. "I don't watch movies where the wife gets sick," I had told her. I said it in a very puffy, huffy voice. I was telling Fanny and not myself about certain movies I wouldn't watch.

This was before our little girl. We had met in town after work and we were in the rental section of the supermarket. We wanted a Friday night film. Fanny loved watching movies. I was pretty much a nuisance to her about them.

I might say, "This is plain damned silly. Isn't it?"

And she would answer, "It's a dream, Jack. Movies are dreams. Can't you think of it like dreaming?"

And I'd get pissy and say, "I don't *like* dreams."

And she would have to answer, "Because you don't get to choose. Because you just *have* them, right?"

The lights in the Grand Union always seemed to hum. The people who shopped always seemed angry. I thought it was because the week they'd worked weighed them down. The movie she picked out was something foreign with *Cleo* in the title. It was about a woman who was dying or who was waiting to find out if she was dying. I asked, "Is she somebody's wife?"

Fanny turned around. She was holding the slipcase of the movie in front of her. She smiled at me like I'd said something clever. Her face looked less tired and less tense. Of course it was cold as hell and she had a knitted cap on as well as her heavy coat. She still looked more broad-shouldered than bulky. She looked streamlined enough. She stood there on her long legs and her eyes gone happy. "What will this particular complaint be about? I never met a man more scared of the dark, of what he'd see in a movie in the dark. It always feels true to you, doesn't it? Isn't that it?"

"Because if she's a wife and it's bad news and she's sick or she's going to die, I won't watch it," I told her. "I don't watch movies where the wife gets sick. Much less—you know."

"They frighten you," she said.

I wouldn't answer.

She leaned against me and raised up on her toes to kiss me on the mouth. She said, "How about we look at *Bad Day at Black Rock* again? I always think of you doing the Spencer Tracy part. *You* always think of you doing the Spencer Tracy. Don't you?"

"He only had one arm," I said.

"And he kicked ass."

"That's me?"

"As long as you don't have to worry about me getting sick, or—"

I put my hand over her mouth, and she bit at my fingers.

This year it would also be Fanny's fiftieth birthday. You shouldn't turn fifty alone.

I got up from the mattress and put water on to simmer while I took a long shower. I changed into clean clothes and poured the coffee water through the filter. I listened to the coyotes and cleaned the rifle. I reloaded the clip and hung the weapon armed but with the safety on back over the door. I should have gone outside and spanked them. It was ridiculous to fire a weapon. I was sure I had thoroughly intimidated the trees around the house and the long-distance coyotes. But I had also made sure that Smith or whoever it was would be thinking now about his own firepower.

"Nobody ever accused you of high intelligence," I said.

No one in the room expressed amusement with my humor.

I was sleepless and surly in the morning when I ordered my breakfast burrito and coffee. Gentry came in a little less slicked with cologne because Georgia Bromell wasn't with him. He ordered enough food for several men. Without having said good morning or hello, he said, "It's for the public relations, Jack. The sheriff made the assignment himself. She wants to write something she can maybe get into the New York City papers."

"But you'd have volunteered to drive her around, Jerry, wouldn't you?"

He grinned what I thought he thought of as a boy's sly grin. "She makes my wife nervous," he said. He kept his voice low, and he was soft-spoken enough for me to need to lean toward him to hear over the clatter of flatware on plates and conversations in the fog of cigarette smoke, maple syrup, strong coffee, and hot oil. "They knew each other in high school. My wife—that's Nina—stayed here, you know, and Georgia went to college at Skidmore. One got out, one got stuck and then got me.

"She's, you know how they say it. She's running out of options," he said. "She ran herself through men and jobs. Word is, she and Mr. Bromell get along terrible. He said out loud on Thursday at the Rotary lunch how sordid her life got. That's his own word for it.

Sordid. Professionally speaking, I guess you'd say she's backed into a corner. Well," he said, "all right. I can understand corners. I'm in the same one I got born into except now I get Social Security deducted. You know what I mean, Jack. She backed her ass right into a corner, so it's shades on at sundown and that's prime ass she's backing. I have to say that."

I chewed at the burrito while Gentry took a gulp of coffee and then made an order of hash browns and fried eggs disappear. He still had a side order of bacon and a side of toast to nibble at while I drank my second cup of coffee.

He said, "There's plenty of people in corners, Jack. Don't you think?"

He pooled sugar and the contents of four plastic tubs of synthetic milk into his coffee.

I asked for another coffee. I didn't talk about Georgia Bromell. I said, "I looked up the school and land taxes, Jerry. I looked through the deeds. This Tyler Pearl I'm looking for is the name on all the documents. He never had more than a couple of hundred bucks, but he owns the land that Smith farms."

Gentry ate buttered toast and I sipped at my coffee. He talked around a wad of pulpy crumbs. "They used him as a front, you're saying?"

"I think he thought he was let in on something large. It's a pretty clever way for them to do it. Smith farms the camouflage as well as the crop. Isn't that how they usually do it? Surround the hemp with something legitimate?" He nodded. I said, "And Tyler Pearl is either some kind of secret hired hand or he's dead."

He said, "There's enough money in it. I guess I can understand they might end up killing him. I don't know why."

"By the time it gets to the killing, the why of it is the last thing we get to understand."

"Often enough," he said. "Did you hear what I said about Georgia?"

"Yes, I did."

"You think we can cooperate?"

I patted his arm. It was like hitting the counter we ate at. I didn't want to give him any more of an answer than that. I decided not to ask him to go after information on Smith. He very definitely wasn't supposed to provide official records to the likes of me. If he wanted to do something informally he'd do it and then I'd hear what he knew.

"I keep waiting for that burrito to come back and bite me," I said.

"Not here. They can cook 'em here. Well. They can anyways put 'em in the microwave all right."

"Coffee's pretty good."

"Gentry nodded. "I'm off-duty today," he said. "Me and Nina, we're driving to Binghamton. There's a craft store there. Well, it's in Vestal, really. They have all these supplies she needs. She makes lawn ornaments, paints 'em up. You come over to the house sometime, you'll see 'em all. The lawn's covered with the shit, to tell you the truth. It's like an outdoor showroom for dwarfs and powder-blue squirrels. I don't know."

"And there's Georgia Bromell," I said, looking sideways to see if he'd take offense.

"Pretty smoky lady," he said.

"She's had troubles," I said.

"You think she'll *make* trouble, you're saying."

I said, "Just ask Nina."

He nodded, and we sat silent a little while. Then I said, "That was a fair enough point, Jerry, about corners."

"What? Oh. Well, you were the one made that particular point, Jack. Listen, I'll see you. I'll be in touch. Leave me word with Nina, or at the department about your number, all right? Once your phone's installed."

I was on my way to buy a radio so I could hear the Bromells' radio station. It was background research. I was conducting it because I didn't have an idea of what I should do except fight with Smith. I put my Linda Ronstadt disk on and punched through the songs until I got to where she sang about all those women with no-account men. I wondered if I'd have fought with my daughter about the clothes she wanted to wear and about her boyfriends.

Well, of course we'd have fought.

But we'd have gotten past that, I thought. We'd have been friends.

How could I not have stayed her friend?

I WANTED TO DRIVE away from the Kwik-Stop but I also wanted to shut the engine down. I sat in the truck. I felt like I was vibrating in place like Smith but from the inside out and not from the muscle. But I didn't care about him. That minute I didn't care about Tyler Pearl or Clarence Smith or Merle or anybody else but me. I held on to the steering wheel and closed my eyes.

I would have been my daughter's friend, I thought. No matter what. I wished I could have been a better friend to her mother.

I was remembering a day in winter, maybe February. It was the time up there when you waited for the thaw. After a while, you begged for it to come. The drifts in the dooryard were mounded high from the town plow. The mounds came up to my rib cage and they were frozen hard and polished by wind. I came outside with the baby in my arms because it was too tense in the house. It was like waiting for an electrical storm to explode. Fanny was also going to explode and I carried the baby away. But it was too cold to stand there so I took her to the station wagon. I started the engine. I pumped the accelerator to get some heat into the cab but we stayed where we were. I had no place to take us.

I held her on my chest in her nest of blankets so I could look down and see her face. What I saw was my daughter looking up at me. They were Fanny's eyes, I thought. But they were also her own. She was a person and she was looking at me. She was still red from crying but she wasn't crying now. She watched me. For all the howling she'd been through, there weren't lines on the soft skin of her face. My palm cupped her head with room left over for my fingers to brush against her ears. She didn't exactly smile. She did seem to notice me and not to mind. The car shook a little and she watched me watch her fall asleep. I sat with her for a long time.

When I carried her into the house she stayed asleep. The dog was at the back of the kitchen near the stairs. His tail brushed the floor. He looked at me. He was serious.

"I didn't forget you," I said. I carried her into the back room and around again to the kitchen. I thought Fanny must be upstairs. The dog stayed at the foot of the staircase.

I said, "Really. I didn't."

I heard Fanny at the top of the stairs and I whispered up to her, "She's asleep."

I heard the floorboards creak when she walked from the steps to our bedroom. Then I heard the latch of the door click shut. It was so quiet in the house, I could hear our baby breathing in her sleep.

In the truck, I closed my eyes and heard the latch again. I couldn't hear the breathing now. I got out of the truck and went back into the Kwik-Stop in Vienna, New York, and bought a container of coffee. Standing outside at the truck, I scalded my mouth drinking it fast. Then I went off on my errands.

I bought a little radio. I found a gun dealer's shop sandwiched between a front-end specialist and an out-of-business ice-cream stand on Route 12 at the southern end of Vienna. I bought a box of .30-caliber military ball for the carbine. The morning had begun with a little breeze and a sense of moisture on its way. By the time I had the ammunition in the truck the sky to the east was gray. I thought I saw lightning jump into the sky and run down to the ground a couple of miles away. Thunder washed over the backs of the clouds and the wind died. I was slicked with sweat from walking through the parking lot of the strip mall by the time I reached the air-conditioned realtor's office.

Ms. Penny Putney looked me over and didn't smile. I thought I might have appeared a little wild to her. She looked chunky and bright-faced in a lightweight suit the color of a metallic mallard's breast.

"Everything all right at the house?"

"Yes, ma'am," I said. "I wonder if anyone was inquiring about me. Looking to find out where I was living, say?"

"Are you that popular?"

"I'm hoping not to be."

She stared at me and then she raised and lowered her considerable chin. Her eyes bulged and I speculated on the weight of the thought that was pressing them from behind. Finally she said, "We respect confidentiality. A real prime tenet of this profession is confidentiality. You could say it's our link with doctors and priests."

I said, "So that's three highly confidential professions."

"Well, there's others," Ms. Putney said, looking at the screen of her computer the way you'd check your notes before giving a speech at the Rotary on a Thursday noon in an upstate New York town. Henry Bromell would be in the audience. He'd be packing away the bread and butter and the prime rib of beef in mushroom gravy. He'd be telling businessmen how offended he was by his daughter's way of life. "But you get my meaning. You've got a right to your privacy even if you're only renting."

"I appreciate that, Ms. Putney, and I want to thank you. I won't take up your time."

She nodded and her smile was full of satisfaction. She was having herself a highly ethical morning.

It hadn't rained but the air was filled with humidity and my knees ached so I knew it would be raining soon. There was a regional commercial newspaper called the *Pennysaver* that you could pick up free at the entrance of the supermarkets. I went through it looking for realtors in town. In my Friend in Pennsylvania notebook I listed five and began to fumble my way in and outside of town to find them. In my third realtor's office of the morning in a small house next door to a tractor showroom and repair shop I met a man named Silverstein who made it clear that he pronounced it Silverstine. His shirt and tie were the same bronze color. His tasseled loafers were brightly shined. His bald head caught the light and seemed to glow in the heat of the office that had no air-conditioning. An oscillating fan made a lot of noise and when its breeze reached him the stiff gray hairs combed over his baldness lifted like a gull's wing. They flapped once and then dropped down as the fan turned away.

"And how are you telling me I would have known to tell somebody where to find you?"

"Oh, I'm not telling you, Mr. Silverstein. I'm asking you. I thought there might be an outside possibility that rentals could be listed with more than one agency. And somebody renting out the place might let the friendly competition know. And somebody asking for rentals recently taken off the market might get an answer from somebody, I don't know, like you." I offered what I thought of as a peaceful smile. He looked away from it.

"And are you alleging it's unlawful of me to give out a little courtesy in my professional capacity?"

"I never knew how deeply you people, realtors, that is, got involved in I guess you'd have to say philosophical considerations."

"What?"

"Just tell me, would you, who asked?"

"I don't know," he said.

I leaned forward in the bright orange plastic chair on the client's side of his desk and clasped my hands on the edge near the long triangular plaque that said MERRILL SILVERSTEIN. "Try to know," I said. "Because then I can get out of your office and stop disturbing your busy day." I tried the smile again.

"There might have been a man," he said, smoothing the gull's wing that slowly lifted and dropped. He patted it like he was perfectly calm but the hair was worried. "He inquired about recent rentals."

"And you were eager to be helpful."

"It's what we do," he said, "we help."

"Blue eyes, very clear blue eyes, and he gives you a very friendly smile? Big man in farmer's clothing. He might talk a little strange."

"The gentleman had eyes that you'd remember," he said, looking away from mine.

When I left the realtor's it was raining heavy, cold drops. The tar of the parking lot steamed. I could go up into the woods and look down at the place and learn nothing but feel a little busy and maybe a little honorable. Or I could go up the road and drive into the farmyard and make trouble. I got out of the truck and walked over to the supermarket. I bought a quart box of raspberries. I thought maybe Elway could grind them up in a blender to use in one of his shakes. The berries and I were pretty wet by the time I was back at the truck.

It had been a busy morning. I had listed realtors in a child's souvenir notebook. I had made a few of them uncomfortable. I had driven the truck from the house to Vienna and I'd voyaged up and down Route 12. I'd bought berries. I owed myself a cup of coffee.

And I owed Merle Davidoff a call. I turned off the main street and went hunting diners but I couldn't find one. I got back on 12 and headed south and drove until I arrived in a town named Greene that was twelve or thirteen miles from Vienna. On a broad main street near a handsome old hotel I found a store front with EAT painted on the glass. A short woman in a spotless chef's jacket and pants with all the cuffs rolled up poured a cup of very rich coffee and smiled like someone's happy child. She was in her seventies, I thought. Her dark hair was thinning. Her nose and chins were giving in to gravity. But she answered me in a voice as strong as the coffee. It was like hearing a musical instrument say, "You're very welcome."

"What kind of coffee is this, ma'am?"

"Ma'am," she said. I couldn't tell if she enjoyed the word or thought it was ridiculous. "You're a gentleman?"

I shook my head. "Just a coffee drinker."

"Our son sends the beans up from New York. French-Italian roast, a very light espresso blend. We lose money on every cup. We break even, my husband says, but he knows nothing."

"You're from Europe?"

"I'm from Coney Island Avenue in Brooklyn, New York," she said.

I held my white china cup up for a refill.

"Our name," she said, "is Stovich. Once it was two syllables longer, but my husband's father thought he should seem more American. Do I appear American to you?"

"You couldn't get more American," I said.

I drank the coffee. Then I went out to the truck and found the dirty Thermos jug that she rinsed for me and then filled. "Mrs. Stovich," I said, "I'll be back."

"Call me Lilian," she said. "If we're still in business when you get here, you could learn to say Lily."

"I'm Jack."

She looked me over and said, "I'd call you American too."

I followed the very wide shopping street and I found a telephone kiosk two corners down. I used my phone card and called Merle Davidoff's number. Her assistant was just picking up when I realized that I had absolutely nothing to tell her about her nephew that wasn't suspicions or bad moods. I could have given her the information about his land purchase. But I owed her something about what that meant. I didn't know yet. So I hung it up and walked back to the truck. I lifted my coffee jug but told myself to wait until I'd either bought more berries or terrorized more realtors before rewarding myself. I drove north on Route 12 to Vienna.

I remembered bringing a cup of coffee to Fanny in the morning after we'd had a bad night. This was in the final year of our marriage and I was impossible for her to live with. I knew that. I also knew I couldn't do too much to make it easier for her. I remembered believing that I was doing everything I could to make it possible for her. But I also knew I couldn't help except by keeping the secret to myself. I might have been right. But this was well before she found out. We weren't having an easy time. Often she would leave our bedroom and move to finish the night in another place. Sometimes it was the empty room upstairs or the extra bedroom next to it. Sometimes it was the sofa in our room downstairs that looked out over the valley to the east. We had rocking chairs near the wall with three windows in it. You could sit and watch the storms coming up to us. In the morning I knew which room she'd moved to by waiting to hear the dog's tail against the floor.

It was a morning in early autumn when I brought the coffee in.

She was lying under just a cotton blanket we kept hanging on the back edge of the sofa. Her bare feet were sticking out of the bottom and I reached to pull it over her toes. I put the two cups of coffee on the table in front of the sofa. Then I went around it to look at the day. Cool air came in through two of the windows that she'd opened. It smelled musky from damp leaves and the sunlight looked golden on everything that was green. I went back to the sofa and lifted the dog's heavy head in my hands to say hello. I was as pleased as I always was that he trusted me with himself. Then I sat on the table's edge and sipped my coffee and waited.

"Hello," she said in a couple of minutes. Her hair was tousled like a child's from rough sleeping. There was a little patch of reddened skin at each cheek and her lips looked dry. Her eyes were heavy-looking. I knew she hadn't slept well and I knew that she had wept.

I said, "I would give anything. I would give up my *hands* if you could be happy."

"Yes, you would," she said. "I know." She worked her way up onto an elbow and reached for her coffee cup. She sipped. She closed her eyes. She sipped again. Then she lay back down. She said, "You want a thought to start the day with? At work, I told this to a friend of mine, she was bitching about her husband—" She cleared her throat, leaned again for a sip of coffee. "I said, 'I could be screwing some man at high noon on the village green and Jack would come over and be about to kill him, but he wouldn't, not right that minute. Because first he would wrap me in a blanket and carry me home.'" She drank a little more coffee. "I believe that, Jack. I know it."

I couldn't think of anything to say. The dog slapped his tail against the floor. No. I could think of plenty to say. It was that I couldn't think of anything safe to tell her. So I ended up moving from the table to the sofa. Then I moved to sit on it near her feet. I reached under the blanket and held on to her ankle. Then I was lying on the blanket against her. I didn't know what to do or what to say. I was lucky because events took care of themselves after that. The blanket fell onto the table and it soaked up some of the coffee that spilled from one of the cups. You might say we were desperate. You might say we were holding on to each other to keep from flying away. I don't know. But it felt like that with the grip we had on each other. You could call it making love. Driving the truck north on 12 back toward Vienna to get through it and out to Elway's, I could feel her skin and taste her breath. It was the first time in years I was able to remember what she felt like.

"Well, get over it," I said, like there was someone on the passenger seat to hear me.

Elway was outside on his front porch and he looked wrong. Instead of turning his head, he turned his entire body when he began to look me over suspiciously. His face wasn't friendly or even familiar. All I could think of was Fanny and me when we hung on to each other in what felt like a shipwreck. We just hadn't stayed afloat long enough.

He turned away to walk into his house. He turned all of his torso and not just his head. I followed him into the kitchen and put the little carton of berries on the kitchen table. He was standing with his back to me. He said, "I suppose you want the information now."

"What'd you get?"

He turned toward me in that strange, stiff way. He looked at me with confusion and maybe with anger. I couldn't tell. It wasn't like being confronted by a man with a weapon. It was more like watching someone you thought you knew turn out to be someone else who just resembled him. Then he slowly unbuttoned his long-sleeved, pale blue shirt. He'd grown softer from his illness and probably just from age but he was still a strong man. I thought of the time I first saw my father naked. Elway stripped the shirt off without unbuttoning the cuffs. The sleeves were inside out when he turned from me and rolled the shirt into a cylinder. Then he opened the refrigerator and stuffed the shirt onto the top shelf.

"That do it?" he asked me.

"What's going on, El?"

He nodded. He put his hand to the back of his neck. "That doesn't feel good," he said.

I stuck my hand out and he took it. I said, "Could I feel your other hand?" It was also very hot. I said, "I need to touch your face a second." He closed his eyes. I felt his cheek and it was as hot as his hand. So was his forehead.

He said, "Sarah isn't here."

"She's at school, right?"

"Sarah's at school," he said. "Much too hot to be at school." He looked at me and smiled. "Jack," he said. Then he forgot who I was. He looked like he might snarl. He said, "You're a foul ball, buddy."

I took his shirt from the refrigerator and pulled the sleeves back out. I asked him, "When did it start to feel so bad, Elway?"

He said in a kind of monotone, "Who's in charge of this?"

I said, "Can you put the shirt on, El?" He held still like a six-foot-tall little boy while I moved his arms into the sleeves and stood in front of him to do up the front buttons.

"Neck," he said.

I said, "I know. We need to take a ride," I said. "Got your wallet?"

He touched his pocket and said, "Wallet."

"Here we go, El."

I took him by the upper arm and walked him through the house to the front door. I wished for the first time in a long time that I was in a patrol car with a radio. I could use someone to clear the roads ahead of me. I belted him in and he sat and looked ahead. I made sure his door was locked. Then I belted myself in and rolled us backward down his driveway. I straightened us and went full bore.

I figured we were fifteen to twenty miles from Vienna. There was a large hospital in the center of it. I didn't know whether he'd been treated there for his leukemia. What mattered was that a doctor could get things started if Elway was suffering from the disease or from something new that was part of it. They could transport him if they had to. The problem would be the small roads. We were on one lane of blacktop. It was crumbling and pitted and potholed from several winters' expansion and contraction. The townships repaired these roads by dumping lukewarm macadam into the holes and backing the town snowplow back and forth over the mess. I tried to avoid the holes, but we were going very quickly now. The truck slammed sideways after a hole I never saw.

"Hang on, El."

"We're in pursuit?"

"Just like it," I said.

I had my headlights on and my emergency flashers. When I took a right toward the two-lane county road the rear end swung out on me.

"I'm out of practice," I told Elway.

"Clumsy son of a bitch," he said in a low, dull voice.

I didn't answer. I wished again that I had a radio. I was in need of help. Rain had cleaned a lot of dust from the road but I could still see rock particles and pieces of twig and cigarette butts and beer cans flying behind us. You'd know from the lights and the tire noise that we were coming. You'd see from the junk descending after us that we had been there. Sometimes Elway panted. He sat with his neck and head pressed back against the seat and his eyes were closed. He seemed to be asleep. I could smell that he'd wet his trousers and I hoped he didn't find out. Driving too far to the right before a left-hand turn, I banged the truck bed against a mailbox post and took it down. I thought how I had become a specialist in knowing what the people I cared about the most should never know.

After that turn I remembered the shortcut. It was a straight drop on an absolutely unpaved narrow road to the county road I needed. I was worried about children in the road and dogs and cats. We hadn't seen any yet. But after a few hundred yards on the unpaved road I came to a farm with the house on the flat to my right and its listing barn on the left. I had to stand on the brake and drop into second to stop in time. Crossing in front of us were eleven white and brown geese marching almost in step. They didn't look at us. I jumped on the accelerator and geared up fast when they weren't quite past my left front tire. I wanted to be that dignified when my fate consisting of six cylinders directed by a large, wild-eyed man came roaring down at me.

"You drive like shit," Elway said, "and I'm sick of it. And keep your fingers off of my *head*." He drooped in the safety belt. He leaned forward against it like he was trying to study his ankles.

"You're doing swell, Elway," I sang to him. "Doing a great job, Elway."

I went through the STOP sign at the intersection of our road and the two-lane where we turned right past an abandoned farmhouse held up mostly by yellow asbestos shingles. Then I made some time. About half a mile ahead of us, I saw a small maroon sedan and started blinking my lights, from full to low, full to low. I leaned on the horn. They didn't budge when I came up. Then they slowed down to punish me for being pushy. I went around them on a curve where it was about as unsafe to pass as it could be. No one killed us in a collision and I had us up to State Route 80. The truck wobbled but not too badly and Elway hung forward in his belt like a man who had fallen asleep or died.

"Nobody dies on *me*, Elway," I lied.

The road curved to the right. Then it suddenly dropped left very steeply. I had to brake when we entered the curve or I'd have lost it. As it was I threw up gravel from the right-hand shoulder. Two cars coming the opposite way pulled over because I came out of that curve in their lane and it took me a while to get back where I should be. I thanked them with a neighborly tap on the horn but I didn't look to see if they were charmed by my manners. Elway smelled bad and looked bad and I was frightened of losing anyone else. I was grateful for the long, straight run into Vienna that intersected with Route 12 from our western approach in the lighted-up truck.

I went through the full-stop four-corners outside of the city without stopping and without slowing. I leaned on the horn and floored it past the waiting cars and one auto tool delivery truck. I saw people watching us go from the feed store on the corner to the right. We went past some houses and one of the banks and then a half-dead strip mall. We shrieked into a left turn through a red light with me pounding on the horn. A kid in a restored orange Chevelle convertible hoisted the extended third finger of each hand. After that it was a few blocks down Route 12 just where it became Main Street and I drove us into the hospital lot.

I turned the lights off and shut off the hot motor. I helped Elway to climb down out of his seat. He said, "This vehicle smells disgusting."

"Sorry, Elway," I said. "I'll get it cleaned up. We need to go inside."

I'd been followed by a municipal police car driven by quite possibly the shortest cop ever hired by any law enforcement agency in the state. I felt sad for him and sorry for whoever he rousted who was tall. The waiting room was populated and probably hostile to anyone else who came in because that threatened to dilute the attention they were barely receiving. I saw two pregnant young girls accompanied by very fat older women. I saw a tall, heavy man with a gray ponytail and an almost gray complexion who looked like a textbook heart attack. Two seats away, an older man in green rubber boots who smelled of the farm sat curled over his lap in bad pain. Two men on gurneys were against a wall of the waiting room. One of them was propped on an elbow joking with an orderly. The other one lay on his back. I figured they were from a car wreck.

I told the triage nurse, "I don't know what's wrong with him. He's got leukemia. He doesn't always make sense when he talks. And his head hurts very badly."

"Neck, you fool," Elway said. He sounded like a very displeased Sergeant Bird.

She said, "Neck?" She had big shoulders and a sweet, tired, intelligent pale face. Her dark hair was pulled tight and gathered in an old-fashioned bun. She reached toward his forehead with the back of her hand and he flinched but then let her touch him. "Ouch," she said. "I need to take your temperature, sir. All right?"

I said, "Would you let me have your wallet, Elway? For the, you know—they need to see your card."

"He has insurance?" she asked.

"Elway has everything," I said.

He looked past her and not at me and not so far as I could see at anything else. He was asleep with his eyes open. His head kept dropping toward his chest and the nurse began to work quickly. I had to leave him to give his information to a secretary around the corner from triage and I was done by the time they were rolling him on a gurney. The little cop and I exchanged a few words and he shook my hand and left.

"How come that black man's so special?" one of the pregnant girls' escorts said.

"State cop," I told her. "Line of duty."

Oh," she said. She asked, "Who shot him?"

I was working on the phone with my credit card getting information and then calling for Sarah. It took five calls before I got a message to her and it took almost forty minutes for her to call back so I could tell her what I knew.

She said he'd never complained about his neck before. "But the fever, good Lord, it's what he had when he came *down* with it. Oh, Jack. It might be starting again."

I didn't know it ever stopped. I said, "Drive very carefully, now, Sarah, all right? I'll be here with him, and you need to be safe."

"How slowly did *you* drive?" she asked.

"And I'll see you here," I said.

It was almost ninety minutes later, but she got there from school and she was pretty composed. She wore a dark brown summer suit that was floppy in what I figured was a stylish way. She had listened to concerts and given them in more cities than I'd heard about. She knew about style. Her large brown eyes seemed not to blink. They just studied my mouth while I told her what I knew. She held on to my hands while I talked. Her hands stayed cold. I couldn't warm them. Half an hour later she was called to talk to a doctor and then she had a few minutes with Elway. Now we were in a dim lobby that was mostly empty space with one hard bench against a wall facing a bank of elevators. It was the kind of room you see in nightmares when you dream that you're lost. The carpeting reminded me of my efficiency floor down South. Sarah's brow was furrowed and her eyes were red. She rubbed her throat. She moved her broad, brown hand slowly up and down.

"He's a little crazy," she whispered. There was no one to hear us except a woman at the information desk. Once every few minutes someone entered or left one of the elevators. "He's very, very *angry*," she said. Her eyes filled.

"He doesn't intend to be mean to you," I said.

She patted my leg. "I know."

"But he's somebody else, isn't he?"

She said, "To you too?"

"Like he never knew me."

She nodded. "That's as bad as anything," she said. "Because he knows you, Jack. The way he knows me."

"It's the fever, they said. But it was like he *didn't* know me. Same way with you?"

"Yes," she said, "but we have to think it's the fever. Terribly high. The way it was when he first came in for it, seven, nearly eight months ago. Closer to eight. One hundred and five, Jack. *Five*. What they think it might be, this young doctor says, is meningitis."

I shook my head. "How do you get it?"

"His kind of leukemia is called acute mylo-something-or-other leukemia. Things like this, meningitis, that's what can happen. According to this doctor who isn't too much older than our son. Oh, he's really sick. He was supposed to do the chemo all over again, right away after he finished it the first time, and he wouldn't. And he needed to, they said! But it was taking me so long to nag him, convince him, to come back into the hospital. We were at it every day. I would have asked you, pretty soon, to talk to him about it. You know Elway. He *cannot* listen. He wouldn't listen to me, he wouldn't listen to Michael. They should do the chemo right now. But now, first, they have to treat his meningitis. They need to pump him full of the right kind of antibiotic. If the meningitis doesn't get him, and they pull him through it, he has to do the chemotherapy all over. Then maybe *again*. It's awful for him. It's bad. It's looking bad, Jack."

I rubbed my hand over her forearm. I stroked it back and forth. "Sarah," I said.

She patted my hand with the hand that was free and we ended up holding on to each other like that. We just sat side by side on the hard bench. We were waiting for nothing. I think we were expecting nothing. We were sitting because we were tired and we had run out of anything else to clutch.

After a while, she said, "This must remind you of the other time."

I said, "With you?"

She shook her head slowly and looked down.

Then I understood what she'd meant. I felt stupid. "Oh," I said. I didn't know what else to say.

"I'm so sorry about them," she said.

"That was years ago."

"I see. And that makes it easier for you?"

"I think people think it's supposed to."

I WENT OUT to the pond in my mucky sneakers and I walked in. I broke the surface that the sunset was turning to a shining red skin.

I thought of myself as a slow but dangerous object when the red shattered. Dragonflies skimmed and hovered and tiny insects jumped along the top. At the far side a bass broke the water chasing a bug. There were no engines on the road to hear, and nothing was in the sky that moment except blackbirds fleeing and then returning to call. Then there was a swift or martin fluttering overhead to dive tightly away. Then it was gone. I lay back floating and looked at the pink sky and thought uselessly about Elway and Sarah and about their grandchild named after a famous Russian. There were plenty of kids to worry about, I thought. Some of them were dead and some of them were alive. One of them was Merle's nephew. He should have been able to take care of himself. I thought he might not have taken good enough care. There were always some to worry about.

I turned over and frog-kicked down. I held near the bottom. I pushed just enough water with my cupped hands to keep myself in place. I opened my eyes and saw some careful small bass at the base of the reeds. In the dyed light of the water at sunset they looked electric blue. I shut my eyes and headed up and climbed out. The temperature had gone down and it was supposed to drop into the sixties that night. When I walked back to the house with my towel around me the weather reminded me for just a second of the coolness and then cold of autumn in upstate New York. Then I thought of the winter. I would be gone before it got chilly, I thought. I would be gone when the snow flew.

I made a pot of coffee and drank a cup after I dressed. I turned on the radio and spread mustard on a boneless pork chop and broiled it in the oven. Bromell's station gave us a solid two and a half minutes of news that was read by the music jockey. His voice was baritone and it was flattened by the upstate accent I remembered—heavy on the squashed *a* sounds so that "cash" came out like "key-ash" said in a hurry. You could hear an accent a little like it in Cleveland or Chicago. But this announcer's sly phoniness seemed all his own. You wouldn't trust the son of a bitch to give you the right change at a toll booth. He ended his report with what I guess you could call a note of humor. He said something about a woman in Decatur, Georgia, whose pet hog ran away and invaded a pet store. He chuckled like the man who repossessed your car. He told us it would be a fair, comfortable night, and then he led us into a medley by Tom Petty. I turned to the FM band and I heard a National Public Radio report on an amputee who was walking from Aberdeen, Scotland, to Liverpool, England, on artificial legs in protest against the decline of the once-reliable British railway system. Someone seemed to be holding the microphone near the hiker's manufactured knee because there was a squeaking above the traffic noises that the reporter told us in whispers came from a plastic joint that would soon require replacement. I went back to the AM frequency as I sat down to my supper. I heard a cluster of commercials read with phony enthusiasm by the program host. I learned about a Nissan dealership that didn't just sell you a car, and a bar that was proud to specialize in serving New York chili dogs along with beer fresh from the tap.

I drank more coffee and looked at Merle Davidoff's notes and my own few notebook scribbles. I wondered why I'd come back. I might have found a way to see Elway and Sarah sometime. They weren't the reason. Maybe they should have been. And whatever I liked about Merle, her Tyler Pearl was no one to me. I could have looked her up in New York City without searching him out two hundred miles north. Maybe I came back to see if I could. Maybe I came back because Fanny and I and our baby were ghosts here.

Janice Tanner was a ghost here. You have to turn and look at the ghosts sometime.

Maybe I would get myself a little television set, I thought. I had a hard time watching it because I hated the laughter on comedy shows. It always sounded like a room filled with drunks. You were never sure if they were laughing at the actors or each other. And the shows about people who volunteered to be frightened or humiliated by groups of other pretty or handsome volunteers were unbearable. When I looked at one I kept thinking that I'd flown to another planet. It was a lot like Earth except everyone here was stupider. But you could see the news on television and maybe it would be useful to know. Of course there were daily papers to be purchased in Vienna. One came from Syracuse and one from Binghamton. One came from Utica and of course Bromell's was published in and for and about Vienna. The headlines seemed to focus on disasters and the decisions of a council concerned with zoning variances. And the board of education was concerned about obscenity in the high school literary magazine. All things considered, I thought, I would listen to the water boil for coffee and guess about the weather and hope that someone in charge would figure out a way of not conducting a war for any longer than it took to get them reelected.

I woke up in my seat at the table. My chest was hammering and you'd have said that I was frightened. But there was nothing new. The coffee had grown cold and I could hear the insects humming. Behind them there was the hoarse, repeated sneezing sound of a deer. I didn't hear any coyotes just then but I thought I soon would. A day of doing nothing can make you very tired. I washed my dinner dishes, rinsed out the coffeepot, and then I carried the cup to the end of the counter. I let some sour mash drip down into it. I went outside and sat on the steps of the small, open front porch. It wasn't much more than a threshold but I could prop my feet and lean my back against the front door and look at the empty road. Bats were silhouetted against the nearby trees as they rolled around and fluttered out of the darker high sky.

I heard an engine coming from the east. It was the direction you would head in if you wanted to make your way to Vienna. Smith had come from the same direction to scare me to death with a truck horn. I thought I should stand and take down the carbine that hung above the other side of the front door. I was going to stand but I was still enjoying the taste of my drink.

"The worst they can do is kill me," I'd have said to the dog.

I was still on my ass when the car slowed and turned in to my place. It lit me up with its country beams. The driver was courteous and dropped to the low beams and then shut down. You might want to stand up now, I thought. But I wanted one more sip. I stayed where I was.

The driver's door opened and closed. She said, "Do you mind that I came out?"

It was a voice I didn't recognize. It was deep and educated. It sounded full of assumptions. Maybe she wasn't entirely sure of herself but she was surer than many others might be. When she came around the front of what looked like a black Mustang GT, I saw Georgia Bromell. She was in her sunglasses and she was wearing a dark leather jacket and a short, flared skirt that was also dark. She walked on high heels like a special kind of athlete. Her back was straight and her legs pushed powerfully. Her neck was a little stiff but not the way Elway's had been. This one was about health. I remembered some of the college students I'd known. I finally recognized from the way her head was balanced that she was trained as a dancer. I used to think these rich kids in colleges were given a lot of lives. I thought it again.

"No," I said, "I guess I don't mind."

"I'd have telephoned and asked, but I couldn't find a listing for you."

"I don't have one."

"I thought Jerry said you were getting a phone. So I tried to call. This is embarrassing. I have no idea why I came out here." She sounded like maybe somebody also trained her for stage acting or movies. I couldn't quite figure out who she thought she was talking to.

I was standing by then. I watched her use her right hand to strike a short wooden match against a box to light a cigarette while she held a file folder clamped to her side with her left arm. I pointed. "It looks to me like you've got an idea," I said.

"It's okay if I smoke," she said rather than asked.

I sat back down and was about to sip. Then I held the cup away. I thought she might want some in a glass. Maybe it looked like I was offering my cup when I said, "Would you like some?"

She stepped in closer and reached up for the cup. I let her. She sipped, made a face, sipped a little more, handed it back. She reversed her cigarette and offered it to me. I shook my head and sipped at the whiskey. I could smell smoke in the cup when I drank and I thought I could taste it a little. Her car had stilled the insects but now their humming rolled back in. I watched her smoke.

Then I heard the coyotes again and so did she. "They're coming back all over the Northeast," she said. "All of us are coming back." She seemed to enjoy the taste of her cigarette. She seemed to like to let the smoke out of her nostrils while she blew it tightly off the bottom of her upper lip. She said, "You think I'm some rich man's dilettante daughter." Then she said, "Do you think I could have a little more of that?"

I opened the door and held it for her. I decided not to watch her look around what was finally a somewhat neatened rural slum. I found her a heavy, squat tumbler and I poured some sour mash into it and then into my cup. "I don't have ice," I said.

"You should," she said, walking back in from what was once the living room. "In case you get a bruise or a burn. You know, for first aid."

"You're right."

"I've lived alone in all kinds of places," she said. "Including sleeping-bag-on-mattress places. But in cities, not the country. You seem to do it efficiently."

I nodded as I handed her the glass. "But you can drink it without the ice?"

"I can drink it without the glass," she said. She sat at the table opposite what was clearly my place because it was marked by the Friend in Pennsylvania notebook and the pencil and Merle Davidoff's oversized brown manila legal envelope. Her very short gray and black hair looked wiry. You could want to run your hand through it the way you roughed a kid's crew cut. She leaned forward with her elbows on the table and she held her juice glass in front of her and swirled the dark amber mash.

"Do you need the sunglasses because of an eye condition?"

She smiled and shook her head. Then she lost the smile. But she kept them on. She said, "You think they're an affectation?"

"It's not too terribly sunny in here."

"I have very weak eyes."

"No sale," I said. I reached across the table and touched them. She held her head in place and let me. I slid them forward and off.

She blinked her eyes. They were very large and light brown. She looked at me. I dropped my glance.

"That's cute," she said.

I looked up and raised my eyebrows.

"The way you looked away," she said.

"I thought I was maybe being forward."

"'Forward,'" she said. "That's cute too."

I sipped. I remembered the smell of her breath in the cup.

"Jack," she said, "Jerry told you I was a writer and you sneered."

"I didn't mean to sneer," I said. "I apologize."

"Everybody's a writer once in their career if they go to college," she said, "and most of them could use getting a couple of sneers a day. That's fine with me. I would like you to let me show you I'm a professional, and I know what I'm doing, and maybe I'm even pretty good. Then you can apologize if you want to. But I'm not after that. I need to write this story," she said. "I need you to help me a little."

"There isn't a story," I said. "I guess what I really would like is for no one to write a word about any of this."

"What's the 'this'?"

I shook my head. She stood. She unzipped the thin black leather jacket. She shrugged it down her arms. She was wearing a black sleeveless sweater with some kind of very delicate gray fabric sewed along the square hem of the neck. Her arms were strong-looking and her figure was athletic and good to observe. She watched me observe it. She looked at me for a couple of seconds and then she picked up the jacket and put it back on. She didn't zip it but she shook her head and sat. "I'm sorry," she said. "It was a little bit slutty, wasn't it? I apologize. I'm not good at that, believe it or not."

"Apologizing," I suggested.

She smiled. It ought to have struck me as an honest smile. It should have seemed as pleasant to see as the rest had been. "Stripping for the crowd."

"It wasn't really a strip," I said. "I'm not a crowd." I also wasn't one of those almost-fifty-year-old men who believed that a good-looking woman in her thirties drove her Mustang GT out on a country road using all eight cylinders to sex up somebody who did everything but laugh at her chosen work. And I wasn't sure that what she said about writing was any truer than the little job she'd done with her jacket. I said, "You were saying you really need to write something. This story. Except it isn't a story."

"What would it be called, then?"

"Would you publish it in your father's paper?"

She dipped her head toward the tumbler she raised. She was hiding. The smell that started to rise when she took off and put on her jacket was stronger now. It was marijuana.

"No," she said. "This isn't about me and my provincial communications mogul father."

"I had the feeling that this place—you know, Vienna, Hamilton County in general—I had the feeling you were down to the last place you could come to. There was this last-stand feeling about you when you came out here with Jerry Gentry. Who did you a favor because the sheriff did your father a favor. Maybe your father doesn't know he isn't your favorite older man."

She said, "He knows. He knows. I rave and squall and tell him every chance I get. I'm a spoiled bitch rich man's daughter. Surprise!" She opened the hard pack of cigarettes. I saw six or seven very neatly rolled joints. "Do you want one?"

I said, "No, thank you."

"Would you mind if I . . . ?"

I shook my head.

They seemed pretty tight little items to begin with but she took one out and licked it all over. She scraped a match and lit the joint and took the smoke in and held it. Then she let it stutter out a little at a time with her words. "I messed things up a couple of times. I don't know if I'm out of chances. I don't know that I had such wonderful chances and messed them up. But you could say I did. Let's say I did. Have you ever read *Boston*, the magazine? No. Why would you? It's very big in, well, Boston," she said, laughing a little. She showed her teeth and her jaw lifted. You could see what she had looked like when she was a kid before she went for the dark glasses and the slinky black clothes. "Or *Preservation*? I wasn't on staff but I wrote two pieces for them. I lived some other places besides Boston. But I was there when I heard about you from the missing-girls story. They covered it here, of course. My parents gave me a subscription to my father's paper for my birthday that year. Like sending you the handcuffs for a present when you're out on parole. You were a bona fide hero, Jack. I don't remember it all, I hope you'll forgive me, but I do remember you got hurt by someone. And that poor child, of course. That was so horrible. And they never found her. You kept trying, though. I remember that. You didn't give up. You don't, do you? So when I heard from Jerry that you were here . . ."

"You've got him thinking with his glands."

She took in more smoke. I went for a saucer she could use as an ashtray. "That was all he ever did in high school too," she said. "He was a nice boy, though. I even liked his girlfriend, his wife now, Nina. She completely hates me, according to Jerry."

"She thinks you're after him."

"I'm not," she said. I liked it that she didn't ridicule the likelihood of her coming down a flight of social steps to chase Jerry Gentry. "I'm after this story. I need to write a good story that really matters."

"So you can get back where?"

She leaned forward and I could smell the tobacco and the whiskey and the marijuana. She said, "Anyplace in a city where they have an orchestra and a museum that shows more than farm appliances from the day before yesterday. And apartments that aren't over the local jeweler's downtown. And an airport you can use for flying nonstop to Europe. Why are you smiling?"

I shook my head.

"No," she said, "I wasn't trying to amuse you."

"Don't be angry," I said. "I was thinking of the job I once had around here. The campus security work and some of the kids I talked to. They were all so set up. They didn't have any idea. They took it for granted they would walk off the college campus and into the life you just now were talking about. They never imagined they wouldn't have it."

"Yeah," she said. She sipped from the tumbler. "Me neither. I might have a little more of this. Is that all right?" I poured about two fingers of whiskey for her. She drank off half.

"I don't like to work with anybody who isn't a professional," I said.

"Because it's dangerous?"

"No. Because I work with professionals. Period. And anyway there isn't a story."

"There isn't a story, you're saying, but you need professionals for it when you work on it in spite of its not existing. Yeah. But listen. I *was* a pro. I wrote words and they gave me a check in return. I just told you that."

I stood.

"You're dismissing me?"

I took a sip of mash. She breathed out more smoke and then it was quiet unless you were listening for the animals at the pond or the coyotes farther out.

"Why do you need the story so much, Georgia?"

She looked up and she seemed to be studying me. I didn't think there was a great deal for her to concentrate on. What she looked at had been sliced, bruised, and broken too many times to be pretty. It hadn't been pretty to begin with.

"Why are you asking me?"

I shook my head. I shrugged.

"Maybe I'll tell you sometime," she said.

"All right."

"Maybe I'll drive back out here sometime."

I didn't answer.

"Maybe you'd like me to." She put her dark glasses back on. "That's called investigatory zeal. You're not supposed to be embarrassed or afraid of asking about anything."

"Are you embarrassed? Or afraid?"

"Guess," she said.

She slid the sunglasses off and folded them. She blinked a little, then looked me in the eye.

She used two fingers to get the roach between her lips and she took in what she could. She held it. Then instead of extinguishing it carefully so she could use the leavings when she rolled more joints she crushed it in the dish I'd set out for her. She let the smoke trickle out. She must have had a very excellent source for it. She might have problems with her father but she had plenty of dope.

She drank off her sour mash and stood up. She extended the

folder she had brought in with her. "Would you look at this?"

I opened it.

"When I'm gone," she said.

But I had seen the first lines. *He is a large man, but light on his feet. You might think, watching him, that he has stepped out of some other, more primitive time. But he is very much a man of these bad times.* I said, "Who's this about, Georgia?"

"Come on, Jack."

"I would rather you didn't do this."

"You're big and tough," she said, "and you want to be in charge of everything. Men, women, and children. But you can't control what somebody writes about you. What I write about you."

"There isn't a story in me," I said. "Why don't you write something else?"

"You're what interests me. Period. Why don't you just wait and see what I do? All right? Wait and see?"

"Aren't you supposed to find out what's true? Don't you want to write that?"

"Oh, it's true," she said.

"It isn't made up?"

"It *can* be made up, some of it. But it's very true."

"So then what does lying mean?" I asked her. The conversation was getting me cranky. I wanted to sit down with my coffee by myself and not have to be her audience.

She smiled the smile you give the mechanic who does a fast job of changing your oil and oil filter. She said, "To be continued. At a mellower time."

I wanted to ask if we really had to. But I also didn't entirely mind the idea.

She stuck her hand out for me to shake.

I said, "I'm not agreeing to anything. And I don't want to read that."

"I'll leave it here. Do what you want. And if you don't want to shake hands goodbye, then you can kiss me goodnight." She took a step closer and took hold of my shirt collar and pulled me toward her. She kissed me once on the corner of my mouth, staying with the kiss long enough to make sure I'd remember it. "Goodnight anyway," she said, and she turned fast to leave.

She walked out and I went back around to sit at the table and smell her smoke and perfume. I did not open the folder she'd left. I went back over the little business she had tried to do on me.

Then I emptied the saucer of its butts and ash. I washed her juice glass. I walked into the living room and looked at what she'd seen. There was the unswept floor with its fragments of leaf and grass and dried-up pond mud. There was the sleeping bag rolled up on the mattress. There was the gear I'd hung on the hook inside the open coat closet door. There were the duffel bags near the mattress and the damp socks and soiled clothes on the floor in the far corner. I sniffed to see if the room smelled of dirty underwear and a sweated-up man. I identified the mildew of the plaster walls and the slow rot in the cellar posts. Something that cut across it was probably a residue of me. I shook my head. What a woman trap I was.

I woke up before the darkness got grainy. It was before birdsong. The temperature was changing and the wet breezes had just begun. I turned onto my back and fell asleep and woke myself with my snoring. I rolled onto my belly and watched a tiny sliver of dark red-orange sunrise move up the wall. When I turned onto my back again, the bottom panes of the window opposite the mattress were flaring. How wise I'd been not to have a telephone. If I had one I would be standing in my underwear holding on to the receiver. I'd be listening to the phone ring in Merle Davidoff's place in Sniffen Court. I'd be trying to think of something to say worth her hearing.

What had got me up was Merle. I understood that later. I didn't think of it that way when I first woke. Looking into the darkness I had thought about how sorry it was to be entertaining long, stoned, dishonest young women. Then I'd thought about how I was spending Merle's money and about how long I had been hanging around this patch of upstate territory with nothing to show for the wait. Then I went on to contemplate what a pathetic operative or searcher or plain damned *friend* I was turning out to be.

Never mind the searcher part, I told myself. I doubled my pillow and leaned back to watch the sun flood up the rest of the window. Because I was done with that. I wasn't searching that way anymore again. I saw the rake handles and shovel hafts sink through the snow. Not that I'd betrayed her, I thought.

I was too good an interrogator to let that one pass. Betrayed who? Which her did you have in mind?

That was a question I was going to skip.

But that's the one you need to answer.

Well, that's the one I won't.

I did think of the shape of Georgia Bromell's muscled arms. I thought of her lips and tongue as she worked the joint. I thought of Merle Davidoff sitting with her hand on the dog. The way I remembered it, the two of them were watching me from the floor. They were waiting to see what I'd suggest. This morning I suggested breakfast and reconnaissance. I was out in forty minutes. I carried some basic gear but no firearms. I was still troubled by the shooting I'd done when the people with the truck had come around. I'd get eight to fourteen years for manslaughter if I shot someone dead. I'd do assault first-class at three to nine if I simply

wounded them. Even up here where firearms were plenty honored
a district attorney wouldn't mind putting away some former cop
gone wrong. And I'd be wrong any way you looked at it unless he
came howling around with a dozen armed bandits. That was
assuming I could hit anything while discharging my weapon.

And didn't that visit by Bromell's angry daughter suggest that
something was beginning to percolate? I thought I remembered
seeing her before. Maybe there were ends of rope that I could tug
on and follow. I ought to be looking for them. And maybe I'd
grabbed hold of something after all.

The morning started out clear but it was clouding by the time I
was at Kramers Barn Road. The skies were overcast when I started
to scuttle uphill. Everything was wet from late-night rains and the
humidity of the last few days. I had no appetite for crawling
through damp-weather fungus and mucky soil. But I did have to
proceed through clearings on my belly. I was swimming across the
terrain. I recalled how I had hung between the surface and the bottom of the pond the evening before and how long I might have
stayed there if I hadn't needed to breathe. I made it to the overlook
in good time. I was soaked and that was all right because the dis-
comfort made me edgy but not too angry to think. I was just on the
border of fighting mad because I still thought about my early
morning considerations and my solid sense of having failed any
number of people. That was useful for now. I felt mean enough to
be difficult if someone grappled with me.

I heard the morning emptiness of a radio program from the
house. It was the same baritone I'd listened to on Bromell's station.
Hanging on to the slimy hilltop I thought of Georgia wanting to fly
nonstop to a major European city from Vienna, New York. Two
ducks went over. They worked their wings hard. I thought it might

be close to migration time. A fat bee went from flower to flower among purple weeds near my head. There was no sound of livestock and none were in sight. It wasn't any kind of farm I'd ever seen.

"I knew you'd do this," I heard in Smith's boyish voice. "I can't read the Tarot, but I know the future from the past. You're all prone, man."

He was standing to my left. I could see half of him. From the waist down he was blocked off by the farthest grassy edge of the rise I was lying on. He held the curved end of an axe handle the way some long-distance slugger might carry a heavy bat to the plate. I sat and then leaned forward to get myself up before he reached me. Then I was standing. He stayed where he was.

"I was informed that even with astral projection and urgent personal whispering you wouldn't stay away," he said. "You just don't get it, man. I am a poor, pathetic fucken farmer. I don't do bad things. I run my farm. I smoke a little reefer. I support the National Rifle Association and the Nature Conservancy. I contribute to upholding the reproductive rights of women. I send a little bit to Accuracy in Media. NAACP. United Negro College Fund. Association of Chiefs of Police. I had my dog spayed. What do I have to do to get out from under you, man? Jack? Mr. Jack. Whoever. What?"

"What's the axe handle for?"

"Oh, that's nonviolent violence," he said. "These hills are full of crazies. You know the Department of Environmental Conservation puts nine-millimeter automatics in the hands of their jackbooted thugs in dark green uniforms? A man has to defend his holdings and himself."

His eyes were huge. He was like a Hallowe'en mask of innocence. I thought of Merle calling me a virgin. He leaned down so that his weight was on the axe handle. His posture made him look crippled. I knew he wasn't. He was full of muscle. He was most likely high on something strong. He was awfully worried about me. That was the good part. I was close to knowing something, I thought.

"I wonder if you would tell me about Tyler Pearl," I said. "His aunt is worried. I could carry word to her and that would maybe end it."

"End what?"

"I think I said end *it*. What I mean by *it* is making myself look silly like this and you feeling like you needed to seek me out and make me wet my pants with fear by blowing your truck horn and lighting up my front porch." I thought of Elway Bird in my truck and the spreading stain on his trousers.

Smith stood up straight. His legs were apart, and there was something in his posture that irritated me. I was angry with myself for being stalked while I was stalking but it wasn't that. He shifted his shoulders and settled his arms and then I understood what I saw. He was posing a little nervously. I thought maybe someone theatrical had coached him for an occasion like this. He looked like he was striking a stance in case a photographer needed to portray a man about to do battle. Weren't we a couple of prime fools, I thought.

"I don't know what you mean about the truck horn, man," he said. "But I think what we need is a conference. We need to meet with our minds. Conflict is resolvable. Is that the word?"

"I'm not the person to ask."

"Problems can be solved. Angers can be dispersed. Power resides in *avoiding* conflict. Do you agree?"

"I don't know what in hell you're talking about," I said. "You're standing there like an armed guard. You're flexing every god-damned muscle in your body at me."

"The mind's the great muscle," he said. "We need to resolve stress."

"Or you'll beat me to my knees with your axe handle?"

"No, man, I told you. The handle's the symptom of my fear. You don't have anything to worry about. Trespassing, no trespassing, haunting me like some mountain spook. Whatever it is, I'm open to a resolution. I promise. You could say I'm trying to get a handle on present events, you know?"

His face was eager. His voice was light. He smiled and smiled. He folded his arms so that the axe handle lay across his bicep and shoulder. He looked like a hunter propping a .308. He said, "You give off the vibes of a man who thinks he's smarter than the rest of us. That can make us edgy."

"Who's us?" I said. "Clarence, tell me who the us is."

"Several of my interior selves plus the usual version I'm presenting out here on the perimeter of circumstances." He set the axe handle down. "See? There's nothing for us to fear. There's nothing for anyone to *see*. Why crawl in all this mud and shit to spy on a farm? Jack, there's no payoff. It's meager business. It's a nonprofit attempt to control the uncontrollable phenomena of the cosmos. You might as well shriek execrations at the moon and expect her to flicker and go out. Are you with me?"

"Clarence," I said, "what have you been swallowing or shooting up?"

He shook his head again and again. He reminded me of a dog with irritated ears. He kept shaking his head. Then he reached for his axe handle. He took maybe two steps but the edge of the rise still blocked his legs from mid-calf down. He felt urged toward me but he wasn't sure he was coming. He said, "I think I could make a case to the state police or a peace justice, let's say. You're trespassing, man. You're harassing. You're probably breaking a half a dozen little laws. I really, really want to believe we can work this out in a timely, friendly, something-else-ly manner. Give me one more word with a -ly at the end, Jack. What's that, an adjective? A subjunctive?"

"I'm the wrong person to ask."

"You feel wrong to yourself, man. That's where this whole deal emanates out of. It's a trespassing self-hatred. You're trespassing, dig this, on yourself! Am I right?" He nodded his head a couple of times.

I held my hands out the way you do when you're inviting someone to back a truck up until you indicate it's far enough. Except I moved my fingers to bring him on. I didn't want any more of his words. I thought I would just fracture some of him and be done with it.

But then I turned my hands and held them up to stop him. "Let's not do this," I said.

"I'm getting through to you."

"I'm getting tired," I said.

"Me too. You know what I'd love? A sandwich made of scrambled eggs and sausages on white bread with ketchup. You want to come down to the house? We'd love to cook for you." He put his hand on his mouth and made a boy's face. His skin looked crimson. He stayed in that pose so I could understand he was in a dilemma. Then he took his hand away. He said, "I misspoke myself, Jack. Forgive me, man, but I need to wrap this up. I'm loquacious. I'm garrulous. I'm—give me one more predicate with a wet noise at the end." He dropped his head like he was studying his shoes.

"Who's the we who'd fry me all those sausages, Clarence? Let's have a conference."

"At another time and place of our choosing?"

"Sure," I said. "Okay."

"So we mediated out of the boxing match."

I said, "We weren't going to have a boxing match."

"How else, man?"

"You were going to flail away at me with the axe handle. I was going to hurt you very badly without one."

"Wow," he said. "We lucked out, then."

"Don't do that drug anymore, Clarence."

"Which one?"

"The one you just took."

"I'm crazy with love and altitude and alertness to the karmic," he said, smiling like a kid. "I come in peace. And several other verbs and antonyms."

"Try and remember this," I said. "I do not want to mess with whatever it is you do here. Or think you do. Or want to do. I'm not prowling for the law. I don't care about profit and loss. I am looking for a kid. That's all of it."

"Never saw a kid here named whatever it was."

"Tyler Pearl." I was going to remind him that Tyler Pearl signed the papers to buy his land. Smith was dirty. But he was worried about plenty more than me.

I turned and walked in long and clumsy paces down the hill and over the old, unused pastureland and under the canopy of evergreens to where I'd left the truck. I drove south on back roads and then on Route 12 to Greene. I wanted some New York City coffee. I didn't know how to begin to think of Clarence Smith and the axe handle he brought in peace or his instructions on how to act and all the parts of speech he slurped up like a child eating spaghetti. I'd been around plenty of drugged-up people. He was scared as much as he was flying.

Lily smiled and brought me coffee.

"What would you say is your business?" she asked me.

"I am a little bit involved in law enforcement and a little bit not."

She nodded as if I'd made sense. "So," she said. She adjusted her chef's hat and pulled at a floppy sleeve. "Which part would you say is the part that is not?"

"The part that drives to Greene and goes to a joint called EAT and drinks coffee."

"Good," she said. "All things considered, I would rather spend my nonprofit time with not law enforcement. I told you I was not local?"

"I guessed."

"Excellent. That would be the detective part of you."

"How else would anyone know?"

She had turned to work at something on the counter. "This is a cinnamon-raisin bread I baked this morning. I command you to eat a piece."

"I surrender," I said. The sweetness filled my head.

"You looked a little, just now, like someone surrendering."

"It tastes beautiful," I said.

Her pale, tired face got bright. "Very few people call a taste beautiful."

"That's what it is."

"Who do you live with—your name is Jack, I'm right?"

"Jack. With nobody."

"Jack with Nobody. Very well," she said. "I'm sorry for it, unless you prefer it. But that's who you are."

"That's who I am," I said.

"You'll eat another slice?"

"With more coffee, please. Will you have a cup?"

"You could be a lady-killer, Jack with Nobody. Did you ever try?"

"I think I never did try since I was a boy," I said.

She poured the coffee and cut my bread. Serving it, she said, "Don't let me make you miserable. My son says I have a gift. It's why he keeps me up here and lives down there. My husband denies this accusation. However, he doesn't have a choice. If I wouldn't live with him, nobody would. This is called family life."

Two men came in to order sandwiches. I drank my coffee and asked for two cups to go. I left money on the counter. Lily called, "Remember your friends."

Coming into the southern end of Vienna I passed a truck-rental outfit, a discount drugstore, and a series of fenced-in metal storage sheds with roll-up locking doors that looked like big garages. I thought I saw Georgia Bromell's muscle car at one of the rental compartments. A woman came out quickly and slid into the car. I closed my eyes and remembered looking down the hill without my binoculars at the door to Clarence Smith's farmhouse. By the time I'd raised the glasses to my eyes she was gone. But I thought she might have been Georgia. I had the same impression now. If it was possible I'd seen Georgia Bromell at his place then maybe the story she was after had to do with him. Think about it the other way, I told myself. If she was with Smith at his place then he was some of the story. I wondered if she would work with him in order to get it. She would work with anyone, I thought. The rental was called Vienna Self Storage. You locked away what you didn't have room for in your efficiency apartment or your rented room. They always were called so-and-so's self storage. I tried to say something smart to myself about paying to store your self. By the time I was parked at the hospital, I had settled on my not owning so much of a self that I had need of the extra space.

Elway was in intensive care, and Sarah looked like she had slept the night in the little dim room opposite the elevators on the third floor where the families of very sick people sat and were allowed into the ward one at a time to visit. We had both been a lot younger when we made our mistake together. It was dishonest, I told myself. But maybe it wasn't only a mistake. I remembered how wild we'd been in the car in the dark forest. But this was about Elway. This was his wife, I told myself. She sat in the far corner. She was hunched over. She was in plenty of pain. She was on a gray metal folding chair near a table crowded with plastic flowers and tattered magazines. I offered the coffee I had brought for her. She smiled real pleasure and took a drink. Her eyes stayed squinted with what hurt her.

"It tastes fresh," she said.

"Did they bring the fever down?"

"Yes, a little. They dipped the poor man in an *ice* bath. They got some antibiotic medicine into him, for the meningitis. He hasn't talked to me yet. I'll go back in soon. But this is wonderful," she said, drinking more coffee.

"And they didn't give him medicine for leukemia? Isn't that what they ought to do?"

"I don't know. I don't think so. I don't know if they think there's any point," she said, shaking her head. She tried to smile. Tears leaked down her cheeks. When she bent over the coffee I wanted to kiss the top of her head but I shoved my hands in my pockets and stood before her like a bodyguard. There wasn't anything in that room or the ward next door that I could guard against. It worked out that I leaned down and she raised up and we laid our cheeks side by side and held on to each other for a couple of seconds.

"Did you call Michael?"

She said, "He wanted to come right away, of course."

"Maybe he's right."

"Let the kids have their lives for a little while longer. Soon enough—"

"But he'll want to be here, I think."

"I know. I know. It's selfishness. I want Elway for *me*, what's left of us alone together in this, just for me. Just a little longer. Then everyone else can come in." She gestured with the hand that held the coffee and then seemed to notice that she held it. She looked at it and drank some. Then she said, "The last few months, I worried I was jinxing us—putting a bad-luck spell over everything. I would think, if we were sitting in a sunny room together, me torturing him by listening to music, or if he was watching his precious ball game and I was reading the newspaper, I would look up and see him just being content, and then I would feel content, and I'd be feeling the feelings I had, but I wouldn't be able to keep from thinking, Someday I will have to sit in this room alone and remember this. How can you survive having to do *that*? I would think. Someday, I will have to drive this drive alone, I would warn myself, and I'd feel hollowed-out."

I said, "Elway is tough, Sarah."

She was good enough not to tell me how useless that information was. She kissed me goodbye while she was forgetting that I was there.

In the elevator down and in the lobby and then in the parking lot out behind the hospital, I wondered the same thing over and over until I was sick of the thought. She had a rich father who owned a house that would be suitable to his success where she could store enough possessions for several lives. Why would Georgia Bromell need to rent a storage unit?

I thought I might drive into the self-storage place and ask some questions but I wasn't sure what to be looking for. It occurred to me to get myself back up to the farm. But what I did was drive home. That in itself worried me too. I didn't like to be thinking of the rented old house as home. I hadn't a home anymore and I needed to know that all the time. It was one of the premises I worked with. I had a truck with a radio that tuned in my engine and played a nasty, buzzing static more than the voices or music of any AM stations in the area. I had knees that answered to wet weather with an aching grind. I hadn't a dog. I had no wife or child. I hadn't a home. It was like the weather. It was like having a bad temper about bullies and a stupid weakness for women in one or another kind of trouble.

I went back to the rented house and I parked the truck in front and took a walk to the pond. The brush was drying out. The sky was clear. The sun was bright on the water and heavy on the back of my neck. Flies circled me. Bluebottles skimmed the surface of the pond. Blackbirds raised a protest. I wasn't there to look at them. I wasn't there to look off to the northwest and see a great blue heron on his slow-motion wings. But I didn't know why I was there. I walked very deliberately around the pond. After two revolutions, I still didn't know. And the feeling of fright just below my ribs and leaking down through the gut got worse. I took deep breaths like I needed the air. It would have been excellent to be able to talk to someone about how I wasn't thinking very well.

I walked to the house and I thought about sweeping up and doing some dishes and cleaning crumbs off the kitchen table. I thought about changing and washing the muddied clothes I wore. I must have looked like hell at the hospital, I thought. I stood there not moving but I was in a real panic. I knew enough to stay away from firearms and sour mash. I was usually good at obeying myself on those two rules. But I couldn't keep myself from ending up on the mattress with my filthy boots on the floor beside my head. I wrapped myself in the woolen blanket I'd rescued like it was very cold instead of eighty-something degrees on an August day. I remember thinking how if I wasn't careful I would find myself here upstate when it dropped to the fifties at night and then I would want a flannel shirt at ten in the morning and then I would worry about getting the furnace cleaned and fuel oil deliveries scheduled.

I slept very deep. I woke to use the john and drink some water from the tap and then I went back to sleep. I dreamed a lot but I couldn't remember the dreams. There was one, though. I did remember one. I don't know if you'd call it a dream. It was a voice and it was telling me what I didn't want to know. The voice was mine partway and it was also Elway's. In the dream or whatever you want to call it we were inside each other's voice. We had known each other a long time and we had worked together a little. I always thought we liked each other a lot. I always hoped that we did. He was one of the people I went to for help. He was the only one left now. So I was going to have to grow up before I grew old. I probably needed to hurry, I thought.

I couldn't describe the voice and I didn't really know it while I slept. I did understand that it was Elway and it was me and both at once.

Somebody stood in front of me who was as straight and taut as Elway had been when he was Sergeant Bird of the New York State Police working out of the barracks south of Vienna, New York. He was telling me the news and I kept interrupting. He wanted me to understand and I didn't want to hear. I kept asking him questions and I was nervous because I was afraid he'd figure out that they were part of the trick to keep him from telling me the news. Of course he did understand. He pointed a finger at me and I could see the finger but not his face. He said, "Eat your damned dinner!"

There wasn't a table or a plate because what I had to eat was information. I swallowed it. I was sick. I was on my knees in the dream and I looked like Sarah hunched over herself in the hospital. I woke up holding my hand against the area of my right kidney. My face was full into the pillow. I was rocking on my side with my hand against myself and my face damp from drooling or sweating or both. I opened my eyes and thought I was awake. But I saw Fanny. She was tall and a tiny bit chunky and as pretty as she was before it happened. Her full lips were turned down. She made a child's face and she held our daughter out to me. I woke up from the dream that I was waking from the dream.

But I still saw her. The dream had been mistaken. She hadn't held our daughter out to me. She had shaken her. Fanny had been crying out and shaking her and the baby's little head swung on her neck. The screaming seemed a kind of roaring to me. I seized them both at once. I had our girl and I had hold of Fanny. She never remembered what she did.

No. It was worse than that. It was that Fanny almost never did remember.

It was Bird's voice that told me to think of it. But of course Bird would know I always did. So maybe it was only my own voice. I was good about nicking myself up over what was obvious. It was ours, I suppose. It was Bird's and mine at once. It was a dream or it wasn't. It was inside his fever or mine. It was inside whatever it was that drove me down and onto the mattress and under the cover and into that sweaty, scared sleep.

Sometimes they miss it, what was now called shaken-child syndrome. I stayed on the mattress and I heard myself pant. I didn't know why but while I waited to fall asleep again or maybe while I slept I thought of Georgia Bromell's car. I might have seen it when I first drove into Vienna. I had made a reconnaissance of Route 12 from one end of town to the other. I'd been looking for a diner and I hadn't found one. I saw a men's tailor, two jewelry stores, a pizza parlor, a movie house, the Salvation Army, a travel agency, some lawyers' offices, the strip mall and the realtor where Ms. Penny Putney worked, lots of places for the sale and repair of various kinds of engines, and then at the far northern end I had spotted and dismissed the self-storage units behind their tall mesh fencing. Maybe in a kind of dream I saw the big, shiny V-8 Ford Mustang with the nearly five-liter engine. Sometimes you miss knowing what you saw. Sometimes you remember. Sometimes they miss shaken-child syndrome. You always remember it. You think of the angle the head lies on the neck.

Then I remembered that Fanny was wearing a soft old tan canvas shirt out over her jeans. She'd rolled the sleeves up. I had seen the muscles of her forearms roll when she swung our daughter and begged her to not cry anymore. For Christ's sake, *please*.

Crib death happens a lot, Bird said to me. I had forgotten his saying that.

And I remembered my answer. But it can't happen.

Or maybe that was part of the dream. When I woke and finally understood that I was awake I walked into the bathroom to fill the basin and plunge my face in. I still heard those voices. They were his in mine or his and mine. I listened to the sink gurgle and I ran the hot water and shaved. I was disturbed by the eyes I saw. They stared at me suspiciously. This guy wasn't going to let me put anything over on him, I thought.

I scrambled half a dozen eggs and ate a lot of buttered toast and drank all of a pot of coffee. I didn't taste the food but I wanted fuel. I put on my clean jeans and a soft old chambray shirt I was never able to convince myself I had worn out. I worked at the mud I'd collected on my boots and I stuck my Friend in Pennsylvania notebook and a ballpoint pen into my breast pocket. When I walked outside I was stopped on the steps by the darkness. I was beginning to understand how much time I had lost. I took a breath and I looked around and I went back in and found my watch and wore it when I went to the truck.

I drove to the hospital. In the lot were some old cars that probably belonged to staff. There weren't any of the excellent cars the doctors drove. It could have been the parking lot of a small school or an insurance company. There were more lights on than at a corporate building. Of course, I thought. They need them for the people who are dying. They don't take the night off and sleep if they're dying. Neither do the nurses or the people with the mops. The nightmare lobby was empty when I walked into the elevator. Sarah wasn't in the waiting room. No one was. I pushed at one of the doors and it gave. When I looked in I saw the duty nurse sitting at her station and writing in a chart. I tapped on the door with a fingernail, then rapped with my knuckles and waved when she looked up.

She came over slowly, pushing her pregnancy in front of her. She was pale and tired and frowning because I had already walked a few feet into the ward to meet her. She held her hands up in front of her and I backed up. She kept moving. She wouldn't talk until I was outside the door near the entrance to the waiting room.

"Intensive Care is open after noon, sir, and only to family."

"I'm Elway Bird's family," I said.

She looked at me. She might have been working it out about

skin color. She shook her head. She stood at the partly opened ward door and she said, "Friends are fine too, but not now. Tomorrow is when you can come. After noon. Mrs. Bird will be here then, and you can talk to her."

"Could you tell me how he is?"

"You'd have to ask a doctor, sir. All I can tell you is he's sleeping."

"Really asleep? Or—could you check? In case he's awake? He'd want to see me," I said.

"Of course you're worried about Elway. I'm worried too. We're all worried. But he is medicated, he is under observation—and I need to get back in there and observe." She smiled a tired, reassuring smile, the kind that mothers learn. "And you'd be disturbing every patient on the ward."

"He's a really old friend," I said.

"Good," she said. "Everybody deserves to have them. Elway's lucky about you. But you'll have to come back tomorrow after twelve o'clock noon."

"How do *you* think he's doing?" I had to ask her.

"Well, you know what he's got. Given that, he's doing all right."

"Given that," I said.

She smiled and I understood finally why I was giving her this much trouble. Who ought to know more about hospital rules than I did? I had heard so often from Fanny when she came off shift about clowns like me who wanted to change the rules to suit their laziness or their sudden jolt of fear. It wasn't because she looked like Fanny. She didn't. But it was that tired patience I remembered. Fanny had a temper and there were times when all of a sudden I didn't know who she was. But often enough she had been able to make me feel like a kid. Nurses see so much and you're always grateful for the good ones. It usually isn't the doctors in those places. It's the nurses who bring you close to crying. It's their patience. No. It's what makes them patient. It's that they know who you are.

"Please," I said, "forgive me. Please."

I sat in the car awhile. I said it again about forgiving because I was deciding to drive back to the house for the pistol before I went up to Smith's farm. I would have to kill the dog, I thought. I couldn't do that again.

I drove slowly because I was very tired. I thought I might fall asleep on the main street and never make it out of town. Vienna was lighted at night from aluminum stanchions with curved arms that hung out over the road and glared a kind of tangerine color. The sidewalks and storefronts and parked cars and even the yellow and white stripes painted in the road for parking and for turns looked wrong. It was a color you simply don't see on the earth in daylight. It made me think of science fiction movies and traveling on the surface of another planet or the moon.

I squinted against the light and heard the voice out of that dream. You were crying, it said. Remember? You crowded into her so the child would be cushioned against your belly and chest as she shook her. You put your arms around Fanny and your daughter and you seized them. You were dripping from the bloody nose she'd given you downstairs in the kitchen when she was so angry about the baby upstairs who cried and cried and never let anyone sleep.

You'd told her what you could. You're a nurse! You know what it's like with babies.

She smacked you hard. She shocked herself. Her mouth was open. O, it said O in her surprise.

You turned to find a dish towel for the blood from your nose and she was gone when you looked back. You followed her upstairs because of the screaming. It was Fanny. It was the child. It was the two voices with one in the other.

Like now, I said to myself in the truck on the nighttime streets in Vienna.

And upstairs you held them. Everyone was shrieking and you held them inside of the noise. It was like a wind and you were holding everyone down so none of you would blow away in it. But you didn't do anyone any good at all.

I sat at the light that had changed. The truck was idling. The green of the traffic signal washed down the windshield in that Martian light. It changed to yellow and then to red. I wondered if the car behind me had honked. When it turned green again I shifted into first and drove on. I would go home, I thought. I curled my lip at calling it home. It worried me how much I needed that. I would go there and I would clean and arm the pistol.

I waited to hear the voice or voices comment on my use of the gun. I heard nothing. I heard the concussion of cooling air at my open window. I heard the weight of the wheels on gravel and dirt as I rolled the country road. I thought of the nurse on Intensive Care and I thought of Fanny. Fanny had been taller than Elway's nurse and she'd been more solidly built. I hoped the nurse was welcoming her baby. I knew how much Fanny had wanted ours. We'd waited a long time to have enough luck in the carrying to term. I had hoped she would leave her work awhile and stay with the baby but she needed to go back. Before she did we took the two A.M. feedings together in the little room I'd Sheetrocked. It was papered by Fanny with sappy big-eyed Bambi repeated every ten or twelve inches. There was a rocker in there and Fanny sat in it with her pajama top open a few buttons. Once her shirt was opened all the way to leave her almost naked to the waist. She fed her while I sat on an old office stool I'd stripped and refinished to watch her chest as much as I watched the child. I had to admit I thought about moving up to her and suckling at the other breast with its blue vein and its long, dark nipple. Fanny was watching me. She knew what I thought. She smiled a tired, wicked smile.

Though now of course I wondered if she was tempting me for sport or out of anger or some kind of punishment for us each. Maybe she didn't feel tempted. Maybe she only felt used and gnawed-at and tired of the baby and tired of me. I could sometimes wonder that.

It could happen to anyone, Bird said to me. It can happen anytime, you'd be surprised, he said on the night when it did. Then he said, Hell, why would you be surprised? You worked in the system long enough. Anyone does anything. End of story. Then he squeezed my shoulders. Of course, it's your anyone, he said. It's your story.

He had me sitting down in the back room at the house. I was at the window where Fanny and I used to watch the weather. He was bent in front of me. He was over me with his hands on my shoulders. He worked the muscles there over and over in a gentle rhythm. He kept looking into my eyes. I kept looking away. The dog was next to us. He watched. He was very anxious. I remember thinking that he counted on us. He was counting on our keeping the world familiar.

Back at the rented house now I stood in the kitchen and tried to remember what I was going to do. I knew it involved the .32 Taurus. I put water on and I washed up some dishes. I stayed away from the gun. I knew to do that. I made coffee and then I filled the sink with hot water and soap suds and threw my laundry in. I drank a cup of coffee while I read what Georgia left behind in the folder. I tried to

read it. It didn't feel right to be reading about myself in her language. *He is a large man* and all of that. I thought I was a man in a
couple of dozen pieces and not one was very large. Not one of
them was sound. I was at a line on the second typed page that said
I had *a kind of hesitancy before speaking, a self-imposed pause, as if
he were waiting to be rescued from speech* because, according to
Georgia, *he is built to act*. She wrote that it was *not because he fears
thought—he is the most contemplative of men, according to GET
STATEMENT/ATTRIBUTIONS FROM PEOPLE AT COL-
LEGE RE HIS LEADERSHIP DURING HUNT FOR GIRL*, it
said. *WHY DID HE <u>NEED</u> TO FIND THE TANNER CHILD?*

I didn't know why she wanted me to see this stuff. It wasn't me.
It was a me she was composing. I thought of the movie with the
creature made out of spare parts dug up from graves and brought to
life by lightning in the laboratory. I thought of the shot when the
bullet entered my dog. I thought of the St. Bernard at the farm and
I wondered if I could do that again to any animal. Georgia would
have me walking through the farmyard dropping bodies onto the
ground right and left.

I drank more coffee. It was a little like having her hands on me
beneath my clothes when I read about myself in her sentences. I
closed the folder, but I thought about her hands scraping a match
along the box to light a cigarette and her anger at her father and
how the cup had smelled of her breath when I brought it to my
mouth. I wouldn't read any more of her writing. I wouldn't carry
the pistol up to the farm and kill another dog. I saw Fanny in the
rocking chair nursing our child. There weren't enough right
words, I thought. There wasn't a way to say it.

CROP

I T WASN'T LATE NIGHT anymore, but it wasn't dawn. I heard an owl's hunting cry off in the woods beyond the pond. I was waiting to hear something dramatic or final, and I fell asleep listening to the distant coyotes and the local pond creatures and the call of the owl. I fell asleep like a man who lived an orderly life. I hadn't been drinking an overload of sour mash and I hadn't hefted a deadly weapon all over the county in search of something to kill. On the counter next to the sink my Taurus was under the old blanket I had washed and folded. Every chamber still contained a cartridge.

I was up a little after seven. I drank coffee and thought about toasting bread. I heard the big motor out front and saw that it was her black Mustang. It was early to be up and out unless you were on an errand. I thought her errand was me. I wanted to know what had happened to push her back upstate and into this corner of her life. I thought maybe knowing that would tell me why she was putting on a play about how irresistible she found me. I wanted to know what she wanted to talk me or sex me into doing. She was made of dance steps and words. She had to write all those words. She had to tell. So she would eventually tell me. I opened the door all the way out and she watched my face from the shelter of her dark glasses. Then she came up the stairs and walked past me. I could smell tobacco and sweat on her clothing. She was wearing jeans and dark blue clogs and an ivory-colored halter. She walked stiff-legged and I thought she felt me study her.

"I needed coffee," she said, "and I thought of the only addict I know who would always have a pot going." I poured her a cup and she said, "No saucer. All right?"

I put it down in front of her. Then I poured some more for myself and I sat.

She drank and made a face and drank some more. "God, you make it strong."

"I don't have any milk for it, I'm afraid," I said.

"That's all right," she said, "I'm man enough." She smiled a crooked smile and looked at me like we'd been friends for several years. Then she shrugged like she was dismissing her own joke and she drank some more. "And one thing you aren't," she said, "is afraid."

"You might be surprised." I watched her light a cigarette and I fetched a saucer for the ashes. When I was sitting again, I said, "And you've been up all night."

"How can you tell?"

I didn't want to say she smelled like it because I didn't want to get familiar about anything physical. "Veteran law enforcement people know these things."

A red squirrel in a dooryard tree was screeching like a movie chimp and when she turned away in the direction of the sound and then turned back I could see how corded her neck was and how fine the skin was at her throat and jaw. She was made for it, all right. "I was up late," she said, "and whatever that is, making that noise, that's what my brain sounded like. I just drove around. Sometimes I parked the car and sat around, waiting to figure out what it was I was trying to figure out. I drove by here, oh, maybe half a dozen times. I didn't come in, though. Well, you figured it out that I didn't, since I wasn't here."

"Do you know what's on your mind?"

"Failing out there," she said, gesturing behind her. "Coming back here. I mean Vienna. I mean this countryside up here. I mean the place where I grew up, if that's what I did. The place I was never, ever coming back to." She put her hand out on the table and patted it. "I had a fling," she said. "My mother calls it 'your fling.' *I* thought I was sleeping with a charming, unhappy man who was married to the wrong woman and he needed me. *He* thought he was screwing a wise-ass girl from the metro department who could drink harder and stay up later than any of his other girls. His *wife* knew he was coming back to her because that's what he always did. It is so sordid, isn't it? On account of it's being so old, and so cheesy, and so boring, and so *stupid*." She raised her brows and flared her nostrils. Then she crossed her eyes.

She said, "What?"

I shook my head.

"You looked like we were having fun. Then you didn't." Her skin was pale and it looked smooth. I thought I could smell her perfume as well as the darkness of tobacco and marijuana and sweat.

"Now you do," she said. Her eyes were very large when she took her sunglasses off and pushed them across the table to me. I set my cup down and folded the wings of the glasses and held them a second. I held them a second more and then put them down.

"I need to tell you something," I said.

Her eyes were on the glasses.

"I hated what you wrote."

She looked up. Her eyes widened. She flushed. She began a smile and then lost it. "Everybody is a fucking goddamned *critic*," she said. "Listen, Jack—"

I shook my head. "I am no critic. I barely passed the only two college English courses I ever took. I'm grateful I can read. No. But I don't want to be in anything that anybody writes."

"You cannot be that primitive," she said. "You think I'm capturing your burly, semi-educated soul? Is that it? Are you afraid—"

"That's photographs. The Indians, or the people in the rain forest a hundred years ago. No. I just don't want you to try and write me down."

She shook her head. She looked at her sunglasses on the table or the table itself or something that wasn't in front of her. Then she sat back like a kid pushing away from the table after dinner. But she stayed there. She drank off the rest of her coffee and lit another cigarette. I watched her lips around the filter. She crossed her legs. She put the left ankle on top of the right knee the way a man sat. She blew smoke slowly and then she drew in more. "You don't want me to know you," she finally said.

I shrugged. I said, "I don't know what it is."

She moved her chair back to the table. She set her elbows on the wood and she leaned in. I watched the way the flesh around the elbow padded out and the ripple that went up her triceps. She saw my eyes. "All right," she said. "But would you tell me—" She shook her head. Her eyes were closed and her face was red. "Never mind if it's you. For a minute, all right? Never mind? Just—what'd you think of the *writing*?" She sat back and stubbed out her cigarette and she waited.

I said, "The writing?"

"The way I wrote it, Jack. The *way* it says whatever you think it says."

"Oh," I said.

She said, "Oh."

"Well, good, Georgia. Very . . . dynamic."

She sat up whooping. She sounded like someone who had nearly drowned. I was startled and she laughed deeper when she read my expression. "Dy-*nam*-ic! Oh, I adore it. I never heard that word with so many syllables pronounced so slowly! Dy-*nam*-ic, Jack."

I didn't want to say anything more. I shook my head.

"You look like the bear with a noseful of bees."

"What bear?"

"*The* bear. Never mind. But I'm writing the piece, Jack."

"Well, I guess that's what you need to do."

"But I won't ask you to read it," she said. "I'm sorry you felt funny, reading about yourself. Take consolation that you're the, let's say, antagonist of sorts. There's plenty more story that you're only a part of. And would you like a little kick to move the morning along?" She opened her cigarette pack and took out a joint.

"Go ahead," I said.

She did all the things they have to do when they light a reefer. She licked the length of it. She put it in her mouth and turned it a couple of times. She lit it with a wooden match. She closed her eyes, sucked in while she shook the match out. She took it from her mouth between her thumb and third finger and she kept the smoke down. Then she let it leak out in little stutters and she looked at me. She smiled. She offered me a toke and raised her brows. I shook my head. She let a little more smoke out and smiled again.

I asked her, "Is that a local crop?"

She said, "You wouldn't believe where I got this batch."

She looked at me like we had just agreed on something. She took a long hit and closed her eyes. I was getting tired of smoke in my eyes and nose and the entire back-and-forth between us. I had

someplace to go because during the night of not sleeping and then
the short sleep and the waking up, I'd remembered again about the
gliding motion of a tall woman in dark clothes at Smith's doorway.
I was certain it was Georgia. And I remembered what I had seen
the second time up there when Smith was running with sweat and
all kinds of English words that sounded like a foreign language
came out of his mouth. I closed my eyes and I saw the rows of corn
in the field behind his farmhouse. I couldn't be sure, but it looked
like feed corn. I think it was supposed to look like a crop that a dairy
farmer would grow to feed his herd. There wasn't any sign of a
herd, though. And the last dozen feet of a couple of rows looked
wrong. Lots of times there were plants that didn't mature right. But
they were random. This was a circle of dirt where a few stalks were
withered and nothing else had grown. It would be a great year for
corn. That was what he'd promised me. I could see that section of
the field behind my eyelids. I needed to get up there and walk the
rows to make sure.

When I opened my eyes she was staring at me. It must have been
strong stuff or laced with additive. Or she must have really wanted
to be stoned. I didn't think she was faking how she thought she felt.
Her eyes were very dark and wet and unfocused. Wherever she was
looking at it wasn't me she saw.

Then she focused. She saw me. She said, "What?"

She stood. She was on the move and she was also waiting. She
prowled along the counter. She went to the doorway and looked at
the carbine. She came back to the sink. Then she reached for the
blanket. She moved its fold and looked down at the pistol. "I knew
you were armed," she said.

"Somebody told you so?"

"No," she said. "You like to be dangerous. Armed, dangerous—

you know." She came around from the counter to my side of the table. She walked close to me and moved her knee between my legs to get them apart. She came in closer and lay her forearms on my shoulders. She set herself against me so that my face was in her halter. Then she folded her arms around my head. She put her chin on top of my head and gathered me in. I was touched by her all over at once. She squeezed hard and I put my arms around her.

I felt her breath on top of my head. I heard her sigh out over me. Then she pulled me to my feet and led me around the corner to the mattress on the floor. She took off the halter and her jeans and underpants. She stared at me while she did. She bent and stooped and straightened as gracefully as anyone I had seen in motion. She was naked and she wore her flesh like a costume. She knelt on the mattress and took a final toke and set the roach on the floor. She reached over and untied my shoes the way you do for kids. And I stepped back.

"Come on," she whispered. Then she said, "Jack." She had a hand around each of my ankles. "Let's leave your socks on," she said. "The way they do in the movies. You know which movies I mean?"

She pulled me by my feet and I moved.

"The ones," she said, "where they start out doing this." Her mouth was around me. Her lips felt hot and her tongue felt cold. I put my hands on her shoulders. It was early on a weekday. I had forgotten what day of the week it was and I had forgotten the time. I kept my eyes closed and after a while it was a little like a fight. It was very much like a fight. I went from standing above her to kneeling almost on her and then rolling her down and flat. I was lying on her. I was lying inside of her. I remember thinking it wasn't possible to get any more of myself inside her. But I tried. Her breathing was never regular. Sometimes she seemed to be scream-

ing with her mouth locked tight. I remember her rolling a condom onto me. I remember thinking I'd been right to figure she
would have some with her. When she did that I was angrier. I
heard myself panting so hoarsely that I seemed to be shouting. I
turned her over onto her stomach. I was pushing her hands down
onto the mattress. She bucked up under me like she was resisting.
Maybe she was. I know I didn't care. I know I was using myself on
her like a weapon. I battered her with myself. Her back and head
went down. Her ass came up. I was in her very hard and deep. I
know I wanted to hurt her. One of us was yelling and yelling.
Maybe it was both of us.

I came the way people cry when they're finally pushed past what
pain or sorrow they can carry in themselves. I'd seen it in the service and I'd seen it on the job. I saw it in my own house. It kept on
going and it was nothing to do with pleasure. We were wet with
each other and it might as well have been each other's blood. After
a couple of minutes of our lying apart on our backs she reached
under me to move me. She tried to push my face onto her breast. I
think she wanted her nipple in my mouth. The breast was wet. I
clamped my lips. I rolled my face away.

I thought about the arrests I'd made for what I'd just done. There
was one in Saigon when a civilian contractor out on a party mistook the widowed mother of a working girl for a whore. He beat
hell out of her upstairs in her apartment and he raped her. The
girl's pimp came to the rescue by jamming a sharpened screw-
driver up into the civilian's armpit. I talked to him about his needing the consulate to send him an attorney at the hospital.

Another time was when I worked college security. A lot of those
prep school boys thought the coeds' bodies came with the tuition
and meal plan their parents bought. One big, handsome kid with

curly light brown hair and a rumpled shirt worth one of my mortgage payments raped a first-year girl because she kissed him with her tongue out at his fraternity's pledge party.

"That's a fucken contract," he kept saying. "That's you fucken give your word." He was wobbling because he was so drunk. He was very red-faced and his handsome shirt was wet with sweat. I was fastening a plastic bag from the fraternity house kitchen around his wrist. I used masking tape from his roommate's studio art course supplies. The idea was to preserve the evidence. The evidence was on his second, third, and fourth fingers from the nails down to the third knuckle. I was certain it was her vaginal discharge and blood.

He said, "You give your word, you keep it. Am I right?"

"Son," I said, "I wouldn't be surprised if I was talking to the next President of the United States of America."

I hadn't beaten Georgia with my fists. I'd beaten her with the rest of me. I'd assaulted her with my cock and my balls. And I had wanted to. Guilty as charged, I thought. I wasn't very eager to open my eyes. We were still lying on the mattress. We were still breathing hard.

I felt her hands around my scrotum. "Aren't you something," she said. I waited for the rest of it. But that seemed all she wanted to say. She cupped me and then took the length of me in her hand. I was still in the condom. I'd been hating her, I thought. And she was too involved with her own terrible dreams to know it. Or that was what she wanted—force, bullying power, rage. She was using me on herself the way a suicide might use the .32.

Her hand left me and I heard wet skin on the sheets. I opened my eyes to find her on her side, one hand tucked between her legs. She was watching me. She said, "You look like you're going to cry, Jack." Then her voice came in a whisper. "Don't cry, Jack."

I took a deep breath. It was like coming back up from holding myself near the bottom of the pond.

I rolled off and got up and went down the hall to the bathroom to throw it into the toilet. I leaned on the wall behind it and I peed. It felt hot coming out and I felt sore outside myself and in. I heard her say, "Jesus." She stood in the doorway with her long, perfect thighs crossed like she was keeping herself from letting something inside of her get out. Her hands were at her sides. "You pee like one of those farm horses," she said. "You just keep on going." Before I was done she walked over to me and stood with one hand on my hip. She brought the other around in front of me and with one of her long fingers she touched the crown of it. She pushed it a little while I peed. Then she leaned in and bit me on the nipple.

"Damn it," I said.

"You can do it back to me. Here." She flushed the toilet for me. "I had a boyfriend once, he was shorter than I am. His cock was the longest I've ever seen. He was a white guy, but he called it a nigger cock. He kept telling me, 'Kiss that nigger cock, baby.' And you know what?" She smiled and she knelt on the old black and white tiles by the toilet. There was a drop of urine on the end of it. She leaned in toward me with her tongue out, and she took me in her mouth. She held me that way and then she let her mouth slide away slowly. "If you have a lover," she said, "you *have* him." She stood and moved to kiss me. I took the kiss. If I was a fraud and a goddamned villain then I had to go all the way with it. I thought I deserved it.

I said it a little too fast for someone who was willing to go all the way when I said, "I need a shower."

"Sure," she said. "I volunteer to apply the soap. I was a medical volunteer, did I tell you? In Pittsburgh. I was living with this guy, a doctor, a first-year resident at Mercy Hospital named Benitez. I always called him Benny on account of that being not only who he was but what he brought home. Well, not *really* bennies, but all kinds of ups. The interns used them to keep awake. I used them just to more or less keep alive that year. I let him do a gyno on me. He loved it. He had the most delicate hands."

We were in the steam together in the small stall and she offered to soap my back. She managed to work a lathered finger up my ass. I wanted to get clean. I also wanted to jam myself inside her again. I also wanted to set fire to both of us because that was the only way I figured we would ever get rid of the dirtiness. She lathered my balls and rinsed the soap off and finished the rinse with her mouth. She made the sucking noises a baby would make. I remembered those.

"You're quiet all the time," she said while she was drying my back with a towel from the resort hotel. "But this, after love—you're even quieter. Jack, don't worry. You were very damned good."

I said, "Whatever I was you couldn't call it good. Or love."

"No commitments, Jack. Don't worry. But we, you know, did get under the other one's skin. To say the very least. And we have time. You know. We'll know each other."

"Georgia," I said, "what do you figure we'll know?"

"You'll know who I am. I'll know who you are. We'll know it by the tastes and textures."

I didn't know what she was talking about. I was working to keep from flaring up and only part of it was her fault. The rest was mine.

We were in the bedroom retrieving our clothes. I told myself to do some work. I told myself to be subtle. I asked her, "You ever hear of a local man named Smith?"

She was putting on her underwear. She was lying on the mattress with her legs planted and she moved her midsection up to work the dark blue silk panties on. She held herself that way. Then she slipped the panties back down, so they were over her calves. She said, "In college, we used to call this taking a guy's picture." She swung her legs apart.

"I never went to college," I said, "I only worked in one." I looked over her because it might have seemed politer than looking away. "Would you call that a turn-on for the boys who saw it or for the girls who did it?"

She pulled the pants up. She said, "That's an excellent question. At Goucher, it would have been called vulgar. At Bard, it was slutty, mildly stupid, but possibly fun and, just, you know, who *cared*? In graduate school, it didn't have to happen. You picked the right man or he picked you, and you got into each other or you didn't. At Northeastern, I had the wrong man at the wrong time. At Pitt, I had the right man, wrong star in ascendancy with Mars turned inside out. The first time I got fired, it was by a man I made the mistake of sleeping with. He liked men better but he didn't know it until I told him. Second time, I didn't sleep with the man who didn't fire me. I had to quit." She was lying down and talking up at the ceiling. I watched her bare breasts move as she lit the joint.

She wanted me to ask. I said, "Why?"

"Some of my facts weren't verified."

"You made it up."

"I used who the woman was, what her situation really was. She was Pearl Toussaint and she was being fucked over by the social services in Erie County."

"That's New York State," I said.

"Just head north and west."

I said, "While you've been doing your research here did you run into someone called Smith?"

"There *is* a farmer named Smith. I did run into him one time." She gasped her smoke around the words. One of them, "farmer," I'd never told her. "He's one of those leftover hippies who live in the hills. He's always a little pharmaceutical, if you know what I mean. Is that the one?"

I caught how a man she ran into once was *always* stoned. I said, "I thought he might have known a kid named Tyler Pearl."

"What about him? Smith and Pearl. They sound like a publishing house. Maybe I should meet them."

"He's why I'm here, Georgia. The story you were looking for? Jerry Gentry must have told you about it. You want to know more. So here's what it might be. This Tyler Pearl kid had something to do with this Smith person."

"Oh, Jack. You're going to think I balled you so I could get the true gen."

"What's gen?"

She said, "It's a writer thing, one of the terms you use in the business. The stuff you look for when you work. So is this missing person presumed to be, you know, past tense?"

"Did you?"

"Fuck you for barter? Well, Jack, I seem to recall being the one who flipped her ass up into the air for you. Right?"

"Yes," I said. "Yes. It was you." Also, I wanted to say, it was me. I couldn't.

She set the roach on the floor when she sat up. Then she made a slow, graceful dip to lower her breasts into her brassiere. "Pearl," she said. "Not that I remember. You want me to ask around?"

"That would be friendly," I said.

"Well," she said, "you know I'm friendly."

She smoked a cigarette while I heated up the coffee. I sat in the

kitchen awhile to wait for it to get warm and then she came around
the corner. She looked careless and happy. She didn't wait to drink
anything.

"Won't take a minute," I said.

"I want to drive about ninety miles an hour and think about you
driving up into me," she said. She kissed me on the Adam's apple.
I knew she'd bite me and she did. I figured she wanted to get to her
car and drive to someplace where she could park and make her
notes. Then, I thought, she just might go to Smith. Of course,
Smith might be working for her, I thought. Why not? I was relieved
she was leaving. I decided I wanted to make a fresh pot of coffee. I
wanted something in me that was new.

"Okay, sweet man," she said. "You know I'll be back."

I called, "Thanks."

She stopped and turned and cocked her head. "For what?"

"I don't know," I said. "What we —"

"Well, yeah," she said. "And the same to you." She kissed at the
air and she left.

I thought of her cigarette ashes and roaches on the floor next to
my mattress. Analyze the contents, I thought, and there would
probably be additives. I wondered if Smith was sharing the speed.

The water was ready and I made a fresh pot. I sat down with a
cup of it to toast myself for giving up my body for the sake of the
investigation. Once I did that, I could tell myself some other lies.

I LOST THE late morning. I lost the afternoon. I had coffee for
lunch. I packed a lot of my belongings into the truck. I thought that
I would leave. I'd find some work someplace. I sat awhile. Then I
brought my gear back into the house. I thought to change my

sheets but didn't have anything clean so I stripped the sheet and pillowcase that smelled from Georgia and me. I brought the blanket in with me and I lay down on the bare mattress. I thought I still smelled us. I hated the smell but I noticed I kept drawing it in. I fell asleep. When I woke up, I made coffee for dinner and then I drove to Vienna.

Elway had to be worse, I thought, because their son Michael was in the waiting room with Sarah. He was taller than his father, but with the same squared-off shoulders and rigid back. His complexion was darker than either of theirs. His nose was broader and shorter. His lips were as delicate as Sarah's and he had her wide, powerful hands. He looked exhausted and confused. Sarah looked exhausted too. But she knew what was going on. She always did. If she didn't, she found out. Elway was also like that.

When I kissed his mother hello she held my face to hers and I reached around her neck and hung on. When I opened my eyes Michael was staring at us. I wondered if he knew half of what he saw. I wonder if he sensed it.

"Hi," I said.

Sarah told him who I was. He remained in his chair. He nodded. "I remember you," he said in a deep voice.

"I remember you too," I said. "You came onto the campus when I worked there. You were with some visiting high school group. I don't remember what it was about. I waved hello. I embarrassed you in front of your friends. I always meant to tell you I was sorry for that."

He stood up and came a few steps closer. He smiled a very good smile and shook his head at himself. He stuck his hand out and I shook it. He said, "I want to thank you for ev—" I could tell that his throat closed down. He shook his head again.

"I couldn't ever do anything for your mother and your father that's enough," I said. I knew that I'd shut down too if I said much more. I patted his shoulder and stepped back.

Sarah said, "You look exhausted."

"You do too, a little."

"Well, I ought to. What's your excuse?"

"I've been working," I said.

"Peeping and prying and poking about," she said.

"Sarah," I said, "I'm almost on my way out again. I'm nearly done."

"Look what you came home to," she said.

In front of Michael's confusion or suspicion, she stepped closer and put one hand on each of my ears. She tugged them a little. I could remember her pulling my head down to her in the back of my station wagon in what felt like the middle of all the forest in the state. My face must have showed her what I remembered. She gave a little laugh. It was almost a giggle but it wasn't. She was on her way to Intensive Care.

Michael and I stood near each other in silence. Then he said, "It looks very serious, with my father. This meningitis. I've told my wife not to come yet, but I'm wondering."

"They think it's that—I don't know the best word."

"Close," he said.

He wore a tan long-sleeved shirt that was buttoned at the neck. He pulled at the collar. Then he pulled at each sleeve. "So—oh, yes," he said. "That's right. I remember. Your dog. I was always scared of dogs when I was a kid. But your dog was all right."

I said, "I know."

"He'd just sort of be there."

"That was his specialty," I said.

"Is he still around? He must be getting along."

I shook my head. "No," I said. "He isn't around anymore."

"That's too bad."

I nodded.

"You must miss him."

"I do, Michael."

It was like the dream. It wasn't only Elway's voice or only mine. It was something of the sound of both of us or what I thought my voice might sound like if I heard it somewhere imitating him. Say maybe in a dream. It was those scolding tones of Elway's. It was the sergeant talking to the misbehaving man in the ranks. It was when I made a call. It was when I called their number in New York State from where I was. It was the longest distance I called. I did it because I thought of Sarah. I must have been in bad shape. I must have hoped she would answer and I'd hear her voice. I wanted someone to be happy to hear from me.

Elway told me what happened. It was the longest phone call of my life.

It was after she left here and after you left, he said. Mrs. Tanner did die pretty much on schedule. She hung on awhile, telling people how Jack might still find her girl, but nobody found her. God knows you needed to as much as Mrs. Tanner needed you to do it, her daughter being the second child you lost. Then word came about you being a long ways gone and living in the hot country. After that field, waist-deep in snow, some places, nobody could blame you for going down there. Though some of us might have appreciated hearing it from you more directly.

Fanny called us maybe six months on. She was in the north country, deep in the Adirondacks. You went south for the heat and she made for deeper snow and ice. She was a nurse outside of

Waterville. She had a rented room, she said. She had some clothing in the room, she had the suitcase that carried it, she said, and
she had the little urn full of ashes. You got to take the dog with you,
she said, and she got to carry the ashes away. She said she was drinking a lot. Sarah tried making a joke about wishing Fanny would try
to forget to drink to forget. Sarah was on the extension. All three of
us managed talking at once when she called. She didn't call a lot.
This time, she said she wasn't drinking to forget. That's what worried her. She was drinking to remember, she said. She was dreaming about the baby. She was remembering things that couldn't ever
have happened, she said.

Sarah was standing in front of me. She said, "Jack?"

"I was—"

"Maybe you'd like to go in for a minute? Just a little minute?
Honey, are you all right?"

"I think I fell asleep."

"Oh," she said. I saw that Michael was staring at me again.

"No, I'm fine."

I took the hand she extended. I suppose she thought I needed
the help. I didn't know what else to do so I raised it to my cheek and
held it against me. I wanted to kiss it. I thought I shouldn't do that
with Michael watching. Then I went out of the waiting room and
onto the ward. Three nurses sat at the station. A heavy-thighed adolescent girl in a pink uniform with hair the color of a purple Tootsie
Pop was swabbing the floor around the station with a mop that
stank of artificial pine. It was very hot in there. The blinds in the
windows of the rooms were drawn against the sun. Elway was in the
room directly across from the station. I thought that was good.
They couldn't help but see him all the time and keep him safe.

He had a drip going into him and a monitor. His arm that was hooked to the drip looked spindly and soft and very bruised. His color had changed from a weathered wood to tan with some yellow in it. His tight face sagged and his closed eyes jumped under the lids. Then he opened them and I needed to resist moving back away from them. They glared pink. He looked past me.

I made myself go closer. I sat in a brown plastic chair beside him. I lay forward a little.

"Elway," I said.

His voice was lighter than I remembered when he opened his eyes again and said, "What?" He was leaving while he was lying there.

"Michael's here. He's outside."

"I know. We talked. I'm sick, I'm not stupid."

"I'm stupid but I'm not sick."

"I know."

"You want me to do anything?"

"Sarah knows what to do."

"I wish she didn't have to."

He patted the sheets that lay across his chest. It was like someone calming a child or a nervous dog. I knew he was patting me. The machine talked to itself in little ticks and clicks. The IV drop hung above the solution in the transparent plastic bag. The clear liquid fell inside like oil without a splash.

"I'll come back," I said.

"All this time," he said, "I'm still sorry about Fanny. We were close."

"Yes," I said.

"Sorry I had to tell you."

"Best, though, coming from you," I said.

We sat like that. I was just about in tears. He sighed. He said, "Jack. Hey."

"What?"

"*Bull*shit, man."

"Bullshit," I finally said. "You're right."

"There you go."

"I'll come back later in the day," I said.

"Will I know it to care?"

"Well, I hope you do, Elway."

"So do I," he said. His pink eyes focused on my face and he patted twice at the sheets.

Between the side of his bed and the doorway to the room where Sarah and Michael waited I had enough time to think about Fanny in a rented place up north with maybe a dark linoleum floor and a soft bed on an iron frame and a pine bureau with some clothing in it. On top of the bureau she would have set the dull-bronze urn that our daughter was in.

It isn't something you can remember or decide to forget. It's the story of your life and it's inside of you. I told myself you got to take the dog with you and she got to carry off the ashes.

Michael shook my hand very hard like I was the one dying or close to it. Sarah and I kissed goodbye. I wanted to rescue them from this the same way I wanted to rescue Elway. It seemed to me I had done a lot of trying with very little success since I'd come back. In the elevator, I realized how much I hated this hospital with its lobby like a country club dance floor and its airless rooms and tired staff. Of course, I hated all the hospitals I'd ever been in, and that included the place a couple of dozen miles to the north where Fanny had worked and where she'd given birth and where we'd brought our daughter. Once or twice I'd had some luck in them. One of the times was when my ribs were fractured by men who'd been sent to kick them in. Another time was when a student nearly died but I'd got her to that hospital in time. But it was a pathetic record, I thought. You'd get fired if anyone kept score. I wished that someone would fire me off this job. That was a large part of my problem. I had no talent except for finding work I couldn't do.

I sat behind the wheel in the truck and I didn't turn the ignition key. I wondered whether Jerry Gentry was following me. I watched in the rearview mirror as a sheriff's department cruiser came slowly into the lot. I knew it was Jerry because the car didn't prowl the lanes of the lot. It came directly for me. It slid into the bay behind mine and hit me with the high beams and then went dark. I knew he wanted me to come out and talk to him. But I sat where I was and after a while he got out in several awkward motions. His impatience might undo him, I thought. Cops ought to be patient. I wondered when I'd learn that.

He came around and opened the passenger's door and levered himself in. He grunted and breathed hard while he folded his stomach down so he could fit his long legs and feet into the narrow compartment.

He said, "Elway?"

I nodded.

"Bad, huh?"

"I think so, Jerry. I don't know anything about what he's got but he looks pretty terrible."

"He made a few inquiries for you."

"He told you about them?"

"Friends told me. They didn't necessarily appreciate the black Lone Ranger asking them for favors. It isn't kosher. Not that Elway's kosher." He gave the sort of laugh you give when you've said something unfunny and you know it.

"So he's not kosher but he is black? I want to make sure I get all the dimensions down. You sure he isn't a black Jew?"

"I heard about you getting all hard-assed over Jews and blacks before, when you worked the college security. You got a friend of mine fired for it."

"Which it, being a Jew or being a black, or making bad jokes about both of them?"

"Fuck you, Jack. You know what I'm saying. He wasn't exactly a liberal, so you kicked him off of the campus cops."

"I remember that. You're right. And you're pissed off at Elway because I got someone fired? Or because he's—well, it couldn't be anything else, Jerry, could it?"

I could smell his aftershave. It seemed to have a base made of all kinds of fresh fruit that was composted for a long time. I could also smell a deodorant that reminded me of baby powder with a layer of grease on top of it. The fabric of our uniform tops didn't help a man stay fresh. It kept the air off the skin. Heat poured off him in the closed cab of the truck but I didn't want to signify his smelling bad by rolling my window down.

An ambulance pulled in with its lights flashing. Its siren gave a burp that was meant to signal its arrival to the ER staff. Jerry opened the door to attend. So maybe he hadn't been following me. But he was transporting all kinds of emotion. He said, "I need to get there. It's an old lady gone toxic or something. She's the color of color-me-dead. How's all that going with Georgia?"

"There's a privileged kid."

"Her old man is major league around here."

"So are you, Jerry."

He stared at me. He was waiting to understand whether I'd insulted him. Finally he said, "You'd like me to believe you just don't give a shit. Am I right?"

"Absolutely wrong," I said. "You're a good law enforcement officer. I hope you have a safe patrol."

He watched my face for clues and then he gave up. He worked his way out and slammed the door and marched with giant strides toward the ambulance. So now I knew he was tight with people who didn't like Elway. That meant to me that Jerry was less than a grade-A man. He still might be an effective cop. I knew he had an investment in Georgia Bromell and maybe it was only sorrow for what he'd lost in high school. It was easy in these towns to live with memories of your teenage years mattering as much as what happened every day of your thirties. That was because you were reminded every day of who you'd been and on the very same spot where you'd succeeded and failed. Every day you felt what was missing in your life and what would never arrive. You breathed the old air of your old times. Sooner or later, it had to hobble you. Strapping Jerry Gentry was halfway to a cripple, I thought.

Jerry wanted a connection with Georgia. I didn't know if it was because of her father or because of the smell of her skin and the look of her arms and the darkness inside of her. Georgia was also who I needed to know. I didn't trust the need part and I didn't trust the know. But I understood to track her. So I left the hospital lot and I drove the big roads and little streets. I cut at random from shopping area to shopping area. Then I headed for the storage units north of town and parked across the road from them for half an hour before I drove back to the south. I saw no sign of the Mustang. I thought to try some country roads and for a while I taught myself to navigate in the hills to the east of Vienna. I stopped to fill the tank with gas and use the men's room and buy a cup of coffee.

I made a note in my Friend in Pennsylvania notebook so I could give Merle an accurate accounting of expenses. Thinking of her was pleasant for a while. I imagined her in her office where she was so competent. I thought of the books in the firm's law library that she could usefully consult. I thought of how sad and defeated she had been in the bar down South and in my efficiency. I remembered her sitting on the floor like a child with her hand on the dog's broad back. I sipped at coffee and watched the customers at the huge variety store exit with large, heavy plastic bags. They looked sadder than when they'd gone in. I wondered which part of the exercise they liked. I was thinking that I ought to call Merle. But I was hesitant. I wasn't sure why. All that was between us was a cup of coffee sweetened with mash, a big dog, a dinner in New York, an embarrassing few minutes at her place, and an assignment I'd accepted. I needed to work and she had a job. She needed information on a nephew and I was someone who dug up information. Look what I used for digging it up.

When I thought of using my shovel instead, I had to think of the missing Tanner girl and how we prodded through the snow of the field. We were hoping to discover her and then uncover her and bear her back across the distance. We would have carried her through our own footsteps to her mother. I drank more coffee and wondered why I rarely thought of her father. He was a decent man and his heart was broken too. But it was the girl's mother who had moved me so much. A friend of mine in those days said he thought I was in love with her.

Blink your eyes and tell me you're in trouble and I'll work up a crush on you, I thought. I thought about buying something for dinner and driving back to the place and cooking. Georgia would likely show up. I knew that I was in no hurry to run into her. At least that's what I claimed. Still, she was a source. Apparently I was too. The situation reminded me of two hill tribesmen I saw in the cellar of a ruined house outside of Saigon that used to belong to a

French exporter. They were killers. They'd been used that way in the early days of the war before we sent the black and brown and redneck amateurs in from the States. Now they made a living by nearly killing each other in a ring marked off by four stacks of bald truck tires in a stone cellar that stank of flesh. It was a dangerous, ugly fight with the two of them locked tight in a painful hold that kept them lying on the floor. The first one to slacken pressure could have a larynx punctured or an eye gouged out. Inside the tension of the hold they were working with small muscle flutters and tiny shifts of leverage. Their faces never changed. I was told they did this weekly. Vietnamese who still had money and GIs who were easily bored or who needed to witness even more pain bet on the fighters. That night one of them passed out and the winner released his pressure and went to his knees to make a kind of bow before he had to lie down again because of the pain.

One of my cracker MPs said, "Those boys work for their dollar, don't they?"

That was Georgia and that was me. We were working for the dollar.

I went back north on 12, thinking that I would reverse in the self-storage lot and then drive back to the house. I saw the black Mustang in the lot. Georgia got out of it carrying two shopping bags into a storage unit halfway down an interior row. I parked to wait. It made so much sense, I thought. You don't need an imagination. All you need is one rented place and two keys to it in each of the bigger cities. You left off the stuff and then the distributors came for it and bagged it and sold it. Everybody got money. Everybody got high. She returned to her car with no shopping bags. I was positive I was right. This was local service. Now I needed to verify my thinking with a storage compartment in Utica or Syracuse up north or someplace south.

She drove south after sliding out of the lot and across traffic without slowing for the cars that almost intersected with her. She started out fast and then she went faster. I had my window open and I could hear her taking it up through the gears. I closed my window and put the air-conditioning on. I stayed close for a while. She didn't seem to be looking behind her. It would be a gift if you could always proceed without looking behind. She was doing over seventy. I let a few cars get between us and went at not quite her speed. She accelerated when we were past Greene. I was thinking of that excellent coffee. Apparently going seventy was just clearing the Mustang's throat. I heard myself grunt. A high-speed pursuit is not an option for civilians.

When we were passing a town called Kattelville and I was trying to figure out how to pronounce it she took a left off 12. I had to speed up to follow because she went out of sight. I caught her as she headed south again on this smaller road. About fifteen minutes later we were on a feeder that went to 81. As far as I could tell we were heading either for New York City or the border with Pennsylvania. She was about ten car lengths ahead of me. She was going seventy-five and drifting across lanes without a signal. I was worried that she would exit so I sped up. I downshifted to get a burst of speed and then I went up the gears. We left the highway on the southern edge of Binghamton and we slowed to follow side streets. I dropped back until I had to squint in the light from street lamps to make her out.

She turned in at Jefferson & Kantwell's Storage. I parked in the street once she was parked inside the mesh wire fence. I waited to see her lug a shopping bag or two. That's what she did. I knew that someone would want to learn the mechanics of the rest but I knew all I needed to. She was the bag man, bag girl, bag woman, bag person. She was that at the very least. I almost didn't care how much else she was involved in, though I had some cruel suspicions. Either she was an investor with Smith but using her father's money or she worked her way into his business using sex. Or maybe she promised to teach him how to speak English. What else would draw her except the story?

I headed back to Vienna. I didn't quite get lost but it took me longer than I thought it should because I couldn't find the road that went from 81 to the Kattelville Road. But I was used to being not quite lost for long periods of time. The idea was to not give too much of a damn. Otherwise you felt like a kid who needed help. I wasn't about to be that again. Although there were women who when they left me could give me that feeling. Fanny of course was most of them.

I made my way to Greene and parked near Lily Stovich's EAT. I thought I would buy some of her coffee and whatever she would sell me to take home for dinner.

She looked me over and shook her head. "You are beset upon?" she asked.

I said, "I need some kind of dinner I could maybe heat up back at my place. Have you got some kind of dinner?" She was wearing her floppy, oversized chef's suit but she walked with what you'd have to call authority into the kitchen at the rear of the restaurant. I said to her back, "How are you?"

"Always, myself, a little bit beset. It helps at these times, I have found, to put on myself a little 4711 lilac water. At the wrists and the neck." She pointed with a little finger at her throat. She said, "You're familiar with the brand 4711?"

"No, ma'am," I said.

"The House of 4711, very elegant German toiletries from the

people who brought you Bergen-Belsen. You're familiar with *it*?"

I thought it best to nod my head.

"Your color isn't good," she said. "You look overworked. Did you work hard enough to look so not very good?"

"No, ma'am, I can't say that I did."

"From John Wayne, the 'ma'am.' You couldn't say, but I could. You look like you could look better. You want dessert? Have a little sweetness. It's a tart, the plums are from California, but the pastry cream is from me. I could cut a slice for after the meat loaf."

"Please."

"It *looks* like meat loaf from America. Trust me. This is made with ground veal, ground lamb, ground beef. I should use pork, but I hesitate. You understand? Not from dietary observance, which we don't observe, but on account of pork is grown lean. Lean, without fat, means tough. I make meat loaf into a *pâté de campagne* you could cut with good intentions, never mind your fork." She carried back plastic containers and a large coffee. "For on the way home," she said, "and with my compliments to encourage commerce. This is something taught to me by my husband's brother who went bankrupt, but who accumulated wisdom on the way."

She looked up, her wrinkled pale face suddenly earnest. It made me see her when she was young. She must have been a serious girl.

She asked me, "Why are you so troubled?"

"No," I said, "I'm not. I'm just busy. Believe me."

"Once I was six feet tall," she said. "Then—life. One and one-half feet later, I am worn away by believing. So pardon me for knowing when someone is troubled. But a secret is a secret, and good luck to you."

"Good luck, Mrs. Stovich."

"Come back," she said.

"You mean now?" I said. I stopped at the door because I thought she needed more money from me.

"You couldn't come back if you wouldn't leave," she said. "Go away, eat well, live carefully, *then* you should come back."

The Mustang was parked in front of my house. I wedged the truck onto the lawn next to her car and went in. I wasn't hungry or thirsty so I put the meat loaf and dessert in the refrigerator. I sat at the table and drank the last cool sips of coffee from Greene. The coyotes were working over the hill across from my place. I wasn't working. I was slumped in a kitchen chair. I was afraid to go in, I thought. That made me decide that I had to go in. Georgia was in the bed. I smelled tobacco and dope and her skin. She'd been toking while I was in Greene. She ran a tight schedule, I thought. She couldn't have got there too long before I did. She breathed like someone who was deep asleep.

I couldn't see anything. I realized that I'd walked in with my eyes closed. Maybe I was dreaming Georgia Bromell. I said, "Is that you?"

"Who else did you want it to be? I got to feeling insular, so I came in here and got under your blanket. Is that all right with you?"

"I brought some food."

She said, "Come here, Jack." I got onto my knees on the mattress. She said, "Where'd you put the sheet? I'm staying over, by the way. All right? Think of it as a slumber party."

"You know, today was a bad day."

"It began right," she said. "Didn't it?"

I heard the rasp and hiss of the wooden match. I was lying down now with my eyes still closed. I heard her take the hit and hold the smoke in. I was holding my own breath. I blew out and then she let go of a little reefer smoke and then a few seconds later she let out some more.

"Jack," she said. I heard her smiling. "Jack, you are a cranky man. How old are you?"

"Why?"

"I want to know."

"You want to say, 'I had sex with a man who was so-and-so years old.'"

"I want to remember us when I was thirty-one and going on thirty-two and when you were—what?"

"I'm forty-nine. I'm almost fifty. I'm too old for you. I'm too old for me."

"You're good, you know, for an older guy. You don't think when you fuck. You don't do the smooth moves, the put this here so she moves here kind of thing. You just do it. And you happen to be an animal. You're authentic." I heard her sigh. "Tell me a story, Jack. Tell me a bedtime story. Tell me about the little girl. When you were looking for her?"

"That's just part of the story you want, isn't it?"

"You're really like regretful about it, aren't you? And suspicious. You should trust me."

"The rest of it has got to be about Clarence Smith."

She took a long hit and stayed behind the usual noises.

"That's all right," I said. "I don't need all of it. I'll find the parts I need. I'm almost there."

"I let you down, huh? Not checking out this what's-his-name person. I'll try. I promise." I heard the air pass around her fingers as she took a hit. "I was wondering, though," she said. She made the strangling noise around the smoke, talking and holding the dope back at the same time. "You might like it," she said. She was on me and holding my throat with her hands. I thought she was going to choke me and I started to move an arm between her arms to break the hold. But I stopped myself. If she strangled me the worst that would happen was not breathing anymore. I thought that. I did. What she was after though was moving her mouth onto my face and at my mouth so she could push her tongue in and blow in her breath. "I was wondering whether you would like a little second-hand smoke."

She licked my lips very slowly around and around. She painted my mouth with her tongue. Then she moved a finger around my lips. Then she stuck the finger into my mouth and waited for me suck on it.

Most of what happened after that was about my lying flat on the mattress and Georgia crawling on me. I thought about animals dead in the deserts I'd patrolled and how the vultures squatted on them to yank at the meat. I remembered how the whole dead crea-ture jerked when a piece tore away. That was me. I made sure my temper was under control. It made me a little slow to respond to what she thought were some very inventive moves. She worked harder. She worked on herself as well as on me. I think she had pleasure. But she was also shutting me up so I wouldn't ask her any more questions. She must have thought she was safe. If they don't see you coming with cuffs in your hand the clever ones end up thinking they're safe. They almost never are. That's why simple men like me stay in law enforcement. You very often nail the ones who think they're safe because they're clever. Clever just isn't usu-ally enough.

She was finished with me below the belt. She crawled up me and rubbed her wet lips on my chin and mouth. "Taste yourself," she said. Then she was lying with her short hair just under my jaw. She was absolutely still except for the pounding of her heart. All of a sudden she moved. It was like a dance, I thought. I hadn't seen any modern dance but I couldn't imagine anything like this happening anyplace except on a stage. She was straddling me. Her knees and heels dug in. She moved her groin back and forth on me. Her hands were on my throat. The thumbs were over my Adam's apple. I waited for her to press and then let go and start the sex again.

But apparently this was the sex. She tightened her fingers. Then she pressed with her thumbs. She pressed harder. She slid down on me so I was inside of her. When we were locked to each other she squeezed with interior muscles. I couldn't help responding. Then she squeezed more with her hands. Then she squeezed more in her groin. She said something but I couldn't hear the words. She sounded far away. It was like drifting on the surface of the pond. Then it was like lying inside the pond under the surface and floating halfway down. It hurt but it also didn't. She rode me and rode me. She kept me from breathing. And I thought, Go ahead and take it.

She was making noises in a deep voice. Maybe it was my voice. Maybe I was making the noises. I came so hard I shouted if you can shout while you're strangling. She did too, I think. She let the air in, and I breathed. I made hard breathing noises and curled my legs up, knocking her sideways. I turned so I would lie with my face away from her while I caught my breath.

I heard the blanket rustle when she pulled it up her body. I slept like a man wobbling around the corner into middle age. It was maybe one in the morning when I moved through the smell of sex and marijuana and cigarettes to get up and out. I carried my clothes and my heavy flashlight and a slice I cut from Lily Stovich's meat loaf that I wrapped in a piece of paper towel. I walked in bare feet over gravel and wet weeds to the truck. I slid into neutral and rolled back down my drive. I dressed in the cab of the truck and started it and got into gear and drove myself to work.

It took me about half an hour to get the truck parked on the side of Kramers Barn Road. I followed the track I had made in sneaking onto the overlook above Clarence Smith's land. This time I didn't sneak. I didn't need to the same way I didn't need much more from Georgia or anyone else. I thought I ought to have done this a week before. I thought I should have called Merle and told her. But first I ought to be sure.

It was tougher walking at night. There was an almost-full moon but heavy clouds moved through every few minutes and shut it off. I had to depend on the flashlight for the bushwhacking. Carrying the long-handled shovel made me clumsy and I walked into some spruce branches and got scratched up. I slipped a few times and banged myself. But that was fair punishment, I thought. I was thinking about Georgia and what she would do to have this story and say it in print. It couldn't have only been about proving something to her father. He seemed like the kind of man whose opinion you could never change. My throat was sore inside and out. I wondered if I wore a black and blue band like a collar on my throat and neck.

I tried to remember Fanny and me in bed but now I couldn't. I could name times and recite places to myself. But I couldn't remember the feel of our skin on each other. I stopped walking because I wanted to close my eyes and remember. I stood there leaning into the angle of the hillside with night birds giving little shrieks and insects whining into my ears. I was holding the shovel I had used to probe the cornfield when I looked for Janice Tanner. It was the same shovel I'd used for burying my dog. I tried to remember what it had felt like to slide inside of Fanny my wife and reach the core of her and feel her jump and then come back down on me while I moved up in her. I could tell myself the words. I said them to myself on the side of the hill I was trying to climb. But I couldn't feel it anymore.

"I'm sorry," I said to her. I could still feel the wetness and slide of sex with Georgia Bromell and everything disappearing while my ears rang with a steady high whistle but I couldn't remember making love with Fanny. I said, "I'm sorry." Fanny was a nurse, I thought. For Christ's sake. She knew what was real in skin and bowels and bone. She knew how finally none of it was only pretty or nice. Fanny would shake her head.

I was walking again. I was holding the Mag-Lite high because I didn't care who saw me. The worst I had to worry about was Clarence Smith. He was only a dopehead and maybe a speed freak and possibly a murderer. That didn't seem like much to contend with. I also needed to be concerned about his dog. It was closer to a couple of hundred pounds of very wide jaw than anything I needed to meet. But neither of them had me too terribly worried. The worst that they could do was the worst Georgia could have done. Kill me, I thought. Kill me.

I came to the little bluff overlooking Smith's farm. The moon was breaking through the cloud cover. I turned off the flashlight and stuck it through my belt like a truncheon. I went slowly because it was a steep descent. But you couldn't say I was quiet or careful. I'd have driven directly into his barnyard if I could have found the rows of crop I wanted to inspect. I had seen them from the hillside so I approached them from there. I remembered how the cornstalks got smaller and smaller and more withered-looking. There was something wrong with the soil there in the middle of all that loam. Something interfered with the nutrients coming up into the crop. It was Tyler Pearl. I would have bet on it. From what I'd heard he would have bet on it too. I had carried a picture of the crop line in my head. I had seen it over and over but I hadn't named it to myself. The field was like a television set that runs in a bar. You look at your beer or you talk to the bartender and all the time the TV's running. Something on it gets stuck in your head but you don't think of it. Then something brings it back and you realize what you saw. That was how I had finally noticed the line of corn plants that never went into healthy growth. I might have been seeing Tyler Pearl, I thought. I could see Smith running with sweat and talking his private language while he dug the kid's grave. I wondered whether Georgia would be able to get it down on the page so you could believe you were hearing a tall, handsome, very youthful man who was scared into being gentle even when he was armed with an axe handle and a huge guard dog. I hadn't brought the Taurus this time. I knew I couldn't kill another dog. I wondered if I could kill a man. I knew how to do it and I thought that maybe I could.

Most of the corn was tall. It was August and the soil Smith worked was good. The cornstalks made a hushing, scratchy noise when I shoved them out of the way with the haft of the shovel. It didn't take me long because he had wanted the planting to reach a good distance from the house out toward the hillside I'd climbed down. It was a giant disguise. I was standing at the far western edge of his field now. I was breathing hard and thinking of a different cornfield in a different town at a different time of the year.

I was wishing I'd brought water along when the rustling east of me began. It moved toward me from the farm. Then it stopped. Then it moved toward me. I inched my hands down the shovel so I could use it quickly if I had to. The rustling got faster and louder. He burst through the row and wheeled. His hind end shook more stalks and his head whipped a trail of slobber when he tried to plant himself. His head came back. Drool slopped down. He stared along his muzzle at me.

"Remember?" I said. I reached into my soggy pocket for the paper towel that was greasy with squashed meatloaf. I held it out. "Sure," I said, keeping it low and casual. "That's the boy. Sure."

He wagged his tail. He didn't have doubts. He wasn't trained to guard. I understood that fast enough. I said, "Do you know how to sit?" I looked him hard in the eye. "Sit," I said.

He slammed his rump down.

He wasn't trained to be anything but a pet. His job wasn't to patrol. His job was to look like a Kodiak bear. Smith counted on size making up for the dog's lack of meanness. Clarence Smith was finally as half-assed about security as anything else. So somebody must have trained him how to act like a legitimate farmer while growing hemp. I didn't care about whoever that was. I cared about what might be in the ground here.

"There you go," I told the dog. "This is for being no damned good at it." I handed the meat loaf over and he made it disappear. "Good for getting the hell out of my way," I said. I wanted to get on with the job. He sat watching me until he got bored. Then he went off. Then he came back. He remembered that I was the source of the meat. He lay on top of low cornstalks and he watched me work. Looking down from the bluff that overlooked Smith's farm I had seen the broad puddle of earth where corn hadn't taken or had taken and then stopped growing. I stood in what I guessed was the center of the bare patch. The dog watched me. When I started to dig he rearranged himself in sections and waited to see. I pressed with my boot against back of the blade on the right-hand side of the shovel. It was stony soil there and I hit some rocks. But he had harrowed it well enough. It was friable earth. I got through. I made myself move carefully. Everything I did here felt important and I wanted to do it right.

I deposited the dirt to the left of the section I was working on. I dug where the corn hadn't grown. The dog was lying maybe seven feet away where the corn came up no more than six or eight inches high. I got into a rhythm and I tried to not think of why I was digging. I stooped and pushed with my foot and leaned back to swivel the blade and lift out and turn and toss. I got a foot down in a decent-sized square. I found nothing. I went down six or seven inches more. I wished I had brought some water but I didn't stop. I was running with sweat. I thought I reminded myself of Smith. That was pure lying. The sweat I saw slicked on my forearms and hands in the green moonlight reminded me of Georgia Bromell in bed with me.

The dog gave up on entertainment and got himself stretched out full length on his other side. I would give it another foot. Then I'd move to a different part of the bare patch.

I sweated enough for my hand to slip on the shovel haft. I was thinking of the cold. I was thinking of the little girl curled under the earth somewhere and none of us able to get to her. I thought of her mother with the blanket around her who sat beside the fire and watched us. The dog watched and so did Fanny. I thought of all of us at work in the cornfield. It didn't get us the result. We wanted the child back. But I still thought it was probably the best work I'd done. It was the last time that I'd felt a good deal more than on my own.

I stood and panted and looked at the sleeping dog. "Okay," I said. "Now you need to move. Move, big dog. Hey!" He lifted his head and put it down with a groan. I said, "Now, please." He looked at my finger and my arm and he looked at my face and then he dragged himself off the withered low stalks and almost stood before he dived for the ground and groaned again. He looked at me. He shuffled his tail in the cornstalks. He set his head on the ground and went to sleep. I started another hole. I didn't fill in the first one.

I found a rhythm again and the second mound grew. Sometimes the clouds screened the moon away. But I knew where to dig. I could have done it with my eyes closed. Maybe I did. I didn't go three feet deep but I got down there far enough to sense if I was close to the body. I knew that I wasn't.

I left the dirt mound. I woke the dog and drove him back a little by pointing and saying nonsense commands that seemed to make sense to him. Move. Get. Hey. Let's go. Go on. He was deeper in the field and so was I. The last of the bare patch was under my feet when I started the third hole. The dog slept. The cloud banks moved in front of the moon and then away. The light looked green whenever the moon stayed bright. I dug by the light and I dug in the dark. I told myself I could take a break pretty soon but keep digging. I didn't listen to myself. I stopped.

I told myself to get back on the job. This time I listened. I pushed and levered and tossed. I thought about Janice Tanner in the ground. I thought about my daughter who wasn't. I thought about Georgia's body slick with sweat in a dark room but with enough light to see the sweat gleaming.

This is what you wanted to do, I thought. This is what you wanted to do.

I dug for maybe twenty minutes more. I toed it in and swiveled back and lifted and tossed and I kept doing it. I could feel him underneath. I kept working and the blade touched something that was hard and also soft. I heard myself make the sound you make when someone hits you by surprise.

But this is what you wanted.

It was the feeling I expected and never got with Janice Tanner or anyone else in any other situation. The body yielded to the shovel blade but also resisted it. The body was what I expected. But it was also nothing I ever felt before.

They'd buried him maybe three feet deep. I thought it was a little less. I dug around it. I didn't want to stand hard on the back of the shovel and stab the dead body. I surrounded him with a trench. Then I worked in. I could see the blue or green plastic tarpaulin in the moonlight that changed the colors of the cornstalks and the earth around Tyler Pearl. I got down onto my knees to work on the soil that covered him. The dog came over when I did that. I could hear him panting behind me. I worked on my knees with the shovel gripped near the blade. I scraped more than I dug. It took me a long time to get all of the tarp exposed.

Either they cut him in half or folded him. It was a small package for a man in his twenties. They had laced him in using white venetian blind cord running through the metal grommets of the tarp. I reached into my jeans for my pocket knife. I hadn't brought it. Wasn't I some Boy Scout. I sawed with the blade of the shovel to sever the cord but it was too dull.

"All you need is the right tools," I told the dog. "Unfortunately, all we have is us."

I stayed on my knees and tried to move the package but I couldn't. I got up leaning on the shovel haft because my knees were sore. Now that I had more leverage I could turn him over. I found the knots. They didn't look like professional knots. They looked like amateurs making a mess. I got back down on my knees and leaned my forearms on the tarp while I worked at the untying. My hands shook a little from digging. I tried to see Smith shaking while he tied these knots. I tried to see Georgia working on them.

She *might* be innocent, I thought.

"Whatever she is has nothing to do with that particular word," I told the dog. He was close behind me now. I could smell his breath. It smelled like a healthy dog's fresh turds. "This will not be meat loaf," I said.

I picked at the knot and I found the part to work on and I began to unwrap Merle Davidoff's nephew. When I had the cord unlaced and I was stooping over him to get him turned, a night bird called. It was a series of short peeps. It did that five or six times and then I didn't hear it again for the rest of the time I was there. I moved fast to keep myself from freezing with fear of what I'd find. I got him unwrapped. He was terrible. He was on his side with his knees drawn up. The body began to relax but it didn't straighten all the way. I stood and used my foot to push his shoulders back. He sighed. I figured it was trapped air coming out. I hoped that's all it was. I leaned close in case there was anything more to hear. Of course there wasn't. I should have known.

At first I smelled mostly damp earth and the chemical smell of the plastic tarp. You could see these bright blue and bright green tarpaulins all over the county. Farmers covered woodpiles with them to weather for a season. They stretched them over trucks filled with trash when they drove to the dump. Along with the shiny white or black hay roll covers they were some of the plastic junk that would never dissolve even after the farmers and their farms had rotted away. The plastic had kept the body from corrupting quickly but the stink of decomposing meat still came up from Tyler Pearl. Every second made it worse. He stayed bent. He looked like somebody folded over to sleep or pray. I thought that would be a good idea. Somebody ought to pray. But I was no good at that.

A few white things crawled on his face and in his nose and eyes. Some beetles ran back and forth. I couldn't tell if the bugs had been inside his body or if I had just let them in. The tight wrapping in plastic must have helped to preserve him. The field was elevated so the air would be drier. That must also have helped to keep him from rotting away. I remembered his haircut in the photograph Merle had given me. As usual on the corpse it looked like it was growing out. I knew it was the skin shrinking back.

I made myself breathe in what I'd found. He'd gone rotten in slow motion. But there was plenty to smell. I told myself this was what I'd been after. How could you have thought you'd make something good out of this? Take a whiff.

His jaws were apart. I wondered if there were creatures alive in his mouth. I pulled out the light and turned it on. I couldn't see anything. I couldn't see his tongue. I wondered if Clarence Smith and his friends had cut it off. If they were hurting him Tyler Pearl might have bitten it off. But I couldn't see Clarence working up the fury for that. Of course, methamphetamine was a miracle drug. It could take whatever was crazy inside you and get it to swallow you up. When you did meth it was the meth in charge.

He'd been corrupting very slowly. I thought they must have buried him in May. There was the marijuana. There was the camouflage feed corn. There was this. Tyler Pearl was also their crop. Soon they'd have been cutting down the corn and grinding it. Maybe they sold it to area farmers for silage. Tyler Pearl would have stayed here on his side with his knees drawn up. His skin would have gone darker brown and then dark blue and gray and plenty swollen. Crawling things would have eaten more and more of him and he would have started turning into the cornfield. Now the skin was a little like brown leather. I didn't want to touch it. I kept the

Mag-Lite close. He did look like his original self if you could get past the snarl and the torn lips and the eyes that looked like the eyes of a bass before somebody baked it. I supposed they would check dental records and see if there was any viable DNA. I didn't think he'd been formally arrested. Probably his fingerprints wouldn't be on file. Now that he was partly uncurled I could tell that his hands were together in what used to be his lap.

I pulled the arm. Under the sleeve of his shirt it felt like wood gone pulpy. It moved when I tugged it. The right hand was made of a whole thumb but not much in the way of fingers above the knuckle joints on the other digits. It was a very clean cut. They hadn't sawed them off, anyway. At least they worked fast. They used something like a big butcher's knife. And any farm would have an axe. I considered that an axe might crush the edges of the stumps but I couldn't tell if that had happened. His mouth was open. Maybe he screamed when they cut off the fingers. Maybe they did them separately but it looked like they might have cut them all at once. That could have been a small mercy. Shock would have rolled into him and then maybe unconsciousness if the kid had any luck.

They must have been trying to find if he'd given them up. It was possible that when Merle asked some upstate people some questions there were people higher in the chain of command who got worried. In planting season they doubted him and tested him and decided that he failed the test. So they planted him in his cornfield where he'd probably have stayed for as long as Janice Tanner would stay in hers. Even in a dead scream of teeth showing through rotten lips it did look like Tyler Pearl's disappointed mouth.

I couldn't see what killed him. It could have been bleeding from the fingers. Maybe they also shot him or stabbed him. The field-colored shirt was stained and maybe with blood but that could have come from the hand. It didn't matter. He was somebody's kid. Then he was nobody's kid. He lived stupidly the way so many people did. And then the world ate him. I turned off the flashlight. I threw the dirt from the mound back over him after I rewrapped him without using the cord. I wanted to keep creatures off him. That included hungry house animals disguised as watchdogs. I left the shovel with its blade stuck in the ground as a kind of marker. I stood above him and thought about kids gone missing and kids gone dead.

It was about their being lost, I thought. It was about their not being lost anymore.

Then I walked along the side of the cornfield with the big wet dog because I wanted a look at the barn. All those years of law work made me want to know some of the details whether I needed to know them or not. The house was dark. I walked past it to the barn. I didn't care who I woke up. I didn't much care what they did about it. When I slid the big door to the side and walked through I found the glow of dozens and dozens of high-powered ultraviolet grow lights in aluminum racks over the high, shining aluminum tanks. A very loud aerator was working and the whole place gurgled. Big spiky plants moved in the currents of air I'd set going and I thought it looked like a leggy crop. My nose itched. I wanted to sneeze. I thought that was all my imagination. It was a very large and very expensive operation with plenty of pipework and tanks so big they could have set Tyler Pearl bobbing through the product for years. I wondered how that would have affected the strength of the plants when they were harvested and dried.

This process would of course go on before someone like Georgia Bromell carried the grass in packets inside shopping bags to storage units for the wholesale customers to retrieve and franchise out to their retailers. All you needed was an extra key to a storage unit in every city you supplied. She had to be doing it to learn the whole story. I couldn't imagine her enough in love with anyone to work as a mule for marijuana. She didn't need the work. Her father financed her. Look at the car and look at the clothes and the leather of her handbag. Look at the leathery skin of Tyler Pearl. But she did want the story. She could write her book or her articles and she could own the life she wanted, including direct imaginary flights from Vienna, New York, to Paris, France.

I thought I heard noises at the house. I didn't care.

I walked slowly through the big barn and looked at every stack of PVC and every carton of plumbing parts. They had garden carts and contractor's wheelbarrows. They had an all-terrain vehicle. They had a short chain saw and a longer one. They had two axes on the wall plus a wood-splitting maul and a long implement with a blade that was wider at the end than under its fiberglass handle. It was some kind of machete. Its blade looked sharp. Someone kept it clean.

When no one showed up I left the barn. During my inspection I had found an electrical panel. It seemed properly installed but no more than half of the circuit breakers were labeled. I thought it was best to pull them all. I cut the power to everything. The aerator stopped gurgling. The water pumps shut down. The grow lights went off.

I patted the dog. He had managed to get the top of his head wet with slobber. I told him, "Stay." He cocked his head and considered. Then he sat. I didn't think he was charming or attractive just because he was somebody's dog. What I had left behind down South was as much of anyone as I had ever known. Smith's noisy, damp dog did not sit for long. He followed me partway to the field

behind the house. Nobody came out of it. Then the dog forgot
what he was doing and stood to watch me go. I went past the rows
of corn and the dirt mounds and the shape in the field and the
shovel that I'd left standing on its blade. I figured Georgia would
have known something to say for the occasion. I knew I didn't.

I went under the spruce trees and came out near the truck. The
sun was coming up. I thought about Lily Stovich's meat loaf. I
sniffed my fingers but I didn't smell pâté. I smelled corpse. I sat in
the truck with the windows down and thought about dead people.
I thought about the little bear doll I'd found in the house and
washed in the kitchen sink and hung outside to dry. I thought
about other dolls in an infant's bedroom and how I found them
upstairs when I returned to the house from working a late shift at
school. It had been a night of freezing rain that was followed by
snow, and the roads on the steep, hilly campus had been treacher-
ous. We'd pulled some kids out of a Volvo that had slammed into a
very old VW camper bus abandoned at the bottom of the campus.
The Volvo hadn't buckled and its frame saved their lives.

The driver said, "My father's gonna kill me."

I'd told him, "He'll be happy you're all right. You were going too
fast for the condition of the road, but he'll know to expect that.
Right? Because he probably knows you're enough of a child to
believe you can go too fast and nothing can ever happen to you?"

He was a burly boy in a leather jacket with a fleece collar and
matching gloves. He was blue-white. I made him sit on the running board of my Jeep. The kid who was hurt had been transported
to the hospital a few blocks away.

"Child?" he said.

"It's okay to be one. Okay to act like one. Disadvantages of doing
so include having to put up with people like me who pull you out

of the wreck." I was blowing on my fingers every few seconds as I took details for my report. I really envied him the fleece-lined gloves.

Hours before that I had helped the college chaplain get her antique Nissan started. I'd responded to a fire alarm at a dormitory. I would respond to an alarm at the same place four times during that evening and night. I made sure there wasn't a fifth by selecting a satisfied-looking kid with a stubby nose wearing a sweat suit. His whiskers seemed more like a smear of marmalade than hair. He was chewing a piece of pizza and watching me check the kitchen when I suddenly wheeled on him and took hold of his sweatshirt where it said CHOATE and pulled him into me.

"You can't do that," one of his friends said. "Can you?"

I said, "Yes."

Sitting in the truck, I remembered how it was when I got the swaying old station wagon home on our country road and came inside to find the dog sitting at the foot of the stairs. That meant Fanny had gone up but he knew his duties included waiting for me to come home. He stayed halfway between the door I'd walk through and the staircase she'd climbed. He seemed very relieved to walk over and lay his big head against my thigh. I scratched his ears. He paused at the foot of the stairs like he was aiming himself. Then he headed up.

I followed and he led me not to our bedroom but to the baby's room. Fanny was sitting on the floor with her back to the wall beside the window that looked over the road. Her legs were stretched out in front of her. She was asleep and our baby was asleep against her chest under a thick maroon wool blanket. They were lit by a small cribside lamp. In the orange light Fanny's chest-nut-colored hair glowed and so did her skin. She didn't look as exhausted as she had for weeks. They both looked better though their sleeping this way meant that the baby had raged and raged against sleep or against something inside her or something we carried inside us. I sat in the rocker. The dog went over to sniff them. He wagged his tail a couple of times and then lay down with his muzzle almost touching Fanny's feet in their gray wool socks. I let my legs spread and wedged my arms inside the rocker arms so that I wouldn't have to hold any muscles taut. I closed my eyes. I opened them to see everyone sleeping while it snowed outside and then I stopped fighting. I knew that when I woke it all would be different. But I was happy to have them there like that while I could.

But now I was in my truck on Kramers Barn Road wishing I knew what to think about what I had seen in Smith's cornfield. I wished I knew how to think about what it was I had wanted to do for so long and then what I finally did. I should have felt more. I should have felt something sizable, I thought.

MICHAEL WAS ASLEEP across three of the brown plastic chairs in the waiting room. He looked like a baby with his mouth open and all the frown lines on his forehead and mouth and at the corners of his eyes relaxed. His hands were tucked between his legs while he slept on his side. That reminded me of Tyler Pearl. A fat Caucasian man in faded jeans, a clean white T-shirt, and dirty barn boots sat across the room and watched Michael sleep. He was studying him the way you'd look at a peacock or a Siberian tiger in a zoo. Next to the man there was someone also wearing dirty barn boots but with a filthy T-shirt that said NO FEAR. He was half a foot and fifty pounds smaller but round enough. It had to be the big man's son. He looked adult but with a mind that was arrested very young. They had the same delicate nose and small, gray eyes and straw-colored hair. Their skin looked like the porcelain you might find on an antique doll.

Sarah came from the Intensive Care Ward. She looked like she'd lost ten pounds. I should have been thinking about her meals. I hugged her and kissed her cheek.

"Elway," I said to her.

"You ever play chess, Jack?"

"He tried to teach me. I wasn't very good. I reacted too fast."

"Well, it's what he would call the endgame."

"I know what that is."

"I do too."

I was almost overwhelmed by my selfishness. I'd caught myself thinking that it was like a family with us. And all the time their child who was the proof of family was sleeping on plastic chairs with his mouth opened wide to the world.

"I need to see him, Sarah."

"They'll let you. They did what they can do. They're waiting, is all. Just the same as we are."

"Can he talk to me?"

She shrugged. Her eyes were covered with tears that seemed to stay in place. I couldn't see their stains on her tan cheeks. "Give him a try," she said.

I pulled her to me and hugged her with my arms across her back. She nodded against my shoulder and I let her go.

"Might as well try," she said.

So I went in through the swinging doors with the smeared port-hole window and past the nurses' station. I didn't see anyone I knew. Looking at them again I thought that any one of them might have been on duty in the hospital to the north when I got the sui-

cidal student in on time and our baby in too late. It was a hot night
and the ward felt airless. I had buttoned my shirt at the throat to
cover the fingerprints I'd seen in the rearview mirror of the truck. I
probably stank with the fever sweat of our sex and then from my
climb up to Smith's and the digging. I waved hello and one of the
nurses stared back.

Sitting in the chair beside his bed I watched him sleep, if that
was the name for what a dying man did with his eyes closed.

"Elway," I said. His fingers were still at the edge of the sheet
folded over his cotton blanket. His bedside lamp was on. The
machine that recorded his vital signs was working. He breathed
very shallowly. The intravenous feed dripped.

I believe that I said, "I never told you the truth about what happened before we looked for Janice Tanner. Before Fanny and I split
up for good. You knew she went upstate to nurse and drink and
begin to remember. You knew I went in the other direction. You
knew I asked you to come to us when our baby died. But you don't
know the rest. I didn't tell you what I knew because I couldn't. I
always thought you may have pretty much suspected it." I folded
my hands on the edge of his bed and I couldn't tell you under
penalty of death whether I talked out loud or only in my thoughts.
But I know that I had gone there determined to say it all to him.

"I couldn't," I said or thought I said. "Fanny didn't know. She did
it and she didn't know. She was a gentle, decent woman with a little bit of monster in her. She was like most of the rest of us. She
worked late shifts, she handled the shit you have to stand up to in
hospitals. Boy with his arm torn off by a combine. Men fat with
butter and potatoes and greasy, bad meat who throw a stroke in
their forties. And then the screaming wife and their little kids. She
saw children who were tortured by their parents. They burned

them up and down their backs and arms. Little *babies.*"

I thought I was beginning to sound just a little like an opera though I'd never listened to all of one. "Of course that's what you saw on every shift. She got the tail end of the traffic dismember-ments that you saw a half hour earlier, didn't she? You worked the same patrol in a manner of speaking."

I said, "A manner of speaking."

I said, "So maybe you knew all along?"

I said, "She was crazy, and she shook the baby we'd waited so long to have. She used to say it was her doing all the work of it. I was just humping away in the bed. You know we did wait a long time to have one."

I said, "It was fury. I saw it in her face. I heard it when she screeched at the baby or the room or the house or maybe me. 'Would you just be *still!*' I heard the screaming. I heard the quiet after it. I ran upstairs because I knew to. She was looking at me out of these eyes. They were like a doll's eyes. Glass eyes. Eyes sewed onto the face. She was holding her out to me. Her little head was flopped back on her neck. I could see how soft her neck was."

I said, "I knew what to do. It didn't work. I knew it wouldn't. But I breathed all my breath into her. I pushed her chest up and down until I knew to leave off. Then I knew who to call. I called you and then the others. Nobody caught it. Maybe nobody even speculated on it. Why would you? The hardworking campus cop. The nice rural nurse."

I said, "Then there was the grieving. It went deeper than words. I never found them. I guess I never thought they could do the job. We didn't talk enough about it. A doctor told me, a psychologist on campus. You knew Archie. Fanny told me. Shit, Elway, you and Sarah told me too. All of you said it: Talk. But it was the secret. It was on account of the secret. I never could tell her. If I told her what really happened, what she did—"

He didn't move. I suppose I wanted him to wake up and turn those small, tough eyes on me the way your old man does when he knows he ought to kick your ass. You think maybe he will. But you know he might also calculate a way to bail you out. It sounded like he panted to himself. It sounded like a kind of chuckle. His chest didn't seem to move but the monitor said he was alive. I heard the little laughing sound of his breath.

I said, "Because Fanny couldn't remember. I didn't want her to. She was in hell. But I knew, I imagined, the kind of hell she'd be in if she remembered. If she knew about our child. What she did."

I said, "If she remembered what she did."

I said, "She left me because I couldn't talk to her. She didn't say that. I know it was why she left. She thought I was sealing her out."

I said, "It was me. It was in."

I said, "I didn't want her to know. And I knew. So I sealed me in."

I said, "I'm sorry that I never could tell her. I'm sorry I never told you. I was afraid of what she would do."

I put my head down on my hands. Then I lifted it up in case he was looking at me. He wasn't. I sat there and my chin went down to my chest. I closed my eyes. I had my hands on the edge of Elway's bed. I was listening to the click of the machine and the sound of his little breaths.

I said, "The one time I called you up, it was the night I let myself miss the people I had left. You circled around the story and then you did what you always do. You talked straight. You said she drank the most of seven hundred and fifty centiliters, that is one entire bottle, of Powers Irish whiskey. She'd used her key for the drug cabinet and she swallowed a very large number, they said, of Percodan tablets. She went outside and she went straight into the heart of it. That was a night of blizzard conditions. You said that county services responded all night to cars off the road, multiple-vehicle accidents due to skids and pileups. It might have been magnolias and peaches and sweaty brows down where I was, you said, but up North you were deep in the deep white shit. I wouldn't know if I ever saw a magnolia down South. She drove out of town. You didn't know where in hell she thought she was headed for from Waterville. You said maybe it was old Navy Point at Sackets Harbor. Maybe she thought she would drive into the Black River Bay off the point. But she ended up on the wildlife management land. She just drove into deeper and deeper snow. She stopped. She finished the bottle of Powers out there. Then she took the Percodan and you said they also found diazepam in her purse. She probably took some of them for dessert. She must have kicked the door open against the snow that heaped around the car. She got herself out and took the urn for a walk in the snow. It was open when they found her. She was holding it.

"'I can see her pushing the door open against the snow. Fanny was powerful. Even though she must have been so tired,' I said to you on the phone that night.

"So it was you, Elway. You had to tell me she was dead. I'd got a little happy on sour mash and telephoned from my efficiency. You said what happened and I said that somebody should have called me.

"'And you'd have rescued her?' you said.

"'I would have tried.'

"'But you're the man without a phone number, Jack. You're the man that no one can find.'"

I leaned into it the way you might lean back against the strong hands of someone who kneaded your shoulder muscles if you could let yourself let them do it.

I said, "And then she died."

I heard Elway panting shallow and fast. And then she died. Almost a year and a half ago, she died.

I said, "It had to be because she remembered."

I said, "Fanny remembered. If she was going to remember, I could have *been* there with her. She could have *stayed* with me. If I knew she would remember. That way, we wouldn't have wasted us."

I leaned back into it.

I said, "Poor Fanny."

He panted and the machine clicked.

I said, "Poor Fanny and our girl."

I leaned back. The panting stopped. Then it started again. I called, "Sarah!"

She'd been standing behind me. Her hands on my neck muscles dug in hard and I winced and fell forward toward the bed.

The panting stopped.

Her hands came off me and we called his name.

WORK

I STAYED WITH THEM awhile but I felt worse than not necessary. I didn't want them to have to think about me. Or maybe I did. But I left Michael and Sarah and what was left to them of Elway and I drove back to the house. Georgia's Mustang wasn't out front. I walked around back to see if she'd parked it there. I thought of her thumbs pressing in. I thought about Tyler Pearl's right hand. I thought that Georgia would be on her way. But there was enough time for coffee. I put the water on the burner and thought of her waking up and seeing me gone and driving over to the farm. They'd see I'd sabotaged their crop. Someone would find the shovel and the mound if they inspected their perimeter.

I checked the clip and slid the safety on and stood the carbine next to the front door. I poured the boiling water through the filter and looked over my shoulder at the weapon. It looked too much like I was worried. I hung it back on its nails on top of the doorway. Then I checked the loads in the .32 and carried the piece around in the kitchen while the coffee dripped. I felt like a goddamned fool in a cowboy movie so I put the pistol away in the drawer. I compromised by leaving the drawer open. I couldn't remember ever seeing Elway Bird with a weapon in his hand.

I had the coffee mug up in some kind of salute to him but I stopped myself. How many ways had I betrayed him? The idea carried over too well to Fanny and our child and to Sarah and other people who had cared about me. I thought about Merle. I owed her a phone call. I'd owed one for days but now I had the news she had sent me after and I should have called. But I sat in the rented kitchen in the smell of coffee and my own sweat and Tyler Pearl's grave. I was waiting for what Georgia would say was the rest of the story.

A cup and a half later it came up my driveway. She wasn't out of control but she pushed some gravel around when she braked behind my truck. She didn't take her keys or shut her door and I could hear the Mustang's warning chime ring steadily. I wondered if you could drain your battery out that way. When she hit the first porch step she slammed hard. She was lighter on the next and then she stood silently in front of the door. I imagined her gathering all those long muscles.

The door opened in gently and she called, "Jack?"

"Come on in, Georgia."

She shut the door behind her and stood. How it played out would start right there and we both waited to see. She wore the sunglasses. She had showered and changed. There was dampness on her short salt-and-pepper hair. She was wearing faded jeans and a white short-sleeved T-shirt and glossy black lace-ups that looked to me like bowling shoes. They were streaked with what I imagined was grave dirt.

She smiled. It was a very tense smile that went away fast. She said, "You're the kind of cop I thought you'd be. A lot less secure, I guess. But you're a stone. You're like some old boulder on a hill. You just roll down it, and roll down it, don't you? You keep on rolling down and then you're there."

I said, "No. That's gravity. Nobody really fights it. Someday you'll be old. Someday your body will droop. It won't be your doing but there you'll be. Gravity. Same thing with cops catching up with you. It just happens because that's mostly the law of things. Cops aren't smart but the system they're in is a little smart. And the bad guys are very often dumber than hell. This was no Albert Einstein deal you were in with Smith."

She said, "His brain's shot. He's ninety percent synthetic chemical."

"You might be in jail when the muscles do go. You can testify against Smith and whoever else worked it. There's some bargaining you could do. But I think we're talking narcotics charges that go maybe ten to twenty years for the feds and maybe fifteen for the state. And then it's capital murder for Tyler Pearl. You bought the big-ticket item, Georgia. Is that a part of the story? You moved in as Smith's girlfriend. You ran his deliveries for him. Maybe you helped him kill off Tyler Pearl. All so you could get the wonderful story and write it all up and sell it to some newspaper? Run it in your old man's newspaper? Jesus Christ. Could you write it in a cell? Would they let you?"

I knew she'd come at me with one of two items. She said, "You wanted me, though. I mean in bed."

"It was work."

She smiled like we were very good friends. She shook her head. "No. Not and whimper the way you did. Not and do the things we did that way. This isn't to flatter me or anything, but let's get honest, Jack. You loved all that."

I said, "You did play me." I had my hand at my throat and I saw her watch me rub at the bruises she had made.

"While you were conning me? Is that what you're saying? You got undercover with me? You were after my story while I was after yours?"

I sipped the last cold coffee in the cup.

She took her cigarettes and matchbox out. She said, "I had your ass, Jack. I did have it."

I couldn't help the sigh I gave. I said, "Well, you did. You kicked over the anthill. You saw the ants."

She scratched the match along the box and we watched it flare. She lit the joint and sucked in the smoke. She nodded and held. Then she let some out and said, "I saw those little guys running in every damned direction, Jack."

She smiled happily. She took in more smoke. We didn't talk. You might have thought we were a couple of lovers who met up a few years after the love and we were having a chat. After another minute, she said, "There were other ways you could have investigated me."

"If I'd been smarter."

"You're smart enough. The cops don't have to fuck with the outlaws."

"Is that how you see yourself? You're an outlaw? You're what's her name. Bonnie? Like Bonnie and Clyde?"

"No way," she said. "Unless I get to be Clyde. Come on, Jack. You could have brought me down without . . ." She waved her hand at the wall behind me with the mattress on its other side. "You found me a little bit necessary, I would say."

I said, "You carry a cellular phone, I'll bet."

"You won't face it, will you? The truth of what happened with us?"

"Here's the deal," I said. "I have to call the sheriff's department. I'm committing a crime if I don't. I have to tell them about the rig up there in Smith's barn and the kid you helped him put out in the cornfield. You did some of that, right? Then I have to call New York. It's embarrassing but I wonder if I could borrow your phone."

Smith kicked in the door. It came up and off the hinges and fell down in front of him. He was very powerfully out of his mind. His skin was red and he looked like someone had turned a hose on him. It looked like he was wearing someone else's eyes. He was standing on the wooden door with his chest heaving. He held the machete in front of him like we were dueling in an old movie.

He said, "Aha."

"Take it easy," I said. "We need to get calm here, Clarence."

"Arm yourself, varlet, and aha," he said. He was talking low, breathing hard, trembling. "Hello, girlfriend," he said to Georgia.

She said, "Oh, boy."

"Clarence," I said, "you probably still feel bad about Tyler Pearl. You cut him up something terrible."

He shook his head very hard. "Appropriate justice," he said. "With probity and scale weights for all."

"Clarence, you cut the poor kid's hand almost off. Did he bleed out? Can you imagine dying of a *hand* wound? We don't want anyone else getting hurt. Am I right?"

He straightened. "We're keeping it calm," he said, "and we want the brain waves level. You furrow your forehead, you understand, and the microwaves settle into the wrinkles up there. Making your complexion rough and red. With the resulting red sky at night, sailors all over the place taking fright, and nobody left to man the mast." He walked over to the stove and took the carafe of coffee off the burner that heated it. He set it to his lips and drank like the carafe was a cup. It had to be scalding hot. He tilted his face up and gargled it.

I said, "Am I right, Clarence?"

He spat the coffee out and shoved the carafe at the stove. It fell onto the floor and shattered. He squared himself to look at me. Coffee ran down his sweat-slicked chin and dripped onto his orange Syracuse basketball shirt. I was staring at the blade. I was thinking of Tyler Pearl.

That made me stupid and slow. I thought Georgia was dangerous to me in other ways. So I didn't watch her walk back around me
toward the door while I turned to face Smith at the stove. I heard
the door shift on the knob that propped it up. Before I could turn
to stop her the strap brackets clattered as she seized it and clicked
the safety off.

Now that she had the carbine I needed to see them both. I
moved while giving my imitation of casual. I went slowly to the
table and hoisted myself up on top of it. I let my legs dangle and I
checked the setup.

Smith still stood with his back to the stove. He held the machete
and he shook. Georgia was facing him. She had the carbine at
something like port arms. She looked very confident with it.

"I can bring it up and aim it and fire it off," she said, "before anybody gets halfway over here to me. Daddy and I hunted with thirty-
oughts every deer season from my twelfth through to my
never-you-mind year. Now, I am about to perform a citizen's arrest.
Well. Actually, it has to be a citizen's self-defense. Jack," she said.
"Reach for my purse on the table and take out three items. You
ready?"

"Steady and slow, Georgia," I said. "I won't rush you. I won't try."

"Jack," she said, "you're talking to me like I'm crazy. I'm dangerous, but I'm not crazy. You should know that by now."

I tried to smile.

"I don't like that smile," she said. "I like the other one. But
get the purse, please. Get my cigarettes and matches and light
me one."

"What kind?"

"Oh. Well, it's a temptation. But I think maybe just the store-
bought kind, please. Steady, right? Slow?"

I got it lit. I started coughing and she smiled like I was telling a joke.

"Lay it on the floor halfway over to me and then walk back to the table."

I did it. She squatted to pick it up. I stayed where I was.

"Kabuki," Smith said. "Ritual dances. Tricksters are flitting and the night air thickens."

"That's my boy Clarence," she said. "He is chemical plumb through the cartilage and down every bone. Right, bone boy?" The cigarette was in her mouth. It moved when she squinted through the smoke and said, "Now get the phone from my bag, Jack, please. Same little trick. Halfway over, floor, and so forth."

"Are you cleared for long distance?" Smith asked her.

She punched numbers with her left thumb. She held the carbine barrel back against her right shoulder with her right hand. She waited, then she said in a high voice, "Sheriff? Sheriff's department? Oh! Please help me? Listen! A man here tried to kill me with a knife! Some big kind of big knife! Jesus God! I shot him! Forgive me, Jesus, but I had to shoot him to keep him away! He busted in the door! He's—he was—he—" She looked up and raised her brows and smiled at me. She nodded while the dispatcher said what they're trained to say. Then she answered, "What? What? Yes. Oh! Yes. I'm at the house halfway down on the little road off of the road off of Route 12 South. It's—"

I was going remind her of its name but the dispatcher must have supplied one.

"No," she said, "no. Uhm. The unpaved road off of Albert Kelley Road? And Albert Kelley's off of . . . I—" She turned off the phone and dropped it to the floor. She took a long drag of smoke. Blowing it out she said, "Now, Jack, *that's* creative. I didn't shoot anyone yet, but I will. So everything I made up comes true. Understand?" Her smile was broad and her face was shining. "Then you and I have come to terms."

Smith was standing politely while she described his death. I wondered why and then I realized that he knew her a lot better than I did. So maybe she'd been describing *me* shot dead, I thought, and maybe he knew it.

"Georgia," I said, "let *him* take the heat for Tyler Pearl. Work your way out of it. Don't try and kill your way out. Don't get the state needle for this. Actually they use two needles."

She said, "You already had me strapped in for it for cutting Tyler's fingers off. All of a sudden you're my legal and spiritual counsel, Jack. You do get a girl confused."

"Damn it." I didn't mean to say that.

She looked at me. I heard the warning chime of the Mustang.

"I talked about his hand. I never said fingers. But you knew fingers, all right." I asked Smith, "Did I say fingers?"

"You said, "Po-taht-o, man. *She* said po-tay-to.""

"Georgia," I said. "You were describing *me* on the phone?" I saw myself face down on the floor with a magazine load of .30-caliber military ball inside my belly and chest. I said, "Well. Well, why in hell not?"

I slid off the table and stood. I checked on Clarence's distance from me. I moved in front of Georgia.

I said again, "Why not?"

She said, "No!"

I said, "Oh, yeah. Oh, absolutely. I mean, *why* not? On account, Georgia, of my absolutely flat-out not giving a good fucking goddamn. That's the why and that's the not." She tossed her cigarette at me and brought her left hand up to the carbine. She'd learned the rules on those girlhood hunting trips. You take a sideways stance with your legs apart and the right elbow cocked ninety degrees from your ribs and you never, ever fire except from a solid shooting position. She raised it to her shoulder instead of firing from the hip. I think that's the move that made the difference of a second or so. It was what I needed.

I got to her and slammed at the muzzle with my left hand. It went off almost in my palm and burned me. I kept moving. I clubbed at her face with my right forearm. But she was also trained as a dancer. She was a good athlete and she rocked back instead of ducking. Ducking would have brought her into the blow. I missed her and fell onto her. She kept her legs moving back and tried firing from almost a squat. But I kept myself driving forward and I was on top of her again. I butted hard into her face with the top of my head and I heard her sigh. I took the carbine from her with my burned hand. She was still scrabbling backward from almost a sitting position. She put one hand behind her for balance. Blood ran from her nose. I smacked her with my open right. She looked surprised. I went in with my right hand yoked and pinned her back by the throat.

She made a choking noise. I kept my hand on her throat but loosened the grip.

She was heaving to breathe but I heard her all right. "Your favorite position," she whispered. She was bleeding and her eyes were flooded with blood. I thought I'd broken her nose.

I took the carbine in my burned hand and looked over my shoulder. Smith was on top of us. I whipped the carbine into him and he changed the direction of his strike. The machete missed me. When I came up I had the carbine in both hands. I brought the wooden stock up into his face. He didn't seem to feel it. I pulled the weapon back, set my feet, then swiveled my hips when I brought it around again. I heard bones in the side of his face break. He came anyway and I dropped into a crouch and drove a boot at his right knee like I was going through it and out the back. I used the butt of the carbine to push myself like a pole vaulter into the thrust. I heard the ligaments go and he went down. Even the amphetamine energy couldn't keep him standing.

I carried the carbine over to the kitchen cabinet and took down my bottle of sour mash. I leaned against the counter and watched them while I gripped the top in my teeth and unscrewed the bottle from its cap. I stood with the weapon in one hand and the mash in the other. I thought I wanted to rinse the taste of her cigarette smoke away. But I didn't take the sip. I tried to set the bottle on the counter and I missed. It fell but didn't break. Some of it gurgled out on the floor. Then it stopped and the room was quiet unless you counted me breathing like a man who'd run a marathon and Georgia forcing her breath easy because of the pain in her face and Smith who was possibly beginning to feel the damage to his jaw and his knee.

I heard myself shouting it at her. "Why not?"

I was as surprised as Smith and Georgia. Now I knew.

The sirens came in. I figured Georgia's call would have brought several cars. I set the carbine on the floor. I was tired enough to sleep standing up. In *Bad Day at Black Rock* Tracy never seemed to get this tired. Jerry Gentry was the first one in. He stood on the cracked front door and looked us over. There was plenty of blood on the floor. There was coffee and sour mash and broken glass. There was Clarence Smith face down, rolling slowly from side to side. Georgia was propped against the far wall to the left of the door. Her face was swollen and her nostrils and lips and chin were bloody. It smelled of cordite from the shots and sour mash and tobacco and sweat and coffee and the high, metal smell of blood. The smell of Tyler Pearl was also part of it.

I moved my toe at the carbine and said, "There's also a handgun in the open drawer under the toaster over there."

"Well, shit," he said. "You *hit* her?" Georgia started to laugh and then stopped and covered her nose with her hand.

"Guilty," I said.

"And him?"

"Yup."

"Well, shit. Anybody else in here? Any corpses? We got a report of some kind of killing."

I said, "That would be up in back of Clarence's cornfield. The kid I was looking for?"

"Did you kill him?"

"I'm afraid not, Jerry."

"Well, shit," he said.

I nodded.

"Did Smith?"

I nodded. "And maybe her. She's been in on the inside of a lot of Smith's work, I think. You remember the famous story. I believe she was getting it."

"No," he said.

I said, "Georgia. I'm sorry about your nose. I found out that I did care."

Gentry said, "About her?" His expression was sour.

"No," I said, "about me. I thought I didn't care if she killed me, but I did."

"Well, shit," Gentry said.

There was another deputy in the kitchen now, and sirens were coming. I turned from them to run some cold water on my hand. When I turned back, Gentry was shaking his head at the other deputy. The deputy shrugged back. The warning chime in the Mustang rang.

"Well, *I* don't know," he said. "I—well, then, shit. Let's just say everyone here is under arrest," he told the other deputy. "How in hell's that?"

THEY TOOK SMITH and Georgia to the hospital where Elway Bird died. I spent two days in the Hamilton County Jail, which was in the center of Vienna across from the public library. I wore an orange boiler suit with a zipper down the center and black felt slippers. The zipper went from the crotch to the throat. If you needed to use the crapper you opened the suit, sat on a lidless toilet in public view, and then you pulled the arms of the suit up your legs and around your shriveled-up nuts and you made your mess. The guard for the weekend took it personally that I didn't eat the jailhouse scrambled eggs and pulpy bread. I did want the coffee even if it was stale and weak. A guard let me see Bromell's newspaper. They called it The Paper like Binghamton, Syracuse, Utica, and anything not in central upstate New York didn't exist.

The Paper mentioned that a man had been injured in an altercation outside of town. Firearms were involved. The sheriff's department and state police were investigating. I wondered if Bromell was involved in the financing of the marijuana scheme. More than likely he was just a sourpuss with a narrow mind who loved money, power, and his daughter. He suppressed the news because of Georgia and maybe because a friend at Rotary or a local surgeon he played golf with knew someone who knew someone.

Bromell might have been told that a lot of inaccurate rumor was jeopardizing some friend's friend who was trying to make a come-back in the dairy business. It was also likely that he was just pro-tecting his very dangerous kid. Somebody ought to tell her that the story was maybe in *that*.

According to what I suppose you would call the news item in The Paper there were speculations concerning the presence in the hills of criminal elements from New England. These were hoods by way of movies or TV from Boston with their odd accents and Roman Catholic ways. They were like the coyotes you could hear from over the hill. They were foreign and threatening and nowhere in sight.

Wasn't it about sight? I thought. Wasn't it about seeing? You should have seen that it was Georgia standing in Clarence Smith's doorway. You should have seen the pattern in the corn. You should have understood it right away. There wasn't any mystery. There wasn't any secret. Everything was there for you to see. Finally you understood to get your thinking past what you *thought* you saw. It was always about just looking. The poor damned kid was always there for you to find.

Merle arrived late Monday. I remembered what she looked like, of course. But in the nasty white lights and the toilet smell of the six-cell lockup she seemed to me to glow. She sat across from me on her side of the little table in the corridor outside the cells. The table was bolted to the cement floor and so were the chairs. The guard outside the cell block watched us from his wooden chair. A little screen like a ping-pong net divided the table in half. She was wearing a very dark blue suit with a tailored jacket and a short skirt. She wore black high-heeled shoes and carried a black briefcase. She didn't at first seem to be wearing a shirt under the jacket but when I saw her at the visitors' table she turned out to be wearing something cream-colored and ribbed. When she sat the air moved from her to me and she smelled good. Her skin was bright. Her hands were clean.

"You look like a cake of soap," I said.

"That's good?"

"It's very good. You smell like one too."

"Jack, you don't. But I'm happy to see you."

"I'm glad you're here. Thank you."

She took a yellow legal pad from her briefcase and looked it over. "Mr. Smith calmed down. They had to give him something in the hospital for his being sky-high and then later, they said, plenty for the pain. You ruined his knee. He'll need corrective surgery for his cheekbone and jaw. Your sexy little friend had to get her nose set and she too will require surgery in due time. They are trading information against each other for any kind of a deal they can work. The gist of what they're trying to trade corroborates you," she said. "The local district attorney and the magistrate—he is a charming man, by the way—he had us over for a kind of a brunch to talk about it. They believe that Mr. Smith broke into the house, in what could only be interpreted as an armed invasion. Ms. Bromell's brandishing of your rifle—"

"Carbine."

"Yes. She's trying to sell it as self-defense on account of Smith-as-assailant, et cetera. Your burned hand— Is that all right?"

"Fine."

"It was noted by the local MD who fills in as sheriff's physician during prisoner intakes. Your burned hand qualifies as a wound suffered in the course of defending yourself from Ms. Bromell. So they aren't buying her version at all."

"It must upset her. Having her story doubted. It's all about the story with her."

She focused on me. She seemed to be repeating my words to herself. She said, "And what was the nature of the relationship between you and Ms. Bromell?"

"I guess you could call her a busted-down journalist. She wrote things. I think she wanted to write about Smith and the operation he ran for whoever he ran it for. I think she wanted to tell the story. She heard from Gentry that I was looking for your nephew. I don't mean she knew Tyler was *your* nephew. You know. And she wanted to find out what I knew. And maybe she wanted to make sure I didn't know more than I should."

"And you want me to accept that as an answer to my question about you and her?"

"If you would, please."

She looked at me and then at her yellow pad. "All right," she said.

I said, "Thank you, Merle."

"All right. The gist of it is, they killed my nephew. He should have been able to live long enough to learn how to have a life. I'd have helped him. He was my sister's son." Her face was hard and her eyes were wet. "The DA will figure out which one did what to which part of him. The marijuana business doesn't involve us. Tyler does. He involves you and me, and you involve me."

"Well, I hope so."

"I'm talking professionally, Jack."

"I'm grateful," I said. "I am."

"I think I can get you out of here fast. You shouldn't be in here."

I said, "I'd be grateful if you could take care of that."

"I'll do it," she said.

"Do I have to put up bail?"

"I'll pay it if you do. But I want you out on your own recognizance. They should grant that. You're a victim here."

"My weapon was—"

"Impounded," she said. "They want them both, at least until her trial is over."

"The pistol wasn't part of it."

"Do you really need it?"

"No, ma'am," I said. "I don't really need any of it. Now, I'm thinking about some property damage."

"I'll pay."

"Somebody needs to take care of Clarence Smith's dog. He's a big, stupid St. Bernard. Would you—"

"Yes." She made a note. "I'll mention it when I leave here."

She looked across at me and I looked back. She had crow's-foot wrinkles at the eyes and seams across her forehead. Her nose, crooked left to right, and her blue-green eyes, were very good to see again.

She took a breath and then said, "May I say something, strictly *not* as your attorney of record?"

"Yes, ma'am."

"How could you not have called me for so long?"

I looked at the angle of her nose. There was a tiny bump of cartilage, I supposed it was, at the top.

"Jack," she said.

"Doesn't mean I didn't think about you, Merle."

She looked at her pad and started to write something, and then she stopped.

We sat across from each other in the stink of the cells. I watched her eyes fill up. The tears ran down her face. She shook her head.

She shook it again and then wiped with the backs of her hands at her face. Kids wiped their tears that way, I thought.

I said, "I'm sorry."

"They just dumped him in a hole in a cornfield?"

"They buried him in a tarpaulin. It kept him safe from animals."

"They tortured him."

"I think he must have passed out right away."

"No," she said, "they beat him and beat him and then they cut his fingers off and he must have been in such terrible pain. And *then* he bled to death, the pathologist thinks. And you know it."

"Yes. That's probably how it happened."

"Poor Tyler," she said. "All he did was look for some kind of halfway decent luck, and he never had it. He never had any."

"Merle," I said, "he had you."

She said, "And we can all see how much good I did for him."

Early the next morning, they released me. There were no charges against me but I was to be available. They thought I could leave but they would want me back for the trial.

Outside the lockup I said, "I need to get a shower."

She said, "What a good idea."

I drove my truck back to the house and Merle drove behind me in her rental car from the airport that was silver and shaped like a bumblebee. There was a great deal of yellow crime-scene tape. It was looped around trees and tied to the railing of the front porch steps. I raised the tape at the steps and she walked through. She was wearing dark denim jeans and brown lace-up shoes. She wore a tan short-sleeved shirt that hung to just about her waist. I was impressed that she had known to bring a scene-of-the-crime outfit.

They had leaned the door up in its frame so I pulled it out of the way. The kitchen looked like a long battle in a small war had happened in it. I started to pick up pottery and pieces of glass and the cap of the sour mash bottle that a deputy had stood on the counter. I was surprised they'd left any liquid in it. I kicked at some of the trash. Later I would gather everything and either burn it or bag it in plastic and haul it to the Vienna dump. "I'll make some coffee," I said, carrying a saucer of ashes to the sink. But she wasn't in the room.

There was an old tin coffeepot in the cupboard. I rinsed it out and stood the plastic cone and a coffee filter in it. After I put water on I went around to where my mattress was. She was in the far corner of the room near the closet. She was staring at the sleeping bag and blanket and a saucer containing ashes and butts and burnt-out matchsticks. She didn't talk. She had her arms crossed and she leaned against the wall.

Without looking at me, she said, "Those bruises on your throat look painful."

"Come have coffee," I said. She looked at me and then followed. She said nothing.

She went to the refrigerator and looked inside while I stood watching the coffee drip down. She said, "There's some greeny-gray meat loaf in here. A piece of cake or pie. And some stale cheese. And eggs and butter. No radishes."

"No, I almost never buy radishes."

"You had a bunch down South. Remember?"

"I must have been going through a salad phase. I remember how impressed I was that you knew to look in that little icebox for a rubber band for your hair. It was like you knew me."

She said, "I didn't, though." She sounded miserable.

I brought two cups to the table and sat down across from her.

"I met you over coffee," she said. "Well, over the rental cowboy and then the coffee and then the sour mash. And your wonderful dog was there."

"The deputies left me a little sour mash."

She shook her head. She said, "No, thank you. I'm dizzy enough."

"Really dizzy?"

"Nah. Fluttery-eyed, damsel-in-distress dizzy. I hate it."

"What kind of distress, Merle?"

She shook her head again. "I'm fine," she said, "really."

"No," I said. "You found out hard stuff. Your nephew was killed. He had a bad dying. It's hard to not think about that."

She didn't answer. The silence went on. I heard flies at the bright windows and crows in the dooryard trees and the gurgle of someone's stomach.

Merle said, "It's terrible about Tyler, and he's all I should be thinking about. But I find myself speculating on whatever private life you might have had here and I guess I feel excluded. I have no right to feel that way. I just thought, if anybody wants to know if I feel a little unnecessary, they're right."

"Merle, it's fine to be with you. Not to mention you came down here and you defended me. You got me out from under Jerry Gentry and the sheriff's department."

"He's the giant one with the baleful eyes? Oh, he's smitten with your friend Ms. Bromell."

"Never a friend," I said.

She nodded but didn't look at me.

I felt like I needed to confess to her. But she wouldn't want to hear what I needed to say and I didn't want to say it. "I wasted all kinds of your money, Merle. They wouldn't give me this lease for less than six months. There weren't too many short-term rentals around and this one was in a good location."

"It's fine," she said. "The money's fine. I make plenty of money. I'll cover the damages. And I intend to pay you more of a fee for this, by the way." She drank her coffee. "You always make excellent coffee. And I am going to be a middle-aged woman soon. Maybe I am one now."

I waited.

"Jack, I don't have all the time in the world to waste."

"I wouldn't want to waste it."

She shut her eyes. She was lit up like a bulb. It made me sad to see her think she needed to hide. She sat still and so did I. Then I walked around to her side of the table. I picked up her hand and tugged at her. She stood and I could smell the soap on her skin.

"If you want to keep your eyes shut," I said.

"I do."

She let me lead her around the corner to my version of a bedroom. I didn't know what to do then. I knew she didn't either.

"Oh," I said.

She whispered, "What?"

"I had my eyes shut too."

"I still do."

"Well, then," I said. I was touching her from the outside of her clothes. I ran my clumsy, burned, chopped-up fingers on her shirt and her hips and then her backside. She took hold of my hands and pressed them harder onto her. We both remembered how grown-ups can undress. We figured out how to kneel down quite a long distance to a mattress on the floor. One of us or both of us made the noises you make when you're shivering cold. But her skin felt hot. I went into the way her skin felt and I burrowed as deep as I could.

The sleep I fell into made other nights of sleep seem like naps. I sank and stayed under. It was dark when I opened my eyes. I was lost for a second. She was next to me. She was wearing a flannel shirt of mine. I could feel it when I reached to touch her. I could see her eyes and I knew that she had been watching me while I slept. I'd slept the way babies do. All of themselves go into being shut down away from the world.

"It's night," I said. "You knocked me out, Merle."

She looked at me but she didn't talk.

"I didn't call you half the times I should have. And I sure didn't get to help your nephew."

"You think you have to be a rescuer," she said.

"I do?"

"You seem to always try and be one."

"I don't know," I said.

"Except who gets to rescue *you*, Jack?"

"You just watched me sleep?"

"Oh, yes," she said. "And I saw how deep the bruises on your throat are. Will you tell me how you got them?"

I said, "No."

"I think I can guess."

I said, "I'd just as soon you didn't."

She said, "You need to have your secrets."

"Everybody has them," I said. "Right?"

"Yes. Everybody has them. I'm afraid I make my living from them. Well, so do you. I think, sometimes, I could try something else."

"Besides lawyering?"

"Except it's what I'm awfully good at. I wouldn't be good at, I don't know, teaching damaged children, or reading out loud for the blind."

"Doing somebody some good," I said.

"Sometimes I think I want to do that."

"*You* want to rescue people, you mean."

She reached over and tapped her knuckles against my forehead. "Nicely done," she said. "You know how to argue."

"I know how to break people's noses and jaws and knees."

Merle rolled onto me and held me around the neck with both of her arms. She wasn't choking me. She was keeping me there. I didn't have any thought of trying to escape but she hung on. She said, "You are the most alone person I have ever met." She kissed my face on either side of my nose and on my jaw and on my forehead. They were slow kisses. They were generous. It was an honor to be kissed like that. I pulled at Merle and held her onto me and then I followed the rhythms that were moving in us.

I woke up in the dark again and this time she was sleeping next to me. I appreciated that because I could look all I wanted to at the skin behind her ears and the muscles of her shoulder outside the old blanket we'd pulled over us. I listened to her breathe.

The rhythm of her breaths changed. Her eyes were still closed when she whispered, "Well, Jack, I finally found you."

We took separate showers and drove in the early morning to eat breakfast at the Vienna motel. Then we went to her room and it seemed natural for us to take off our clothes and get into bed.

When she was wearing her suit and carrying her briefcase, Merle conferred with the district attorney's office and once more with the magistrate. On the day of Elway's funeral she and I had iced tea and sandwiches at the motel restaurant. The funeral was for immediate family and I surely wasn't that. I had used up my immediate family. Merle looked creamy again. I'd watched from the motel bed while she got that way.

In the parking lot, I slid her bag onto the back seat of the little silver bumblebee. Merle said, "You have to come to New York." She wasn't looking into my eyes and she had avoided them all morning. I thought we were both working on how to tell each other goodbye.

I said, "I intend to." She smiled a smile I didn't think she meant. "Really," I said. "But I was wondering what you thought about Maine."

"The entire state?"

"The coast near Portland."

"I painted some of it."

I nodded. "That's what I thought. One of the pictures in your apartment and one in your office. I recognized Maine. Or I thought I did."

This time she did look directly at me. It was good to see her eyes straight on. Her smile went away but it came right back. "It's fine country," she said.

"I wondered if you might want to visit me there."

She had her serious lawyer look. She got it when she focused her attention. "You think?"

"I was wondering," I said.

"What do you think would happen?"

"I don't know. Maybe something."

"Maybe what?" She was looking away again.

"Well, Merle, I don't know what. Maybe only paintings of rocks. Maybe not."

She said, "Maybe not?"

"Yes."

"That's not an invitation, Jack. That's more like a prayer." She smiled. Then she lost the smile. Then she reached out to touch my throat.

I said, "All right. Then that's what it is. I'll get to someplace where I have an address and I'll get in touch with you. And we'll meet up near Portland."

"When?"

"I need to get myself there first."

"And I'm supposed to go home and wait to hear?"

"If you're willing to."

"And wait to hear, if I'm willing to wait. But also maybe not to hear."

"No," I said, "you'll hear."

"Because you're saying I will."

"That's right."

"I'm a realist, Jack. I think I am. I try to be. I know how to wait, and I know when to trust someone. I trusted you. I'll trust you again. So that's all right," she said. She came a step closer and said, "But it would be good, when you come and get me at the little airport in Portland, if you have a dog on the seat next to you."

"There wouldn't be room for you in the truck if I did."

"If it was a puppy, there'd be room," she said.

OUT AT THE HOUSE, I sat on the stoop and drank coffee and listened to the chugging of the insects at the pond. It sounded like an engine and I thought of my truck and being away in it. I walked out to the pond in the dusk light. It all went silent except for a bird in the pines at the far end. There were fewer scolding blackbirds. They might have started migrating south already. Fall was coming on. I listened for the coyotes and then I heard them.

In the morning after a tin pot of coffee I set my clothes in stacks on the kitchen table. I assembled my tools. The deputies had taken the ammunition and my guns. I pulled together my shaving kit. I knew I'd throw away the housekeeping supplies. I used the claw hammer to take out the nails I'd pounded in above the front door to hang the carbine on. Merle had told me that a term people use when transferring a house is "broom swept." You clean it up but you don't have to scrub down the walls or pull out all the nails. But the nails hadn't been there when I came.

I gassed up and checked my tire pressures and my oil level and the level in the master cylinder. I checked the radiator and filled the windshield washer tank. I packed my gear into the cap and left the doorless house.

I went south to Greene. Lily Stovich smiled when I came in with my coffee jug.

She said, "What do you have in store for yourself today?"

"I'm on my way away," I said. "I'll miss your coffee."

"And me, of course, you'll miss more."

"I was about to say so."

"You American cowboys never know how to reassure the girl, do you? She waits and she waits and the cowboy is kissing always the horse instead of her."

I leaned across the counter and she leaned too. I kissed her cheek and she patted my face.

"Thank you," I said. "I will miss you. And the coffee."

"Tell your friends, the other cowboys," she said. "Free coffee for the first one buys the restaurant. God bless your life."

Then I did what I'd been putting off for so long. I drove slowly and drank coffee. I might have looked like a handyman taking a break. But I was on what you could have called a mission. I went north again and then cut west before I got to the college. I put my coffee down and took the narrow roads with both hands on the wheel. It looked like I remembered it. The road was potholed and crumbling from frost heaves. There had been a lot of winter kill and soft trees like aspen were bent in half or sheared. A lot of birch had gone down with the weight of ice and wet snow. The field I came to before I came to the house was turning gold. It would go tan soon and then the autumn would have come. The dog and I used to walk out here in the deep snow. Sometimes we went there because I couldn't think of anyplace else. The big spruce in the side yard looked healthy and full. The house looked bad. It needed a roof and new siding worse than the Birds' did. The pickets of the fence looked scuffed and the porch sagged. It looked like somebody's last chance. I went past very slowly. I looked up at the window of the room where we kept the crib. A lot of it happened up there.

I stopped. I backed up a little. I sat across from the house with the engine running. I looked at the upstairs window and tried feeling what I thought I ought to feel. It wasn't there in the house any more than it was in the cornfield where I dug until I finally found them. A motion downstairs drew my eyes. I thought I saw someone at the upper glass panes of the front porch door. The door opened out a little and the screen door outside it started to swing. It was a thin shape. It was someone very short and slender or a child. I remembered seeing Georgia at the door to Smith's farm. The door stopped moving.

"Hello," I thought I would say. I tried to think of what else I might tell them. I could have asked to look inside the place I used to live in. I could maybe have talked my way upstairs by smiling like an aw-shucks countryman. I could maybe have stood outside the little room our daughter slept in when she slept. It was where the dog and Fanny and I and the child had fallen asleep together a few times. I thought I could breathe in its air.

But then I'd have to breathe it out if I kept on breathing. So what could I keep? What good would I have done for anyone? So I did what I'd been doing for quite a while. I said so long.

I took the cutoff at Bill Potter Road and went to the other final place. It was maybe a twenty-minute drive from the house we used to live in. I remembered making it in twelve or fifteen minutes during the days when I was looking for the Tanners' stolen girl. The town wasn't much more than a crossroads with a church in one corner. The old farmhouse in front of the field where she'd been buried was painted up and planted with evergreens on the front lawn. The old barn behind it still listed to the right. I parked in the road and rolled the window down. I smelled wood smoke and cut grass. The grass went away and the smoke felt thicker and harsher. I thought of us in the field when it was covered with snow and crusted with ice and Mrs. Tanner sat by the barrel of burning wood to watch us dig for the child we all needed to find. I was wet with sweat and my throat stung from the smoke I was remembering. I wanted hot coffee. Then I remembered the cup that Lily Stovich had poured me.

I drank some. I wiped with my forearm at my sweaty head and started the truck. I thought I was pretty much done.

I drove to the Birds', where a handsome woman in her middle twenties opened the door for me. She thought I was law or trouble and I admired how she stepped forward and not back for safety. She was making it clear with her body that I could not come in. Her skin was the color of darkened copper. Her face was long and so were her nose and ears.

"Film studies," I said, "right? You're the younger Mrs. Bird?"

She solemnly repeated, "The younger Mrs. Bird. Well, I suppose I'm also that." Her voice was low. She said, "Then you can't be anyone but Jack. We all know about you. We're all in the back. We're—well, we're sitting around being sad. Come in and be sad with us. I'm Marion, by the way. The younger Mrs. Bird."

Sarah stood when I came in. She hugged me very hard. Michael sat with a boy on his lap. It must have been Sergei. The boy was maybe three, I thought. He stared at what I carried.

I kept an arm around Sarah. With the other I held out the scuffed-up bear doll. "If Sergei isn't too old and if his parents don't mind," I said, "I found this where I was living and I cleaned it up. It's the kind of bear that ought to be living with a child someplace."

Marion took the bear and looked it over. She watched her son consider it.

"Boys need bears," she said.

Sergei nodded.

"What do they say, *if* their parents let them accept the bear from a friend? *If* their parents know the friend very, very well?"

That all sounded complicated to me. But it was a dangerous world for children. I figured they were right to set up rules about surviving it.

"Thank you," he whispered. He was his mother's color, and his features were polished and bright like a statue's. But he was flesh. He was up and after the bear.

I said, "You're welcome, Sergei."

He smiled when I said his name. I could see spending a while trying to get another smile like that.

He held the bear. He looked at its dark glass eyes. He said to it or to me, "My Pop-Pop died."

I thought I ought to answer so I said, "I know. I'm sad about it."

Sergei looked up from the bear and asked, "What do you know about heaven?"

Marion put her hand over her mouth and Michael shook his head.

Sarah smiled and said, "Tell him, Jack."

"What do I say?"

She said, "Tell him the truth."

I looked at Elway's grandchild. "Nothing," I said.

Sergei waited. He looked at me. He said, "You need to use your 'magination." Then he stuck the bear under his arm and walked back to sit with his father.

Sarah looked at me. I could imagine her thinking that she needed to tell Elway about what his grandson said. Then it must have struck her again that she couldn't.

"I believe you're right," I said to Sergei. "I'll work on that."

Sarah said, "You and I need a conversation, Jack." Michael looked surprised and then annoyed. Marion studied us.

I said, "Yes, ma'am."

She took my arm and walked me out of her living room and out the front door. She let go of my arm and took my hand. We went around the house and through the backyard and into a field that sloped up to a series of hills. Cattle grazed on the farthest of them. There were dozens of old apple trees that were full of small green and red apples no one would want to eat. We walked past the orchard and when we were screened from the house she stopped. So I did. I thought of her when we were together and I saw how easy it was to get tangled with her. It didn't hurt in those days that I knew her to be so much smarter than I was and so educated.

She said, "Look at me."

I did.

"You know this face."

"Yes, I do."

"I remember that you kissed it. You kissed me under each eye when I was crying. I was in your car. We were lovers."

"Yes."

"So you will understand how much I mean this. I am saying to you please do not disappear again. Please stay in touch with me."

"Yes," I said. "I will. Yes."

"I do not want to be the widow in your memory and nothing else. I'm your friend. Don't be surprised to learn you sometimes are not a consolation and a comfort to your friends because of your tending to hide away. Do not hide away from me."

I said, "No." I said, "Elway loved you so much, Sarah." Wasps were patrolling the small apples in the crooked, low trees. "Did he know about you and me, do you think?"

She sighed and stepped back. "I hope not," she said. Her brown eyes were steady on me. "I hope that was only ours." She said, "At that time—at those times—it was necessary. You were necessary. Hoping for anything more, or trying for it—that would have been absurd. Now, don't you *pout*, Jack. You do know that."

"I do. Yes."

"But it was wild for a while, wasn't it? It was beautiful for a while, even when it was crazy. You made me feel . . . cherished. That's a delicate thing for a large man to do. I loved you for it." She stood in front of me. Then she raised herself up on her toes and put her hands on my cheeks and kissed my mouth. She nodded. She was going to say something but then she stopped. Then she said, "One early evening, when you were working at the college, I was in the library. Up in the stacks, off in the corner that looks out on the path you can take to the art building. I don't remember what I was looking for, but it wasn't you. I didn't know you very well. I was most likely, in those days, looking for *me*. But I did find you. It was when you were taking courses. You were improving yourself. Remember?"

I waited. She knew I remembered trying to be better.

"You were standing in front of some of the shelves and you were looking. Just looking. You were taking books down and reading in them and putting them back on the shelf. Which, you remember, you weren't supposed to do. You were supposed to leave them for the staff to put back correctly. But that would be you. You'd want to clean up after yourself. You were . . . grazing. You were working the range. You were reading maybe just because there was so much there you could read at if you wanted to. I looked around the corner and I found you because I heard you singing. You were standing there in your uniform and you were singing. You sing off-key, Jack. You were singing quite terribly to yourself, very low, the same dozen notes, over and over. It was from 'Sh-boom.' Remember? About how life could, you know, be a dream? You sounded so dopey. You sounded so *happy*."

"I shouldn't sing. I can't." Crows were yipping in the taller trees surrounding the Birds' land.

"But you gave forth a joyful noise, Jack. That's my point. That's why I remember that time when I think of you and the other times. It wouldn't be in a course you take, and it probably couldn't happen in a library. But I do believe it is available. You were *happy*. You could be a happy person is what I want to say."

Her eyes were enormous and wet.

I nodded. I got my voice unstuck. "Thank you."

"Yes," she said. "Now I'm going back in. Come with me, please."

I walked back to the house a step or two behind her. When she went into the living room, Michael stood up and made sure she saw him shove his hands deep into his pockets. His face was angry and puzzled.

She said to him, "You hush."

I said, "Good luck with the film studies, Ms. Bird. And good luck to you too, Michael."

She nodded. Michael said, "Jack."

Sergei said, "Jack."

"Yes?" I said.

"His name is Jack," he said, looking up from the bear at me.

"Oh," I said. "Then thank you. Thank you very much."

"Jack the Bear," Sarah said.

At the door, she hugged me. I put my arms around her back and shoulders.

She said, "You make very sure I know how to get hold of you."

"I'll call you. I will."

"You have to be better about that. I want to hear your voice."

I hugged her again and we both hung on.

In the truck I drove quietly for a while. Then I said, "Well."

Then I turned up the volume on Linda Ronstadt singing about poor poor pitiful me. I left the bear behind. I left the invisible coyotes behind. I left Elway Bird and Sarah behind. I left my firearms and I left the shovel. Little birds were lined up on electric wires and the tips of the sumac were swollen and red. Canada geese flocked in fields. Soon they'd fly in deltas.

When I drove away from there I made for Route 88. It went northeast to Albany. I'd pick up the Thruway to the Berkshire Extension of the Massachusetts Turnpike. I intended to get myself north through Massachusetts and a little of New Hampshire into Maine. Portland would be a good day's drive. There were all those little coastal towns above it that I knew when I was a kid. I thought I might find work there.

NOTE

I am grateful to Ernie Cutting, Undersheriff of Chenango County in the State of New York, for his courtesies. Thanks to Dr. Joseph A. Roedling and Dr. Loren Wolsh for providing important information. Vienna, New York, as well as its hospital and the nearby college, do not exist except in my imagination. You can follow the Hosbach Trail in Norwich, New York.

FB

NORTH

FREDERICK BUSCH

A Reader's Guide

A Conversation with Frederick Busch

*This conversation took place in November 2005. Frederick Busch
passed away suddenly on February 25, 2006.*

Geoffrey Becker is the author of a novel, Bluestown, *and a
collection of stories,* Dangerous Men. *He teaches fiction writing
at Towson University in Baltimore, Maryland.*

GB: Both your short story "Ralph the Duck" and your novel *Girls*
feature the same narrator as *North*. What was it about Jack that
made you want to continue working with him?

FB: I couldn't get his voice out of my head, and after I had written
A Memory of War, which was such a different kind of book, so full
of complexity, I was hungry to get back to writing a simpler voice. I
love his voice. The other thing was the situation where you have a
man who is telling the story—so he's using words—who finds it
impossible in his situation to use words. He can't name his dog. He
can't tell his wife. He can't tell his friend Bird, his best friend for
various reasons, some of which involve his own sins. I was very
interested in those paradoxes.

GB: In *Girls*, he says he's taking a class to learn to "express himself."

FB: Exactly. And he can't. And he won't.

GB: One of the things that he can't express is the secret that you begin this novel with.

FB: "In a marriage you have to tell your secrets." Yet he wanted to have the marriage, and he did love her, and he still loves her.

GB: I think it's fair to say *North* is a dark book. And yet something I really admired about it was the humor. I wondered if you were thinking about that.

FB: I'm so glad you found humor in there. I like to think that a lot of my writing has a kind of dark humor in it. Apparently not— according to Judy, my wife. She'll ask how the writing is going, and I'll say I'm writing this funny story, and she says, "And then you'll bring it down and I'll read it and I'll start to cry. That's your idea of a funny story." I like the idea that you can tell true stories about grown-ups' lives and still have some kind of humor.

GB: In a setup right out of Raymond Chandler or Dashiell Hammet, Merle Davidoff hires Jack to find her missing nephew. Even her name, Merle, seems from another era. How consciously were you channeling the world of hard-boiled fiction, or of films like *The Maltese Falcon*?

FB: I wasn't, I was just desperate to find a name for her. I've never used a Merle. Probably I'd just seen a movie with Merle Oberon. If I was channeling anything, it wasn't just the 1940s or certain hard-boiled writers. I think I was trying to work with the whole genre of the detective story in which you followed, roughly, a form, and yet didn't resort to the clichés of the form. You know, so they don't meet cute at the bar of the resort when she picks him up and falls into his arms and says, "You big hunk of stuff, I need help finding my nephew." Instead he gets interested in her, she gets interested in him, and then as far as he's concerned, they're never going to see each other again. Then catastrophe strikes his small life on the Carolina coast and he's suddenly homeless and without work — he moves from job to job and I think he defines his life by work — so when they meet up again, it's because he's looking for work. I was trying to write the usual, in the sense of the usual private cop story, without using those clichés.

GB: If James M. Cain had written this novel, Merle would have been a femme fatale.

FB: Oh, absolutely. She would have been implicated in the death of the nephew or something like that.

GB: I was glad it didn't go that way.

FB: Me, too. I was hoping they were going to get together, myself. And they might.

GB: The novel has a palimpsest quality to it, with the past constantly becoming visible to us through some tear in the fabric of the present. For instance when Jack pulls over at the rest stop overlooking the Hudson River and is transported momentarily back to that same field that figures in the opening of *Girls*, Jack seems almost adrift in time. Did you think of him this way?

FB: Yes. I didn't realize I was doing it, but I've had a project that has been lasting since 1996 or 1997 when I wrote *Girls,* and then *The Night Inspector,* and then *A Memory of War,* and now *North.* In all these novels, I have been dealing with characters for whom the past is not over, and in whom the past keeps presenting itself with power equal to the present. I was interested in their apprehension and understanding of time, with their contending with time, because I believe that is what art—and literary art—seek to undo and to resist: time. That's the enemy—to the writer. Not to the characters . . . but maybe to the characters, too. It interested me because it was such a difficult writing assignment to give myself. How are you going to write about these people who are adrift in time, while still anchoring them to a specific time and place so that the reader (a) understands what's going on and (b)—most important—cares? There's no point in writing unless your reader feels something important and strong. That's what I wanted to achieve. When I finished *North,* I felt that I was done with that, at least as a primary concern. That the next book would have to be radically different from everything that's gone by.

GB: For all his toughness and apparent competence, Jack is also a lousy shot.

FB: I wanted that. I don't know why I did, but I wanted that from the beginning. Again, I wanted to violate the notion of the cowboy as played by Tom Selleck, or the detective as played by some B-actor on television who is a great fistfighter and a great shot, and he can track human spoor better than a dog. I love the idea in *Girls,* when he's in a small kitchen with the guy, and he unloads a whole revolver's worth of ammunition and he can't hit him, and he virtually scares him into confessing. The same thing here, where he's got a carbine, he's got a pistol, you'd think he could take anybody out, he's totally protected, and he can't even hit the front of a car from twenty feet away. He's probably flinching, doesn't like the shot. I enjoyed that. It's my sense of humor, I guess. He's not an official hero.

GB: Let me ask you some craft questions. John Irving claims he doesn't start writing a novel until he knows the very last sentence. Other writers will tell you they don't have a clue where they are going, they'll just get an image, or a voice in their head, and they'll start writing. How does this work for you? How much do you have laid out in advance, and how much do you figure out as you go?

FB: I am among the clueless. I usually write something to respond to a question I have about—oh, it could be an image. I may see a man and a woman together in a situation and I want to know why, how'd they get into that situation. I may start in response to a line of poetry—poetry is very important to me—I may start just responding to a rhythm of something I've heard. I can't start unless I know the vocation of the protagonist. I need to know the protagonist's job, where they edge into the public world from their private world. That's my own silly habit. And then I write to find out what the hell is going on in what it is I seem to be writing. So it's draft after draft as you try to figure out why in heaven's name you wrote this, or are writing this, and what it's about. What does it want to be about? I've come back to short stories six months after beginning them, thinking they were done, realizing that I still haven't figured out who the characters were, and I have to rewrite the end, and then finally I knew why that situation matters to me. I'm like a sculptor. I try to find what is the shape in the block of wood or the chunk of stone that is to be represented, that's in it to be expressed.

GB: Do you often find that where you begin is not the beginning?

FB: Yes. *North* did not begin where it begins. *Girls* did not begin where it began. *A Memory of War* underwent many, many changes, and *The Night Inspector,* the same. Most of my novels. I just keep writing until I get it right, or until I think I've got it right. No doubt some critic will tell me whether I got it right or not.

GB: It occurs to me that *The Night Inspector* begins with someone commissioning a mouth.

FB: "*No* mouth," he says. I believe that's the first line of dialogue, maybe the first line of the book. Because he's gone to a professional woodworker to make a kind of papier mâché mask to cover his maimed face, and the man who is crafting it for him was going to make a mouth—a circle through which his lips could speak—and he doesn't want that. Didn't want to have a public caricature of a face. But in the end, he says, he made me a mouth. That's again a story about talking versus not talking.

GB: I used to believe I had a lucky T-shirt. Kent Haruf wrote a novel with a hat pulled over his eyes. Any superstitions involved with your writing process?

FB: I work in a modernized room on the second story of a barn across from the house. I work in a corner that has a blank wall; I keep the blinds and the curtains drawn. Although I live in a beautiful area, I'm really careful not to look out at physical reality. The only pictures I have inside are family photographs and some stuff that my wife has given me, and a poster by Wyeth illustrating *Robinson Crusoe*, which was a seminal book for me. But I don't look at reality, because I want to manufacture reality. I don't know that I have other quirks. I try to write five or six pages a day.

GB: First thing in the morning?

FB: First thing in the morning. I go to work. Just like grown-ups. I go across the field to my workroom and I lock myself in and I go to work.

GB: No e-mail.

FB: I don't check the e-mail on writing days. No consciousness coming in. Nothing but the characters. When I wrote *The Night Inspector*, I sat above photographs of New York in the 1860s, which I was writing about, and I just stared at the photographs. I fell into that place—it was a kind of a self-hypnosis. Usually I don't have anything like that to help me. I just sit down, do the damn work if I can. And if I can't, I write letters, pestering my friends. I try to make words. You must have a similar experience—I think everybody does. Every time I sit down to work at my computer, I wish I were sitting down at a typewriter. I used to love to pound really hard on a typewriter, so I'd work up a sweat—it felt like manual labor.

GB: Why don't you do that anymore?

FB: I can't get a good typewriter that will stay in tune, you know, and produce what I want to produce. My friend Ward Just still writes all of his novels on a portable typewriter. He was a war correspondent in Vietnam, and he keeps it up. I'm a fast typist—I've gotten to the point where I like the convenience of the smart typewriter. That's all I use my computer for. It remembers what I've written.

GB: Do you keep any old typewriters around?

FB: All of the tops of the bookshelves in my workroom are littered with the corpses of typewriters I've pounded my way through.

GB: So what are you working on now?

FB: I have finished a book of stories called *Rescue Missions*, and I am wrestling with a novel I've begun, which I think is going to be incredibly difficult to do right, and I expect that to occupy me for the next two or three years. Maybe just figuring out what it is will take a while. I've just finished an essay for *Harper's* magazine on my older son's time in Iraq as a combat Marine officer, and that was a very interesting and satisfying thing to do, especially now that he's come home.

READING GROUP QUESTIONS AND
TOPICS FOR DISCUSSION

1. "It was a warm day for upstate New York but mild compared to where I'd been living. I had gone there to get away from the cold. I thought maybe the cold made me feel the other feelings stronger." (page 81)

    Girls, the novel in which Jack and his dilemma are introduced, takes place in the coldest part of winter in upstate New York, and *North* takes place in late summer in the same region. How does the weather affect Jack? The story? How might *North* be different if it took place in winter?

2. "Why did you really come back? . . . You were *right* to stay away. So I mean why *really*? This is where it all blew up in the air in pieces on you and the pieces never all came down. Why in hell would you ever come back?" (page 67) Why does Jack return to upstate New York, the place he had to leave?

3. Merle Davidoff calls Jack a rescuer. Do you agree?

4. Jack was too late to save Merle's nephew, but he managed to find

him. In what ways was this discovery significant for Jack? What else
had Jack been looking for?

5. How does Jack react to Elway's illness? How is this a reversal of
their roles?

6. "I thought how I had become a specialist in knowing what the
people I cared about the most should never know." (page 172)
    Jack keeps grave secrets to protect others. Why does Jack shoul-
der this burden? Do we all do this?

7. Could Jack and Fanny have saved their marriage, or was their
paradoxical secret an insurmountable problem? Do you think Jack
could have saved Fanny?

8. Jack reveals his secrets to the reader very slowly and in pieces.
Did you trust that he would reveal the whole story?

9. Why does Jack tell Elway the truth about his daughter's death?
Would Jack have told him if he were conscious?

10. One night, Jack abstains from adding sour mash to his coffee and thinks, "If I started in treating myself too generously,
I thought, I might come to expect that sort of kindness from me
all the time." (page 127) Why does Jack have trouble being kind
to himself?

11. What was Jack seeking in his affair with Georgia Bromell? Was
he just looking for her part of the story, or, as she claimed, did he
want her for other reasons? What about his affair with Sarah? What

did he seek from her? What might he find with Merle if he pursues their relationship?

12. Clarence Smith charges that Jack doesn't like the idea of losing control. He says Jack *is* control. What hasn't Jack been able to control? How has his need for constant control influenced his choices?

13. When Jack realizes that Georgia plans to shoot him and not Clarence Smith with the carbine, he says, "Oh, yeah. Oh, absolutely. I mean, *why* not? On account, Georgia, of my absolutely flat-out not giving a good fucking goddamn. That's the why and that's the not." (page 278)

What makes Jack realize he *does* care if she shoots him? What makes Jack want to live?

14. "How many ways had I betrayed [Elway]? This idea carried over too well to Fanny and our child and to Sarah and other people who had cared about me." (page 271)

In what ways has Jack betrayed them? In what ways has he been loyal and good to them?

15. How has Jack changed over the course of the novel? Do you think he'll keep his word and be in touch with Sarah and Merle?

16. Sarah tells Jack that he could be a happy person. Does Jack agree with her? Do you agree with her?

FREDERICK BUSCH is the author of twenty-five books. *A Memory of War*, Busch's twenty-first work of fiction, was a *New York Times* Notable Book. He received the PEN/Malamud Award in short fiction, and, from the American Academy of Arts and Letters, the Award of Merit. His books have been finalists for the PEN/Faulkner and National Book Critics Circle Awards. He died in February 2006.

Lizzie's

1

4

HARPETH RIVER BRIDGE

TO NASHVILLE

FORT GRANGER

CARTER'S HOUSE

COURTHOUSE

MASONIC LODGE

CLIFFE HOUSE

FIRST PRESBYTERIAN CHURCH

MARSHALL HOUSE

TO MURFREESBORO

5th AVE.

USE

MCNUTT ACADEMY

LEWISBURG PIKE

ROYCE COTTAGE

CK'S GROVE

FRANKLIN

TENNESSEE

1864

Copyright © 2012 by Margie Gould Thessin

Illustrations and cover art: Col. Samuel A. Whitson

Cover design: Beth Merrill Hart

Layout and design: Margie Gould Thessin

Photographs pages 121 and 122 courtesy of the Battle of
Franklin Trust, Carter House collection; page 123
courtesy of the Battle of Franklin Trust, Carnton
Collection; page 134 courtesy of J.T. Thompson, Lotz
House Foundation; pages 124, 125, 130, 131, 132
courtesy of Rick Warwick, Heritage Foundation of
Franklin and Williamson County.

Special thanks to Macey Baird, Rob Cross, Lisa Patton, Jay
Sheridan, Joanna Stephens, J.T. Thompson, Rick
Warwick, and Sam Whitson for his amazing drawings.

ISBN-13: 978-1479110988
ISBN-10: 1479110981

First printing: September, 2012

Margie Gould Thessin

Illustrated by Col. Samuel A. Whitson

To Rick Warwick, historian, and
Calvin LeHew, preservationist

MGT

To Pvt. Samuel Whitson, Co. B, 42nd Tennessee Infantry
Regiment (CSA) and every American soldier before and
since.

SAW

We saw the lightning and that was the guns and then we heard the thunder and that was the big guns; and then we heard the rain falling and that was the blood falling; and when we came to get in the crops, it was dead men that we reaped.

Harriet Tubman

CONTENTS

Glossary of Terms 11

1. Dawn 13

2. A New President 19

3. U.S.A. or C.S.A.? 25

4. The War Comes Home 37

5. Franklin is Captured 45

6. A Visit from the Colonel 53

7. Sad Times 59

8. A Budding Friendship 63

9. An Unexpected Visitor 73

10. In Hiding 83

11. The Longest Day 93

12. The Day After 111

Epilogue 119
Questions 137
About the Author 139
About the Artist 140

GLOSSARY OF TERMS

Some of the following military terms may be unfamiliar to the reader.

Artillery: Big weapons such as cannons and the soldiers who operate them

Bivouac: A temporary camping place used by soldiers

Cavalry: The part of a military force composed of troops that serve on horseback

Furlough: A leave of absence or short vacation given to a soldier

Hardtack: A hard saltless biscuit or cracker provided to soldiers

Haversack: A canvas bag for provisions or equipment, carried on the back or shoulder

Infantry: Soldiers or military units that fight on foot with small weapons

Musket: A heavy weapon with a long barrel, later replaced by the rifle

Muster in: To enlist into service in the armed forces or military

Sentry: A soldier who guards or prevents access to a place

Army Names:

The Northern soldiers were called **Union**, **Federal**, or as a nickname, **Yankees**. A typical Northern soldier was nicknamed **Billy Yank**. Their uniforms were dark **navy blue**. The Northern armies were named after rivers. There were the Armies of the Cumberland, the Tennessee, the Ohio, the Potomac, the James and the Mississippi.

The Southern armies were called **Confederate** or as a nickname, **Rebels**. A typical Southern soldier was nicknamed **Johnny Reb**. Their uniforms were **gray** or a shade of brown called butternut. The Southern armies were sometimes named after states. They were the Armies of Tennessee and Northern Virginia in addition to the general Confederate army.

Chapter 1

Dawn
November 30, 1864

Lizzie Courtney awoke with a start to voices murmuring and feet stamping outside her bedroom window. Suddenly a man yelled, "Halt! We'll stop here."

Lizzie threw back the covers, jumped from her bed and ran to the window. Soldiers—hundreds of them—crowded into the family's backyard. Last night when Lizzie went to sleep, her backyard held a wash pot, a rick of firewood, and the remains of the summer's vegetable garden. Now it was crammed full of soldiers, horses and equipment. And not just in her yard. Everywhere Lizzie looked was a sea of blue—out to the Columbia Pike and beyond—on up to Carter Hill.

The soldiers, as far as Lizzie could tell in the early morning light, appeared very tired. They dropped their

muskets, haversacks and canteens in piles on the ground. Some soldiers squatted on their heels, digging through their packs as if looking for something, while others collapsed to the ground to sleep, using their haversacks as pillows. Lizzie ran to her mother's room, and saw she was awake too and staring out the window.

"Mama—soldiers! There's so many..." Lizzie's voice quailed like it did when she was nervous. Soon Lizzie's 18-year-old sister, Fannie, joined them, all three staring in astonishment out the window.

Just then someone banged on the front door. Pulling on her dressing gown, Mrs. Courtney opened the door and stared apprehensively at the officer standing on their doorstep.

"Ma'am, I'm sorry to bother you," the man said. He tipped his hat to Mrs. Courtney and introduced himself. "I'm Major Luther Sabine, 44th Illinois Infantry, United States Army. The Army of the Cumberland is marching into town now. We'll stop here for a few hours. The men need a few hours' sleep before moving on to Nashville. We'd like to bivouac here."

"That will be fine. The men may rest here. And won't you come in, Major Sabine? I'd be happy to make you breakfast," Mrs. Courtney offered, relieved.

"I'd be grateful," said the major, wiping his feet as he stepped inside the Courtneys' neat brick house near the edge of the village of Franklin, Tennessee. He glanced around the house, spotting the Courtneys' 34-star American flag hanging on the mantelpiece. "You folks Union?"

"Yes, sir, we are," Fannie spoke up. "Mama, Lizzie and I are all loyal to the United States of America."

"Well, praise heaven for that. I'm glad we've got a few friends down here."

"Unfortunately just a few, Major Sabine," Fannie said.

Lizzie shivered. She hoped the officer wouldn't ask any more questions. She wouldn't want him to find out the truth about her family. Yes, she, mama, and Fannie were loyal. But what about Brother? William was anything but loyal.

Lizzie was only eleven years old in 1864, but she still remembered peaceful and happy times from the past. All of that seemed so long ago now. It was five years ago when Papa got sick. When it became clear he would not recover from his illness, he solemnly told William, "Son, you will soon be the man of the house. Take care of your mother and sisters." And of course, William promised he would. And he did his best.

Then war came and decisions had to be made. Mama and Fannie made an unpopular one. They didn't want Tennessee to leave the United States of America. They loved their country and its heroes like George

Washington, Thomas Jefferson and Andrew Jackson. Why, Mama even talked about the time she had tea with First Lady Sarah Polk at the McEwens' house, when President James K. Polk came to town. They just couldn't imagine not being part of it. So in the end they stayed loyal.

Brother William, though, he was a different story. He was a student at Professor McNutt's Academy, and all the boys there talked of nothing but war. As soon as Tennessee voted to leave the Union, they all joined up and marched off to fight, as flags waved and children cheered and women wept.

William was gone, and Mama never stopped worrying. At first, Fannie tried to tell Mama that the War would surely end soon. But that was in 1861, more than three long years ago! Would it never end?

Lizzie thought back four years to when it all started.

COURTHOUSE

Chapter 2

A New President
November 7, 1860

"*Lincoln Elected! New President Lincoln!*" The newsboy shouted out the headlines from a *Western Weekly Review* newspaper on Main Street in Franklin. The news shot through town: Abraham Lincoln was going to be the next president of the United States. Lincoln was not the choice of most Southern voters. Not a single Tennessean had voted for the man from Illinois; he wasn't even on the ballot. But he was popular among Northern voters.

Men gathered together in circles in front of the courthouse, debating the election. Lizzie was coming home from running an errand for her mother when she heard one of them say, "We just won't stand for this. We can't!" Another one said forcefully, "Now, surely it won't come to that." Then another one shouted, "Just you wait and see!" Lizzie could tell these were not the ordinary snippets of conversation she was used to overhearing. These men were full of wrath, as they raised their fists and pointed at each others' red faces.

Lizzie raced home and found her mother and sister peeling potatoes for supper.

"It was scary! The men downtown sounded so angry. I thought they were going to start hitting each other. What do those men mean, won't stand for *what*? Wait and see *what*?"

Mama put down her knife, wiped her hands and sat down in her rocker. She took Lizzie in her lap and stroked her hair. "The men are just talking the way men do when they get upset about things. You needn't worry, my darling."

Fannie spoke up. "I don't know about that, Mama. I think this is serious. I was talking to some of my friends earlier today and they said if the rumors are true, states might secede—and soon."

"*Secede?* What does secede mean?" Lizzie asked.

Fannie explained, "It means to separate. Some folks think Tennessee and some of the other southern states might just break from the rest of the country and form a separate country."

"Can they do that? I thought we were the *United States.*"

"They think they can. But some folks in South Carolina tried that about 30 years ago over a tariff. Our President Jackson wouldn't stand for it."

Fannie, Mama and Lizzie lapsed into silence, each lost in her own thoughts. They could hear the clock ticking on the mantel. Finally, Lizzie spoke up.

"Fannie," Lizzie said, "But why do they want to secede? Why don't they like Mr. Lincoln?"

"Mr. Lincoln doesn't want slavery to expand into the western territories of the United States," Fannie told her. "And without that, slavery could end. Some people who own slaves are afraid they'll lose them."

"Lose them? How do you lose someone?" Lizzie asked.

"Well not *lose* like you lose a toy. *Lose* like slavery might be outlawed as it has been in some states in the North. Slavery was once legal in many parts of the country but up North, it just didn't work anymore. Down here, where we have a lot of farms and plantations, the slave owners really need those slaves to do all that hard work. So they don't want to give it up. But they think that if there are more free states than slave states, pretty soon the slave states will be outnumbered and outvoted in Congress."

The Courtneys owned slaves, as did most of their friends. Their slaves, a married couple named Jim and Annie, lived in a house in the back yard. It was a simple log house with a fireplace and a sleeping loft. Grandpa gave Annie to Mama as a wedding present. When Annie and Jim wanted to get married, Papa bought Jim so he and Annie could live together. Mama and Papa prided themselves on treating their slaves well, almost as members of the family.

Not like some people. Some slaves lived in awful shacks, and their children ran around ragged and hungry. Some of them got whipped too. Mama would never do that. Then those terrible auctions! Seeing a mother crying for her child on the auction block, and the child screaming for her mother—it gave Lizzie a sick feeling in her stomach when she saw it. The feeling reminded her of when Papa died.

Afterwards, she asked Mama, "Why did that girl have to be taken away from her mother?"

Mrs. Courtney thought for a minute, and then said, "Lizzie, it's just the way it is . . . it's just the way it is."

"But *why*, Mama, *why*?" Lizzie asked.

Her mother just shook her and turned away.

Lizzie had a lot to think about.

Secession.

Anger.

Fear.

Slavery.

Annie and Jim were happy, weren't they? They *seemed* like they were, didn't they? They were always so bright and cheerful, Jim whistling and Annie singing gospel songs. *Of course they were! Why shouldn't they be?*

Lizzie thought about all those things as she lay in bed that night and felt scared all over again. Then her mind wandered past the unpleasantness of the day and she thought of supper. Roast pork, green beans and boiled potatoes, with Mama's biscuits and honey for dessert. Mama's prayer for unity in the nation as she said grace over their meal. The family in the parlor gathered around the fireplace, Fannie reading, Mama sewing, and Lizzie working on arithmetic—to the dim light of candles. Brother William coming home from hunting with school friends and showing off his string of quail. Mama's hugs and kisses goodnight, as Lizzie settled into her soft feather bed, covered with woolen coverlets. Soon Lizzie was asleep, and dreamed only happy dreams . . . of life as it was, and as it had been, when Papa was alive, and before red-faced men quarreled on the streets of Franklin.

McEWEN HOUSE

Chapter 3

U.S.A. or C.S.A.?
April 21, 1861

L izzie and her friend Jennie McEwen rolled their hoops through Franklin's streets. Mrs. Birdsong's Female Academy had dismissed for the day and the girls were enjoying the early spring day as warm weather finally came to Middle Tennessee. It had been a brutal winter, with several deep snowfalls and many days near zero degrees. Even though the girls lived just one block in either direction from their school at Five Points, some days they thought they'd turn to blocks of ice just walking to school. But as soon as they got inside their school, a roaring fire blazed through the chill and warmed them through and through.

This afternoon, the friends decided to race from Five Points to the courthouse on the square. Five Points was where five streets joined at one intersection. The Public Square was two blocks northeast down Main Street.

"*Ready, set, go!*" called Jennie. Off they ran, rolling their wooden hoops with a stick along Main Street. Hoop and Stick was one of their favorite games. Jennie was usually faster, but today Lizzie edged her out, tapping first on the courthouse column that always marked their ending spot.

"Now let's go to my house," Jennie suggested. "Today is Jane's baking day, and she will have a treat for us."

Jane cooked all the McEwens' meals. She made delicious sweets for Jennie and her family.

Lizzie loved going to Jennie's house. Her eyes feasted on the paintings, fabrics and silver that adorned the house. Some of their furniture came all the way from Philadelphia; their porcelain china even farther—Paris! A dressmaker fitted Mrs. McEwen and the four McEwen girls for new silk and lace dresses every season. The famous Mr. Washington Bogart Cooper, up in Nashville, painted their portraits just last year.

The McEwen house was Franklin's finest. It was enormous—12 rooms on 11 acres with a kitchen garden, orchards of plum, peach and apple trees and a pasture for their horses, cows and hogs; and of course, slave houses in the back. Graceful arched windows and spacious front and side porches looked over Fair Street. The ruby red glass window over the front door told everyone what they needed to know about Jennie's daddy's bank account.

John McEwen descended from one of the pioneer families who travelled over the mountains from North Carolina to seek their fortunes in the new state of Tennessee, around the turn of the 18th century. John practiced law and started several successful businesses. People said that everything John McEwen touched turned to gold.

Mama laughed when Lizzie told her that Mr. McEwen had magic powers. She explained that just meant that Mr. McEwen was just really good at making money.

Lizzie wondered . . . Jennie told her that to turn clear glass red, the glassmaker mixed real gold into the sand. Maybe Mr. McEwen really did have the touch of gold!

Lizzie and Jennie linked arms and walked down Main Street to Jennie's house. Franklin hummed with activity this afternoon. Forging tools clanged at the blacksmith shop. Horses neighed and stamped at the livery stable. Women chatted as they shopped at the dry goods and grocery stores and men quietly conferred outside lawyers' offices.

"Look! There's Dr. Cliffe," Jennie pointed at her family doctor urging his horse and buggy down Main Street. "He could be on his way to my house. I hope no one is sick."

"I'm sure everyone is fine, Jennie," Lizzie told her. Ever since Jennie's brother Richard died last year, Jennie worried a lot about her family.

"Lizzie! Jennie! Wait up!" Hardin Figuers, a Franklin boy about their age, raced towards the girls, accompanied by a young friend named Park Marshall.

"Quick, Jennie, run! Park's ok, but Hardin!" Lizzie exclaimed. "The last time we let him walk with us, he made all those goofy faces and strange noises."

"Oh, Hardin's not so bad. Father thinks he has quite a future in front of him."

"As a daredevil maybe! The last time I saw him, he was climbing on the roof of the courthouse."

Jennie laughed. "Well, I guess he's brave anyway."

"William said Hardin's returned to school at the boys' academy," Lizzie said. "He couldn't go for awhile after his father died."

"Father is paying his tuition. After Richard died, he and Mother decided to help other boys who couldn't afford to go to school." Jennie looked sad for a minute.

Lizzie bit her lip. She knew Jennie missed Richard terribly. She ached for Papa just the same.

Hardin and Park caught up with the girls and the four youngsters found Jane out back of the McEwens' house, in the brick kitchen, preparing boiled custard. Jane's eight-year-old granddaughter, Elisa, was picking the stems and blossoms off a pile of gooseberries for Jane's gooseberry fool, a delectable concoction of the juicy red berries, custard and sugar.

Jennie and Elisa were about the same age and had played together as toddlers. But, since Jennie went to school now and Elisa had to work, they didn't spend as much time together. Slaves weren't allowed to go to school, or even learn how to read and write.

"Lordy, children, look at you four, circling like hawks around a field mouse," Jane said. She always had funny expressions but the children all knew just what she meant.

"Please, may we have something to eat, Aunt Jane?" asked Jennie. Jane wasn't really Jennie's aunt. White folks called some slaves "Aunt" and "Uncle," although Jennie didn't really know why. Neither did Lizzie. That's just what everyone did.

"Your Mama told me not to allow you children to spoil your supper, so no, you can't." Jane usually sneaked a tasty morsel to the children, but they could tell that today there was no use trying. Jane had something on her mind.

"This here is for your father, Jennie, for him and his men friends in the house."

"Men friends in the house? At this time of day? Father should be at his law office." Jennie sounded surprised.

The children remembered the whispered conversations they had overheard lately among adults. They saw the newspapers with the big ugly headlines and strange names and places: *"Fort Sumter." "Secession." "States' Rights." What did it all mean?*

"Let's sneak into the house and listen," Jennie demanded. "Father wouldn't like it but I want to find out what they're talking about."

The children ran around the house and slipped inside the side porch. They crouched under a wicker table in front of a window. Luckily, Mrs. McEwen had taken advantage of the beautiful spring day and opened all the windows, airing out the house after the long winter.

"Perfect," Jennie whispered. "We'll be able to hear everything."

The first voice they heard was deep and commanding, and Hardin recognized it immediately.

"We simply cannot allow ourselves to be pushed around. We must take action!" a man's voice roared.

"That's Professor McNutt!" Hardin said under his breath. The professor ran the boys' academy that Hardin attended with Lizzie's brother William. The professor's drama-filled voice could make even history class seem exciting.

"My good sir! Do you know what you're saying?" another man asked.

"Yes, Daniel, I do. We have not asked for this. We simply want to continue our lives the way we always have. But this latest transgression by our so-called president is the last straw. Resupplying Fort Sumter was an act of aggression."

Hardin murmured to his friends, "*Daniel*. That must be Dr. Cliffe."

"What you're suggesting is treasonous," Dr. Cliffe exclaimed.

"I *cannot* support secession," Franklin judge and lawyer John Marshall insisted.

Lizzie said, "Park, that's your father!"

Park began to speak up but Jennie quickly shushed him. "South Carolina has every right to defend herself!" another man shouted.

"Hear Hear!" a chorus of voices joined in.

"And Lincoln is asking for 75,000 troops!" the professor continued. "That can mean only one thing. He plans to invade the South!"

A voice cried out, "Governor Harris simply must call another election!"

Seven Southern states had already seceded, but Tennessee was not among them. An election for secession had failed in February, and while many folks were relieved, others were still angry.

The men continued to squabble and debate back and forth for awhile, then one by one, left the house and all was quiet. The young friends slumped back on the porch and looked at each other with worried faces.

All of a sudden Lizzie really wanted to be home, so she could talk to Mama and Fannie. She told her friends goodbye and ran home.

Mama and Fannie were talking together, but they stopped abruptly when Lizzie walked in the door. Lizzie ran to Mama and buried her head in Mama's apron.

"It's scary! What the men were taking about at Jennie's."

Mrs. Courtney sighed deeply. "It's being talked about all over town, honey. War is coming." She looked at her daughters sadly. "Heaven help us."

~~~~~

In June, Tennessee Governor Isham Harris called for another election.

This time the voters approved secession, overwhelmingly. Tennessee left the United States of America to join its sister Southern states, and became the 11th and last member of the Confederate States of America. The United States was at war—with itself.

McGAVOCK'S GROVE

Chapter 4

The War Comes Home
February 14, 1862

William had been gone eight months now. Lizzie thought back to that day in June when he came home and told Mama he'd decided to join the army. Mama hadn't liked it, not a bit. Nor had Fannie. They both begged him to change his mind.

"William, you're barely 18," Mama cried. "Can't you wait another year?"

"If I wait it may be over before I have a chance to get in the fight," William insisted. "We'll whip those Yankees in no time."

"But William, why do you want to fight?" asked Fannie.

37

"We're doing it for *you*, Fannie. Don't you care about Tennessee?" William asked her. "Don't you care about the South?"

"I am an American first, William," Fannie declared.

William had made up his mind. So he went to Mr. McEwen, who was raising up a regiment, and mustered in along with many other young Franklin men. Within days, they began drilling and marching at McGavock's Grove. The McGavocks lived one mile from town on a big plantation called Carnton, and their many acres of property gave the men plenty of space to drill and march. All the town children envied their friends Hattie and Winder McGavock, who got to see the soldiers marching and firing guns every day.

Franklin throbbed with excitement about the coming war. Franklin ladies like Mrs. McNutt and Hardin's mother Mrs. Figuers gathered in the Masonic Lodge and stitched uniforms for the soldiers. Lizzie and Jennie assembled little mending kits with a needle, thread and spare buttons that the soldiers called "housewives."

Mrs. Sallie Ewing Carter sewed the first Confederate flag in town and hung it from her porch on Third Avenue. Soon it seemed the whole town flew the new flag.

Finally, the day arrived. William joined dozens of smartly-uniformed young men, marching through town toward the train depot on East Margin Street. Everyone cheered, waved flags and sang songs like "Dixie" and "Bonnie Blue Flag."

Lizzie, Fannie and Mama stood in a little knot on the platform, watching William march toward them. When he saw them, he broke ranks to say goodbye. They hugged and kissed him until he laughed and said, "You're going to crush my new uniform. It'll be ruined!"

And with that, William jumped on the train. He rushed to a window and bellowed over the din of the crowd and the screech of the locomotive, "Bye, Mama, bye, Fannie and Lizzie. Now don't y'all worry . . . I'll be home by the end of the summer!"

II

The Courtneys eagerly awaited William's letters, which arrived every several weeks. He told them about the train ride to Camp Cheatham, north of Nashville, where the soldiers first trained.

"We are ready to go fight the enemy," William wrote.

After that, the army boarded the train eastward, through Knoxville, and into Virginia.

"We arrived one day too late to join in the action at Manassas," William wrote. "It looks like we might just miss this war . . ."

Manassas, or as the Federals called it, Bull Run, was the first major battle of the War, and a Confederate victory. Surely everyone would turn around and come home now, Lizzie hoped.

But they didn't. The fighting continued.

Life at home without brothers, sons and fathers was difficult for those who stayed behind. Hardin's older brother and two of Jennie's cousins enlisted along with William. Dr. Cliffe joined the Confederate army as a surgeon, leaving behind his wife and daughter Belle. Mr. McNutt's school didn't have quite as many students as usual, but the professor's voice was often heard on the street encouraging the war effort.

Bad news arrived in William's next letter. "Measles has broken out at camp. Also dysentery and camp fever. Many men have died or mustered out. It seems these illnesses are proving to be more destructive to us than any army."

As winter came on, the men began to feel the effects of the weather. "Western Virginia's terrain is very rough," William wrote. "We have had difficulties crossing over the mountains. We have had to swim across icy rivers. Our uniforms (and we have just one) are worn and tattered. Often we cannot get enough to eat."

Mama, Fannie and Lizzie all wiped tears from their faces. Their precious son and brother, suffering so!

By February, William's regiment had lost a quarter of its men to illness or death without fighting a single battle.

Back home, the news turned as bleak as the winter weather. Jennie's cousin Henry died of measles in Virginia. Another Franklin soldier died from dysentery. Still, Confederate supporters remained optimistic that their side would win the war.

Then one mid-February day, a traveler arrived in town carrying the news that the Union army had attacked the forts protecting Nashville.

"Union soldiers have captured Fort Henry," Fannie told Mama and Lizzie. "Fort Donelson is next. U.S. General Ulysses S. Grant is invading Tennessee through Kentucky."

"Oh, my!" Mama exclaimed. "That is good news. Surely this war will end soon and William can return home."

"Yes, Mama," Fannie said. "And our country can be reunited."

Fannie, Mama and Lizzie held fast to their Unionist views, although Mama and Lizzie kept their opinions to themselves. Not Fannie, though. She was outspoken, and never hesitated to voice her view that the country ought to be united.

At first, Fannie's old friends made fun of her and called her a home-grown Yankee. They stopped laughing and soon turned bitter when Franklin's newspaper, the *Western Weekly Review*, reported that Nashville had been invaded by the U.S. army and was now under Union control. *Would Franklin be next?*

MASONIC LODGE

Chapter 5

Franklin is Captured
March 23, 1862

It was a cold early spring Sunday morning. Church had just let out all over Franklin when Titus, a slave from the farm of Jennie's grandfather Christopher McEwen, galloped into town with the news that hundreds of Union soldiers were marching down the Nashville Pike toward Franklin.

"They were almost to the house when Master Christopher told me to race to town to tell the news," Titus told Mrs. Cliffe, who was walking home from church with her daughter Belle.

Those McEwens lived on their plantation called Aspen Grove, three miles north of town, on the Nashville Pike.

News travelled quickly through the village. Professor McNutt, John Marshall and John McEwen hurried to the third floor of the tallest building in town, the Masonic Lodge, which gave them a bird's-eye view of town and its surroundings. A large crowd quickly gathered on the street underneath.

Sallie Carter called up, "What do you see? Are they coming?"

"All I can see right now is a big cloud of dust—it looks like it's about two miles north," John Marshall shouted down to the crowd.

"That must be the Yankees! Mayor McEwen, stop them!" Mrs. McNutt cried out.

"This is terrible!" Mrs. Figuers said. "We must keep them out of Franklin."

Franklin's voters had elected John McEwen mayor in October of 1861. He had no idea he would soon be called upon to make the biggest decision of his life.

Mayor McEwen came downstairs and immediately called a meeting of Franklin's city leaders. Several men wanted to resist.

"We can stop them, we must fight!" one said.

"We can't!" said the mayor. "They are armed to the teeth and we are but a few old men, women and children. If we fight, they might destroy the town and who knows what else. My decision is we surrender the town—to save it."

Before long they heard the rat-a-tat-tat of drumbeats, the clomp-clomp of men marching and the clip-clopping of horses trotting. Soon dozens of rows of soldiers in navy blue uniforms, accompanied by officers on horseback, marched across the Harpeth River Bridge and entered Franklin.

Mayor McEwen met the soldiers on the town square.

"My name is John McEwen and I am the mayor of Franklin," he said to the senior officer sitting astride his horse. "I pray that you will not harm our people."

U.S. Lt. Col. George Grummond dismounted.

"I will speak to the people soon. But first I must do something," he said.

Col. Grummond crossed the road to the courthouse, where the Confederate flag flew from a flagpole. He yanked it down, wadded it in a ball and threw it on the ground. He pulled out a colorful bundle which he carefully unwrapped. It was the Stars and Stripes. He solemnly raised it up the flagpole while all the soldiers saluted.

Fannie, Lizzie and their mother looked at each other and smiled.

Around them, the mood was tense. No one said much as they waited for the officer to speak. Everyone looked around nervously. Most of the white folks in town were Confederate supporters, called Secessionists or

Secesh by Union supporters. *Would they be arrested as traitors? Would their property be confiscated?*

Then there were the Unionists. They had remained loyal to the U.S. and were thankful the U.S. Army had arrived. The Courtneys, however, felt uneasy because William was a Confederate soldier. *Would they be punished because he was the enemy?*

Elisa and Titus stood at the back of the crowd. Their eyes stared down but their hearts soared. *Maybe,* they thought, *this soldier might somehow bring freedom at last!*

Col. Grummond went to the courthouse's second floor balcony, and addressed the citizens of Franklin.

"We are here to maintain order," Grummond shouted to the crowd below. "We won't hurt you if you do what we say,"

"That's a relief," Lizzie thought. She was worried about Jennie, Hardin, Park and their families.

The colonel continued, "First, every head of household must step up and sign the loyalty oath."

"The Oath" was a written promise that citizens would stay loyal to the United States of America. This was the first time that U.S. citizens had ever been required to sign a loyalty oath.

For Mrs. Courtney, this was no problem. She *was* loyal. However, for the McEwens, the McNutts, Mrs. Figuers, John Marshall, Mrs. Sallie Carter… to sign went against their beliefs.

"What if we refuse?" someone shouted from the crowd.

"Then we'll have no choice but to send you beyond the lines," Grummond shouted back. "We'll give you three days to get your affairs in order . . . then you must leave Franklin."

"What about our homes?" a voice yelled.

"And our property?" another asked.

"Sign or leave, that's your choice," Grummond told them.

Grumbling could be heard from the crowd but no one said another word. Lizzie and Jennie looked at each other.

"Jennie, will your father sign?" Lizzie whispered to her friend.

"I don't know what he'll do . . ." Jennie's voice trailed off.

Lizzie felt sorry for her friend. How difficult the choice must be for her father. She hoped he would sign the oath so her friend could stay in her home in Franklin.

Hardin and his mother stood in the crowd too. Lizzie saw them talking softly together, looking anxious. Mr. Marshall had his hand on Park's shoulder. Mrs. Carter was whispering to Mr. McEwen. Mrs. McNutt cried as the professor spoke quietly to her.

Franklin was now under occupation as heads drooped and hearts sank.

But Titus and Elisa raised their heads high.

"Titus, we may soon be free!" Elisa whispered to her friend.

Titus smiled. His older brother Charley had been sold three years ago. Titus didn't know where he was but he missed him something terrible. *Maybe,* he thought, *just maybe, he'd be able to see him again someday.*

HARPETH RIVER BRIDGE

Chapter 6

A Visit to the Colonel
Later that week

Fannie and Lizzie walked to the town square, looking for Col. Grummond. They spotted him in front of the courthouse surrounded by soldiers awaiting orders.

Fannie Courtney snaked her way through the men. She approached Grummond.

"Sir, I must speak with you," she said to him.

"What is it, Miss? We have jobs to do. Make it quick."

"I must tell you about my brother, William. He is a Confederate soldier. But my mother, my sister and I do not support that cause. We are loyal and always have been," Fannie said firmly.

Grummond stared at her through narrowed eyes.

"Do you *really* expect me to believe that?" Grummond asked her.

"You can ask anyone in town. They all know our allegiances. They're Secesh and don't like it much," she retorted.

Grummond shot back, "Why are you telling me this?"

"I don't want you to hear about William from anyone else. In spite of William, you won't get any trouble from us." Fannie abruptly turned and left, grabbing Lizzie's hand and pulling her through the crowd.

"Fannie, I can't believe you spoke that way to that man," Lizzie said as the sisters hurried away. "He looked angry."

"I needed to tell him the truth," Fannie said.

Col. Grummond looked thoughtfully after the young woman, realizing how brave she had been to tell him about her brother.

Then he went back to work. He had a job to do.

~~~~~

The army needed a building to use as a headquarters, and Col. Grummond quickly chose the courthouse.

Just four years earlier, in 1858, the county leaders decided that Franklin's courthouse was just too small for growing, prosperous Williamson County. So they had it torn down and a new one built in its place.

Franklin's citizens took great pride in their beautiful Greek Revival courthouse with its cast iron columns, hand-carved woodwork and walls three bricks thick. Now Union soldiers came and went all day long with their muddy boots.

The judges and lawyers who worked there were irate when they were told they could not use their own courthouse without getting permission from Col. Grummond. But there was nothing they could do about it.

Grummond's next task was to find places for his men to sleep. Soldiers on the march usually slept on the ground. But there would be soldiers in Franklin for the rest of the war—however long it lasted—and Grummond needed barracks for them.

He did not force Franklin residents to share their homes with soldiers. That was against the law. So he looked for empty buildings, and found two.

The first was the Masonic Lodge. Although the Masons met in the building every week, no one lived there. *Perfect*, Grummond decided. The second was St. Paul's Episcopal Church. Two years earlier, the church's congregation had gotten so small that they could not afford a full-time rector and stopped holding regular services. It was vacant most of the time. *That would work.*

Soldiers moved in and made the buildings their temporary homes.

Then Grummond needed to secure the town, meaning no one could come or go without permission. That was easy to do because of the town's location.

The village of Franklin is bounded on three sides by the Harpeth River. To enter or leave town from the north, east or west required crossing a bridge. That made it easy to keep folks in or keep folks out. All Col. Grummond had to do was post a sentry at the bridge. Heading south there was no river in the way. So Col.

Grummond posted sentries on all the roads coming into town from the south.

The first time Jennie's father tried to visit his parents at Aspen Grove he was turned away at the bridge.

"You've got to get a pass," the sentry, a private from Indiana, informed him.

"A pass? Where do I get a pass?" John McEwen asked.

"From the courthouse. Go ask the officers there and they'll decide if you can leave or not," the soldier said. "Otherwise I cannot let you cross this bridge and leave town."

"This is an outrage! I'm just going to visit my father."

"I'm under orders. I can't let you go."

Mayor McEwen turned around and went home.

"What have we come to?" the mayor asked himself. *"What have we done?"*

LOTZ HOUSE

Chapter 7

Sad Times
March, 1863

One year had passed since the Union army came to Franklin to stay, and life had changed. A sad feeling shrouded the town. People didn't laugh much anymore—especially not since soldiers arrested two ladies for laughing on Main Street as a soldier's funeral procession passed by. Although the women tearfully explained they hadn't noticed the funeral, they were threatened with banishment from town if it ever happened again.

Professor McNutt did not shout out his opinions the way he used to. No one gave an opinion on the war anymore, at least not in public. Even husbands and wives whispered to each other.

Food was scarce. Cows, horses and chickens disappeared from barns overnight—often stolen by soldiers. Soldiers cut down entire groves, trees their owners had planned to sell or use to build houses, barns and fences.

Fabric for clothing was hard to get and costly. Simple calico cost four times what it had before the war.

Old friendships soured because of the war. Some families even broke apart over it.

Lizzie and Jennie stayed best of friends, even though their parents held opposite views of the conflict. For Fannie, though, life had become very difficult. Many of her old friends had stopped speaking to her.

"Thank heavens for Belle Cliffe," Fannie told Lizzie. "She's the only friend I have left."

Belle's father was Dr. Daniel Cliffe, who joined the Confederate army as a surgeon. He was captured in Kentucky after a battle in Mill Springs and was to be sent to a Northern prison when he made an important decision.

"Father changed his mind about this war," Belle told Fannie. "He no longer supports the Confederacy. He's now a Union man."

Dr. Cliffe resigned his commission in the Confederate army, signed the loyalty oath and returned home to his family and the practice of medicine.

"Belle, I'm so glad your family is Union now. It was so hard feeling like we were the only ones."

"You weren't, though. The Lotzes, I think they're Union too."

"Oh, I don't know about that," Fannie said. "I'm just not sure they care much one way or the other."

Johann and Margaretha Lotz emigrated from Germany in 1849, and later built a beautiful two-story wood house on the Columbia Pike across the road from the Carter Farm. Mr. Lotz was a master carpenter and wood carver who also made pianos. He carved all the mantels and moldings for the new courthouse.

Lizzie and Jennie attended school with Matilda Lotz at Mrs. Birdsong's Female Academy at Five Points. Matilda was a good student but she especially loved drawing. When the girls played outside, Matilda often grabbed a stick and drew in the dirt.

The girls loved visiting Matilda at her home and listening to her parents speak German to each other. When Mr. and Mrs. Lotz spoke English, they peppered their conversations with German words and had deep guttural accents. Their food—*schnitzels* and *tortes* and *sauerbraten*—wasn't like the dishes served in Franklin homes. But *rote grutze*—red fruit pudding—tasted just like Aunt Jane's gooseberry fool.

One day Matilda missed school. When school let out, Mrs. Courtney met Fannie and Lizzie at the door.

"My daughters, I have some sad news for you." Mrs. Courtney told them.

Lizzie held her breath as Fannie put her hand to her throat, eyes wide. *Was it William?*

"It's the Lotzes. Their precious babies are no more."

"Mama!" both girls cried. "Julian and Julius have died?"

"Yes, and it's a terrible thing."

How the older girls loved the Lotz twins. Chubby, fair-haired toddlers, the children were always laughing and chattering together. They seemed to have their own secret language that no one else could understand. Even at two years old they got into much mischief, to Mrs. Lotz's consternation. She was forever chasing after them as they ran off to explore.

"What happened? How did they die?" Lizzie asked.

"I don't know, but Mr. and Mrs. Lotz think the army killed them."

"Babies! Who would kill little babies? How cruel!" Fannie said.

"I don't know. But Mr. Lotz said the soldiers poisoned a well and the children drank from it."

"Could that be true? Why would they poison a well? They might accidentally poison some of their own soldiers." Fannie pointed out.

"I don't know, dear girls. All we can do is pray for the bereaved Lotz family. And we must just hope that this terrible war ends soon."

II

Col. Grummond visited the Lotzes soon after the funeral.

"Mr. and Mrs. Lotz, I have heard rumors that you are blaming our soldiers for the deaths of your children," Col. Grummond told them.

"*Ja!* Yes!" Mr. Lotz shouted. "Julian and Julius were poisoned!"

Mrs. Lotz added, "You did this!"

"Sir, we did no such thing! Have we done any act like that since we've been here?"

"*Ja!* You take food, you cut down our trees, you arrest ladies for laughing. Why don't you leave us alone!"

"This is war, sir! And you Southerners started it! While we mean to win this war, we do not murder children. We have children of our own. We are not evil."

"Who cares who started it? I come from Germany to seek new life in new world, and then this!"

"Mr. Lotz, it was a tragic accident. An *accident*. You saw that we had begun building earthworks just south of here. We have to protect the southern end of Franklin because there are Rebels out there, planning attacks. Remember all the rain we had recently? Water filled the trenches. I think your poor children drowned in one of the trenches."

"*Nein*. No. I cannot believe that. *Danke*, thank you for coming, but please, *go*."

Col. Grummond sighed. This was one of the most difficult parts of his job. How could anyone think American soldiers would murder children?

COURTNEY HOUSE

Chapter 8

A Budding Friendship
April, 1863

A few days later Col. Grummond stopped at a brick house on Church Street and knocked on the door. When Mrs. Courtney opened the door, she was concerned to see the Union officer standing there.

He smiled and tipped his hat. "Ma'am, may I speak to your daughter?"

A look of alarm crossed Mrs. Courtney's face. "You mean Fannie? Has she done something wrong?"

"No, ma'am. She has not. I would just like to talk to her for a few minutes, if I may."

Mrs. Courtney said, shutting the door, "I will ask her if she will receive you."

She went to the kitchen where Fannie was washing up after supper.

"Fannie, I do believe Col. Grummond has come to pay a social call."

"Do not joke about things like that, Mother dear," Fannie replied.

"I am not joking. He said he just wants a few minutes to talk to you."

Fannie dried her hands on her apron and went to the front door. She opened it and saw Col. Grummond standing there, hat in hand.

"What is it?" she asked him.

"Miss Courtney, I realize now I misjudged you," Grummond told her. "That day you came to see me at the courthouse, I thought you were lying. I now see how brave you are."

"It's not brave to do what one thinks is right," Fannie said firmly.

"I wouldn't want to be in your shoes. It would be much easier if you lived in the North," Grummond said.

"This is my home and I'll stay here. Someday I may be needed here."

Col. Grummond didn't say anything for a while. Neither did Fannie. They just stared at one another, sizing each other up.

Finally Fannie said, "Would you like to come in?"

Col. Grummond answered quickly, "Yes, I would very much like to come in."

"Mother, Col. Grummond would like to visit for a short time," Fannie told her as they walked into the parlor.

"I'll just do some mending while you are talking," Mrs. Courtney said.

Lizzie came into the parlor from her bedroom when Col. Grummond sat down. She asked him, "What are you doing here?"

"Lizzie, hush! Don't ask rude questions!" Mrs. Courtney said.

"I'm sorry, Mama. It's just that Jennie said it's never good when a Yankee shows up at your door, is all."

Mrs. Courtney turned red. She spoke to the officer, "Col. Grummond, you know what she hears around town. I'm just grateful that Lizzie is still accepted by friends like Jennie McEwen, Hardin Figuers and Park Marshall. Unfortunately, the same can't be said for Fannie. She only has Belle Cliffe."

"It's difficult living here when our allegiance to the United States is unpopular," Fannie said. "And to think just four years ago we would have been called traitors *not* to feel as we do."

"I cannot imagine how you must feel," said Col. Grummond. "For me of course, I am the enemy. It's so different from the last war, the one against Mexico in '46."

"Yes, you are so right, Col. Grummond," said Mrs. Courtney. "Here too, I remember when all the men came back with such stories of the brave soldiers they fought with, from all over our nation. Northerners and Southerners were friends then. I wish it were still the case."

"Yes, ma'am. I didn't fight in that war because I was too young, but many of the officers talk about it a lot. It's sad that our country has come to this."

"We quite agree," Fannie said, "And you are welcome to visit anytime you wish."

And thus began the special friendship of Miss Fannie Courtney and Col. George Grummond.

FORT GRANGER

Chapter 9

An Unexpected Visitor
March, 1864

As 1863 crept toward 1864 the war slogged on with no end in sight. Christmas was a sad occasion as no one was in the mood to celebrate. New Year's came and went with barely a hurrah. By now, most families had suffered the loss of a loved one.

The Courtneys wondered where William was. *Did he fight in that big battle at Gettysburg? Was he at the siege at Vicksburg?* It was impossible to know. The mail system was no longer reliable. The local newspaper had shut down. The only people who knew the truth were Union officers, and they weren't talking.

Long after midnight one spring night Lizzie was awakened by tapping on her window.

"Fannie! Wake up! Do you hear that?"

"Someone's out there," Fannie said.

The girls rushed to the window, and saw a familiar, but in some ways, different face.

William!

They threw open the window, and grabbing at his arms, pulled him inside head first. The three siblings hugged and kissed and laughed and cried as they fell in a pile on the floor.

"I thought I might never see you again," Lizzie said.

"Oh, dear sisters, I missed you so much," William told them. "I had given up hope of seeing you again too."

"Mama will be so happy," Lizzie said. "Let's wake her up."

The three Courtneys lit a candle and tip-toed into Mrs. Courtney's bedroom.

Fannie gently shook her mother, whispering, "Mama, we have a surprise for you. But you must not cry out."

William moved to his mother's bed and whispered in her ear, "It's me, William."

Mrs. Courtney said softly, "Is this a dream? It can't be . . . my dear William?"

"Yes, I've come home," William said, embracing her.

Mrs. Courtney pulled back and her eyes searched William's face.

"Son, you have had a difficult time, I can tell. You have suffered."

"Yes, I have. Just as every soldier in this army has suffered," William answered her.

The family went into the parlor and settled in close to the remains of the fire in the fireplace. Fannie threw a blanket around William and ran out to the kitchen to prepare food for him.

"How is it that you are here, William?" Mama asked. "Have you . . . deserted?"

"No! Of course not. Our army is in camp south of Murfreesboro and I was able to get a pass for a three-day furlough."

"Wasn't that dangerous? If you're caught here you'll be sent to prison at Camp Douglas."

Camp Douglas was a Union camp in Illinois for Confederate prisoners of war captured by the Union army.

"I traveled at night and stayed off the pikes," William explained. "I waded across the Harpeth and sneaked into town."

"You'll have to hide in the basement during the day," Fannie said, as she brought him a bowl of steaming hot soup. "Someone might see you and you'll be arrested."

"What about Mary and Jim? Will they turn me in, do you think?"

"They're gone," Mama told him.

"Gone? Where?" William asked.

"Ran to Nashville, I suppose. After the Emancipation Proclamation a lot of the slaves took the opportunity to run away. We woke up one morning and they were gone."

"I thought they were happy here," William said.

"We all thought that," Fannie said. "Anyway, eat your soup before it gets cold."

William gulped it down. "We rarely get nourishing food. I don't think I will ever feel full again. There's just not enough food to go around . . ." His voice trailed off.

"And make sure you're quiet when Col. Grummond comes to visit!" Lizzie piped up.

"Col. Grummond? A Yankee is coming to this house? Why?"

"He's a friend of mine," Fannie said. "And it's lonely here too, when almost every friend I ever had refuses to speak to me. Col. Grummond is a kind man and I enjoy his company."

William looked disgusted.

77

Mrs. Courtney said, "Children, let's not spoil William's homecoming. We must spend what few days we have with William remembering the good times."

"And fattening him up!" added Lizzie. "He looks like a scarecrow!"

"Yes, William," Mama said. "You do have a gaunt look about your face. We must find provisions for you to keep your strength up."

"Is it difficult to get food here, too?" William asked her.

"Oh, yes. There's just not enough to go around, with both armies living off the land in the South. Soldiers from both armies forage and many outright steal too."

"Did you notice anything different about the town, William?" Fannie asked him.

"It was awfully dark, but I thought maybe some of the timber had been cut," William said.

"Yes, that's one difference. The army cut down hundreds of trees to build Ft. Granger."

"Where's Ft. Granger?" William asked.

"It's on top of Figuers Bluff, you know, the hill on the other side of the river overlooking the railroad tracks," Fannie said.

"So they have weapons and ammunition up there?" William asked.

"Yes, and there are four cannons pointed this way. That frightens people who think they could fire those cannons on the town at any time."

William's face darkened again. "They better not do that!"

Fannie spoke forcefully. "William, Confederate cavalry have attempted twice to raid the fort, and they didn't fire the cannons. If they didn't do it when being attacked, I don't think they're going to do it now."

"What happened during the raids?" William asked.

"Well, the Rebels came up from around Spring Hill into town but they never made it across the river. The Federals met them around the McNutts' house and they skirmished there. The Rebels retreated after that," Fannie said.

"I was in school when we heard the guns going off," Lizzie told her brother. "Mrs. Birdsong led us down to the basement. We were scared to death!"

"And after that the army ordered the McNutts and Mrs. Royce to leave town. They were suspected of spying," Mrs. Courtney said. "The Royces' house was completely destroyed. The McNutts' place has been taken over by the Union army and badly damaged."

"Professor McNutt and his Academy. It meant everything to him," William said. "Where have they gone?"

"Mrs. Royce and her two daughters are in Alabama last we heard, and the McNutts are in Virginia."

Fannie asked William, "Do you remember that Mr. Royce was the rector at St. Paul's Episcopal Church?"

William nodded. The Courtneys attended First Presbyterian Church but had several friends who attended St. Paul's.

"If he ever makes it back and sees the church . . ." Fannie hesitated.

"If he ever makes it back and *what?*" William asked her.

"Well, some of the soldiers chopped up the pews and burned them to heat the building. And then they stole the pipe organ and somehow sent it up North."

"I'd like to get my hands on those Yankee scoundrels!" William said.

Lizzie added, "And they threw the pipes down Main Street and the boys rode them like stick horses."

William sat back in the chair, sighed and shook his head.

"I knew Franklin had become occupied. But I guess I just didn't think it through. I see now that this war is not just between armies and soldiers. It's everywhere. It affects everyone. I never thought it would be that way."

"Nor did we, William," his mother gently told him. "Nor did we."

MCNUTT ACADEMY

Chapter 10

In Hiding
March, 1864

William stayed two nights, hiding out in the basement during the day and creeping upstairs after dark to sleep in his bed. He slept soundly, snoring so loudly that his mother and sisters worried that someone would hear from the outside. William laughed and said that he was not accustomed to sleeping on a soft feather mattress and pillow, covered with blankets and coverlets. It was a far cry from his usual bed of the hard ground, cold and wet in the winter, and hot, dusty and buggy in the summer.

Mrs. Courtney was afraid to wash William's filthy uniform. Someone might notice the gray uniform as she boiled her laundry in the big iron pot in the yard. She did mend holes and seams and was able to scrounge material to make William another pair of pants.

William stuffed himself at every meal. It was heavenly eating good food—biscuits with gravy, beets and tomatoes put up from last summer's garden, and ham and bacon—and quite different from his usual diet of hardtack, dried corn and, if he was lucky, a piece or two or stringy boiled pork. William could hardly remember the past when he ate until his stomach felt full.

But the best part was being home with his family. Yes, they disagreed on the war, but all the Courtneys knew their mutual love and devotion would never end.

On his second night home, William had already come upstairs from the basement and was sitting in the parlor with Fannie when someone knocked on the door.

"Oh, no! William, you'd better go hide in one of the bedrooms. It could be Col. Grummond. I'll tell him I'm not feeling well enough for a visit tonight," Fannie told him.

William ran toward the back of the house, careful that his footsteps not be heard.

Fannie slowly walked to the front door and opened it.

"Good evening, Col. Grummond," Fannie said softly to her friend.

"Hello Miss Fannie, may I come in?" He smiled tenderly at her.

"I've been feeling poorly lately," she said. "I'm not sure I'm up for company tonight."

"It's important that I talk to you. I have news for you that I want to share."

Fannie rubbed her forehead. "Can you come back tomorrow? I have a terrible headache."

"No—that's just it. I'm being transferred first thing tomorrow morning. I just received orders tonight."

"Oh, dear!" Fannie exclaimed. "Yes, do come in."

Col. Grummond removed his hat, entered the parlor, and sat in William's recently vacated chair. He glanced absently around the room, clasped his hands together in his lap, and finally began to speak.

"Miss Fannie," Grummond said slowly, now gazing into her eyes as she sat on the settee opposite him. "I find myself becoming very much attached to you. I hope you'll not find my words too strong, but after this war ends I would very much like to return to Franklin. I would like to ask your brother for your hand in marriage, if he and I make it through this war."

Fannie blushed but said nothing.

"I'm not asking for a word from you now, and if you don't want to accept my proposal, you need not receive me when I return."

"I will look very much forward to your return, Col. Grummond," Fannie said quietly.

Col. Grummond's eyes lit up. He threw his head back and laughed heartily.

"Wonderful! Well, goodbye, Miss Fannie. I hope to see you soon."

"Goodbye, Col. Grummond."

Fannie extended her hand, and the colonel softly kissed it.

After the door shut, William came back to the parlor.

"Do you mean to marry that man, Fannie?" William demanded.

"I like him," Lizzie piped up. "He's very nice to all the children, even the Secesh."

"I like him, too," Mrs. Courtney said. "He seems to be a great family man. He loves to visit here in our home. Like you, William, he's lonely and misses his family. You can understand that, can't you?"

"Yes, I do. But he's a Yankee. He's not from here. Where is he from anyway?"

"Michigan. It's a very nice place, from what he describes," Fannie said.

"Well, I hope you'll think about it a long time before you go and marry someone so different from you, Fannie."

She shot back, "Not so different. We both salute the same flag."

II

William was due to return to his regiment the next night. He waited until darkness fell, and began to pack his haversack.

"Are you sure you must go back?" Mrs. Courtney asked him.

"It's my duty, Mother. Being home these three days has reinforced my belief that I am doing the right thing. I'm sorry that you, Fannie and Lizzie don't see it this way, but I do."

Mrs. Courtney said, "Even some of the biggest Confederate supporters around town are starting to question whether they can win it."

"Who?" William quickly asked. "Do you know this for sure?"

"Well, there are many rumors but some say that Mayor McEwen is softening his support. I know that his businesses have taken a beating. His law practice is making no money."

"There are others?"

"Dr. Cliffe. You knew about that, didn't you?"

"No!" William buried his face in his hands.

"Yes, he was captured in Kentucky, returned to Franklin on parole and is now the biggest Union man in town."

William was speechless.

"And it's a good thing he's here," she continued. "He's the one everyone goes to when they need permission to travel. And as much help as he's given people, his old friends shun him and refuse his services as a doctor. The whole family has suffered."

"What about you, Mother? You and Fannie and Lizzie?"

"Your serving with the Confederates has helped, William. They won't ostracize me because of you. Lizzie's close friendship with Jennie McEwen has kept her from loneliness. And thankfully, Fannie has Belle Cliffe."

Suddenly Mrs. Courtney's eyes filled with tears. She took William into her arms, hugged him tightly and cried out, "How many more years must we endure this? When will this horrible war end?" William shook his head and said nothing. He looked sadly at his mother as she wept.

A few minutes later, her tears dried, Mrs. Courtney said to William, "Son, I guess it's time for you to go."

She gave him a bundle filled with meat and bread, as much as he could carry, along with the new pants, and a newly-knitted pair of socks. He was ready to go. Fannie went to the front door, checking for the sentries who patrolled the town.

After looking up and down the street, Fannie whispered to William, "It looks clear, you can go. Be careful."

William whispered back, "Goodbye, I love you all."

He crawled out the back window, melting away into the darkness through back yards and gardens. Fannie slipped out to the street and glancing east, saw her brother vault over a fence just south of the McNutts' ruined house. Beyond were the train tracks and then the Harpeth River. Fannie had warned William that the tracks were often patrolled so he knew to be wary. He crouched down next to the tracks and after checking for sentries, jumped across the tracks and scrambled down the river bank.

William splashed across the water holding his pack and clothing above his head. He made it quickly to the other side, crawled back up the bank and headed east toward his regiment in Murfreesboro.

At home, Fannie, Lizzie and their mother cried and cried.

They didn't know when they would see William again. They didn't know *if* they would see William again. As it turned out, they would see him again—eight months later, on November 30, 1864.

CARTER HOUSE

Chapter 11

The Longest Day
November 30, 1864

Major Sabine dug hungrily into the eggs, bacon, grits and biscuits Mrs. Courtney prepared for him for breakfast. After he sopped up the last of the egg with his biscuit, he pushed back in his chair.

"Delicious, and thank you, Ma'am," he told Mrs. Courtney. "It's been awhile since I've had anything this tasty. Where we've been no one's offered to cook a meal like this."

"I'm glad to do it," she said. Then she asked nervously, "What is happening here? From the looks of it, there are a lot of soldiers here. We've not had this many since last year when they were marching through to Chattanooga."

The Union army's garrison in Franklin rarely had more than several hundred soldiers in it. At the moment, that many were jammed in the Courtneys' backyard.

"Ma'am, we're heading to Nashville. We've been ordered to stop at nothing to get there to defend the city."

"Defend from whom?" she asked. As far as Mrs. Courtney knew, there were no Confederate soldiers anywhere near Nashville.

"The Confederate Army of Tennessee, of course." Sabine told her. "They're on the march, hoping to retake Nashville. They're trailing us up from Spring Hill, where we sneaked by them last night. Before that they were in Alabama, and before *that*, Atlanta, where we got 'em good. So I expect we'll be out of here soon, ahead of them. I don't think we'll see any action until we get to Nashville."

"Then why have you stopped here?" Mrs. Courtney asked.

"We can't cross the Harpeth River bridges. Someone damaged them so badly that we cannot get our heavy cannons and supply wagons across them. And the water is almost flooding the banks from all this rain. So we are rebuilding the bridges now."

"Have you and the Rebels fought in Tennessee this year?" she asked him.

"Just skirmishing here and there. Nothing major. Why?"

"I have a son in the Army of Tennessee. We've heard nothing from him in months."

"But you're Union folks . . ."

"Yes, we are. All except William." Mrs. Courtney looked sad.

"Well, ma'am, I can promise you we'll do more than skirmish when they attack us at Nashville. I hope the best for your son, and you."

Major Sabine doffed his hat to the ladies and left.

Mrs. Courtney turned to her daughters. "It doesn't sound like they'll be fighting here today. That's a relief. "

Lizzie burst into tears.

"Darling! Whatever is the matter?" Mama asked.

"I was so afraid we would be in trouble because of William. I'm just happy is all."

"Oh, you little silly," Fannie said. "We can't help what William does. We won't be punished because of him."

Mrs. Courtney hugged her daughter.

"Well, you run along for a little while. I've got dishes to do."

II

Mrs. Birdsong cancelled school because of the activity in and around town. Of course, all the children found excuses to go outside and explore.

Lizzie walked toward Main Street where the streets swarmed with soldiers, horses, supply wagons and big guns such as cannons. A stranger, a boy about 12 years old, sat on the ground, leaning back against the low stone wall around the Presbyterian Church.

"You must be a drummer boy," Lizzie told him, noticing a snare drum on the ground next to him.

"Yes," he said listlessly. "I'm trying to sleep. We marched all night and the day before to get here."

"Would you like something to eat? My mother will feed you breakfast."

"I'm mighty hungry," the boy said, suddenly wide awake. "But my brother told me not to leave this spot."

"I'll bring you food. Wait right here," Lizzie offered.

The boy sat up straight as Lizzie ran home. She returned a few minutes later with two ham biscuits.

"Here. Take this. If you need more, my house is right there." Lizzie pointed behind her. "My mother will give you whatever you want. I'm going to visit a friend."

The boy grabbed the food and wolfed it down. The last time Lizzie looked, he was running towards her house.

III

Lizzie headed for the McEwens' house and knocked on the door.

"Florence, is Jennie home?" Lizzie asked when one of Jennie's older sisters came to the door.

"Yes, she's in the parlor. You may come in."

Lizzie entered the parlor and saw Mrs. McEwen working on her mending and talking quietly with her daughters.

"Hello, my dear," Mrs. McEwen greeted Lizzie. "Does your mother know you are out and about today?"

"Yes, ma'am, we had a Union man at our house for breakfast."

"Visiting Fannie, I suppose," said Florence with a sly smile. "She sure is popular with those Union men."

"Hush, Florence!" said Mrs. McEwen. "I'll not have that kind of talk here. You apologize right now to Lizzie."

"I'm sorry, Lizzie," said Florence, as her cheeks got red. Mrs. McEwen never allowed unkind talk in her home.

"So Lizzie, dear, you were saying, a Union man for breakfast . . ."

"Yes, ma'am. He said that the Union army was on its way to Nashville and he didn't think there would be any fighting here in Franklin today."

"Oh my goodness! That's wonderful news. Let's all pray that there isn't."

Jennie asked her mother, "May I go out for a little while with Lizzie? We won't be gone long."

"Yes, dear, but at the first sign of any trouble, run back home as fast you can."

"Mother, may we take Elisa with us?" Jennie asked.

"Yes, if it's alright with Jane. I don't think there will be much work done today."

IV

Lizzie and Jennie went to the slave quarters behind her house and found Elisa sitting with her grandmother kneading dough.

"Elisa, Mother said you can come with us if Jane gives you permission."

"Where?" Elisa asked.

"Just around town for a little while to see what's happening. We're going down to see Hardin."

"Granny, can I go with Miss Jennie and them?"

"Yes, if Mrs. McEwen says so. Children, you be careful."

The three girls skipped down West Main Street to Hardin's house and found him there with Park Marshall looking up the big oak tree in his front yard.

"Hey, girls," Hardin said excitedly. "Looks like there might be a battle here today."

"I sure hope not," Jennie said.

"I sure hope *so*," Hardin shot back. "And I'm going to get a grand view of it from right here." He looked up the tree and pointed to a big branch extending out about 15 feet.

"Hardin! You're going to climb the tree and shimmy out on that branch? You could get killed," Lizzie said.

"Nah! I'll be up out of the way. I just want to see a real battle. It'll be exciting."

"You won't catch me up a tree, that's for sure," said Park, as the three girls nodded in agreement.

"See those soldiers down there?" Hardin pointed down the street away from town. "Let's go down there and see what they're doing."

The five youngsters walked down West Main Street where hundreds of soldiers were busy digging trenches and piling up the dirt behind them, in piles even taller than the children. The children watched for a while then cut over to Columbia Pike toward Carter Hill.

Old Mr. Carter, the widower Fountain Branch, lived in his brick house at the top of the hill with his son Moscow, four of his daughters and nine grandchildren. Two of his sons, Tod and Francis, and all of his daughters' husbands were serving in the Confederate army. When the husbands decided to enlist, Fountain Branch urged his daughters to come home with their children. He didn't think it was safe for them to be alone and away from family. Lizzie and Jennie had gotten to know Alice, one grandchild who'd come all the way from Texas.

At the moment the house and yard bristled with activity. As the children watched, it seemed that the Union army had taken over the house; blue-clad soldiers were coming in and going out in a steady stream. When they passed by the back of the house, Alice waved at them from a window.

"I wonder if she can come outside," Lizzie asked.

"I'm sure not going to knock on the door and find out," Jennie remarked.

The children crossed the street and headed down the hill back toward town. As they approached the Lotzes' house, they saw Mr. Lotz in the yard arguing with a Union soldier.

"You're stealing from me. *Das not gut!*" Mr. Lotz looked agitated as he spoke to the officer.

"There's nothing I can do, sir," the officer told him. "We've got to protect our army and this is the only way to do it."

Mr. Lotz stalked into his house and slammed the door.

The children watched as soldiers began to dismantle Mr. Lotzes' board fence, taking it apart piece by piece. Then the soldiers headed to his back yard, where they hacked away at his barn, work shop and outhouse with axes and shovels, tearing the buildings completely down to the ground. Then the soldiers piled all the boards on wheelbarrows and hauled them up the hill where they stacked them around the breastworks they dug near the Carters' house. The only thing standing on the Lotz family's property was the house, the big white frame house on the hill. The rest—gone.

The children looked at each other.

Finally Lizzie said, "That's bad." The other children nodded.

V

By noon, rumors were flying thick and fast:

The Confederates were stuck in Spring Hill.

The Confederates were marching up the pike.

The Federals were making a stand in Franklin.

The Federals were leaving Franklin for Nashville.

There would be a battle.

There would be a skirmish.

There would be neither.

Everyone was on edge wondering what the day would bring. Tension filled the air. Finally the children wearied of it all and headed home.

By mid-afternoon, Mama, Fannie and Lizzie sat down for their last meal of the day. After grace, Mama ladled out vegetable soup; the family picked up their spoons and began to eat, while listening for noise outside.

The day's furious activity had died down. Many of the soldiers were sitting around campfires drinking coffee and talking quietly. Some were writing letters. Others were lying on the ground, grabbing a few minutes sleep, and warming themselves in the late afternoon sun of the bright Indian summer day. The soldiers were waiting for final repairs to the bridge crossing the Harpeth River. When that moment arrived, they'd be ordered to march out of Franklin, ahead of the Confederates' arrival, and head to Nashville, 15 miles north. Fighting the Rebels would wait for another day.

~~~~~~~

Suddenly, BOOM! A thunderous roar of artillery fire rocked the house. Plaster dust swirled through the room as the ceiling cracked. The oil lamp over their dining table started swinging. Deafening blasts of gunfire filled the air.

Lizzie and Mama shrieked, as Fannie bolted out of her chair and ran to the nearest window. Poking her head out, she saw screaming men, women and children, hands cupped over their heads, tearing north on the pike toward town. More shots burst out: BANG! BANG! BANG! BANGBANGBANG! Clouds of smoke choked the air. Riderless horses and untethered mules stampeded. Dogs circled in panic, yelping and whining. Howling cats leapt on roofs and clawed their way up trees. Then a sound chilled the air: the Rebel yell! *The Rebels were attacking*!

"We can't stay here!" Fannie shouted over the din

"Where can we go? It's too dangerous to go outside to escape!" Mama shouted back.

Lizzie burst into tears, for the second time of the day.

Fannie cried out, "To the cellar. . . it's our only chance!"

The three flew downstairs, grabbing blankets and a candle on the way.

"We've got to get away from the direction of the attack," Fannie yelled. "It's coming from the south, so we have to go *there*." Fannie pointed to the north side of the basement.

A constant barrage of battle sounds assaulted their eardrums as they swaddled themselves in the blankets on the dirt floor of the cellar. Lizzie sat in her mother's lap, while Mama hugged her tightly. Fannie stuffed a coil of rope over the south-facing cellar window to stop any stray bullet that might find its way into the house.

Over the next five hours, many times Lizzie feared for her life—and William's. He was surely in this fight. She hoped and prayed he'd survive, although she wasn't sure *she* would. Artillery fire—cannons—boomed from Fort Granger. One of those cannonballs could easily crash through their roof! Soldiers shouted right outside the basement window. *Were they fighting right here?* Lizzie didn't know. A voice cried out, "Water, water." Fannie crept upstairs and out to the front door where she found a Federal officer bleeding. She quickly gave him water, covered him with her cloak and ran back downstairs. Then—footsteps over their heads. Strangers were in their house. *Why? What were they doing inside?* Then the strong smell of smoke. *Was something on fire? Could it be their house? There'd be no way out. They'd be burned alive!*

Around midnight a voice yelled from upstairs, "Mama! Where are you?"

It must be William!

Fannie grabbed a wood-handled rake and knocked on the ceiling of the basement.

They heard footsteps racing downstairs and a grimy, disheveled man appeared, barely recognizable in the candlelight. The man coughed, then spoke in a raspy voice, "It's me. I'm home."

It *was* William. He made it through the battle, at least so far. Lizzie was so happy she cried all over again as the family embraced.

Suddenly a loud explosion rocked the town, interrupting the family's tearful reunion.

Lizzie shrieked and started shaking.

William said, "That's the last of the Federals. They've left town and blown up all the ammunition they can't transport so we can't have it."

"Is it over? Is the battle over?" Fannie asked him.

"I think so . . . they're mostly gone. The town is in Confederate hands now."

"Oh my," Mama said. "What will happen now?"

"It's bad out there, Mama. I've never seen anything like it in three years of war," William said.

"Can you stay home now?" Mama asked him. She knew the answer and William gave it to her.

"I've got to rejoin my regiment, if I can find it," William said.

"Son, must you?" Mama pleaded with her eyes.

William said, "I can't desert the cause now. We've suffered great losses. Some of our finest officers. Many foot soldiers. We need every man."

They quickly hugged and kissed good-bye. William raced upstairs two steps at a time and left the house; they could hear the front door bang behind him. The exhausted mother and her terrified daughters lay down again on their blankets, huddling close together. Lizzie could not stop shivering—she wondered, was it the cold or the fear? Mama stroked her hair and rubbed her neck and whispered tenderly to her. As Lizzie began to settle in, Mama began to sing Lizzie's favorite lullaby.

Sleepyhead, close your eyes.
Mother's right here beside you.
I'll protect you from harm,

You will wake in my arms.
Guardian angels are near,
So sleep on, with no fear.
Guardian angels are near,
So sleep on, with no fear.

Finally, long after midnight, Lizzie slept.

FIRST PRESBYTERIAN
CHURCH

Chapter 12

The Day After
December 1, 1864

Lizzie woke up at dawn on the cellar floor. For one brief, merciful moment she was spared the memory of the day before. Then the terrors of the battle came flooding back, and Lizzie cried out and jumped to her feet. Mama and Fannie were gone. The gunfire had stopped, but sounds coming from outside and from the room over her head were just as terrifying.

Voices, mostly. Moaning. Wailing. Screaming.

Lizzie ran upstairs and found wounded soldiers in the family's beds. Fannie and Mama were busy tending to them, cleaning and bandaging wounds, ladling out soup and pouring coffee.

111

Lizzie answered a sharp rap on the door. It was Dr. Cliffe.

"Lizzie, get your mother and sister. They're needed at the Presbyterian Church. We've set up a field hospital there and we have nobody to help. Bring these men with you."

Fannie ran in from the bedroom.

"I'm not sure they can be moved, Dr. Cliffe," she said.

"We need help. You come with me and leave the men with your mother."

"I'll be right there," she promised. "Lizzie—come with me. Mama—you stay here."

The sisters went outside and walked to the church. It was light out—barely. Through the early morning mist, the girls stared in all directions. They were not prepared for the sight.

Hundreds of dead and wounded men lay before them. They were strewn up and down the Pike, along with dead horses and mules. Wrecked wagons, equipment and weapons littered the ground. As the sisters made their way among the men, many cried out for help and tugged at their skirts.

The church doors were propped open as men carried in the wounded on stretchers. Dozens of soldiers had already been brought inside and laid on the bare floor. Most men had thin clothing and no blankets. Unlike the day before, the weather had turned bitter cold. A weak fire burned in the fireplace. Men crowded up next to it and each other.

"The Federals are gone from town. They withdrew the army last night when the bridge repairs were completed," Dr. Cliffe told them. "So it's only the wounded who are left here. It's going to be up to us local Union supporters to help out our boys."

Fannie and Lizzie looked at each other. They could not say a word. They just got to work.

II

Food was the first priority. The army's food supplies were gone; the soldiers had not eaten in two days. So Fannie sent Lizzie home to tell their mother, who quickly prepared as much food as she could spare for the men. Lizzie's job was to transport it. She also distributed her family's extra blankets and coverlets to the men.

By noon, Lizzie was exhausted from dozens of trips back and forth between house and church. She went outside for a breath of fresh air. She looked toward Fair Street and saw Jennie on her porch.

"Jennie! You made it," Lizzie called out to her best friend. "I've been so worried about you."

The two friends met in the middle of Five Points and embraced as they talked.

"It was terrible," said Jennie. "We spent the night in the basement scared half to death."

"We did too," Lizzie said. "I've never been so afraid in my life."

"I saw Hardin and Park earlier today heading out to the countryside to find food," Jennie said. "And Jane and Elisa are cooking up a storm for our soldiers."

The girls saw Hardin and Park coming down the street pushing a wheelbarrow full of turnips, cabbage and potatoes.

Hardin called out to Lizzie, "Everyone alright at your house?"

"Yes, we made it through," she said. "What about you?"

"Spent most of the night in the cellar," Hardin said, in a quiet voice.

"What about that tree you were going to climb?"

"I did climb it. But when I saw a soldier shot dead right in front of me I jumped out and went inside."

"How about you, Park?" Lizzie asked him.

"A big cannonball blasted through the back wall of our house and hit an armoire. But everyone's safe."

The friends looked at each other and shook their heads. Hardin took a deep breath and began to speak.

"First thing this morning I walked where we went yesterday. Remember yesterday? How we watched the soldiers tear apart Mr. Lotz's barn and outbuildings? And how they stacked up all the boards? That's how the dead are at Mr. Carter's—stacked up like firewood. And their house is full of wounded, and Tod Carter's there and he got shot a bunch of times and they don't think he'll make it. I saw old Mr. Carter and he looked…well, I can hardly say how sad he looked. When I came back this way and saw the Lotzes' house from the south—the whole south wall collapsed from cannon balls and bullets and there are giant holes in the roof where cannonballs came through. The Lotz family hid out in the Carters' basement with them and they're all safe. But their property is almost destroyed. And some people were talking about Carnton. They say Mrs. McGavock has over 300 wounded soldiers in her house. . . I wonder how Hattie and Winder are doing?"

Hardin paused, and his eyes filled with tears.

"Then I saw a drummer boy—dead. He'd been shot. His drum was on the ground next to him . . . He was about my age . . ."

The children stood silently, each lost in thought.

So much had happened since yesterday. At first, Lizzie struggled to remember. Then the memories buried deep in her brain bubbled to the surface. Waking up early to the sounds of soldiers outside. Their feverish preparations, the tearing down and building up. Then that quiet dinner, interrupted by the screaming attack. The gunfire and cannons. The howling animals, crying men, moaning and groaning with their painful wounds. The dead.

Lizzie could not forget all she had seen and heard. She would not forget the hungry drummer boy leaning against the church wall.

"Oh! I met the drummer boy yesterday," Lizzie told her friends. "He was hungry and I brought him food."

Yesterday the boy lived and breathed and dreamed of home. He had left that home to join a cause. He died for that cause. His dreams ended at 12 years old.

That was hard to think about.

The children said goodbye, and returned to cleaning up the messes men made.

None of them would ever forget it, any of it.

The End

EPILOGUE

There is always the moment in childhood when the door opens and lets the future in.

Graham Greene

Over 2,000 men died in the five hour Battle of Franklin, with another 8,000 wounded, captured or missing. These 10,000 casualties represented almost one-quarter of the two armies' strength that day, staggering when considering the relative shortness of the battle. The Union army withdrew from the battlefield starting about 9:00 p.m. and by morning was completely gone, leaving the town in Confederate hands for the first time in almost three years.

So the Confederate Army of Tennessee (what was left of it) and Franklin's townspeople (about 750 men, women and children) cared for the wounded and buried the dead. The Courtneys pitched in, as did the McEwen girls, their parents, Hardin Figuers, his mother, Park Marshall, Sallie Carter, Fountain Branch Carter and his large family, Carrie McGavock, Jane and Elisa, Dr. Cliffe, Belle and the family, and so on. In fact, the entire population of the town. It was unavoidable. And the horror lasted for the better part of two solid weeks.

The Confederates dug graves and buried the dead.

For the wounded, forty-four field hospitals served. Homes, businesses, doctors' offices, the Courthouse, Masonic Temple, First Presbyterian Church, St. Paul's Episcopal Church—all were hospitals. Shelter. A place to take the wounded to warm up, eat, be treated, live . . . or die.

On December 17, the Confederate army retreated back through Franklin after fleeing Nashville utterly defeated. The Federals chased them and for a while it looked as though there might be another battle in Franklin, but there wasn't, to everyone's relief.

The war ended April 15, 1865, four months later.

The Confederate supporters in town were disappointed, to be sure, but it was a relief that the suffering stopped. The slaves were quickly freed, those who hadn't already escaped, and rejoiced.

In the years following the war, most folks tried to put it in the past and move into the future. Some were more successful than others.

But they never forgot. Their memories were (unfortunately) crystal clear on what had happened that day.

Here's what Fountain Branch Carter's granddaughter **Alice McPhail** said about it:

You know how little eight year old girls don't remember very much after 65 years have passed by, but there are some things that impress a child and they never forget it and that one thing is the Battle of Franklin. I can see it all now in my mind, and I wish I had the language to express the impression it made on me.

Alice was one of the Carter daughters and grandchildren Fountain Branch sent for from Texas. When the War came, he was glad to have them there, thinking he could protect them. Of course, as it happened Alice ended up living through one of the most terrifying, dangerous experiences anyone could ever imagine. Alice, her family, their slaves, and the Lotz family from across the street spent the night in their basement as the epicenter of the Battle of Franklin raged over them.

In the morning she remembered her Uncle Tod being carried into the house after falling on the battlefield. She saw him placed on "Aunt Annie's lounge. I can see his limp boots and arms now with his captain's uniform and cavalry boots and spurs. I can see Uncle Tod lying in the parlor in the last casket that could be gotten in Franklin with a bandage across his head."

Aunt Annie's lounge can be seen at the Carter House museum, and Tod's grave with its modest headstone can be found at Franklin's Rest Haven cemetery.

Alice McPhail later married James Nichols. The family lived in Franklin where she died in 1933.

Like Alice Nichol, **Hattie McGavock** remembered in great detail the day of the battle, when asked about it in 1931, 67 years later.

I can still sense the odor of smoke and blood. I recall how the startled cattle came home from the pastures, how restless they became, sniffing and excitedly running about the place, bewildered by the smell of the battlefield. I can still see swarms of soldiers coming with their . . . comrades and lying them down by the hundreds under our spacious shade trees and all about the grounds. I was only nine years old then, but it is all as vivid and real as if it happened only yesterday.

Twenty years after the Battle of Franklin, Hattie married Lt. George Cowan, a cavalry officer who fought in the Battle of Franklin.

Hattie McGavock died in 1932 and is buried in Mt. Hope cemetery in Franklin. Her younger brother **Winder McGavock** died in Franklin in 1909.

Park Marshall grew up to be a lawyer, historian and mayor of both Franklin and Nashville. He wrote a

detailed account of the Battle of Franklin as part of his *History of Williamson County* in 1917. His memory, like that of so many others, was sharp. On the morning after the battle, he, his mother and sister walked on the battlefield.

He recalled: "The battle-field was a gloomy scene, the Confederate dead filling the trenches and lying thickly in front, while the Federal dead were thick in the inner trenches. . . When one looks upon the streets and field, quiet and peaceful as this suburb now appears, it is hard to believe that within the memory of men now living this place was such a scene of desolation and carnage . . ."

Park Marshall never married, and died in his home on Third Avenue South in 1946 at 91 years old. He could well have been the last citizen of town to witness the battle.

Hardin Figuers wrote an article for *The Confederate Veteran* in 1915.

When the Federal army arrived in town, "the Federal soldiers were at once put to work constructing fortifications entirely around the south margin of the town. They worked like beavers, using houses, fences, timber, and dirt in their works . . ." Later, Hardin reported he "spent the entire afternoon upon the top of the barn and woodshed, in a tree top, and other high places, seeing all that could be seen. At the time the first assault was made, the bullets were flying and whizzing by around everywhere to such an extent that I concluded I was as liable to be hit as a soldier, and I retreated to the cellar."

On the morning after the battle, Hardin saw his first dead person, "a little Yankee boy, about my own age, lying in the middle of the street with his hands thrown back over his head, pale in death. The sight of this boy somehow impressed me more than the thousands of dead men I was soon to look upon."

In the days following, Hardin worked with the rest of the town to alleviate suffering.

> Food got scarcer and scarcer each day. Many a day I went out through the country in an old dump cart hunting for food. We would take a large wash kettle, holding about twenty gallons, and make it full of soup with plenty of red pepper. For this soup I brought in from the country Irish potatoes, cabbage, dried beans and turnips, and in making it we used any kind of meat obtainable. The soldiers

thought this was great diet; in fact the best they had had for more than a year.

Hardin Figuers moved to Maury County, became a lawyer, married and died there in 1917.

Upon the request of the U.S. Sanitary Commission, **Fannie Courtney** wrote an account, in March, 1865, of the battle, along with the condition of the hospitals and the wounded.

On the morning of the 30th of November the retreating army arrived at this place, tired and many almost exhausted. But, notwithstanding this, they commenced immediately throwing up breastworks . . . We felt uneasiness of mind, fearing there would be a great battle. We asked of almost everyone passing if that would be the case. They replied, 'we will only skirmish with the Rebels till we get our wagon trains away, and then we will invite them to Nashville.

Fannie and her family felt relieved. Suddenly:

About half past three o'clock I was sitting at the dinner table when I heard the roar of artillery. I ran into the yard to listen. There was skirmishing for a few minutes only, when, with a tremendous yell, the Rebels made a charge along the whole line. The bullets were falling so thick it was unsafe to remain longer . . . Men, women, and children were running in every direction . . . I hastened to the cellar with the rest of my family.

Fannie described the terrible fright of being trapped in the cellar. "Soon a fire broke out in town. It was fearful enough, for we thought of nothing else but being burned alive in the cellar . . ."

Later that night, Fannie was nervous when the door bell rang.

I opened the door, who should stand face to face with me but my own dear brother and cousin . . . They were just from the field. Words are inadequate to express my happiness . . . My mother was overjoyed that she was once more permitted to clasp her boy to her heart . . . He remained with us one day and one night, and then joined his command near Murfreesboro.

After that:

Early the next morning after the Battle I went to the field. The sight was dreadful. It seemed I could scarcely move for fear of stepping on men either dead or wounded . . . I could not look upon such sights long, but hurried back to care for the wounded.

After the war, Fannie married **George Grummond**, and accompanied him to Fort Phil Kearney in Wyoming Territory where he was killed in battle against the Sioux tribe. Fannie arranged to bring his body back for burial to Franklin, and he is buried in Franklin's Rest Haven cemetery. Later, when Fannie applied for a widow's pension, she discovered he was already married. Later she married another army officer and spent the rest of her life in New England, where she died in 1911.

William Courtney mustered out of the army after the war ended and returned home. He met Fannie in St. Louis and helped her bring Grummond's body back to Franklin. He died in Franklin in 1928.

Jennie McEwen's father **John McEwen,** Franklin's mayor, thoroughly soured on the war after the

Battle of Franklin. He wrote a letter to his brother-in-law Richard Graham, who had moved to New York City:

> I thought I hated secession as much as anyone could hate anything but I was mistaken. I find I have a much greater hatred for the Mississippi fire eaters than I had for anything else save the demon himself . . . I have determined to get out of the way. And if you can think of a place that we can go to North or East, suggest it and we will go there until the war is over . . . [I] wish to get to some quiet place where there are good schools at hand . . .

 The family stayed, and John McEwen got back on his feet. John died in 1903.

Jennie McEwen married the son of former Tennessee governor Newton Cannon, also named Newton Cannon, and died in 1935 in the house where she was born.

Following emancipation, the U.S. Freedmen's Bureau required anyone hiring a former slave to enter into and sign a labor contract requiring payment for work. **John McEwen** and **Mary Jane** and **Elisa** entered into this contract:

> . . .this 1st day of January 1866 between James and John L. McEwen . . . and Elisa and Mary Jane agree to work faithfully on the plantation of the said McEwen when required to do so during the present year and the said McEwens agrees to give them twenty five dollars apiece and allow them to spin and make clothing for themselves when not required to work out and also to feed them should they lose time from any cause it will be deducted from their wages.

Belle Cliffe married U.S. General James P. Brownlow in 1865, whom she first met when he was wounded in a skirmish in September, 1864 and brought to her house for treatment. They lived in Franklin and had two children.

Sadly, first the children, then Belle died of consumption, or tuberculosis, in 1878. Within a year,

James died too and was buried among his family in Rest Haven cemetery. At his funeral, many of his former enemies eulogized him:

> We citizens and ex-Confederate soldiers of Williamson County have heard with deep regret of the untimely death of our fellow-citizen Gen. James P. Brownlow. He came to us during the war a stranger and an enemy. Yet he won the admiration of *our* soldiers for his valor, and the kindness and justice to civilians. He was imbued with courage and chivalry of the Tennessean. He lived long enough with us after the war to change our esteem and respect into affection. We deplore this early death, which has taken from us one of the noblest and truest of men, and blighted our hopes, which looked toward his future usefulness as a man and a citizen. We send our heartfelt sympathies to his mother, brother and sisters, that we received as a sacred trust his mortal remains to be deposited in the soil of the much-loved county of his adoption.

Mrs. **Sallie Hines McNutt** wrote about her family's experiences during the war.

Mr. McNutt went out for observation. He first saw a large number of tents pitched in our pasture near the bar, and scores of soldiers at work erecting others several hundred feet distant. Then he went out into the back yard and such destruction, such pillaging had gone on there, we supposed it began the moment the troops arrived . . . First the smokehouse was broke into, the door slivered, all the bacon, hams, dried beef and tongue of which there was a large quantity taken. The poultry yard fence and house was torn down and all the chicken, ducks, turkey taken . . .

Sallie recounted the damage to St. Paul's: "The Episcopal Church, the handsomest and best equipped one, was robbed of its pipe organ, one of the few in the state." Of their banishment from town, she said, "Sunday, April 26th 1863 was the day we were to give up our home. The destruction of it was unparalleled!"

After the war ended, the McNutts returned to Franklin and found their house in ruins. They moved to Nashville. **James McNutt** later took his own life in despair. Mrs. McNutt died in Franklin in 1923.

The **Lotz Family** spent three years living in the basement as Mr. Lotz struggled to rebuild the house and business. In 1869 he made a piano on which he carved an image of the eagle grasping the Confederate flag. The newly-minted Ku Klux Klan heard about it, paid him a visit, and threatened to murder him. Within 10 days, the Lotzes sold everything they couldn't take, packed up what they could and moved 2,300 miles to San Jose, California, leaving behind what turned out to be a nightmarish period of their lives.

Matilda Lotz, remembered in Franklin for drawing in the dirt with a stick, moved to Europe by herself at 18 and began a successful career as a painter. She married for the first time at age 55 to an Austrian man, and died in 1923 at age 65 in Tata, Hungary. Today her works can be seen at the Lotz House museum, as well as museums around the world.

Titus's story comes from a true story of a slave whose brother Charley, like Titus's brother, was sold out of the family. This slave never saw his brother again. After he was freed, he decided to take as a last name "Charley" to honor the memory of his brother. His descendants still bear that last name today.

The character of **Lizzie Courtney** is based on several Franklin children. Her story is universal.

QUESTIONS

1. When Lizzie saw a slave child sold away from her mother, she said she felt like she did when her father died. Why was the feeling the same?

2. Jennie and Elisa played together as toddlers but later Jennie got to go to school and Elisa had to work. What should Jennie have done about this unfairness?

3. What do you think Jane had "on her mind" the day the children hoped to get a treat and she refused?

4. While everyone else had strong opinions about the Civil War, the Lotz family didn't seem to care "one way or the other." What was different about the Lotzes?

5. The Courtneys were surprised when Jim and Mary ran away to escape slavery, since they always appeared to be happy. How do you think Jim and Mary felt while enslaved?

6. Hardin said that although he'd seen hundreds of dead men on the battlefield, he felt most affected by seeing the dead drummer boy. Why did seeing one dead boy affect him more than seeing hundreds of dead men?

7. William Courtney argued with Fannie about Grummond and disapproved of their relationship. Yet he met her in St. Louis to help bring his body back after he was killed in Wyoming. What does this tell you about their family?

8. Sixty years after the War ended, Hattie McGavock said the events of the Battle of Franklin were "as vivid and real as if they happened yesterday." What events from the past do you think your elderly friends or relatives remember the most?

ABOUT THE AUTHOR

Margie Gould Thessin is the owner and co-founder of Franklin on Foot, offering guided walking tours, bike tours and food tours in historic Franklin, Tennessee since 2003. Margie graduated from the University of Florida (B.A., history, 1977) and Catholic University (J.D., 1981). After practicing law in West Virginia for seven years, she retired to a life of child-rearing and volunteerism in Franklin, which led her to the Heritage Classroom program where she served as teacher from 1998-2004, and 2011-present. Margie was director of sales and marketing at Carnton Plantation from 2004-2007 and served as Interim Executive Director from 2008-2009. She is a member of Franklin's Battlefield Preservation Commission. Margie is the author of *Ghosts of Franklin, Tennessee's Most Haunted Town.* She is married to Mark and is the proud mom of Anne, Tyler and Molly, and son-in-law Ryan.

ABOUT THE ARTIST

 Colonel (Retired) Samuel A. Whitson, a professional soldier with a lifelong passion for art and military history, served 26 years in the Regular Army with combat service in Iraq. Sam was raised in Nashville, currently lives in Franklin, attended M.T.S.U. (B.S., 1976), University of Oklahoma (M.P.A., 1985) and the U.S. Army War College (1998). Sam serves on the Carter House Board of Directors and as Vice Chairman of Franklin's Battlefield Preservation Commission. He loves his friends, neighbors, family, dogs and especially his sons, Brad and Brian, grandchildren and his high school sweetheart and wife of over 38 years, Pam.

54572231R00087

Made in the USA
Charleston, SC
08 April 2016